MOUTH TO MOUTH

Also by Michael Kimball

FIREWATER POND
UNDONE

MOUTH TO MOUTH

MICHAEL KIMBALL

AVON BOOKS NEW YORK

This is a work of fiction. Names, characters, places and incidents
either are the product of the author's imagination or are used fictitiously.
Any resemblance to actual events, locales, organizations, or persons,
living or dead, is entirely coincidental and beyond the intent
of either the author or the publisher.

AVON BOOKS, INC.
An Imprint of HarperCollins*Publishers*
10 East 53rd Street
New York, New York 10022-5299

Library of Congress Cataloging in Publication Data:

Kimball, Michael.
   Mouth to mouth / Michael Kimball.—1st ed.
      p.   cm.
   I. Title.
PS3561.I4163M68   2000   99-39876
813'.54—dc21   CIP

First Avon Books Hardcover Printing: February 2000

Printed in the U.S.A.

FIRST EDITION

QPM 10 9 8 7 6 5 4 3 2 1

www.harpercollins.com

For my son Jesse

And in memory of three good men:

Al Pope, my father-in-law
Dr. Bob Mackey
Professor Terry Plunkett

They were warm, joyful, hard-working, open, and caring people.
Wherever they were, they made life much better.

thanks

Chris Fahy, Nancy Graham, Glenna and Jesse Kimball, Tabby King, Chuck Landry, Paul Mann, Howard Morhaim, Nessa and Pete Reifsnyder, Brenda Reimels, Frances Sullivan, and Mildred Schmalz . . . for wading through early drafts and telling me what was right and wrong

Howie Nielsen, Karen Wachtel Nielsen, and Glenna Kimball, for listening to an oral version of this entire novel while imprisoned in my car on a drive back from Montreal

Aaron Bourassa, the esteemed professor Bob Steneck, and the folks at York Beach Scuba, for diving info

Nancy Graham, for help with computer editing in the homestretch

Sarah Haskell, for her knowledge of tapestry making and weaving

Susan Hayes, Nanney Kennedy, and Joe Miller, for answering my questions about sheep

Arthur Kyricos, for his knowledge of firearms

Fred Muehl, of York Harbor Marine Service, for answering my boat questions

Pat and Al Philbrook, for medical and engineering info

Stan Ross, of York, Maine: good man, hard-worker, straight-shooter, for helping me find a house

Reverend Betty Stookey, for her help with biblical questions

Jill Schultz and the Maine Writers and Publishers Alliance, for doing good work

The Automatics, for their permission to quote from "Hangin' Out at EJ's," the quintessential pop-punk song of the twentieth century (from their CD *The Automatics,* Mutant Pop Records, 5010 NW Shasta, Corvallis, Oregon 97330)

Special thanks to Jennifer Hershey, my U.S. editor, and Bill Massey, my U.K. editor, for their wisdom and encouragement

Abner Stein, my U.K. agent

As always, to my U.S. literary agent Howard Morhaim . . . and to fisherman Earl MacVane Jr., for pulling him out of the ocean off Peak's Island one day and not throwing him back when he found out he'd rescued a New Yorker

And, as ever, to Stephen King, for his generosity

Neglected last time:
From the U.S. edition, Meredith DeLoca, ace photographer, who went uncredited for her author photo in *Undone*

Alan Williams, my first editior, for teaching and encouraging me

Note: In order to sell a few more books, I borrowed names from some of my friends; however, personalities, relationships, and events in the novel are completely fictional.

Revenge is a kind of wild justice . . .
FRANCIS BACON

. . . I will repay, saith the Lord.
ROMANS 12:19

MOUTH TO MOUTH

one

On the crest of the hayfield, outside her sheep pasture, Ellen Chambers stood calmly under a green canopy tent while her son-in-law smothered her daughter with wedding cake. Randy was apparently teaching Moreen the first lesson of their married life, getting even with her for smearing his goatee with frosting while she'd fed him his slice. The wedding guests laughed. Even Moreen's high school friends thought it was funny, as Moreen tried to duck away from Randy, her swollen belly straining against the silk of her wedding dress. But when Randy wiped his hands on Moreen's dress, then stalked away from her, Ellen finally lost her composure and went to head him off at the beer keg.

"Is it my imagination, or is the groom not the son-in-law of your dreams?" Ellen heard the voice behind her. In her heels and close-fitting skirt, her friend Maddy was doing her best to keep pace with her.

"He's twenty-seven years old," Ellen said. "She's a junior in high school."

"Shy girls always marry outlaws," Maddy said. "You did." She gently took hold of Ellen's arm, stopping her. "Anyway, you don't want to make a scene today."

Ellen shut her eyes, took a heavy breath. Madeleine Sterling had been her closest friend since high school and usually gave good advice—it helped that she was a psychotherapist.

"So," Maddy said, changing the subject as she turned them around, "do I see more sheep in your pasture?"

Ellen laughed, finally grateful for Maddy's intervention. "We need the wool," Ellen told her. "The phone company's threatening to shut us off, the barn's falling down."

Maddy gave her friend a sympathetic look. "El, if it's just money, you know I'd love to help."

Ellen shook her head. "Thanks. But we'll be fine. The wedding set us back a bit, that's all."

"Mm," Maddy said. "I also can't help but notice that the minute Moreen moves out, you expand your flock."

"Oh, Maddy, no analysis today." Ellen turned away and found herself making eye contact with a young man standing in the shade of the oak tree beside her house. She averted her eyes, as she had done twice already. Large and strikingly handsome, with dark eyes and long black sideburns, he nursed a Styrofoam cup of coffee. The cuffs of his white shirt were rolled up.

"No one seems to know anything about him," said Maddy, observing the direction of Ellen's glance.

"I'm sure you've asked around."

"Discreetly."

Ellen mustered a smile.

"His hair," Maddy went on in a low voice, covering her mouth. "Would you call that wavy or curly?" Maddy ran her hand through her own jet-black cut, which matched her black silk designer suit. Though Ellen loved Maddy, the friends couldn't have been more different. Twice divorced, Maddy was always on the lookout for her next conquest.

Ellen had been married since her teens and looked homespun, even when dressed up. Her hair was long and mahogany-colored; it fell down the middle of her back in a thick braid. She was tall, but with a curve to her hip and breast. At thirty-six, Ellen felt strong and healthy and young—much too young to be a grandmother.

"How old do you think?" Maddy asked, eyeing the dark young man. "Thirty-three? Not a day younger than thirty."

"Dream on. Twenty," insisted Ellen, just as the young man glanced over at her again. Uncomfortable, she turned to look for Scott, her husband, spotted him leaning against the paddock fence with their new son-in-law. The two men were smoking cigars and talking intently. Scott, with his easy manner and ready smile, worked hard to make sure nobody in Destin disliked him. It bothered Ellen to see him trying so hard with Randy.

She heard a sudden burst of singing, and turned to see Moreen standing at the beer keg with her friends, posing for snapshots with her arms around them, swaying and singing along with the three-piece band.

Unavoidable, Ellen supposed, the way Moreen mirrored her own young life: the rebellion, the recklessness, the careless pregnancy, the misfit husband. But somehow, across all these years, the reflection seemed so warped—almost as though Moreen was knowingly orchestrating her own destruction.

"I feel like she's drowning herself, and there's nothing I can do to save her," Ellen whispered to her friend.

"Don't you think that's a wee bit overstated?"

"Maddy, I don't even know her anymore," Ellen said, sorrow almost closing her throat. "It's like I just opened my eyes, and here we are."

Maddy gave her a look. "You're both growing up," she said. "That's called life."

"Call it what you want," Ellen said. "It's not the life I wanted. For her or me."

"Ladies and gentlemen, get out your hankies," the singer announced, his amplified voice booming over the valley and echoing back off the wooded hillside. By now Ellen's sheep had flocked to the farthest corner of the fenced-in pasture, down to the right, where the stream came out of the woods. Ellen imagined the gray coyotes, whose nightly baying she'd been hearing for weeks, slinking down the hill beyond the fences and stream, stalking them.

"Because right now, ladies and gentlemen, I'd like to get the bride and her father up here on the dance floor—"

Ellen turned, saw Scott stub his cigar out on the gate, set his drink on top of the cedar post, and start walking toward the canopy. Eyes sparkling, he still maintained some of his youthful charm—his tourmaline stud and black ponytail countering the fullness of his face. Everyone knew he was about to lose his hardware store—this, after he'd been one of Destin's most prosperous young men only ten years ago—but he carried himself with a staunch, countrified dignity as he searched the crowd for his daughter. When he ducked under the canopy and stepped onto the dance floor, Moreen was there waiting, dark eyes staring off dazedly as she reached for him and wrapped her arms around his neck. Daddy's Little Girl.

"You gonna cry?" Maddy asked.

Ellen folded her arms, not answering.

"I just hope Randy knows how to waltz," Maddy added.

Ellen looked askance at her. "Why?"

Maddy patted her arm. "He's the groom, and you're the mother of the bride—you're on next," she said, moving off. "Be sweet. I'm going off to do my sultry thing."

Ellen turned, spotted Randy sauntering toward the beer keg with his hands stuffed in the back pockets of his leather pants. With his matching leather vest and dark shades, and his cropped ponytail, he must have imagined himself swashbuckling.

Waltz? Ellen had never even had a real conversation with Randy—not that she'd made the effort. According to Moreen, Randy had studied art at some community college in Florida, yet now he worked part-time for a sea-urchin diver, who was also his best man today. On the side, Randy made airbrush paintings depicting endangered animals killing humans—building up his portfolio, Moreen had explained on the night she told Ellen and Scott she was pregnant.

Really, what was there to say to Randy? I'm so happy that my daughter has chosen you to father her children. And how cool that you wore shades to the wedding. Not to mention that little nod you and Scott exchanged when he brought Moreen to the altar.

Now, as Ellen watched Scott dancing with their daughter, she wondered again how he'd given his consent so easily, while she tried to talk to Mo about adoption and even offered to help raise the child herself, to keep Moreen in high school—and to keep her from marrying Randy. But the conversations had been cut off each time by Moreen's breezy indifference, by Scott's reluctance to argue.

Ellen gazed at her daughter. Dark-haired and beautiful as a pregnant Irish-American girl could be, Moreen had the deep brown eyes of her father, a dusting of freckles on her nose like her mother, and a pretty, cherubic mouth that was all her own.

Moreen had told Ellen that Randy was an uneducated genius. She said he was sensitive and ambitious and funny, and that he'd be a wonderful father. Moreen told her mother a lot of things. For instance, that the first time in her life she'd ever felt loved was the first time Randy had looked at her.

Right now, Randy was at the keg making another girl feel loved, judging by the way he was allowing her to pick the frosting out of his goatee. She was maybe fifteen years old, and wore denim shorts ripped off so short they seemed to have no crotch.

"Now I'd like to have the groom and the bride's mother join in," the singer announced, snapping Ellen from her reverie. She set her glass down and came forward to the dance floor, while she watched Randy wrap his arm around the girl and fill her cup from the keg.

The singer leaned into the mike: "Randy, your mother-in-law is waiting for you. Get used to it, man."

Some of the men laughed heartily; some women booed. Randy glanced over at Ellen while he fed the girl her first sip of beer, laughing as it spilled down her chin.

Ellen looked toward Moreen, who rolled her eyes, as if to say, *Randy is just so independent.* Ellen eyed Scott next, wishing he'd rescue her, but he just gave her a look, a shrug. Then a hand touched her back.

"Dance with me," the voice said, and before Ellen could decline, her right hand was firmly in the young man's left, and his arm was around her back.

His shoulder was solid, as was his arm, his fingers thick and long. His face was symmetrically constructed, his nose straight, his chin square. Though cleanly shaven, she could tell his beard would be heavy in a few hours. She could detect a tinge of fresh perspiration about him, a close, energetic scent. She could feel the champagne she had drunk.

"He may not be the groom," the singer announced, "but I don't think you mind, do you, Mom?"

Ellen felt her face flush as she glanced up at her partner. He gave her a bemused smile that she took for sympathy. His brown eyes, she noticed, were as dark as Moreen's.

"I guess your son-in-law has one redeeming quality," her partner said to her, as the small dance floor filled with other couples.

"What's that?"

"He left you unattended."

His smile was warm and easy and somehow seemed familiar. Then she became aware of fingers spreading on the small of her back, and she felt her heart pump. She inched away from him.

"I'm Moreen's mother," she told him.

"I know," he said. "Your name is Ellen. And you've been standing over there wondering if it's possible to get away with murder."

"Close." Laughing uncomfortably, she hadn't realized her feelings toward Randy were quite so obvious.

"Anything's possible." he said quietly.

Reflexively, she pulled back another inch, to study him, to ascertain that he was joking. He gave her another smile.

"Are you a friend or relative?" she asked.

"Relative, you might say."

"Okay," she said, tiring of the game.

"Of the bride."

Ellen stopped dancing. She pulled her hands from him, his features suddenly snapping together like puzzle pieces. His smile broadened.

"It's nice to see you, Aunt Ellen."

Ellen embraced him. "Oh, Neal," she said happily.

"I wasn't about to miss my only cousin's wedding day," he said, as he took her hand again and they continued dancing, Ellen's heart drumming, her mind whirling, remembering Neal the last time she had seen him, at his father's funeral—two days after his twelfth birthday. Now she held him tightly, suddenly wanting the song to end, wishing Scott was near so she could tell him—*Your nephew Neal is here*—then wondering whether to tell Scott at all.

"Moreen will be so happy you came," Ellen said.

"I wouldn't have recognized her."

Ellen sighed, but said nothing. They danced some more, while they both absorbed the reunion.

"And Uncle Scott—I heard he's still running the hardware store."

"Fifteen years now," Ellen said.

"Or it's running him—?"

Ellen looked closely at Neal and saw a knowing glint in his eye. "Into the ground," she acknowledged quietly.

"I probably should mind my own business," he said. "Anyway, there's another reason I came here today. I didn't know if you heard about my mother."

Ellen looked up at him again, then pulled him closer as they kept dancing.

"Now that she's gone," he said, "you're the only family I have— you and Uncle Scott and Moreen—and I was hoping we could, you know, exchange Christmas cards at least."

"Oh, Neal," she said again, wishing she could think of something else to say, trying to rectify her feelings in the face of the old wounds, the persistent scars.

"Mind if I cut in?" asked Scott suddenly at their side, one hand on his nephew's shoulder, the other on Ellen's.

"Not at all," Neal replied, backing away, giving Ellen the glance of a steadfast ally.

She took Scott in her arms, held him in a familiar way, felt the softness of his back as he began moving his knees in time to the music, shuffling his soles across the makeshift plywood floor.

"Holding up?" he asked. Ellen smelled the cigar on his breath, tinged with whiskey.

"I'll be glad when it's over," she answered. *Tell him. It's his past too, more than mine.*

He drew her closer. "They'll be okay, El. Don't forget, you were the same age when we got married."

"Have we been okay?" she asked pensively.

He smiled easily. "I think we've been great."

She nestled her face against his, relieved to let someone else answer the hard questions.

"So who were you dancing with?"

"Neal," she answered, just as the song came to an end and the drummer began a faster beat.

"Friend of Randy's?"

Moreen's arm around Ellen's neck interrupted them. Ellen let go of Scott, turned, and took her daughter in a hug. Moreen was so drunk that she almost pulled her mother over, and Ellen wanted to admonish her for drinking while she was pregnant—for drinking anyway at her age—but Ellen restrained herself. It was a hug from her daughter, who had grown so distant lately that Ellen relished any connection with her.

"You look beautiful today," Ellen told her.

"So do you," Moreen said. "Are you happy for me?"

Ellen pulled her daughter closer. "I'm trying, Mo. I really am."

Just then, a cry came from the direction of the barn. All three of them turned.

"Jesus," Scott said, heading for Maddy, who was next to the paddock fence, covering her face with her hands. Ellen recognized Neal standing beside her, though his back was to them.

"Who *is* that guy?" Moreen asked.

As Ellen fell in step with Scott, hurrying to see what had happened, Neal lowered his head and walked away.

Ellen reached her friend first.

"Mad?"

"I'm fine," Maddy told her, even as she rubbed her eyes with her fists.

"What happened?" Scott asked, watching Neal disappear around the front of the barn.

"I'm fine," Maddy repeated. "I touched your electric fence and splashed my drink in my eye."

A few other wedding guests gathered around to see what was wrong. "She got bit by the fence, that's all," Scott told them.

"If you want, ma'am, I'll arrest that fence," said Sugar Westerback, the town's only full-time policeman, then he laughed at his joke along with the other guys. Sugar was built like a hydrant, with massive arms. His hair was shaved within an eighth-inch of his skull, and he wore a black, tight-fitting T-shirt that said D.A.R.E. TO KEEP KIDS OFF DRUGS, and loose-fitting pants, the kind favored by weight lifters, with a pager hooked to his belt.

"So glad I can entertain you all," Maddy told him, squeezing her eye shut. "Does anyone have a napkin?"

Scott pulled a clean handkerchief from his pocket and handed it to her. "Sure you're okay?"

"I'm not going to sue, if that's what you mean," Maddy replied, dabbing the corner of her eye.

Sugar nudged Scott with his elbow. "Scotty, if this fence don't keep them kii-otes away from them sheep, that scream of hers sure as hell will." Sugar laughed as he walked away, and as the other men also dispersed, Ellen picked up Maddy's plastic drinking glass a few feet away in the deep grass.

"I thought it was a very sultry scream," Ellen said to her friend, affectionately.

"Here he was, all by himself, and I'm coming over, doing the walk—remember Kathleen Turner in *Body Heat?*—and just as I say, 'You don't have an older brother, do you?' I lean against the fence and throw my drink in my face."

"And you're thinking he wasn't impressed?" Ellen said with a smile.

Maddy's face changed. She turned and stared at the fence, a realization overtaking her. "He was holding onto it," she breathed.

"Holding what?"

"The fence. The electric fence. He was standing right here, leaning against it, holding it in his hand."

"Are you sure?"

Maddy looked up at Ellen in disbelief. "The entire time he was standing here, he was baiting me."

Even though Ellen found this a little hard to believe, she didn't question her friend. Maddy had always been a little dramatic. "Remember Neal?" she said.

Maddy scowled darkly. "Neal, your nephew?"

"Neal, Scott's brother's son."

Maddy gave her a look. "Does Scott know he's here?"

Ellen shook her head.

"Well, I hate to be the one to tell you, kid, but Scott's brother's son could use some serious professional help."

"And you just happen to know a psychotherapist with free time?"

Maddy shook her head grimly. "Not on your life," she said. "That's way more than I can handle."

While the crowd was distracted, Neal Chambers walked into the barn. There were stalls running down the left and right walls, with a small dusty window lighting each, and a double door on either side of the barn that opened onto the ewes' and rams' paddocks. A thick chain and hook hung down from the center beam. As Neal passed under the hook, another young man stepped out of the last stall on the right.

"You want something?" the kid said. He was Neal's size and build, possibly a year or two younger. He tipped a bottle of Pabst Blue Ribbon to his mouth in a way that made his biceps flex.

Neal continued to approach, saying, "Before I left, I wanted to say goodbye to Randy."

The kid cocked his head and drawled, "Better for you to wait outside. He's busy now."

But Neal didn't stop; he walked right up to the kid and looked into the stall where Randy was kneeling in front of an overturned wooden crate. The young girl in the denim shorts sat on the crate, her knees pressed against Randy's sides. She looked up vacantly at Neal.

Randy glanced over his shoulder. "Good fuckin job, Gator," he said. A hypodermic stuck like an arrow in the head of a green hummingbird tattooed on the girl's forearm. A length of slender rubber tubing was tied around her left arm.

"It's okay, Randy, I'm Mo's cousin," Neal said, stepping through the narrow doorway of the stall. "I just wanted to say goodbye before I left."

Watching Neal closely, Randy left the needle hanging from the girl's arm, reached around behind her and picked a double-edged razor blade off the crate. "You want to say goodbye?" he said, rising to his feet.

Neal came toward him, extending his right hand.

"Randy, finish me," the girl protested.

Randy stuck out his left hand to shake, still grasping the razor blade in his right.

"One other thing," Neal said, as they clasped hands.

"Yeah?"

"Well," Neal said, "I think you need to start showing a little more respect for the family."

At first Randy didn't react beyond a slight narrowing of his eyes, as if he were trying to read the glint in Neal's eye. Then the corners of Randy's goatee lifted in a kind of grin. He blinked his eyes. Once. Twice. And all at once he snapped Neal's hand around and laid the razor blade flat against the pale underside of Neal's wrist. Timing.

"Stay very still, cousin," Randy whispered, steeling his grip on Neal's hand to make his point. "Very, very still. 'Cause now I have something to tell you."

"Randy, are you gonna finish me?" the girl complained, pushing limply to her feet. Gator snickered, leering over the stall at her.

A bright speck of red winked on Neal's wrist where the point of Randy's blade touched his skin. Neither man saw the blood, however, intent as they were on each other's eyes. Neither did they see Gator sidling into the stall with a three-inch punch blade protruding from his fist. "See, I don't know what your actual problem is," Randy said to Neal. "Fact is, maybe I didn't even hear you right—"

"Ran-dee," the girl sang again, knees bending, holding the syringe in her forearm so it wouldn't fall out.

With the hand that held the punch blade, Gator reached out and caught the girl's breast between his thumb and finger. As she let go of the syringe to clutch at his wrist, he plucked the syringe from her arm.

"You're a little brat," Gator said, giving her nipple a twist until she rose onto her toes. "Anyone ever teach you not to interrupt?"

Tears welled in the girl's eyes. Then he released her. She staggered backward, into the doorpost. "Asshole!" she screamed. Gator jumped at her with his punch blade, and she ran out of the stall.

Then, turning back to Randy and Neal, Gator raised the syringe upright in his hand and tapped the barrel with his ring finger. Squeezing the punch blade in his other hand until the veins on his arm rose fat and blue, he carefully sank the needle into his bloodstream and pushed the plunger. He hissed through his teeth as the drug went in, all the while studying Neal and Randy.

"Well, then," Gator said, tossing the syringe on the floor, "looks like we got ourselves somebody else that needs a lesson in politeness."

He pushed himself off the rough-boarded wall and ambled closer to them both, pale eyes shining intently, until he stopped arm's-length from Neal, staring at his neck the same way he had stared at the girl's breast.

But even as Gator's punch blade flashed with the window's reflection, Neal kept his eyes fixed on Randy.

"Yup," Gator said. "Seems like nowadays everybody's forgettin their manners."

"Hey!"

Suddenly Gator jerked backward, snagged in the oversized hand of a very tall man who had silently entered the barn behind him and yanked him out of the stall. It was Rooftop Paradise, Randy's boss and best man, and he seemed annoyed at Randy.

"This is a wedding," he scolded, ducking back into the stall.

Suddenly Randy flinched. He looked down at his razor blade, one corner of which had sunk between the bones of Neal's wrist, while the opposite corner had thrust up into his own index finger. Dumbfounded, Randy watched the blood well up out of both of them. Then he returned his eyes to Neal's steady stare. "You some kind of mental case?"

"What the heck are you doing in here?" Rooftop demanded of his friend.

"What does it look like?" Randy answered sourly. "I'm having a discussion with an asshole."

Rooftop turned to Neal and asked quietly, "Your business done here?"

Neal's eyes left Randy's but didn't meet Rooftop's. Instead, they tracked Gator sneaking into the stall again, his punch blade peeking out of his fist.

"I said behave, you," Rooftop told Gator, his long right arm swinging back, stopping him short. "And you," Rooftop said, returning his attention to Randy. "It's your wedding day. You're supposed to be out there with your wife."

"Fuck," Randy said.

Rooftop turned to Neal again. "Okay now?"

"I think I made my point," Neal replied, backing into the cob-webbed corner of the stall, casually taking a handkerchief from his pocket and pressing it against his wrist, though his eyes remained keenly focused on the three men in front of him.

Randy tried to flick the razor blade off his bloody fingers. "Dipshit," he said, finally flinging it toward Neal's legs. "Stick around, maybe you can give me some more marital advice later on, when we won't be interrupted."

Rooftop peered down at the floor through wire-rimmed glasses that looked tiny on his face. He slid his huge wingtip forward and toed the syringe out of the hay, then bent his head toward Randy. "What the heck is this?"

"How should I know?" Randy answered. "It's a sheep barn, probably some vet left it." He did not make eye contact with Rooftop, who was staring at him. Then the giant took a clean handkerchief from his back pocket and stuffed it in Randy's hand.

"I don't know what that little girl was doing in here, but she's young enough to get all you guys locked up," said Rooftop gravely. "Now go take care of that hand."

"Since when did Ann Landers die and put you in charge?" Randy grumbled, wrapping his finger with the handkerchief.

"Cop comin," Gator said quietly, sticking his head back in the door.

"Mind your manners," Rooftop said, pointing a long finger first at Randy, then Gator. Then he turned toward Neal, accidentally gouging his shoulder on a nail sticking out of the ceiling.

"If you were planning to leave," he said, "I'd go ahead with my plans." Then he ducked out of the stall.

Sugar Westerback stood about ten feet inside the barn with his hands on his hips, watching the three men come toward him. "Hey, we had a little girl come runnin out of here a minute ago all upset about something," he said. "You boys know anything about that?" He looked down at the bloody handkerchief in Randy's hand.

Randy held up the injured finger. "Old barn," he said. "Nails stickin out every which way." He grinned at Sugar, though the everpresent scowl seemed to deepen on his brow.

"So you boys don't know anything about the girl?" Sugar said.

Randy shrugged, then nodded to his two cohorts. "My associates were just giving me some pointers on my wedding night."

"I had to take that cake knife away from that girl," Sugar said. "She had it in for somebody."

"Not me," Randy said and started walking toward the door.

As they proceeded toward the daylight, Gator moved around behind the policeman, his right hand buried in his pocket. Rooftop inserted himself furtively between the two.

" 'Dare to keep kids off drugs,' " Randy recited, reading Sugar's T-shirt.

"That's me," Sugar said, turning back. "I go into the schools dressed up in a dog suit, talk to 'em about drugs."

Gator snickered.

"But you know what's funny? What I got in my car: pot. About this much." He spread his thumb and finger an inch apart. "I show the kids what it looks like, you know, in case somebody offers 'em any, they'll know enough to turn it down."

"That's good," Randy said, as they emerged into the sunlight. "You keep this fuckin town safe."

"That's exactly what I do," Sugar said, and he gave Randy a wink. "So I'd watch myself, if I were you assholes."

two

For Ellen, the last week before summer vacation seemed endless. Home in the afternoons, she worked in her garden, picking rocks, preparing the soil for another planting of green beans and late corn. On Tuesday a customer came by and bought two brown fleeces at sixteen dollars a pound, and she was able to make a payment on her phone bill. With shearing behind her and her spring lambs almost ready for weaning, the sheep required little of her time, besides feeding and watering.

At five o'clock every day, she went into her pantry where her weights were set up and put herself through a brutal workout. Where normally she'd lift every other day for forty minutes, this week she worked out every day for an hour. She also raised her bench weight from 120 pounds to 125. The exhaustion did her good.

Evenings she graded final exams and filled out report cards in the kitchen, and if she finished at a reasonable hour, she'd go up to her spinning room and work on her tapestry, a seascape commissioned by a Portsmouth interior decorator. As much as possible, she filled her time with work that enabled her to avoid the living room.

In fact, she avoided Scott, and she was aware of this. At first she thought it was Moreen's glaring absence, the reason she preferred her solitude. But there was more to it. Even on the weekend, she had barely spoken to Scott when they awoke in the morning or passed in the kitchen. Maybe she didn't want to tell him about how it felt to be grading papers of kids who were Moreen's age and planning for college, when Moreen was pregnant, married, and gone. Maybe she didn't want to confront her husband about his cavalier attitude in giving their daughter away. Or maybe she was afraid she might tell him what she'd been thinking—that without Moreen home to care for, there wasn't a whole lot keeping her there anymore.

No matter. He never asked her what was wrong, so she kept it to herself.

But on Sunday afternoon, a week after the wedding, when she went into the pasture and found her oldest ewe bloodied and sprawled on the crest of the hill, Ellen's cry rang full of her frustration. It also sparked a movement below them that she spotted with a heart-thumping start. *Coyotes.* Three of them, gray as sticks, slinking down at the far right corner of the pasture, where they'd gotten through the fence. Timid as coyotes tended to be, these must have been famished beyond reason, the way they stood their ground once they'd seen her.

Ellen glanced behind her at the rest of her sheep, tightly flocked in the paddock. She turned back to the coyotes, realized they were edging up the hill toward her. She thought of Scott's revolver in the bedroom but was afraid to leave her sheep to fetch it. For the first time this week, she wished Scott was here.

"*Go on!*" she shouted, tearing off her baseball cap and waving it at the predators. The dying ewe raised its head and Ellen put her hand on its bloody shoulder, then saw the blood-saturated grass under its belly.

Halfway up the hill, with seeming calculation, the coyotes separated. Bowing their heads, fixing their yellow-brown eyes on Ellen, they spread left and right. Ellen raised herself high on her knees, although she realized that the visage she presented was hardly threatening: a woman in a green tank top and frayed jean shorts, her only weapon a baseball cap.

Hearing the familiar diesel engine up on the road, she was almost afraid to hope it was Scott, but to her relief, the old Mercedes pulled into their driveway. She waited until the door closed, then she called for him. When he didn't answer, she yelled louder.

"Hold your horses!" he yelled back. She could hear in his voice that he was wounded by her week of silence.

"*Get the gun!*" she cried. As if understanding her words, the coyotes stopped and sniffed the air.

"Where are you?" Scott shouted.

"Down here! Get the gun!"

Scott came to the paddock fence. "What's the matter?"

She pointed down the hill. *"Coyotes!"*

"Ellie, get out of there!"

But Ellen wasn't about to leave her sheep. Besides, as close as the coyotes were, and as bold, she had a better chance standing and fighting than turning and running. Scott remained at the fence, holding his briefcase, as if wondering whether or not to just charge down after the predators barehanded. Instead, he turned and ran for the house.

Katie, the bloodied ewe, let out a mournful bleat and tried to get up again. Ellen held her down. She knew the animal could smell her killers nearing. Then Scott's voice called out:

"Ellie, where the hell did you hide the bullets?"

Ellen shouted back: "In the freezer!"

She looked toward the coyotes again. Seeing them resume their skulking ascent up the hill, she got to her feet, presenting her full height, grateful for the additional half inch her work boots provided. She raised her arms over her head. The coyotes balked.

Ellen looked back, as the side door of the barn opened against the sheep pressed together there, and Scott came marching through their midst, holding the revolver at his shoulder.

Seeing him, the lead coyote hunched his bony shoulders and lowered his head.

Scott stopped walking, straightened his arm and aimed. The animal's ears went back. The gun fired. The coyote wheeled and raced toward the corner of the pasture. Scott ran a few steps, then got off a second shot. A divot sprayed up to the left of one of the remaining two animals, and they too bolted for the gully. When Scott reached the crest of the hill, right in front of Ellen, he fired again, three times, the echo of his shots slapping back off the opposite hill, as the trio pushed under the livestock fence and disappeared into the tangled gray shadows of the stream bank.

"Nice shot," Scott said sarcastically to himself.

Ellen knelt beside Katie, running her fingers gently over the stiff, cropped wool beside her ear. Scott turned toward her, blowing a sigh that was tinged with frustration. "Want me to call Merrifield, see if he can fix her?"

Before she could answer, Ellen noticed that Scott's ponytail was gone. In fact, his hair had been barber-cut and parted neatly down the center. And he was wearing what appeared to be a uniform—light blue blazer, red necktie. An insignia embroidered on his breast pocket read

MAINELY HARDWARE, under which grinned a dancing stick figure holding a hammer in one hand and a pipe wrench in the other.

"I'm buying into the franchise," Scott said, responding to her stare.
"First thing they said, no earring, no ponytail." He raised his brow in
a show of futility. She could tell he'd been drinking.

Ellen looked off beyond him. Scott must have seen a change in her
eyes, because he turned and stared. "Who's that?"

They watched the young man duck under the electric fence and
come steadily down the hill, black hair, black sweater, black corduroy
jeans.

"Do we know him?"

In her week of silence, Ellen hadn't mentioned Neal's presence at
the wedding. "It looks like Neal," she said now, fitting her cap back
on her head and pulling a loose strand of hair behind her ear.

"The kid from the wedding?" Scott asked.

"Neal," she said flatly. "Your brother's son."

Scott turned fully toward the barn, peering off against the low sun.
When he looked back at Ellen again, he was still squinting, as if trying
to register too many facts through too much whiskey.

"Wolves?" Neal called as he came.

Scott watched him with a scowl.

"Coyotes," Ellen replied.

"Neal?"

"Hello, Uncle Scott," Neal said. "If you want to go after them,
we'd have better luck with a shotgun."

Scott reached the pistol behind him, tucking it in his waistband.
"Jesus Christ," he said, grabbing Neal's hand, grinning, then looked at
Ellen again, his face registering the reasons she hadn't told him.

"Pistol's the only gun we have," Ellen explained to Neal.

"You want to go after them?" Neal asked again.

"Nah, we'd better get the sheep to the vet," Scott said. "I'll bring
Ellie's truck down."

Neal knelt beside the animal, placing his hand gently under its shoulder and raising it a little. He laid his face on the ground and peered
underneath the sheep, then said matter-of-factly, "You can't save her."

"You don't know Jake Merrifield," Scott told him. "For fifty bucks,
he'll bring the dead back to life."

Neal got to his feet again, shaking his head. "They've opened her
gut." He turned to Ellen, as though for her decision, and she became
aware that, bending over the sheep, her tank top was opened to him.

She straightened, kneeling upright. "Neal's right," she said to Scott. "She's dying."

"Want me to bring her to Justin?" Scott asked, consolation in his voice. "Justin Briscoe, the butcher," he explained to Neal.

Ellen shook her head. "They might've had rabies."

"Not likely," Neal replied. "Rabid animals travel alone."

He reached behind him and withdrew a knife from a sheath, a four-inch blade with a worn leather handle. "At least we can save the pelt."

"Wait—" Ellen rose to her feet.

"Go up to the house if you want," Neal said, "but we need to take care of her. She's suffering."

Scott pulled the revolver from his waistband.

"Scott—"

"El, go on up to the house," he told her gently, then said to Neal. "This is the only thing she lets me do on the farm, but she hates me when I do it."

He placed the barrel behind Katie's ear, but Neal reached out and touched his hand. "The other sheep are spooked enough," Neal said, taking the revolver from Scott and handing it to Ellen. "I've done this before. Lift her by the hind legs, backside to you."

Scott looked down at his blazer.

"Quickly," Neal said. Scott, nonplussed, nevertheless stooped and got his arms around the animal's flanks. He grunted once as he raised the sheep off the ground.

Neal knelt in front of the ewe and held the back of its head. Ellen felt her knees shiver. Neal looked up at her. "Okay?"

She nodded. Although she had never watched when Scott put down one of her sick or injured animals, there seemed something less offensive about Neal's doing it. His questioning look on her lingered. She nodded again. Then he turned back to the sheep, threaded his knife blade carefully through the wool at her throat.

"Hold her still," he said softly to Scott.

"Got her," Scott replied.

Neal's arm barely moved. The sheep kicked once, and Ellen saw the dark blood gulp over Neal's thumb before she turned and left them, walking quickly toward the barn. She moved through her flock, hiding the still warm revolver under her arm, then hurried through the paddock, across the dusty dooryard and onto the porch, into her kitchen, where she closed the door behind her, wondering why she had stayed to watch.

She went into the pantry, stepped around her weights, and slid the pistol on top of the cupboard, then returned to the kitchen, where she washed the ewe's blood off her hands, then sat at the table and unlaced her boots, pulled off her wool socks. Through the open windows, she could hear Scott's voice out in the barn, the dull clatter of the chain being dragged across the same wooden beam that Neal's father had used to hang himself.

She went into the bathroom, stripped off her top and shorts, and stepped into the shower, lathered and rinsed herself thoroughly, wanting to wash away every trace of Katie's death.

When she was through, she wrapped a bath towel around herself and went upstairs to dress, putting on a crisp, white long-sleeved shirt and pair of faded jeans. Wide leather belt.

She rolled up her shirt cuffs and returned downstairs to the pantry, where she kicked a ten-pound dumbbell out of her way and took some frozen lamb chops out of the old chest freezer. Putting down an animal now and then was part of farming, she told herself. All part of farming. The screen door opened.

"That sheep did not feel pain, I guarantee it," Scott said, tossing his new blue blazer on the kitchen table. His khaki slacks glistened red and brown. He seemed to study her.

"Take off your pants," she said. "I'll throw them in the wash." The old linoleum felt cool under her feet.

"You okay?" he asked her.

"I've had better days," she answered, even though there was more to his question than her slaughtered sheep. They both knew it.

"Toss me a couple brewskies?" he said.

Ellen opened the refrigerator, found two cans of Pabst and put them in his hands. He smelled of sheep, of fresh blood. It bothered her, the thought of them drinking beer over Katie's carcass, but she didn't say so.

"Neal's got some ideas about the barn," Scott said, going back out the door, his pants riding low on his hips. Ellen followed him out, went around the side of the house to her salad garden, where she picked some spinach and chives, then returned to the kitchen to rinse them.

"Amazing," Scott said, coming in again behind her. "I mean, it was like he was putting her to sleep."

"Mm." *You told me.*

Scott unzipped his pants and stepped out of them as he went into the bathroom. He turned on the shower. Then, with the water running, he opened the bathroom door again.

"I invited him for dinner," Scott told her, standing there in his jockeys. "I didn't think you'd mind."

She took a knife from the maple holder. "Scott, you never told me about the franchise."

"It's business," he said. "I didn't tell anyone."

He went back into the bathroom and showered, then came out with a towel wrapped around him. "You know, Neal's a carpenter by trade. He's built a couple of barns before, post and beam, he's got pictures. Beautiful."

Ellen started cutting the chives, her back to him. A moment passed.

"El, is this hard for you?" he asked. "I mean, Neal showing up."

"It's not hard for me." She kept the knife moving.

"Maybe it's a little uncomfortable for me."

"Maybe it is." *Should be.* Chop, chop.

"He looks so much like my brother."

"I thought he looked like April."

Scott paused. Ellen could feel his eyes on her. "Anyway," he said, "he's between jobs, and he was talking about fixing up the barn. Actually, building us a new one."

Ellen stopped cutting.

"He says it'll take less than two weeks. We buy materials, give him room and board, that's all he wants."

Ellen turned. "Scott, where are we going to get money for lumber? We can't pay the bills we've got."

"Hey," he said, scratching at his new haircut, "we're middle-class now. I get a salary." It was hard to ignore the defeat in his voice.

"You still haven't told me where you got the money to buy into the franchise," she said.

"El, how does any business get money? I took out a loan."

"With *our* credit?"

"It's not important. Look, you've been telling me for years the barn's falling in."

"But have him stay here?"

"Mo's room is empty. Why not?"

Ellen took a breath and let it out.

"I didn't give him a definite answer," Scott said. "I told him I'd talk to you."

Ellen scooped the cut chives into her hand, sprinkled them over the spinach, then brushed her hands together over the salad bowl. She chose her words with care. "Scott, if this is your way of making up to him—"

"Free labor, that's all it is." Scott took his beer off the counter and took a long swig, then tossed the empty can in the wastebasket. "That's what the silent treatment was about, right? Neal shows up and you get a chance to crucify me a little more."

"Scott, you brought Katie into the barn and hung her from the beam," Ellen said. "With Neal standing right there."

Footsteps on the porch silenced them, as Neal appeared outside the screen door, looking in.

"Here he is!" Scott said, finding a welcoming grin. "Come on in, man." He threw the door open and Neal caught it, then stood awkwardly in the doorway, wearing a black T-shirt, his black sweater bunched in his hand. His arms, Ellen noticed, were long and sinewy, like a swimmer's. His neck and shoulders looked strong. A far cry from the boy she remembererd.

"Name your poison," Scott said, opening the refrigerator. "Another brew?"

Neal lingered at the threshold, looking in at Ellen. "Maybe I picked a bad time."

Scott waved his hand. "Don't be crazy, come in. Hey, show her the picture of the barn you built. I've almost got her talked into it."

Ellen gave Scott a warning look, but he pretended not to notice.

"Seriously," he said, "Ellie and I need to talk it over. Have dinner with us. Tonight you can sleep in Mo's bed. In the morning we'll have a decision for you."

Neal looked at Ellen again, checking for consent.

She smiled at him. The smile he returned was tinged with sadness— or sympathy.

She served broiled lamb chops, along with the spinach salad and some fresh-baked rolls. She used her good stoneware, and Neal ate heartily. To Ellen, the meal seemed like those when they'd first bought the farm from Scott's parents, and Moreen was just learning to walk. The old farm kitchen was meant for meals like this, with its cast-iron cookstove and old oak chairs.

"So, Neal," Scott said. He was working on his second whiskey and ginger. "Where did you learn so much about sheep and barns and things?"

"When I was fourteen," Neal answered, "I spent a summer on a sheep farm in Vermont and helped them build a barn. It's basic stuff."

"What were you doing in Vermont?" Ellen said. "I thought you moved to Massachusetts."

"The state sent me off to boarding school when I was thirteen. I don't know if you heard; they checked Mom into the hospital. She had a little breakdown. Well, more than one."

Ellen studied his face, thinking of her own mother.

"Stupid goddamned thing," Scott interjected. He was turned in his chair, looking at his blazer folded on top of the washing machine. "MAINELY HARDWARE. Isn't that clever? Mainely. Mainely bullshit.'

Neal laughed a little. "So, Uncle Scott, when's the grand opening?"

"Hold on," Scott said, laying his fork on the table. "If you're gonna live here, you can't be calling me 'Uncle.' "

Ellen caught his eye, annoyed that he was acting as if it were already settled that Neal would move in. She got up from the table and started collecting the dishes.

Scott crumpled up his napkin and tossed it at her. "Come on, hon, you know you want that barn." He turned to Neal with a grin. "See, she refuses to look at the picture."

And there it was, the snapshot already stuck to the refrigerator with a DESTIN HARDWARE magnet, a beautiful building, tall and stately and bone-white against the dark green hills, almost churchlike in the way its silo rose up above the peak. Hearing the silence in the room, Ellen turned to see both men watching her.

"You know you want it," Scott teased.

She laughed a little as she shook her head. "Like a couple of little boys," she said, although she realized she'd made up her mind the minute she heard the suggestion. "Neal, I'd love you to stay here and rebuild the barn."

Scott responded by sitting back in his chair, turning and giving Neal a wink. Neal smiled, but kept an uncertain eye on Ellen.

"So what's for dessert?" Scott said.

"Yesterday's rhubarb pie," Ellen answered. "Neal, would you care for some?"

"Maybe later," Neal said, sliding his chair back. "I want to get started on the barn tonight."

"Hold on, I'll give you a hand," Scott said.

"Know how to handle a hammer?" Neal asked, straight-faced.

"Hey," Scott said. " 'Mainely Hardware: Serving Maine's hardware needs.' "

"Ellen, thanks for dinner," Neal said. "It was wonderful."

"Very wonderful," Scott added.

"Yeah, yeah," she said, waving them off. Despite her slight annoyance at the way Scott had steamrolled her, Ellen felt good about how the two men were getting along. Still, she couldn't help but wonder just how much Neal knew about his uncle—or the day his father died.

three

"Next left," Rooftop Paradise said, and Randy turned the dark panel truck onto the Phipps Road, its headlights sweeping over the dark, green woods. A magnetic sign attached to the side of the vehicle read XYZ DIVERS—DIVING IS OUR BUSINESS. But tonight, fifteen miles inland, the men were not looking for water.

Rooftop moonlighted as a collection agent for Ray LaFlamme, a seventy-two-year-old financier who owned the Belle Atlantic Restaurant in Old Orchard Beach. LaFlamme's philosophy was simple: Property in southern Maine, particularly around the southern coast, was gold. Although he owned thousands of acres of it, he knew there were still farmers who owned thousands more. And there wasn't a farmer alive who wasn't in some kind of financial dungheap. LaFlamme would lend them as much money as they wanted—for whatever reason. At 20 percent interest, what did he care? As long as they put up their property as collateral.

"Turn left up at the curve," Rooftop said. "Then look for a big potato barn and a burned-out foundation."

Randy worked for Rooftop in both ventures, collections and diving, not that Randy had any particular expertise in either. Randy had signed on a year ago, right after Rooftop finished a three-year stint in Thomaston State Prison and resumed these particular lines of work. He had served time for a drunk-driving, resisting-arrest conviction in which the oversized young man had taken two bullets in the thigh and another in the chest, and still managed to send four state troopers to the emergency room.

Their assignment tonight was not a collection, per se, but what Rooftop liked to call an encouragement session—meaning after it was over, the borrower would seriously consider signing his deed over to LaFlamme. A couple of guys named Humphrey and Jimmy Burdock, who lived in a trailer on sixty acres of land in Eliot, had borrowed forty thousand dollars from LaFlamme to start a company—and they still hadn't made their first payment. Which was not all that surprising, given that the product they were attempting to market was pickled french fries. By the time the assignment reached Rooftop through one of LaFlamme's bodyguards, the message was garbled and vague, but the upshot was they'd get an even four hundred bucks for a routine, ten-second beating. And four hundred more if the session resulted in a deed transfer.

"Two of 'em. Maybe we shoulda brought Gator-Aid along," Randy suggested as he turned onto the old road.

"I don't know," Rooftop said. "That Gator's pretty bad. I think he gets a thrill out of hurting people."

"What, like you don't?"

Rooftop ignored Randy. He leaned forward in his seat, watching the mobile home slide past them, sitting in front of a pair of white block chimneys. A huge barn sat behind everything, with a satellite dish high on its roof. A wooden, hand-painted sign banged into the front lawn said:

BUrDOCK'S FAMOUS FrICKLe'S
LIVe BAIt WeDDINg CAKe'S

" 'Frickles,' " Rooftop said. "That was the place."

" 'Wedding cakes?' " Randy added with a smirk. "Prub'ly a couple of faggots. Hey, I'll pound faggots for free."

"Actually, I think these guys are brothers," Rooftop said. "They got the same last name."

"Whatever. They borrow forty grand from Ray LaFlamme and then blow it all gambling, they deserve a pounding."

Rooftop shrugged. "Some people can't control their instincts."

"Fuck. Then they burn down their own house for the insurance money, and the fire investigators find three points of origin. They deserve a beating just for being so stupid. Besides which, *pickled french fries*?"

Randy drove to the dead end of the road, where he turned the van around, then stepped on the emergency brake. He looked over at Rooftop and said, "What do you do it for?"

"Do what?"

"Fuck people up."

"I don't believe I ever hurt a person for fun," Rooftop said, "even when I used to drink."

Randy snorted. "So how come you're still working for LaFlamme?"

Rooftop stared straight at him. "Mr. LaFlamme helped my mother put me through Saint Joseph's. I'm paying him back for my education. That's the only reason I do it. Plus sometimes I feel like I'm educating others in return."

Randy smirked. "Gator-Aid'll educate your ass," he said. "Doctorate in pain."

They shared the rearview mirror and straightened their hair. Sometimes they'd pretend to be Jehovah's Witnesses, but in neighborhoods like this you never knew—the people answering the doors might be Witnesses themselves. Not to mention these guys might have wives or kids living there, who could go for the gun while the old man was busy getting beaten. One thing Rooftop had learned, people that lived in places like that—with the junk cars and mud-strewn yards and NO TRESPASSING signs—they always had guns. Some of them were fearsomely dumb, some were downright crazy. And you never knew which wayward relative might be lurking in the shadows.

"I don't give Gator much in terms of life expectancy," Rooftop said, as they got out of the van. "Personally speaking, I wouldn't be associated with him if he wasn't related to Mr. LaFlamme."

"Who isn't related to Ray LaFlamme?" Randy said, sliding the side door open. "Some alcoholic bastard third cousin got a stepson in Baton Rouge, Louisiana, supposably swallowed by alligators escaping from his chain gang. And we get to train his crazy ass."

"Like I said," Rooftop told him, "I got a debt to Mr. LaFlamme. If he says, 'Show the kid the ropes,' that's what I do."

He lifted the carpet and pulled out the pair of magnetic signs that said MAINE STATE LOTTERY COMMISSION and stuck one to the side of the van. Randy took the other sign and stuck it to the other side. Then they got back in.

"You know what I think?" Randy said, as they drove back to the trailer. "I think LaFlamme's groomin the Gator for bigger things."

"What bigger things?"

"I don't know exactly, but I get a very dark feeling," Randy said.

He shifted into neutral and stepped on the parking brake. "Call it a premonition."

They left the motor running while they walked to the trailer and climbed the two porch steps. Randy reached in his jacket pocket and took out a small, green jalapeño pepper and popped it in his mouth while Rooftop knocked on the aluminum door. June bugs and spindle-legged flying insects bounced off the bare yellow light bulb. Chewing the jalapeño, Randy's eyes watered, his cheeks reddened.

When the door opened he smiled warmly, as if he was about to make this guy rich. But it was a woman who stood there, wearing a blue, threadbare bathrobe, possibly the smallest woman Randy had ever seen. Not that she was a dwarf, but she definitely looked undernourished. Her hair hung straight to her shoulders, her eyes were ringed with dark, concentric circles. In fact, one eye was bruised, as though she'd been punched. Her cheeks were hollow. She could've been seventy, could've been twenty-five. A cigarette glowed between her fingers.

"Whadda you guys, goin fishin, need worms?" she said, squinting up at them. Case like this, Rooftop would usually detain the wife while Randy walked inside and did his business with the old man. Rooftop hated doing that, the way some of these wives fought. He was afraid of accidentally breaking their arms.

"Is Humphrey or Jimmy at home?" he asked.

Sweat ran down Randy's forehead. He looked back over his shoulder, working up a fiery saliva as he checked the dark road.

"Right here, I'm Jimmy, whaddya want?" the woman said, her speech a rapid-fire burst of syllables. She peered out at their van. "What's this, I win some kinda gimmick or what?"

Rooftop looked at Randy, then back at the woman. In all the jobs he did for Ray LaFlamme, he'd never had to collect from a woman. He said, "I thought Jimmy was a man's name."

"No friggin man around here."

"No Humphrey?"

"You lookin for Humphrey, you can find him on the gamblin ferry tomorrow night," the woman said. "And when you do, you can tell him for me I don't want him back."

Randy didn't say anything, just hauled off and spat a greenish spray in the miniature woman's eyes, then followed with a quick hard punch to the face. Rooftop saw one of her bony feet lift out of her slipper as she shot out of sight.

Rooftop gaped at his partner, amazed, then looked into the trailer, where the woman was sprawled in her kitchen, just starting to move. Her cigarette smoldered on the floor beside her.

"For crying out loud," Rooftop said to Randy. Then he ducked into the kitchen, picked up the cigarette and dropped it in the sink. Turning back to help the woman up, he saw that she'd already pulled herself onto one elbow. Blood ran thinly from her nose down her cheek and lips, but she seemed more concerned with her burning eyes, squinting and rubbing them with her flimsy bathrobe sleeve, like a raccoon washing itself.

"Dirty bastard," she slurred.

"Never mind that," Rooftop told her. "You need to take responsibility for your financial obligations."

He stooped and gently lifted her to a sitting position. Indeed, she weighed about as much as a raccoon.

"See, when you borrow money from a man and don't pay him back, you might as well be stealing from him," he said to her. "Now you people have missed your second payment, which means you owe Ray LaFlamme five thousand dollars, plus six hundred in late fees. I don't think anyone's going to complain if you pay half now and half on the weekend."

"Uh," the woman replied, reaching her skinny hand into the pocket of her bathrobe.

"This'd be cash, not check," Rooftop explained, but then he saw that what she pulled out of her pocket was not a checkbook or cash but a tiny revolver, and he ducked his head and charged out the door, knocking into Randy on his own way out, just as the shooting started, *bang-bang-bang-bang-bang-bang*, she fired the gun the way she talked, all six shots popping off before the men had made it down the steps.

"You hit?" Rooftop said as they jumped in the van.

"No, you?"

"Nope."

"Christ, who keeps a gun in their bathrobe?" Randy said, ramming the shift into D and screeching the tires on the road. Rooftop looked back at the trailer's lights as the van tore up the country road.

"That's what I call paranoid," Randy said. "She in pursuit?"

"Nope."

Randy checked his rearview. "Want to go back?"

"What the heck for?"

"I only hit her the once."

Rooftop shook his head. "Once was once too much for a lady. What's the matter with you?"

"Some lady," Randy said. "Friggin witch, if you ask me. We best get home anyway. I don't want the wife askin a lot of questions. I told her we had to dive in the dark tonight so we wouldn't upset the sea turtles."

"What're you gonna tell her about tomorrow? Looks like we'll be spending the night on a gambling ferry."

"I don't know, some story. Dumb bitch believes anything I tell her."

Rooftop gave him a look, kept right on looking at him until Randy said, "You got a problem?"

While Scott and Neal worked on the barn, Ellen folded laundry and finished her report cards, then made her way up to her spinning room. She had two looms and a spinning wheel in the room: the smaller loom for her commissioned pieces, the larger one for her art. Tonight she sat at the large loom. She'd been creating the tapestry for almost two years now and hoped it would be done by summer's end. It was her homage to parents, hers and Scott's, all of whom had died in recent years.

As soon as she began, she lost herself in her work, lulled by the sounds of the night, the water falling over the dam, an occasional sheep crying, its bell ringing, the creaking and banging of her barn coming down. She had worked for three hours or more when she realized that the hammering had stopped and the men were downstairs talking softly. Only vaguely aware of dishes and silverware ringing, or the footsteps on the stairs, she didn't even hear the door open behind her.

"You are amazing."

Startled, Ellen turned to see Neal standing there, staring over her shoulder at the tapestry. Now she heard Scott snoring across the hall, in their bedroom.

"I plug away," she said.

"You plug away," Neal replied, gently mocking her modesty. "That's a museum piece."

Ellen smiled, unsure how to respond. It was a wide tapestry, four feet wide, and nearly five feet high. Centered in the work was a scene from an old photo, of her mother, crouched beside a sand sculpture in the Ogunquit dunes on a misty day. Her mother, an artist, had spent the entire day working on the sculpture, an Indian woman lying on her back watching the stars. Ellen's woven image was done in undyed wool, the natural browns, blacks, and off-whites of her flock, made to resemble an old, sepia-toned print. In both the photo and the tapestry Ellen's mother appeared uncomfortable posing. She had been thirty-six at the time—Ellen's age—and quite beautiful. But while her sculpture gazed skyward, her own head remained bowed self-consciously.

"How many hours do you have in this?" Neal asked.

Ellen shrugged. "I haven't counted."

"And I thought you were so practical."

"I am, about most things."

"Is this your mom?" he asked, pointing.

"Yeah. She was a sculptor. Metals mostly. She died a few years ago, choked on a piece of candy." Ellen laughed a little, bitterly. "A lemon sour ball."

Neal was silent for a moment.

Ellen went on. "I'm sure she always thought she'd be struck by lightning."

"I hope you don't mind the interrogation," Neal said.

Ellen shrugged off his concern. "I'm flattered that you're interested."

Along the top quarter of the tapestry, where Ellen had yet to inlay the shed, the bottoms of five sepia-toned wheels showed. In the top right-hand corner, the lower half of a full, yellow moon sat in a black night sky. Ellen had made the yellow dye with the skins of onions she had grown.

The entire bottom border was a frozen lake. A jagged break in the ice revealed swirls of creamy white water. From the left and right corners grew gnarled, bare-limbed trees that crackled upward like flames, the tops of which protruded through the central image as dune grass.

"White water?" Neal ventured.

"The reservoir, where Scott's parents were killed."

"They drowned?"

Ellen nodded. "Christmas morning. Your grandmother was helping Rolley deliver his milk—she did that every Christmas. It was snowing and his truck slid off the road."

"So that's going to be the milk truck," Neal guessed, pointing to the pair of wheels on the upper left, where four butterflies—the small wooden crosses around which were wound different-hued yarn—hung from the unfinished image.

Ellen nodded.

Neal touched another butterfly, one that hung from a larger wheel in the center of the design. "This is going to be a spinning wheel?"

"Scott's mother's—your Grandma Chambers. She taught me to spin and weave."

"And?" Moving his finger to the right.

"My mother's motorcycle, an old BMW."

"So tell me," he said, putting his hand on her shoulder and tapping the yellow butterfly with his long finger, setting it gently swinging. "Is this the moon or the sour ball your mother choked on?"

"I haven't figured that out yet," Ellen said, turning to look up at him. "It's almost funny, isn't it?" she asked grimly.

"Not at all," he said. His hand remained on her shoulder, and his dark eyes met hers intently. Then, abruptly, he removed his hand and stuck both hands in his pockets, showing some discomfort. "Ellen, I feel like you were coerced into letting me stay here."

She shook her head dismissively. "I just don't handle surprises well," she told him. "But you're family, Neal. You're always welcome here."

"I may be Scott's family," he said. "As far as you're concerned, I'm just the son of someone who used to be your brother-in-law."

"Whoever you are," she replied, conceding the point with a smile, "I'm glad you came."

He returned her smile, easily. "So am I," he said, but he seemed to study her.

"Neal, how long do you think it'll take, realistically?" Ellen asked, hoping he wouldn't mistake her question for eagerness to have him finish and be gone. She just needed to know how long he'd be there so she could prepare herself emotionally. Feeling disjointed as she did, with Moreen's departure, she still wasn't sure this was a good idea, having him here.

"Realistically?" he said. "Twelve days."

"Twelve?" Was he teasing her? She met his eyes again.

"Twelve," he repeated. "Why?"

She shook her head. "You seem very confident, that's all."

Neal shrugged. "What can I say? This is the first of July. I'll be done on the twelfth." He gave her a last look, a kind of polite smile. "Well, I guess I'll leave you alone and try to get some sleep." he said, and he left the room.

"Night," Ellen said, hoping she hadn't insulted him.

★   ★   ★

When Ellen got into bed, Scott stopped snoring. He lay still for a moment, then rolled over to face her. "He's just like his father was, another Superman," he said. "Supposedly he's gonna help me too."

"Help you what?"

Scott smirked. "With the business."

"I thought Mainely Hardware would be making all the decisions now."

"Hey, between them and Neal, how can I go wrong?"

"*Shh.*"

Their bedroom door was closed. Ellen could see the light under the door—she had left Mo's bedroom light on for Neal. She glanced at the clock. One-eleven. She rolled over to face Scott, ran her fingers through the soft warmth of his chest hairs. He covered her wrist with his hand. She could feel his heart beating.

"Scott, he's your family," she said quietly. "If you'd rather not have him here, tell him we've changed our minds."

Scott sighed. "I've got to admit, the kid's a hell of a worker," he said. "Incredible energy."

Ellen softened her voice to a whisper. "I didn't tell you what Maddy said."

Scott grunted again. He wasn't a big fan of Maddy, and it was as much interest as he could muster in anything she might have had to say.

"At the reception, she told me that Neal was holding the electric fence."

"How the hell could he hold onto the electric fence? And *why?*"

"I don't know. To make a fool out of her."

"She doesn't need any help there."

"But if it's true—"

"Ah." Scott rolled over, facing away from her. "I don't know what you see in that woman."

Ellen rolled onto her back and listened to the quiet night. Just a sheep's bell jingling down in the pasture and the waterfall whispering beyond.

"Do you think he knows?"

Scott took a breath. "Doubtful," he said quietly. "I know his mother wouldn't have told him."

Ellen closed her eyes, listened to the waterfall. So many years. Let it go.

★   ★   ★

Second of October. More than twelve years ago. Why keep the date? But you do. A Tuesday afternoon. Ellen's first year teaching. Neal's twelfth birthday.

Scott's older brother, Jonathan, convinced that his son's behavioral problems were the result of his unchallenged genius, had bought the boy a state-of-the-art computer for his birthday and stored it at Scott and Ellen's. Neal's mother, April had arranged to pick it up the day of Neal's birthday, while the boy was at school.

Over the years, Ellen came to believe that intuition had brought her home that day. At the time, however, she thought she was just stopping in to check on her sheep. A hurricane had been moving up the coast all week and was due to hit Maine sometime in the evening. But it had reached Cape Cod hours ahead of schedule, and Ellen wanted to make sure the sheep were safe in the barn.

The wind was already loud when she pulled into the dooryard. April's Jetta was parked beside Scott's Mercedes. Figuring he had come home for lunch, as he often did, Ellen stopped in the house before going to the barn, to say hi and to see if April needed her to bring anything for the birthday party later.

Despite the rain and wind outside, the farmhouse was strangely quiet when Ellen went inside. In the living room she found wrapping paper spread on the floor, the carton containing the monitor sitting in the middle of it. Then she heard a noise upstairs.

"Where are you guys?" she called and started up the stairs, unsuspecting. Then her bedroom door slammed shut.

"Be right out," Scott yelled, but when Ellen went up the rest of the way and pushed open the door, she found the two of them standing on either side of the queen-sized bed, their backs to her. They were getting dressed. April turned first, with a kind of smile—more of a grimace, really. Ellen did not remember looking at Scott. What she did remember was the sound of his voice as she left the room and escaped down the stairs, through the house, and back onto the porch into the loud wind, where the watering pails had overturned beside her black rubber boots and piles of brownish clouds tumbled angrily over the barn.

Leaning on the porch rail, staring wildly off at her farm, the entire scene flattening before her eyes, Ellen finally heard Scott's words. "You didn't see anything," was what he had called to her.

Then it was raining and she was in her car, turning onto Main Street, a calendar-image, double-wide New England boulevard bordered by white colonial homes and wide sidewalks, crimson and yellow leaves ripping from ancient maples. Her new white pickup truck—her anniversary gift from Scott—sliced through it all, the rain, the plastered leaves, rippling this perfect place with confusion.

The white-pillared town hall stood on one end of the town commons. A white-domed bandstand sat in the center. At the other end of the wet green stood the white Assembly of God Church and parsonage—April and Jonathan's residence—the Reverend no doubt closeted in his oakwood study, preparing Sunday's fire-and-brimstone sermon.

Ellen pulled into the driveway without a thought about what she was going to say to Jonathan. She hadn't planned to come here. She had meant to return to school and try to finish out the day. But here she was, at Jonathan's house. Pastor Johnny, Scott called his brother, though never to his face.

Jonathan was a charismatic faith healer who had recently earned his master's in theology from Harvard Divinity School. Brad Beecham, Destin's first selectman, claimed that Jonathan had cured his throat cancer with a touch of his hand. Marianne Clancy, a receptionist at the tax office, swore that Jonathan had driven the muscular dystrophy from her body. Similar testimony of his healing powers issued from scores of adults and children all over New England, who had been cured of their ailments at Jonathan's hands. His church boasted nearly 500 members— 475 more than the congregation who had attended services until 1985, when he had taken over.

Maybe it was because Ellen felt that she needed healing that day, the reason she went to Jonathan and not to her best friend, Maddy Sterling—who, after all, was a counselor—or to her mother, who would have only acted as if she'd seen it coming.

When Jonathan let her in, Ellen asked if she could use his phone.

"Is everything okay?" he asked as she dialed.

In fact, she could not think of a single aspect of her life that was okay or would ever be okay. Everything was poisoned. She called the elementary school to have the bus drop Moreen off at Scott's parents' house up the hill from the farm. Then she called the high school. When Arlene Glanville, the secretary, answered, Ellen told her that something had come up and she wouldn't be back. Arlene told her not to worry, that school was letting out early because of the hurricane. Arlene asked if everything was all right. Fine, Ellen said.

"Because Scott just stopped by, looking for you," Arlene told her.

"Thank you," Ellen said, and hung up.

All the while, Jonathan stood across the kitchen table from her, dressed in his white shirt and black necktie, watching with growing concern. "You seem troubled," he said. In years to come, Ellen would wonder if Scott's infidelity had been a brotherly thing—Jonathan, older than Scott by six years, academically superior, athletically superior, morally and spiritually superior, the favored son. Had this been Scott's way of evening the scales a bit?

At the time, Ellen did not care about the brothers' rivalry. In fact, standing in the pastor's kitchen, she felt suddenly foolish that she had come here. Furthermore, she knew—with absolute certainty—that if there was any hope of salvaging their lives, that hope would be dashed if she told Jonathan. But here she was.

"Did something happen to April?" he ventured.

A short laugh escaped Ellen. April's betrayal did not surprise her. President of the Destin Historical Society, the Concerned Citizens Coalition; April, with her colonial home and community standing. No, April did not surprise her.

But Scott—

—who had always ridiculed his brother's high and mighty attitude, his sister-in-law's hypocrisy. More honor among thieves than preachers, he'd say, at least a thief only wants your money.

Jonathan leaned his fingers on the table, his face clouding with concern. "Ellie, what is it?"

"Nothing. I just found them in bed together."

Disbelief. Jonathan raising his long body, seeming to float on his feet.

"Scotty?" he answered. Wind rattled the windows. "Not Scotty. And *April*?"

Ellen gave him another sort of laugh, as if this were Jonathan's own fault—or maybe she'd just thrown him an affliction that he couldn't heal. He pulled a chair back from the table as if to sit, then leaned heavily on its back. "Are you sure?"

"I don't even know why I'm here," Ellen said, turning to leave, when the door blew open and April flew in, carrying a cardboard box that read MONITOR.

"She didn't see anything," April said to Jonathan. Then she wheeled to Ellen, her lipstick smudged, her cheeks a deathly white.

Jonathan left the room.

April dropped the box on the counter and pursued him, saying, "Jon, she didn't see anything!"

As her voice trailed away, Ellen saw Neal's head pass the window. The door opened.

"Aw-right!" he said, seeing the monitor on the table. He must have read the turmoil in Ellen's face, because for the moment they just stared at one another while the trees roared outside and the rain beat at the windows. Neal was a bright boy, dark and quiet and exceptionally gifted, and Ellen wondered if he had any idea how his life was about to change. "Maybe you should go outside and play for a while," she told him.

"Yeah, in a hurricane," Neal said, and he turned toward the living room just as the footsteps drummed down the stairs, April's voice echoing through the parsonage, *"Jon, would you wait?"* Jonathan burst into the kitchen with his trench coat flung over his arm, Neal tracking his father silently as Jonathan threw open the storm door and walked out into the wind.

"Jon, are you going to listen to me?" April cried.

Neal studied Ellen, as his mother trailed off in pursuit, the sound of her voice chiming against the glass.

"It'll be okay," Ellen told him. Then she left too. Out in the driveway, in the rain, she walked past April while Jonathan started his car.

"You didn't see a *thing!*" April yelled at her.

Ellen got in her truck and followed Jonathan out of the driveway, past the white church and down the road. When Jonathan turned right, Ellen went left, and she drove for the rest of the afternoon with no destination, the trees waving her wildly on, the rain and wind buffeting her pickup, the road signs shivering, windshield wipers dashing madly. Everywhere she went, houses were plastered with yellow leaves, roads littered with branches, limbs torn from trees.

Sometime that night, in the full violence of the storm, she made her way to York—a neighboring coastal town—and knocked on Maddy's apartment door.

Maddy was a counselor then, with the Department of Social Services, and she had a small, private practice in the basement of a pizza place. She was in the process of divorcing her first husband, an anaesthesiologist, while waiting for her next husband—a surgeon at the same hospital—to divorce his wife.

When Maddy opened the door, she just stared at Ellen, an odd look of wonderment on her face. "Everyone's looking for you," she said, trying to hand Ellen a cordless phone. As if they'd all met and sorted it out while Ellen had been out driving.

Ellen gave a sneering laugh, refusing the phone. "Do you have something to put me to sleep? Valium? Anything?"

"You don't know?"

"Know what?"

Maddy took a breath, kept her eyes on Ellen. "Call Scotty."

Ellen heard the gravity in Maddy's voice, and her heart skipped.

"Jonathan," Maddy told her. "He hanged himself."

Ellen felt the building shake with a gust of wind, and she thought it was going to collapse around them. Hanged himself . . . She wanted to ask if Jonathan was dead, but she wasn't able to get the words out. Then she didn't need to.

"He did it in your barn," Maddy said. She paused, staring soberly at Ellen, then added, "El, school let out early today."

Ellen expelled a long breath of air, vaguely wondering what school letting out had to do with Jonathan's hanging himself. Then it hit her.

"Moreen?"

Maddy was already nodding. She took hold of Ellen's arms. "Mo found the body. She's okay."

"Oh, God, no." Ellen leaned heavily against the door jamb.

"Moreen's okay," Maddy said again. "The bus dropped her off at Scott's folks' house, but they weren't home, so she walked down the hill."

Ellen turned. "Have you seen her?"

"I've been waiting here for you. Ellie, what happened?"

"I've got to go," Ellen said, opening the door.

Maddy captured her, held her arms. "El, talk to me."

Ellen could feel herself trembling, spiked to the hilt with adrenaline, way too much to manage. "I've got to see Moreen," she said, stiffening, wanting to pull away.

"She's at Jonathan's."

"At Jonathan's," The words didn't register. Jonathan was dead. Hanged himself.

Maddy nodded, kept their eyes connected. "Everyone's at Jonathan's. April and Neal. Scotty and Mo. Scott's parents are there too . . ."

Again Maddy tried to hand her the telephone.

"Scotty doesn't know where you are. He wants you to call him before you go over."

Ellen shook her head, desperately needing to see Moreen, but just as desperately wanting to avoid everyone else; she especially did not want to talk to Scott.

Maddy's eyes darkened. "If this is what I think it is," she said, pressing the phone in Ellen's hand, "you'd better get your stories straight before you go over there." She seemed confident in what she was advising, so Ellen took the phone and dialed.

Scott picked up after the first ring. "Ellie?" he said anxiously.

She didn't respond.

"Everyone's here." His voice was low and slightly slurred, as if he'd been drinking. There was talking in the background. The television, Ellen realized.

"Where's Moreen?" Ellen said.

"She's fine." There was a pause, and then the background noise quieted. Ellen pictured Scott closing himself in a closet so no one would hear him. "El, I know we need to talk," he said softly, and then he paused. "Did you say anything to Maddy? Nobody here knows. It'd kill my parents."

Ellen listened angrily, not about to answer.

"I wish it was me," he said. "Babe, I love you so much—"

Ellen hung up the phone.

The steeple bell was pealing and a vigil gathering outside the parsonage when Ellen drove down the street. Townspeople wore rain gear, substituted flashlights for candles in the rain, looking as if they were preparing to storm the stockade fence, a structure that had been originally erected in 1711 as a defense against Indians, but now protected only the parsonage swimming pool. Not wanting to talk to anyone, Ellen considered stealing in through the church basement; an underground tunnel connected the cellars of both buildings. But, in deference to her claustrophobia, she pulled into the driveway, keeping her eyes straight ahead as she parted the mourners.

Scott was waiting in his brother's kitchen, his face dark with remorse, when Ellen came through the back door. He wore his tweed jacket and tapered slacks—his dressed-for-success look—and he came forward to hug her, whispering, "I told them one of the sheep got hurt in the storm and you brought it to the vet's. I'm so sorry." She held out a hand, to keep him back.

"Where's Mo?" she said.

"Up in Neal's room reading," he answered. "She's okay."

Ellen started to walk away from him, but he took hold of her jacket sleeve. "Ellie," he whispered, and she smelled the alcohol on him. It took all of her restraint to keep from lashing out at him. She pulled away and walked through the arched doorway, where she saw Scott's father, Rolley, sitting on the carpeted stairs, leaning forward with his arms on his knees, staring down into the living room; Neal sat over in the corner, on the piano bench, working intently at his new computer. Scott's mother, Thelma, was sitting on the couch beside April, both of them absently watching a medical drama on TV. There was a box of tissues on the coffee table between vases of flowers and plates of cookies and brownies. A few used tissues lay crumpled on the couch. When Ellen walked into the room, April's eyes shone intensely at her.

Thelma lifted herself off the couch and met Ellen in front of the coffee table, where they embraced.

"How can you believe a thing like this?" Thelma said, the bones of her arms suddenly seeming very frail. Scott came over and placed a hand on both of them.

"It was just like Jonathan to keep his sorrows private," Thelma continued. "Never complain, never burden others with his troubles."

Except for hanging himself in his brother's barn for a child to find, Ellen thought bitterly. She looked over at Neal, whose eyes remained fixed on his computer monitor. She said to her mother-in-law, "I need to see Moreen."

Thelma nodded. "You go see her," she said. "I left her in Neal's room, away from the adults and all the blubbering. It must have been such a shock for the poor thing, but we're all very proud of her, she got right to the phone and called 911."

Thelma released Ellen. Scott didn't.

"How's the sheep?" he said, feigning concern, anxiously massaging Ellen's shoulder.

Ellen paused, to decipher his words, to decide how to answer him. Indeed, whether to answer him at all.

"Was the leg broken like you thought?"

Ellen saw the halting glance Thelma gave her son at that moment. Then the old woman turned her gaze to April. There was no flash of revelation; in fact, it was the way Thelma's eyes just sank, unfocused, that told Ellen her mother-in-law had just seen through the charade. Ellen backed away from Thelma then, ashamed to have been part of it, and she went up to find Moreen.

Rolley glanced up at her as she passed him on the stairs. "Some God, huh?" he said. "Let the good one go."

Ellen was stunned. Although his casual cruelty toward Scott was no surprise—she'd never heard her father-in-law say a kind or complimentary word about Scott—Rolley had always been the most unquestioning believer Ellen had ever known, a fearsome Christian, the eldest son of parents who believed that every form of enjoyment was a sin. Now Rolley chuckled bitterly, as if every belief he'd ever held had just vanished along with his favorite son. "Yup, he's a real beaut."

In that moment Ellen realized that nothing would ever be the same, not with any of them: Rolley sitting on the stairs so small and devastated, Scott standing in the middle of the floor pretending he hadn't heard the old man's invective, Neal eyeing Ellen from behind his new computer, April watching her too carefully, and Thelma walking off to the kitchen, knowing everything. Thelma would not tell Scott that she knew, Ellen was sure. She would not even tell her husband.

And six years later she would die with the secret.

four

Two in the morning. Ellen stared up at the darkness while Scott snored beside her. Although the waterfall spilled loudly over the dam, to Ellen the sound was as quiet as breathing. With Moreen gone, the farm seemed quieter than ever. Then she heard the jingle of a single sheep's bell.

Aware of a faint illumination in the room, Ellen raised her head and saw a line of light bleeding under the door. She got out of bed, careful not to disturb Scott. Putting on her robe as she opened the door, she walked down the hall and discovered that Neal was not in Mo's bed.

She went downstairs, thinking that he might have fallen asleep on the couch, but the living room was empty. She went into the kitchen, took the flashlight off the counter, then went out onto the porch.

She walked down the steps and across the dooryard to the paddock fence, and saw one of the ewes pacing nervously, pursued by two of her lambs. Opening the gate, she went in to quiet them—and her heart jumped.

Peering down past the pasture fence, she saw something—was it Neal?—sitting up on the crest of the hill. She aimed her flashlight, but the beam was weak, so she crept through the bustle of ewes and quietly pushed open the gate.

He appeared stationary on the crest of the hill. But as she crept closer, his body suddenly took shape, wrapped in a blanket, his right elbow moving rapidly up and down.

Ellen stopped abruptly, felt her heart beating in her chest, wondering whether to come ahead and risk embarrassing him, or to turn and leave—and risk embarrassing him even more.

Then he turned his head.

"I didn't want to wake you," Ellen called softly, keeping her distance. His arm continued to move.

She wondered whether she should just go back to the house, but she found herself venturing a few steps closer, until she was no more than ten feet away.

"I got worried," she said. "You weren't in the bedroom." She drew a breath and shone the light on him.

Wrapped in his blanket, he was spinning yarn with a drop spindle, alternately feeding wool from the bundled dark fleece he held in his lap and working the spindle with his right hand. She stepped closer, shone her flashlight on the fleece in his lap—Katie's, she guessed. He stopped spinning and took Ellen's hand, forcefully directing her flashlight down toward the right, the gully. Four tiny eyes shone back at her like stars.

Ellen's muscles clenched. Coyotes. He moved the light thirty feet farther to the right: another pair of eyes. The rogue, she guessed. She lowered herself to her knees.

"What are you doing out here?" she whispered.

"I'm presenting them with a dilemma," he explained. "They're very hungry, and I'm very confident."

"Oh, Neal," she said, hearing her own words coming back at her.

"Don't apologize," he told her. "A stranger comes to your house, you have a perfect right to ask how long he intends to stay."

"You're not a stranger," she said, putting her hand on his shoulder. "Now will you please come back inside?"

Neal continued spinning the yarn. "When the sheep are safe, I'll sleep in the house," he said. "Besides, I like it out here, the way the moon reflects off the water."

Ellen sighed. A breath of wind came up, rippling the pond on its way over the dam.

"Back when Scott's parents moved up on the hill, and we first had the farm to ourselves," she remembered, "we used to have parties down there all the time. We'd build a fire, and Scott and the guys would play music, and we'd all get wasted on homebrew and blueberry wine and go skinnydipping."

Neal gave her a look.

"There was nothing sexual about it."

"Of course not."

It was hard not to hear the sarcasm in his voice, but she let it go. "Sometimes Scott and I would wake up in the middle of the night and be the only ones left. And we'd just lie out under the stars listening to the frogs and the nightingales. Those were the best times. Mo was a baby, I was finishing school, we had plenty of money." She shivered a little.

"Want some?" He dropped a corner of the blanket off his shoulder so it fell on her knee. She moved closer to him and pulled it around her own shoulder. In the paddock behind them, the sheep kept moving. Neal's arm felt good against her, generous and warm.

"Can I ask you something?" he said softly.

"Yeah?"

"Did you have a chance to make amends with your mother before she died?"

Ellen took a long breath and let it out, while she considered her response. "We probably never talked about what we needed to talk about."

"What's that?"

"I guess I hoped she'd let me off the hook," Ellen said.

"For what?"

"I don't know. For not measuring up. But I don't think she ever forgave herself, either."

Neal kept spinning. "Forgiveness isn't all it's cracked up to be."

They sat quietly for a few moments. Then Neal stopped spinning and looked at her.

"Is it true your dad was an astronaut?"

Ellen laughed a little. "That's the family myth, isn't it? Actually, on my sixth birthday my mother took me to a restaurant and told me that my father was either an astronaut or a convicted murderer. Evidently, she only consorted with men who held titles."

Neal smiled, resumed his spinning.

"She was an art professor in Baltimore at the time," Ellen continued. "NASA had commissioned her to do a piece to commemorate the country's first manned space flight. At the dedication she met candidate number one—Drew McDermott, the astronaut. Candidate number two was a guy who had two original Cezannes hanging in his bedroom. He'd stolen them from a gallery in New York. At the time he was the most wanted art thief in America—I guess it inspired the romantic in her. Four years later he killed two museum guards in a holdup and got life in prison."

"You must be curious about which one was your father," Neal said.

"It mattered to me a lot when I was younger," Ellen admitted. "Being an optimistic kid, naturally I was convinced it was the astronaut. Then when I was in junior high, he did a space walk. Colonel Drew McDermott. I told all my friends, and my teacher brought a television into the classroom so we could watch him. I never felt so proud. But then they interviewed his wife at home, and I saw that he had two daughters of his own. When they cut back to him walking in space, I wished his tether would let go. That was the end of my father fascination."

"Fathers can fuck you up," Neal said.

"I got over it. But sometimes at night when I'd look up at the sky, I'd feel like I secretly had something in common with the stars."

Neal looked up, and she saw that he was smiling contentedly. She lay back on her elbows, raised her face to the blackness, the infinitesimal billions of scattered, silent worlds.

"Mothers can fuck you up too," she said.

She remembered the restaurant in Baltimore. Their table was at a window, high enough so they could see the Atlantic stretch out beyond Chesapeake Bay. While they ate strawberry shortcake, her mother told her they were moving to Rome. She showed Ellen a picture of bone-white pillars, she showed her the sculpture of David, naked.

Instead, they moved to Maine.

She remembered sitting in the window loft of a ramshackle garage they rented from a fisherman, watching her mother kneeling in a shower of welding-torch sparks, backed by the cold ocean, wearing leather work boots and a filthy T-shirt, making useless shapes of abandoned iron and steel.

Another memory: her mother hanging out dirty laundry in an April rainstorm, saying, "This way we don't have to wash them."

Or the afternoon when Ellen was called to the guidance office and told that her mother had been taken to a hospital, and that Ellen would be living with the Nielsen family for a while. Later she learned that her mother had tried to drown herself by walking headlong into the ocean, but the waves kept driving her back.

She remembered carrying a plastic trash bag of her clothes and school books into the Nielsens' spacious house, and the way the family—husband, wife, and daughter—stood in front of the kitchen table while Mrs. Nielsen introduced them. The table was set in a bay window with a view of perennial gardens and a small duck pond. One of Ellen's mother's sculptures—it looked like an exploded lighthouse—stood on a small rock island in the center of the pond. That's what Mrs. Nielsen wanted Ellen to see. What Ellen noticed instead was that the way the table fit into the bay window, there was room for only three chairs. So for the nine months that Ellen lived with the family, she straddled the corner leg.

Ellen took the blanket off her shoulder. "Neal, we have a bedroom for you. Now come on, I don't want you sleeping out here alone."

He laughed softly, pulling the blanket around him. "If you don't want me sleeping out here alone, go get your sleeping bag and join me."

An image intruded on her unexpectedly, the two of them cradled in each other's arms. It surprised her, and she pushed to her feet.

"We can listen to the frogs and nightingales," he teased.

"Yeah, and them?" She waved her flashlight down toward the gully, moving the beam down the green hill to the thick, gray brush . . . but there was no sign of the glowing eyes.

"I told you," he said, "we have an understanding, the coyotes and me."

Ellen sighed a kind of laugh. She really did admire his confidence. For a moment, she almost considered sleeping out here beside him, curled up in her musty old bag. But she had to get up for work in three hours, her last day of school—

"Ellen."

"Hm?"

"Go to bed."

She smiled, shone the light once more down along the stream bank, the pond, the dam.

"Please be careful," she said, touching his shoulder again. He reached for her hand, but she drew away from him and headed toward her house.

five

Ellen awoke to the sound of hammering the next morning. Her bedside radio was playing, Scott had gone to work over an hour before. When she saw it was seven-forty, she jumped out of bed, gathered her clothes, ran downstairs to brush her teeth, grabbed her car keys and cap, and was out the door.

She spotted Neal high off the ground, straddling a roofing truss, pulling nails out of the ribs. Amazingly, the barn was already stripped to its posts and beams on two sides. Looking straight into the sun, Ellen pulled her visor down. "You be careful up there."

Neal raised his hammer to wave, and she caught her breath. She noticed that he had also removed the paddock fence from the corner of the barn and constructed a temporary pen for her two rams inside the ewes' pasture.

"Think it's safe having them so close to the ladies?" she called, watching Buckminster, a small but muscular brown Merino with curled horns and extremely valuable wool, pacing incessantly inside the pen, intermittently springing at the Z-boarded gate with a loud *whack*. Mike, the less passionate of the pair, huddled in the slim shade of the barn, content to blaat his lustiness over the nervous bawling of the ewes around him.

"I thought we could add some excitement to their lives," he replied, looking down at her with a sort of scowl. "You're not going to school—?"

She figured it was her casual clothes that had confused him: khaki shorts and a baggy cotton shirt; red Converse All Stars on her feet. No socks.

"Last day," she explained.

"In July?"

"Class trip. We lost two weeks this winter, snow days."

Hearing a car pull off the road, she looked back to see the dark green panel truck coming in, hauling an open, seventeen-foot Boston Whaler.

XYZ DIVERS

DIVING IS OUR BUSINESS

Randy pulled up just short of the porch, and Rooftop Paradise unfolded his seven-five mass from the passenger side, to let Moreen out. Mo looked curiously at the dismantled barn, then came over to Ellen and gave her a quick kiss on the cheek. "The guys need neckties. Can they borrow a couple of Dad's?"

"Neckties? Come on in," Ellen said, uncomfortably aware that she had just invited Mo into her own house.

Moreen walked up the steps, seeming to labor under the weight of her pregnancy. Despite the hazy warmth of the morning and a forecast for a record-breaking heat wave, she wore a black, long-sleeved jersey under a black wool shift. Her forehead and cheeks shone with perspiration.

"Mo, you look so hot," Ellen said. "Let me find you something cooler."

"That's okay, they're in a hurry," Moreen replied, coming into the kitchen, the silver ball in her tongue clicking against her teeth as she spoke.

Ellen led the way into the living room then started up the stairs. "What color ties?"

Moreen remained below. "Anything," she answered. "They've got a meeting, and they want to look spiffy."

Outside, the van's horn blared. That didn't take long, Ellen thought, but she kept it to herself. She went up to her bedroom, found a couple of Scott's neckties, then went into Moreen's room to find something short-sleeved. Downstairs the horn blew again.

"Mom?" Moreen called up to her.

Ellen sighed. She left Moreen's room and brought the neckties down. "Thanks, thank Daddy too," Mo said, reaching for the ties, but when her sleeve pulled up, Ellen saw a dark bruise on the inside of her forearm.

"Mo, what's that?"

"What's what?"

Ellen caught her sleeve and lifted it, revealing four distinct marks side by side, like fingerprints. The horn blew again.

Moreen shrugged. "Must've bumped it, I don't know. Mom, I've gotta go." She pulled the sleeve back down and headed for the kitchen.

Ellen followed closely, her mind tripping over images of Randy grabbing her arm, wondering if the reason Moreen came in the house was to show her the bruise.

"How do you bump the inside of your arm?" Ellen persisted.

"I'm coming!" Moreen called, pushing the screen door open. "Gotta go," she said to her mother.

"Wait, before you leave," Ellen said, coming onto the porch behind her, suddenly hating to see her daughter go back to that van. "Is it okay if your cousin Neal uses your room for a week or two?"

"Not my room anymore," Moreen answered with a shrug, then caught sight of Neal, who was standing beside the van, talking with Randy. "You mean that guy at the wedding was *Neal*—who used to baby-sit me?"

Randy blasted the horn, glaring up at her.

"I'm coming," Moreen called, then turned and rolled her eyes at Ellen. "I'm gonna be late for work."

"Work? We've got school."

Mo wrinkled her nose. "You don't think I'm going to Fun-town—?"

Again Ellen felt that horrible sense of Mo slipping away. "Honey, are you sure that bruise is okay?"

"Love you," Moreen said to her, then started down the steps, the horn blaring.

Rooftop hadn't noticed Neal at first. He'd been standing beside the van, staring at the farmhouse and sucking on his asthma inhaler, when he heard the sound behind him. And there was Neal, claw hammer in hand. Rooftop stood well more than a foot taller than Neal, and a good deal heavier, and when he recognized Neal, he aimed a ready stare through his thick glasses.

But Neal ducked down to see Randy inside the van. "How's it goin?" he said, and he walked around the front of the vehicle, with

Rooftop following close behind. As he approached the driver's door, Randy sat slightly back in his seat, taking his hands off the wheel, keeping an eye on Neal's hammer.

"Listen, I was way out of line the other day," Neal told him, offering his hand.

Randy replied by leaning on the horn.

"I was hoping we could get started on a better foot," Neal said.

Randy regarded the hammer sullenly. "You wanna discard that thing?"

Neal gave a self-effacing smile. "Sorry," he said, and tossed the hammer on the ground. His right hand remained offered. "Really, no hard feelings?"

Randy smirked. He looked away as he stuck his hand out the window.

"So, where you guys diving these days?" Neal asked, shaking hands.

"Here and there," Rooftop answered. "Got a couple of moorings to put in down in Kittery." His deep voice was drowned out when Randy blew his horn again.

Up at the house Moreen came onto the porch. Ellen caught the screen door behind her.

"I'm coming," Moreen called, then came down the steps showing Randy the neckties.

Ellen leaned on the railing, watching, as Moreen walked toward the van then stopped about ten feet from Neal. "Hey," she said to him. "Don't you remember me?"

A smile formed slowly on Neal's face, and he replied, "Of course I do."

"You grew up," she said.

"And you got pregnant," he replied.

"Hah!" she said, giving him a thumbs-up. Randy blasted the horn again, and it continued blaring, even when Mo got back in the van and Rooftop ducked in beside her.

Moreen draped the ties around Randy's neck, but Randy whipped them off; in doing so, he caught her in the eye. She lowered her head, poked him with her elbow.

The horn stopped, the van rocked, and Ellen, without thinking, bounded down the steps and was there at the van reaching through the window, bunching Randy's white shirt in her fists.

"What are you doing to her?" she heard herself say.

"Hey, hey." Randy laughed, raising his arm to deflect her.

But Ellen yanked him toward the window, ripping his shirt open. He stopped laughing then. "Hey, *bitch*—"

"Mom, I'm okay—"

"Don't you ever touch her," Ellen said to Randy.

"Hey, mind your own fuckin business." Randy found the shift, gunned the accelerator and the van shot back toward the barn.

Neal caught Ellen in his arms, to keep her from falling. "Love you," Moreen called, as the van jumped ahead again, swerving as it sprayed gravel at the boat. At the end of the dooryard it chirped onto the pavement and went roaring up the hill.

"God, I'd like to kill him," Ellen said, as she watched her daughter going away.

"Proverbs sixteen, thirty-two," Neal replied, taking a hand off her and waving cordially, as the van dipped out of sight. " 'He that is slow to anger is better than the mighty.' "

He reached behind her and retrieved her cap, which had fallen off her head and hung from her braid. He threaded her hair back through, then squared himself to her and fit the cap on her head, a glint of admiration in his eye.

"Which means, let's take our time," he added.

Agitated as she was, Ellen's heart raced even faster in her chest. *Take our time?* Had Neal just let her know he was planning some kind of revenge against Randy, like maybe picking a fight with him sometime when Rooftop wasn't around to defend him? Ellen couldn't deny that she disliked Randy with an intensity that she'd never felt toward anyone. Still, something Ellen had heard in Neal's voice chilled her, even dampened her rage somewhat. Or maybe it was the way he smiled as he looked up the road where the van had gone.

Let's take our time. His words echoed round her head.

Already late for work—and not knowing Neal well enough to ascertain if he was serious or just posturing—she turned away from him without saying a word and walked to her pickup truck.

But it wasn't Neal that distracted Ellen as she stood there in Funtown, watching her kids dressed in bathing suits and shorts and sunglasses and sandals, running from ride to ride. It was her worry for Moreen that shadowed her all through the bright, hot day, like a storm cloud looming.

"Moreen?" Scott had said in disbelief when Ellen called him from the teachers' room. "She's the biggest tomboy that ever lived. Don't worry, Mo's not gonna take shit from him or anyone else. Are you kidding?"

He was right about Moreen. Having grown up on a farm, even as a little girl Mo had been strong and fearless and physical. Ellen could remember her stacking firewood when she was five; trying to carry a wayward lamb back to the barn, hauling pails of water to the trough, even throwing hay bales onto the flatbed. When she was older, between mosh pits, skateboarding, and ice hockey, her body was constantly bruised—not to mention the rings and studs she'd had poked through her flesh lately. Moreen, though sweet and loving, was not without the ability to defend herself.

But it wasn't sweetness or toughness Ellen had seen this morning. Behind Mo's cheery smile and easy kisses, Mo clearly wanted to show her mother that she was out of her care and living with a cruel and dangerous man. And Ellen had no idea why.

The front doors were propped open on the sidewalk, but the store was not open for business. Beside the 50% CLOSE OUT SALE was a much larger sign, in day-glo orange: ANOTHER MAINELY HARDWARE COMING SOON!

Inside the building, a crew of laborers moved walls of shelves, un-packed crates, and carried trash out to the dumpster, while carpenters sawed and hammered. Down in the back, across the alley from the laundromat, Scott unlocked the back door to let the young men in. Randy wore a jacket and tie. Rooftop carried a briefcase. Scott locked the door behind them, and the men walked down an aisle of steel shelving stripped of merchandise, except for a few bags of rock salt.

"Feels like old times," Randy said, "us giving you money for a change."

"Feels pretty good to me," Scott replied, leading them through a door to his office. Rooftop and Randy took a seat on the leather couch in front of a wide, glass-topped coffee table. Rooftop hunched over his briefcase and pulled out a manila folder, started thumbing through the papers inside.

"Mr. LaFlamme's attorney did a title search and found everything in order," he said. "We didn't need a survey. No building inspection, either. We stopped over this morning, saw that you're making improve-ments to the barn."

Scott wheeled his desk chair over to the table.

"Oh yeah, we took a couple of your ties," Randy told him. "Hope you don't mind."

"As long as you don't take my house," Scott said with a laugh.

Randy chuckled with an air of authority. "No way we're gonna let that happen, Scotty."

Rooftop gave him a look, then slid a document in front of Scott.

"This is your promissory note," he said. "You can read it, if you want. Basically, it states that Mr. LaFlamme is loaning you the money, eighty thousand dollars, at 20 percent interest, so you can buy into the Mainely Hardware franchise."

Rooftop took a red pen from inside his jacket. "This is the mortgage deed, and you need to sign this binder agreeing to keep a hundred percent damage insurance on your home and name Mr. LaFlamme as the mortgagee, same as you did with the store on your previous loan."

Scott looked the documents over. "So now I owe him a hundred and a half."

"Well, plus the interest," Rooftop told him.

"I know it probably feels like a big risk," Randy said.

"Yeah, you know that, huh? Like, if the franchise goes belly-up, Ray LaFlamme not only gets the store, he gets my house and farm too? Is that what you mean?" He looked at Randy straight-faced for a moment, then winked.

It took Randy a second to realize that Scott wasn't seriously busting his balls, and he laughed. "I like that sense of humor," he said. "See, we think alike, us two."

"Just don't tell Moreen about the loan," Scott told him.

"Hey," Randy said, raising his hands in mock surrender.

"I don't want my wife to know, either," Scott added.

"Be discreet. Exactly."

Rooftop set a certified bank check face up on the coffee table, turned it to face Scott.

"Mainely Hardware, here we come," Randy said, picking up the check and handing it to Scott. "Really, I think this is a very wise move."

Scott folded the check and stuffed it in his pocket as he stood up. "Guys, thank you very much. I'd invite you to have a drink with me, but I'm a company man now. No drinking on the job."

"Just as well," Randy said. "You ever give this guy a drink"—he hitched his thumb at Rooftop—"you best be sure you're either caught up on your payments or you're in a fast fuckin car."

*   *   *

By noon, the temperature had swelled to ninety in the shade, and the school bus back from Funtown felt like an oven. As soon as Ellen's home room emptied out, she loaded her pickup truck with cartons of her personal things and headed for home—and summer. Unfastening the third button of her cotton blouse as she drove, she fanned the fabric away from her chest to let the air circulate around her skin.

Before her truck was within sight of her farm, she heard the miserable crying of her sheep and realized that Neal must have begun the weaning. She pulled into her dooryard and saw that her ewes were separated from their lambs into their respective pastures, both groups bustling at the wire-mesh fence that kept them apart, all of them bawling frantically.

Ordinarily, she would have isolated the ewes in the cellar of the barn and withheld their water until they dried up. But now the barn was almost completely skeletonized, stripped to its posts and beams and a few stalls standing off the old wooden floor. She spotted Neal carrying a wide plank from the barn to the toolshed, where he had stacked the lumber in four separate piles. Despite the heat, he was still wearing the black wool sweater and corduroy jeans.

"How can you stand all that crying?" she said to him as she pulled off her sneakers.

"I've heard it all before," he answered.

She got out of the truck barefoot, the fine gravel of her dooryard burning the still-tender bottoms of her feet.

"How was your last day?" he said, heaving the plank onto the pile. His sweater was covered with sawdust and wood chips, his hair and face similarly caked.

"Hot. Want something cold to drink?"

"In a while."

Ellen watched him walk back to the barn, thinking she should talk to him about Randy—clear up their earlier conversation—but, deciding that he didn't look like a young man contemplating a fistfight, she went out to the pasture to feed the sheep.

She started with the rams, hoping to quiet them before she tended to the others. The gate of their pen was fastened with rope at the top and a hook-and-eye on the bottom. Showing Buckminster the bucket, Ellen unfastened the rope from the top of the posts and pulled the gate back just enough so she could fit the pail through. She kept her bare foot behind the post. But the instant Bucky spotted his food, he sprang with enough force to split the diagonal board and rip the eye screw from the post, knocking Ellen to the ground and pinning her ankle beneath the frame. As both rams escaped, immediately all thirty-seven ewes broke for the pasture with Bucky in feverish pursuit, burrowing into their ranks, mounting one after another. Mike, less aggressive, nevertheless took advantage of the stragglers.

Ellen's ankle burned and bled. Afraid it was broken, she raised herself onto her elbow and reached to gingerly lift the gate off it, when she heard the bells of her flock and saw them charging back up the hill toward her.

She pushed the gate off her ankle and started to pull herself up, when Neal's arms went around her, lifting her effortlessly to her feet. He turned and snapped the gate's broken board off its frame, then went wading into the marauding flock. While Bucky was preoccupied with one of his nieces, Neal swung the board down hard, driving two nails into Bucky's rump. The ram twisted and let out a sorry blaat, raising his face in protest, at which instant Neal smashed the side of the lumber down on his ear, and the animal's legs crumbled beneath him. Dropping the board, Neal lifted the ram by its horns and heaved mightily, swinging him into his pen. Dust flew. The other ram, Mike, trotted into the pen of his own accord. Neal shouldered the gate closed, looped the rope over the tops of the posts, then propped the broken board against the front of the gate.

He turned to Ellen, who was leaning on the pen for support. "Are you all right?" he asked.

"He's got a beautiful fleece," she answered, flexing her toe to test her ankle, "but a nasty disposition."

"Then you have to be nastier," Neal said. He glared into the pen, and the ram let out a sorry complaint.

Allowing a little more weight on her foot, Ellen took a couple of cautious steps, saying, "Once summer's over and I see how the ram lambs develop, maybe I'll replace him." She wanted to show Neal that she could be practical about these things. He took hold of her shoulder and brushed off the back of her blouse, then, more tenderly, the back of her arm.

"Sure you're okay?" he asked, and he kneaded her shoulder a bit with his thumb. She took a deep breath and released it, allowing the tension to spill out of her. She flexed her neck. *Talk to him.*

"Neal, I appreciate your help—"

She turned to face him, then noticed that two more buttons of her shirt had come undone; she fastened them.

"I'm talking about Randy," she said. "And Moreen. I guess I want to figure things out for myself."

He gave her a look she couldn't quite decipher, an almost paternal frown. "What's going on with her?" he said, bending to brush the side of her shorts, the side of her leg. "She seems to be angry at you for something."

Ellen stepped away from him, reached back and dusted off her own seat.

"Just let me deal with Moreen and Randy in my own way. Okay?"

He turned away and stepped on the angled board, securing it against the gate. Behind them, the lambs kept bawling. Ellen straightened her cap, folded the sides of her visor down. "I'm sorry," she said. "It's the heat. And I can't stop thinking about Mo."

"I know," he told her. "Wanna take a swim, cool off?"

"Me? I've got way too much to do."

His dark eyes glinted playfully at her. She didn't like the way he always seemed to question her truthfulness.

"Come on, you've got the whole summer off," he said.

She sighed. She had to admit she had a school's-out-for-the-summer kind of itch. "Maybe," she told him, "if I can find my bathing suit." She turned for the house. "Do you want one of Scott's?"

"I thought we'd go skinny-dipping." He raised his eyebrows at her, still teasing.

"I'll get you a suit too."

"There's nothing sexual about it," he called after her.

She climbed the porch steps and went in the house, favoring her sore ankle. She stopped at the telephone and called Moreen's house, let the phone ring several times, but no one answered. Hobbling upstairs, she pulled off her blouse and dropped it in the straw laundry basket, then slid the cardboard box of summer clothes out of her closet. The room was easily ten degrees warmer than outside. A line of perspiration ran down her arm.

The first suit she found was a faded denim two-piece, one she'd had since high school. These days the top showed more cleavage than she cared to reveal, and the bottom rode too low on her hips. She still liked to wear it when she was alone, down at the pond or in the garden, never in public.

The suit she found at the bottom of the box was one she couldn't remember buying, a black one-piece. She unbuttoned her shorts and stepped out of them, pulled off her bra and panties, and stepped into the suit. It was snug in the thighs and the elastic was strong, which she was glad of. She fit her breasts in the cups and crossed the straps over her shoulders, then went to the mirror with apprehension. She was pleasantly surprised. A slight rounding of her stomach, but not bad for a thirty-six-year-old who ate three meals a day. Hang it, she was too hot to worry about it. She pulled Scott's bathing suit out of the box, checked to see that it wasn't falling apart, then went downstairs and grabbed two clean bath towels from the linen closet.

Making her way barefoot down the dusty farm road and around the cinder-block pump house, the farm pond came into view. She could see Neal doing a lazy breaststroke up the middle of the narrow pond, working against the current, his body long, white, muscular—and naked.

She stopped for a moment to rest her ankle, which had begun to throb, and from the corner of the pump house she watched him. The pond water looked brownish against his back, his firm white buttocks reflecting the sun. His shoulders were broader and more muscular than she had imagined, his biceps solidly defined. She imagined a strong, lean buck. Suddenly he looked back at her, as if he'd known all along that she was watching him.

Embarrassed—and dismayed at herself for spying on him—she lowered her head and followed the dusty tire tracks down to the water, aware that Neal's eyes were on her all the way, conscious of her long white legs, and the high cut of the bathing suit on her hips. Hobbling up the grassy bank onto the granite blocks of the dam abutment, she tried to talk some sense into herself. This tension she felt around Neal—Scott's nephew, for godsakes—was ridiculous.

"I brought you Scott's suit," she said, tossing it indifferently to him. "It may be too big for you."

He retrieved the bathing suit then lowered his arms and legs underwater. In a moment, he was swimming again, the bright orange suit reflecting the sunlight from below the surface.

"Is the water cold?"

"Not at all," Neal answered, watching her.

"I'll bet."

Neal dived underwater again, disappearing into the darkness, and the water pulsed over the dam, splashing down on the other side. The pond was little more than forty feet long and only twenty feet wide at its widest, but quite deep at the dam. The body of water had once been a sleek granite cascade along the Agamenticus River. In 1828 the river was reduced to a stream when its headwaters were dammed to create a reservoir for the town of Destin. About the same time, Scott's industrious great-great-grandfather—the first of four generations of dairy farmers to inhabit the property—decided to dam up the gorge to restore his water supply.

He constructed the dam of granite keystone blocks that bowed in toward the pond, its arch effectively resisting the tons of water that pressed against it. In 1930, after a midwinter earth tremor had realigned some of the blocks, Scott's grandfather had pumped the pond dry and sealed the upstream face of the dam with four inches of cement. To aid future repairs, he had also embedded iron rungs down the left side and installed a drainage pipe at the bottom.

Because the sides of the pond were steep, there were only two ways in: climbing down the rungs or diving. Not given to slow torture, Ellen always chose the latter, so now she sat on the edge of the abutment and lowered herself down to her diving rock as Neal rose out of the water, shaking the hair from his face. "You're stalling," he said, his eyes fully on her.

She took a breath, braced herself for the shock and sprang out, arms stretched over her head. Entering the water with hardly a splash, she knifed down where it was icy and dark, then turned upward and broke into the sunshine with a yell.

"Not cold?"

She slapped the water at him. Neal laughed and splashed her back, his hair lying down his forehead in shiny black ringlets. She started a lazy sidestroke, and as the sun warmed her cheek and shoulder she experienced a sudden and unexpected feeling of euphoria. Nine weeks of freedom lay ahead of her. Even though she loved teaching—and she was good at it—there was nothing like having her life to herself for a couple months a year.

"Ohhh!" she cried, and plunged again, straight down where the water was cold enough to drive the tension from deep inside her. She opened her eyes and looked up to see Neal's silhouette rippling the bright sky, then scissor-kicked powerfully and broke water beside him, taking a deep breath of air.

"Feel better?" he said, smiling affectionately at her.

"Mmm," she said, a luxurious moan. She took another full breath to buoy herself and rolled over on her back, floating on the surface so she could feel the sunshine soak into her black suit.

Neal let the current carry him to the bowed center of the dam, where a clear sheet of water, maybe four inches thick, flowed over it. The top of the dam was a flat surface of concrete that overhung both sides of the dam by six inches, to enable foot passage across the top during the dry months. Five heavy-duty eye bolts reached out of the lip, suspending a steel cable twelve inches above, to keep swimmers or stray animals from being swept over the top.

With his back to the dam, Neal reached up and grabbed hold of the cable, spreading his arms wide and pulling himself up out of the water so she could see the thick cords of biceps and the hard ripples of his stomach.

"Careful up there," she said. "It's a long way down the other side."

Neal glinted down at her in a way that made her look down at herself and see the impression of her nipples showing through the bathing suit. She let herself sink in the water.

"I saw the coyotes again," he told her.

"Today?"

"Just now, up in the woods. Don't you have a shotgun around?"

"I got rid of it a few years ago," Ellen answered.

"Where does Scott keep his revolver?"

"He hides it in the bedroom." Just after she'd said the words, a wild notion rose unbidden in her mind, that he might have been thinking about Randy. She swam away from him, wanting to change the subject.

"The bedroom where?" Kicking off the dam, Neal skimmed across the surface on his back, pursuing her.

"I don't know," she answered honestly. "He hides the gun, I hide the bullets."

"And the plan is, when the burglars break in, you'll have a meeting."

They moved around the center of the pond, circling one another, Neal holding up his bathing suit—which was way too big for him—with one hand. Ellen enjoyed his playfulness. She rolled over and treaded water as he swam past.

"Scott had some trouble with depression a few years ago," she explained, "after he went into bankruptcy. It just seemed like a good idea." She thought back to that time, how she had worried about him, the way he'd sit on the porch for hours, staring off at the barn and pastures. She had loved him so passionately in the early years of their marriage—before his infidelity had cast a chill over everything. Eventually, after she'd forgiven him, she had learned to love him again, but in a different, perhaps more mature, way, without the blind devotion of young lovers. In fact, they grew to become more like partners—in parenting and homesteading—mutual caregivers. So when Scott's financial problems grew worse and worse, concerned that he might hurt himself, Ellen sold his shotgun and began hiding his handgun.

"How is he now?" Neal said, snapping her from her thoughts.

Ellen shrugged. "Oh, fine," she answered, though she was stuck wondering if it was really enough in a marriage for a husband and wife to be caregivers.

"Well," he said, swimming toward the bank, "if I'm going to finish that barn on time, I'd better get back to work."

"Why twelve days?" Ellen said, swimming behind him.

"Twelve," Neal answered, pulling himself onto the diving rock. "Twelve is the heart of the universe."

"Yeah, how's that?"

Sitting on the rock, he looked down at her matter-of-factly. "Twelve months in the year."

"That's because the moon revolves around the earth twelve times." Using the strength of her arms, Ellen hoisted herself onto the rock beside him.

"Twelve hours on a clock, twelve inches in a foot," he said. "Twelve in a dozen."

"Maybe it's because twelve is so versatile," Ellen suggested, "divisible by two, three, and four. It was probably good for trading." She reached up to the abutment and grabbed her towel.

"So you're saying twelve is practical," he replied. "There are twelve tones in Western music. That's not practical, it's sound waves. Pure physics." He grinned up at her, eyes sparkling.

"Twelve-volt battery," she offered, pulling her long braid over her shoulder and wrapping it in the towel, loving the sun's heat on her back. "Twelve-step program for alcoholics."

"Twelve-bar blues, twelve signs of the Zodiac, twelve Caesars, twelve tribes of Israel."

"Twelve disciples," Ellen said.

Neal's eyes snapped at her, suddenly intent. "Christ knew all about the twelves." He seemed to enjoy instructing her, and it put her slightly on edge. "You've heard of the twelve legions."

She shook her head.

"Christ's fatal mistake," he explained, standing up on the rock. "When the Romans came to arrest him at Gethsemane, Peter sliced off a guard's ear, and Jesus told him to put down his sword. Remember that? Jesus said, if he wanted to, he could summon twelve legions of angels to slaughter every last one of his enemies."

"That's right," Ellen said. "He was teaching us to forgive our enemies."

Neal smiled at her, then dived into the pond again. When he surfaced, he turned to her and said, "That's the popular misconception. Actually, what Christ was teaching us was that forgiveness can cost you your life."

Ellen shielded her eyes from the sun and peered down at him, to see if he was kidding.

"Come here," he said, and he jackknifed down.

Ellen dropped the towel at her feet, took a full breath of air, and dived into the water after him, deeper and deeper, until her ears plugged and the sunlight all but disappeared. She could see Neal descending farther, the pale kicking of his feet, but when her lungs called for oxygen she turned and pulled for the light, yawning to pop her ears on the way up. She surfaced and held on to the cable at the top of the dam as she caught her breath. She looked down in the water, expecting to see the brightness of Neal rising, but the sun's rippled reflection obscured the view. She waited. She watched.

Suddenly afraid that he might be in trouble, Ellen filled her lungs and dived for the bottom, kicking through the water with all her strength, and as her world grew steadily darker and colder, she spotted him. He appeared to be working at something at the bottom of the dam. When Ellen's lungs demanded air this time, she ignored the call and pulled herself deeper, until finally she reached him. She touched his arm. He turned and pointed his finger upward. Together they sprang off the rocky bottom for the surface. Ellen broke water first, with a gasp. Neal came up beside her.

"Are you okay?" she cried.

"Yeah, why?"

The current carried their bodies against the dam, and they both reached up for the cable. When Neal turned to face her, his thigh moved forward in the current and stopped against hers. She drew her leg away.

"It's almost twenty feet deep there," she said. "I thought you were trapped."

He laughed at her. "I have exceptional lung capacity."

"Neal, you're so talented," she said, unable to resist the sarcasm.

"I've known a couple of women who think so," he answered, giving her a look.

She flicked water at him.

He grinned. "Did you see that pipe in the dam?"

"It's for draining the pond," she told him.

"So, if you wanted to drain it, you'd have to hire a diver, wouldn't you?"

If there had been any doubt in her mind, now she knew for sure that he was talking about Randy, about luring him over here and doing some harm to him. But whatever Neal was suggesting, Ellen wanted no part of it—no matter how much she despised her son-in-law.

"Neal, do me a favor," she said, looking straight at him. "I asked you not to get involved in this."

His dark eyes stared back unblinking.

A cry sounded in the distance. They turned their heads toward the pasture and heard it again, along with the sudden ringing of bells.

"It's Mo," Ellen whispered, and she called out, *"Down here!"*

Ellen looked up. At the top of the hill, her flock of sheep came thundering down the slope, Bucky the ram in hot pursuit.

"Mo?" she shouted. She waited only a moment for a response then dropped off the cable and grabbed one of the rungs on the face of the dam and pulled herself up to the abutment. Hobbling down the bank barefoot, then across the farm road, she tore open the pasture gate and started up the green hill, ignoring the burning in her ankle. Reaching the crest of the hill, she could see Moreen sitting just outside the rams' pen, her head bowed, holding her stomach. Ellen ran to her, fell to her knees.

"Honey, what's the matter?"

Doubled up in pain, Moreen sank to her side in the grass.

"Bucky got out," she moaned. "I think I did something." She

looked up at her mother, her eyes swimming in fear, her hands pressing up on the underside of her rounded belly, as if trying to hold her baby inside. She was strikingly pale and soaked with perspiration.

Bells suddenly pealed, and they heard the drumming of hooves. Ellen looked back and saw Bucky herding the flock toward them.

"Hey!" Neal shouted, vaulting the fence with one hand on the post, the other hand holding the oversized waist of his bathing suit. Fixing his eyes on the ram, Neal stalked forward. If sheep possessed any degree of reasoning, it was clear that Buckminster was putting his to use, the way he nonchalantly dismounted his partner and trotted back to his pen. Mike, his cohort, followed eagerly. Neal pursued them both and swung the gate shut behind them, pushing the looped rope down over the top of the two posts, then fastening the hook and eye at the bottom.

Ellen looked up at him helplessly. "We have to get her to the hospital."

Neal came and knelt beside them, laid his hand on Moreen's knee. "Where did he get you?"

She moaned, as the ewes moved in closer to watch.

Neal pressed his thumb on Mo's ankle. "Can you feel this?"

She winced.

"This?"

"Hnn!" Hunching up, Mo reached for her mother.

"Oh, God," Ellen whispered.

"I'm going to see if you're bleeding," Neal told her. "Okay?"

Moreen peered at him fearfully. He lifted her dress, looked underneath. "No blood," he said to Ellen, "but she's cold. And pale. I think she's going into shock."

Mo was about to miscarry, Ellen was certain of it. "We've got to call an ambulance," she said.

Neal shook his head. "It'll take them too long to get here," he answered. "I'll drive her."

Ellen stared at him, aware that she was too frightened to think clearly, aware also of how she was relying on him. "Mo, honey?" she said helplessly, touching her daughter's face.

"Tell Randy I'm sorry," Moreen gasped.

"You're going to be all right," Ellen told her.

"Okay," Neal said, fitting his right arm under Moreen's thighs, his left under her shoulders. "Ellen, hold my trunks," he said.

Distracted, Ellen didn't understand. She was thinking that if she had been in the house or working in the garden, this wouldn't have happened.

"I'm going to lose 'em," Neal said, rising with Moreen in his arms. The bathing suit fell halfway down his bottom. Ellen grabbed it, pulled it back up as he started walking, and she kept pace, holding the back of his trunks with her right hand and brushing Moreen's hair with her left.

"Don't tell Daddy, okay?" Moreen said. She was beginning to sound delirious, and it scared Ellen.

"Honey, try to relax," Ellen said. She thought about her reason for keeping the ornery ram—to get another few pounds of fleece, another few dollars.

"What were you doing?" Moreen whimpered.

"What do you mean, honey?"

"You're wearing my bathing suit."

Ellen shook her head, having no ready answer. "It was the only one I could find," she said.

"It looks good on you," Moreen said, wincing as she tried to smile.

"Open the door," Neal said, reaching his truck. Ellen did, and he ducked inside, gently laying Moreen on her side. "Try to keep still," he said.

Ellen started to get in with her.

"Go in and call the hospital," Neal said. "Where is it?"

Ellen ducked out of the cab, trembling. "Sanford," she told him. "Take Route 91 from the center of town."

"Tell them we're on the way," he said.

Before Ellen could question him, he started the engine.

"Love you," Mo whispered between breaths. Ellen looked fearfully at her.

"Tell Randy I'm sorry," Moreen said again.

"Sorry for what?"

"Just tell him."

Ellen called 911 and told the dispatcher to watch for Neal's pickup truck. Then she drove her own truck to the hospital, made it in fifteen minutes and left the motor running in front of the EMERGENCY EN-TRANCE NO PARKING sign.

Neal was waiting when she came limping through the door. The receptionist looked sympathetic. A nurse appeared behind her and brought them into a small room that had a table, a television, and a small refrigerator and microwave on a counter. "Moreen's placenta became separated from her uterus," the nurse said after she had closed the door.

Ellen tried to grasp the meaning. "She lost the baby?"

The nurse picked up the remote control and clicked off the TV. "Would you like to sit down?"

Ellen stared dizzily at the table under her hands.

"In order to stop the bleeding," the nurse explained, "the doctor had to remove the uterus. It was the only option."

A great breath escaped from Ellen's lungs. "*The*" uterus, the nurse had said, not *her* uterus, as though it were a thing apart now, discarded. Neal put his arm around Ellen's back. "Sit down," he said. He pulled a chair up and Ellen dropped heavily in it.

Hysterectomy.

The nurse continued talking, but Ellen barely heard her. She stared numbly at the floor between her bare feet, feeling as if there was not enough oxygen in the room.

"We were able to leave her ovaries," the nurse said.

Ellen nodded.

"Here," Neal said, handing Ellen a cone-shaped cup of water. She took the cup, touched it to her lips and drank, grateful for its coldness, despite the way she shivered from the air conditioning. She had thrown a T-shirt over her wet bathing suit. She noticed that Neal's bathing suit was held up with a winding of duct tape.

"It would help if we knew what happened to her," the nurse said. "Her pelvic area is bruised."

"My ram attacked her," Ellen said. She turned to Neal and said, "Didn't you tell them?"

Neal nodded. "It was the ram," he said. Something in his lack of conviction niggled at the back of Ellen's mind, but she was too distracted to focus on it.

The nurse said to her, "I know you'd like to be with Moreen in recovery, but we're keeping her pretty heavily sedated. She'll probably sleep through the night."

"I'll stay," Ellen said.

The nurse studied her, looking as though she had more to say, but Neal placed his hand gently on Ellen's shoulder. "Want me to call Scott?"

Ellen heard him vaguely. "No," she said, remembering Moreen's plea. "If he gets home before I do, tell him I went to see Maddy."

An hour later, in the recovery room, Moreen opened her eyes. "How are you, hon?" Ellen asked, taking her hand.

Moreen stared for a moment, tried to smile, then closed her eyes again. Ellen watched fluid dripping slowly into the IV tube that was taped to her wrist. She watched the slow rising and falling of her daughter's chest. Inside her own chest she could not relieve the terrible weight of her negligence. She sat at Moreen's bedside for another two hours, then left the hospital.

She didn't cry driving home. In fact, it wasn't exactly sadness she felt, more a deep sense of regret. She was thinking about all the ways she had neglected her daughter over the years, the way she had filled her own life with work, with her art and her animals, and now one of them had robbed Moreen of her own motherhood. It felt as if something had been torn out of Ellen's own womb.

She pulled off the highway onto Reservoir Road with one thought. She would call Justin Briscoe the minute she got home, she would have him come and haul Buckminster to the slaughterhouse and be done with him. She'd give Justin the meat in return for his services. She did not want the animal even in her freezer.

Pulling into her driveway, she got out of her car and walked directly into the house, picked up the telephone, and started to dial.

"Ellen, wait—"

Neal's voice startled her. He came in from the living room just as Briscoe answered his phone. "It's Ellen Chambers," she said to the butcher. "Can you come over and take care of my ram?"

Neal put his hand on her arm. "Tell him you'll call him back." He nodded, with some urgency.

"Justin, I need to call you back," she said, then pressed the cradle with her index finger while she held the receiver to her ear. "What?" she said to Neal.

"The gate wasn't broken," he told her.

Ellen closed her eyes and took a breath, to calm herself. "Neal, I don't blame you," she told him. "I should have gotten rid of that animal a long time ago."

"Do you think the ram let himself out?"

Ellen's scowl deepened. "What are you saying?"

"I'm saying that Moreen let Bucky out."

He reached out and took the receiver from her hand.

"Ellen, Mo was already hurt when she came over here," he said, lowering his voice. "Your ram did not do that to her."

Ellen stepped back, her mind whirling, her head shaking in disbelief.

"It was a boot," Neal said.

Inside Ellen's chest, a boiling started, slow but volcanic in its intensity. Leaning forward on the kitchen counter, trying to catch her breath, she felt as if her body was gathering energy from the atmosphere. She pictured Randy the way one pictures an enemy, alone and defenseless. In furious glimpses, she beat him to the ground with an iron pipe, she smashed his face, she stabbed him through the heart with a steak knife, she strangled him with the strength of her fingers and thumbs. It was relentless, the destruction she wreaked on her son-in-law, but it gave her no relief. Adrenaline tore at her heart.

"You don't know that," she said. "How can you know that? You don't know he kicked her."

"Do you want a drink?" Neal asked softly.

She noticed that he was once again dressed in his black sweater and corduroys. She turned away from him, went to the kitchen table and sat down, feeling all the day's heat pressing in around her. She tore her arms out of the T-shirt, pulled it over her head and flung it across the room, then sat there in her bathing suit trembling. Moreen's bathing suit. She stood up again.

Neal set a juice glass beside her, filled with whiskey. "Have a drink," he said gently.

Ellen picked it up and took a sip, coughing after she swallowed, feeling for a moment as if she was going to vomit. She would have welcomed the chance to get rid of this bile any way she could. She drank again, forced down the whiskey, then spun away from him and threw open the door, stormed onto the porch, intent on, what—walking? running? getting in her car and going after Randy? Despite her protestations, deep inside her she felt there was truth in what Neal was telling her.

Now, as Neal came out, she turned and pushed past him, went back inside to the phone.

"What are you doing?" he said, coming in behind her.

She started to dial. "I'm going to have him arrested."

He thumbed the cradle down.

"Neal, stay out of this."

She glared at him, her chest heaving.

"Take a walk with me," he told her.

"I don't want to walk."

"Ellen." He took hold of her hand, tugging her toward the door.

She closed her eyes, not releasing the phone. "Please let me handle this," she told him evenly.

"Fine," he replied. "But first we walk."

"Neal—"

"Take the bottle with you," he said, letting go of her. "Or put it away. I'll wash the glass so Scott doesn't see."

Scott.

Moreen had begged her not to tell Scott, and Ellen knew why. Scott would go over there with his gun, and nothing would be able to stop him. Though Ellen had fired the revolver only once, she knew well its incredible power, the way flames shot from the muzzle and the gun jumped in her hand. She imagined the black satisfaction of shooting Randy, firing all six slugs through his body, then watching him collapse to the ground and melt out of Moreen's life.

"Ellen," Neal said. He was holding the screen door open.

With an angry sigh, she replaced the phone in the cradle and came out on the porch. The sun had set and the greens of the pasture and woods were already darkening.

"Down back," he said.

She decided not to protest, but went with him down the steps and headed left, around the pump house and down the farm road, not talking. A pair of ewes inside the pasture fence started following them, bleating.

"I forgot to feed them," Ellen said.

"I took care of it," he told her.

They were walking fast, Ellen setting the pace, going down toward the stream below the pond, feeling only a dull throbbing in her ankle, the whiskey already blurring her pain. But it had done nothing to suppress this wild electricity inside her.

"Why are we doing this?" she said.

"Because I don't want you going after him."

"I told you, I'm going to call the police."

"Do you really think Moreen would be willing to press charges against Randy?" he asked quietly.

She stopped but did not answer him. Then she started walking again, faster, toward the pond. The waterfall was loud, a heavy black sheet oozing over the dam and crashing on the rocky bed below, boiling and foaming away down the granite hill.

"I'll press charges myself," she said.

"On what grounds? You didn't see him hurt her."

She stopped walking, and finally the surge rose up from her chest and closed her throat. Tears burned at her eyes and she turned away from Neal, gulping a deep breath to keep from crying. She felt like collapsing. Once again his hands found her shoulders.

"Let me help you," he whispered. "Let me help Moreen."

The roar of the waterfall was like the roar building inside Ellen's head. She looked at the water moving, at the woods pressing darkly in beyond it. Then she started up to the farm road again, returning to the house saying, "I'm going back to the hospital."

"Scott's going to be home soon. What should I tell him?"

"Don't tell him anything. I'll call him from the hospital."

"Ellen—"

She paused, not turning.

"Just tell Scott she had a miscarriage," he said. "Don't say anything more."

She looked back at him, saw a look of arousal in his eyes that made her heart skip.

"Tell him," Neal repeated.

She resumed walking.

six

Ellen took the winding road to Sanford, her mind spinning in blackness. Although she no longer had any doubt that Neal would do anything to Randy she might ask of him, she forced the notion from her mind, vowing to do everything in her power to convince Moreen to have Randy arrested for what he'd done, and then to divorce him. What to do about Randy was clear enough.

The idea that Moreen had not only lost her baby but also lost the ability to ever have children was too much for Ellen to grasp. Her mind refused to accept the information all at once, the same as when she'd heard that Jonathan had hanged himself, or that her mother had choked to death on a piece of candy. Logically, of course, it was not incomprehensible. Moreen would not be the first woman to live her life childless—nor was she the first woman to marry a man who beat her. Still, Ellen's mind could not begin to fathom the depths of all those hard facts.

When she got to Sanford, instead of driving to the hospital as she had intended, Ellen followed the back roads that led to the house where Moreen was living with Randy and Rooftop. She came to a stop at the railroad crossing, then turned left onto Basin Road. The neighborhood was poor and rural, a smattering of old mobile homes interspersed among older farmhouses, a seemingly random assemblage of mismatched additions and roofs surrounded by overgrown fields and undernourished woods. Sheds were collapsed. Cars sat on blocks.

The evening was warm. Ellen had on a beige T-shirt, a brown

cotton skirt and sandals, and she'd tossed her white blouse in the cab
in case it cooled off.

A mile down the road stood an abandoned chicken barn, easily a
hundred feet long. On the other side of the barn was the old house
that the chicken farmer had built in the 1940s, sided with green asbes-
tos shingles.

Ellen stopped her pickup truck in front of the house and looked
out at Randy's new black Cherokee parked in the driveway. What was
she doing here, anyway? Looking for a confession? An apology? She
shut off her lights and engine and opened the door, slipping her blouse
over her T-shirt as she stepped out of the cab—not that the evening
had grown any cooler, but she wasn't wearing a bra, and she was afraid
of what she might do if Randy started gawking at her breasts. She
walked up to the back porch.

Emboldened by anger, she didn't knock but pulled open the screen
door and walked into the empty kitchen. A half-eaten chicken sat on
the counter, surrounded by flies. Dirty dishes lay strewn across the table.
The house stank of stale smoke and old beer.

She tiptoed through the doorway into the living room, where three
of Randy's paintings hung. Framed in rough pine lathing, and air-
brushed on black velveteen, they depicted a bull moose upending a
woman canoeist in the river; a brown bear rearing up over a doomed
female camper; an elk butting a woman off a cliff. In all three paintings,
the victims were back-to-the-land type women wearing skimpy shorts
and tops that had either ripped open or come unbuttoned.

Ellen walked into a hallway off the living room, where she noticed
an open door with dim light coming through. A red fire extinguisher
was fastened to the right side of the doorway. He was in the cellar, she
realized. She stepped softly to the door and looked down. A plywood
hatch cover on hinges was raised over a two-foot-square opening in
the floor, where a set of open treads, a ladder of sorts, led down to an
oily, earthen floor. Ellen listened for another sound but heard nothing.
A dank, musty smell rose up. She stepped down to the first tread,
wishing she had worn something other than the skirt. Her legs felt
vulnerable.

She stood there listening for a moment or two. Then, moving
quietly, she took three more steps. As soon as her head ducked below
the floor joists, a hand shot from between the open treads grabbed her
ankle. Ellen cried out and started to fall but caught the stairwell wall
above her head. She kicked with her heel of her other sandal, caught

the side of his hand. Then another hand emerged through a higher tread, wrapping around the front of her thigh and pulling back on her.

"Feels like my lucky day," came a voice, not Randy's. The rough hand slid off her thigh, while the other kept hold of her ankle. Then the young man ducked out from under the riser, grabbing her swollen ankle with his free hand and jerking her leg in the air. She hobbled and held onto the walls of the stairwell with both hands to keep from falling.

When she got a glimpse, Ellen recognized him instantly, one of Randy's friends from the wedding, the one they called Gator. He was solidly built, maybe nineteen or twenty years old, with baby fat under his chin and a menacing gleam in his eyes.

"I'm Randy's mother-in-law," Ellen told him, trying to kick free. He squeezed harder, and her ankle flared with pain.

"Now I know where Mo-reeen gets her long legs," he said, a Southern twang in his voice.

"Where is he?" she demanded. "Where's Randy?"

He leered up her skirt with a dangerous grin. All her adult life Ellen had wondered how she would feel and what she might do if she were attacked by a man. Now she knew. She wanted to kick him in the face as hard as she could, break his nose if she got the chance.

"You need to let go of me," she said, her voice full of false bravado. "The police know I'm here."

He released her ankle and folded his arms, still grinning. "There, you're let go of." He grinned, and she saw that one of his bottom teeth was missing. Evidently, he'd been kicked before.

Blood pumped behind her ears. Adrenaline surged. But she restrained herself, afraid that if she made any sudden move, he'd tackle her and haul her down. Backing up a single step, she said, "Just tell me where Randy is."

"We in some kinda hurry?" he asked. " 'Cause as far as I know, we won't be interrupted. The boys went out for stripers, hopin to catch the midnight tide."

He placed his foot on the bottom step, his eyes settling high on her thighs. "As long as the cops don't come, you and I got all night."

Ellen glanced behind her, saw that she was three steps from the top, with four steps separating them. She lifted herself one more tread, and so did he, his eyes rising to her breasts.

"Yup, far's the gov'ment's concerned, I was swallowed by alligators two years ago. Far as they're concerned, I'm just some family's dirty little secret."

She took another step up, and her head rose through the opening. Shifting her eyes, she saw that the hatch cover was held up by a make-shift latch, a small wooden block that swiveled around a nail.

"So no matter what happens here between you and me," Gator continued, "even if you decide to tell someone, it'll be like you imagined it. Cops wouldn't have the faintest idea who you was talkin about."

Ellen turned to face him, targeting the underside of his nose.

"So why don't you just relax and enjoy yourself. We got the whole place to our—"

She saw the flash in his eyes, but her foot was faster, glancing off his nose with enough force to snap his head to the side. He lunged blindly for her legs, but she was already bolting up the last two steps just ahead of his hands, which slapped at the treads behind her heels. Leaping out of the stairwell, she punched the wooden latch and slammed the hatch cover down just as he caught her swollen ankle in his hand. Fueled by fear, she jerked her leg, yanking his arm out of the hatchway. In the same motion she threw herself back onto the hatch cover, the plywood slamming off his shoulder and landing with a satis-fying crack on the wrist that still clutched her ankle.

He called her a cunt. His fingers opened and she scrambled to her feet. As the cover flew up again, she grabbed the closest thing—the red fire extinguisher—tore it from its rack and swung it by its valve just as Gator's face rose into its arc. The steel cylinder bounced with a hard ring across his forehead.

"Hah!" he said. Still grinning, he groped at the air for a second, then dropped noisily down the stairs, as the hatch cover slammed down.

Ellen stepped back, keeping the fire extinguisher in her hand, ready for the hatch to open again. In a moment or two, once her adrenaline subsided, she picked up her sandal and walked quickly out of the house, trembling.

"Moreen had a miscarriage," Ellen explained to Scott over the telephone.

At first Scott didn't reply. It was almost 9:30.

"I'm at the hospital," she told him.

"What happened?" Scott said gravely. "I'll be right there."

"Nothing *happened*," Ellen told him, sounding more defensive than she wanted. "She had a miscarriage."

"Okay. I don't know about these things."

Ellen sighed. "I'm sorry, it's been a shitty day." She had already decided to keep her encounter with Gator secret, since, technically, she had entered his house uninvited and may have fractured his skull.

"All things considered," Scott said, "a miscarriage probably isn't the worst thing that could've happened to her. What room is she in?"

"Scott, she doesn't want you to know."

"Is that what she said?"

"She's embarrassed."

For a second or two, Scott remained silent.

"I'm going to stay with her tonight," Ellen told him. "She's going to be asleep all night anyway."

On the other end of the line, she heard Scott sigh. "I guess it happens, huh?" His voice was soft, as though he were nervous, or close to tears. Or maybe relieved.

"It happens," Ellen said. "I've got to go."

America Sings and Dances was the name of the stage show aboard the ferry. Rooftop and Randy sat at a table toward the back of the lounge, where it was dark. Randy worked on his fifth hurricane, the rum concoction the crew was pushing, while Rooftop drank Diet Pepsi. An overnight gambling ferry wasn't the best place in the world for a recovering alcoholic, with all the drinking that went on. Small wonder—no casino ever lost money making people drunk. And this casino sure wasn't losing money tonight.

The low-ceilinged room smacked of makeshift luxury, with its royal-red carpeting and hundreds of stuffed captain's chairs surrounding little round tables. In the center of the floor, a chandelier hugged the elevated ceiling above a circular stage, where a ring of young, sequined dancers kicked to the beat of a four-piece stage band. Running the length of the interior wall, a polished cherry bar was decorated with fish netting and nautical brass—in case the sliding ashtrays or occasional stumble of the dancers weren't enough to remind passengers that they were fifty miles from land, muscling their way through a dark and frigid and particularly unfriendly Atlantic. Already during the show two members of the audience had staggered between the pitching tables vomiting into their napkins.

At one in the morning when the show ended, a couple of crew members wheeled a karaoke machine onto the stage. By now, the seaworthy audience had dwindled to maybe thirty, and they were all pretty well tanked, all but Rooftop Paradise.

The cocktail waitress started things off by singing "Top of the World," by the Carpenters, smiling and nodding confidently through the whole thing. It wasn't hard to see she'd sung the song before, probably every night of the week.

"I'm thinking about getting out of the collection business," Rooftop said after the first chorus.

"And do what?" Randy asked.

"Dive full time."

"No future in divin, for an asthmatic."

"Well," Rooftop said.

"Well," Randy said, lighting another cigarette.

"I happen to like diving," Rooftop told him. "Anyway, ever since I quit the booze, this other stuff's not settin right with me."

"Tell you what don't set right," Randy said. "Me, tending on your diving jobs for seven bucks an hour. That don't pay a married man's bills, not to mention I got payments on my Cherokee and a baby on the way." The ashtray slid over to Rooftop; he slid it back.

"Nobody said you had to quit collections," Rooftop said.

"Fuck. Only way Ray LaFlamme even tolerates a nonfrog like me is 'cause I work with you."

Rooftop took his asthma inhaler from his pocket and sucked on it, as he looked left and right, to make sure they weren't overheard.

"You know what I mean," Randy said. "Anyways, how the fuck does Gator, that asshole, get made a bodyguard, while you keep doin the freelance shit. You got seniority over that punk."

"Gator's family," Rooftop said.

"No, there's more to it," Randy said. "LaFlamme's got something going with the Gator."

"Like what?"

"I think he's got Gator-Aid doin hits. Terminations."

Rooftop scowled, looked over his shoulder. "Keep your voice down."

"That's what it is," Randy said. "LaFlamme knows you wouldn't go that far. That's the only reason you got passed over."

Rooftop sipped his Pepsi skeptically.

Randy leaned forward on the table. "Hey, what do you think LaFlamme pays for a hit?"

"I wouldn't know."

"Ten, fifteen?"

"Not in Maine."

"Six or seven thousand, I bet. That's some serious re-numeration, bud. Work five days a year, spend the winter in Hawaii, dive to your heart's content."

Rooftop shook his head soberly. "We'll educate this guy tonight. Then I'm giving my notice."

Randy stared at him, sat there staring and smoking and thinking. "This guy tonight," he said, "Humpty Dumpty?"

"Humphrey Burdock, the potato farmer."

"Yeah, pickled french fry farmer, real fuckin noble vocation. He takes a huge loan from Ray LaFlamme, which he's got no intention of payin back because he's too busy feedin LaFlamme's money to slot machines, not to mention he's probably sleeping in his truck because he beat the shit out of his old lady once too many times because he's a drunk and a low-grade character. And you seriously got a problem inflicting pain on this asshole?"

"You're the one that hit his wife," Rooftop said, "which was way overboard as far as I'm concerned."

"Yeah, overboard, huh? I say we throw Humpty Dumpty overboard, make a little example to LaFlamme's other deadbeat clients. Who knows, maybe if LaFlamme sees you got the gonads to do the deed, you know? Little promotion?"

Rooftop took a wheezing breath, then sat there staring right back at Randy through his thick lenses. "You're not God. Neither am I. Besides, you don't kill a man that owes you forty thousand dollars."

"Well, then, I think it's time he had some major whip-ass laid upon him."

Rooftop sighed.

There was a couch in the recovery room, which the nurse had made into a bed for Ellen, with a light wool blanket and cotton sheet. The room was warm and lit with a small night light. Ellen lay in the semidark for hours, listening to the steady rhythm of Mo's breathing, hearing voices in the hallway that would rise and fall with her own consciousness.

Periodically she would get up and check her daughter to make sure the blankets hadn't fallen off or that her IV tube wasn't crimped. When it got to be three o'clock and Ellen was no closer to drifting off than when she'd first lain down, she gave up trying. She concentrated on her breathing, as she'd learned in yoga. Deep breath in . . . Deep breath out . . . Pause . . . Peace . . . Repeat.

★　　★　　★

For some reason, she pictures Scott's mother, Thelma, walking down the road to their house. It's twelve years earlier, on a cold autumn day, two weeks after Jonathan's burial. Scott is off working at his store. Moreen's upstairs reading. Ellen stands in the pasture, surrounded by her sheep, watching the old woman hobble down the road.

She has known that Thelma would come eventually, to sit in her kitchen. In fact, Ellen's been waiting. Now, while she builds the season's first fire in the cookstove and they talk about the twenty new sheep Ellen has bought, they hear Moreen close her bedroom door upstairs, and Ellen thinks it curious the way Mo has been avoiding her grandmother since her uncle's suicide, especially considering the special relationship the two of them always shared.

"I'm so scatterbrained lately, I can get lost in my own backyard," Thelma says over her cup of tea; then she says the words that Ellen's been expecting. "But I think I know what happened with my boys that day."

The women avoid each other's eyes at first. Thelma looks out at the barn and pauses for a number of seconds. "Oh, I don't doubt April felt neglected, as much time as Jonathan devoted to his ministry. And Scotty, such a troublemaker, always trying to put one over on his older brother." Thelma turns back to Ellen at that point, indeed seems to scrutinize her. "Now Scotty's done a terrible thing and he's torn right up about it. Any mother could see that. If his father ever suspected—"

Thelma closes her eyes and stops for another moment.

"When it comes to holding a grudge, I've never in my life seen anything like these Chambers men."

She pulls the kitchen chair close to Ellen's and looks in her eyes.

"Ellie, don't you be like that," she says. "Scotty's going to have to live the rest of his life knowing what he did, and I know how it'll eat at him."

Ellen looks away from the woman, raises her face defiantly to stop the aching in her throat. Thelma puts her hand on Ellen's arm.

"I don't want to lose both my boys. Now, listen. Scotty loves you more than life itself, and he needs you to forgive him."

Ellen stares implacably down at the wood-grained table.

"Life's a long road," the old woman tells her. "If you don't come to terms with what he did, you may never be able to get past this awful way you feel."

Clench as she does, Ellen can no longer hold back the tears. She pulls away from Thelma and cries for a few seconds, until she's able to stop. Then she dries her face with her flannel shirtsleeve and stands up.

"I can forgive him," she says. "I can try. But I don't think I'll ever get over this."

The old woman rises from the table, far more hunched than Ellen has ever seen her, and makes her way to the door. As she takes hold of the latch, she turns her head and says one thing more, something that Ellen will not understand.

"Forgiving Scotty is only the beginning, Ellie. If you want to save Moreen, sooner or later you're going to have to face the truth. And then you'll need to forgive yourself."

With that, the woman walks out the door.

"Forgive *myself?*" Ellen says to herself, and she throws open the door and strides out to the porch, catching the rail in her hands.

"The truth about what?" she calls, but the woman walks on.

At three in the morning the casino manager shut the power off, and that's when Humphrey Burdock tried to pull the slot machine over, which was about the time the Jamaicans escorted him from the casino. It took all four of the little uniformed bastards, too, and then they locked the door on him, so Humphrey went out on the deck to smoke a cigar.

Three in the morning. The karaoke music had stopped. The bells from the slot machines had stopped, the loudmouthed drunks from Massachusetts had gone to bed, and now Humphrey stood alone under the lifeboats watching the ocean rush past him, trying his damndest to light his cigar against the gale that whipped across the deck, while this monster of a ship hummed and vibrated and crashed its way through the waves, its twin smokestacks blackening the low clouds above.

Twenty bucks to his name. So tomorrow when he got off the boat, maybe he'd stop at the liquor store and buy Jimmy a big bottle of coffee brandy. At least he'd have something to give her for their anniversary . . . if she'd let him in when he got back. Wouldn't surprise him one bit if she'd already changed the lock on the door. Couldn't blame her, really, after he went and lost the gas money on Megabucks the week before, then blew two hundred at Grange Casino Night, then belted her one when she complained about it. And now losing the rest of the Frickles money on the gambling boat?

Humphrey hunched over his last match. The wind snaked around his shoulders and snuffed it out, then laughed in his ear. He stuck the cigar back in his pocket.

Yup.

Change of luck, that's all he needed. Like maybe in the morning he takes that last twenty to the Wheel of Fortune. Why not? One shot, forty to one. Now there's a story. The day I won your grandma back.

Behind Humphrey, the door slammed open in the wind and someone came out on the deck.

"They rob you too?" Humphrey said.

"Humpty, right?"

Humphrey turned. In the instant of understanding, Randy stuck out his chest and let fly a full spray of pepper juice. Problem was, he spat against a wind that whipped the acid back over his own shoulder.

Now Humphrey, seeing Rooftop duck through the door, raised himself to his full height, his head grazing the overturned lifeboats. "We're in international waters," he said. " You got no rights out here."

"Keep your voice down," the giant told him. "Mr. LaFlamme needs his twenty-eight hundred tonight."

"Yeah, well, I had it a minute ago," Humphrey said. "Anyway, I'm planning to talk to the old man tomorrow about reconfigurin my loan repayback schedule, so to speak. I didn't figure advertising in my budget."

"Oh yeah? Well, reconfigure this," Randy told him, and he launched his steel-toed boot at Humphrey's groin.

It wasn't the first time someone had tried to kick the farmer. He sidestepped and caught Randy's heel in one hand and stomped Randy's crotch with his own boot, dropping him in a pile on the deck. Then he wheeled around to take on Rooftop, whose huge fist caught him square in the shoulder, knocking him so that he slammed into the side of the ship. But he sprang back at Rooftop like a bee-stung Angus, his wild backhand swing catching Rooftop's ear and knocking the glasses from his face.

"Everyone stop," Rooftop said, dropping to his knees, his blind hands crawling around the deck, looking for his glasses. But Humphrey was too busy trying to get to the door—then his big rubber boot came down with a sickening snap. For the moment, everyone did stop. Randy lay on the deck groaning and holding himself, while Rooftop paused on his hands and knees and angled his ear toward the crunching sound he had heard.

Humphrey lifted his boot. "Okay now?" he said, toeing the broken glasses toward Rooftop. "You ready to listen to reason now? What I'm tryin to explain is, there's a company in Portland that can get me on television—marketing, promotion, the whole works—they'll give out free samples all over New England. All's I need's another twenty thousand."

Rooftop squinted blindly at the rubber boots in front of his face. Then he wrapped his arms around Humphrey's legs. At first it seemed that the giant was only trying to raise himself to his feet. But as he stood, he lifted the farmer clear off the deck and lumbered toward the rail with the man slung over his shoulder.

Humphrey reached up and grabbed the seat of the overhead lifeboat. "What I'm saying—hold on a minute—"

Rooftop never heard a word. He pulled toward the rail with all his might, and the big farmer held onto the seat with all his might, as the lifeboat slammed back and forth on its cables.

"Slow down," Humphrey said. "No one said I can't get by on ten thousand."

Behind them, Randy rose unsteadily to his feet, stuffing another jalapeño in his mouth and starting to chew. Then, positioning himself under the lifeboat upwind from Humphrey, he raised his face and blew a thick, hot spray into the gale. The farmer's head snapped back. He let out a howl and lost his grip on the lifeboat, rubbing his eyes with one fist and beating Rooftop's head with the other, while Rooftop hoisted him over his shoulders and hurled him, flailing, over the wet, upturned hull of the overhanging lifeboat. Somehow Humphrey managed to catch the far gunwale on his way down, and he hung there by one hand, flipping in the wind like a gaffed tuna while the ocean raced past far below him.

"I'll get your money!" Humphrey shouted. "I'll have it by Friday, every dime!"

"You had your chance, you big dumb weak-willed bastard," Randy said, dragging a deck chair over and setting it down underneath the lifeboat.

Rooftop squinted over as Randy climbed up on the chair. "I guess we'd best pull him back," he said. "He's only made half a payment."

But Randy, caught up in the moment, jumped off the chair and caught the near gunwale in his hands. The lifeboat rocked back and forth, squawking like a parrot.

"You want the farm, take the farm!" Humphrey bellowed.

Randy kicked his knees up to his chest, his body coiled as though in a single, taut C-shaped muscle.

"You call that a farm?" he shouted. "A barn full of pickled fuckin french fries!"

With that, Randy launched into a vicious, full-bodied convulsion that set the lifeboat slamming back and forth against its moorings.

"Whoa, whoa!" Humphrey objected, then without another word, he dropped off the other side.

Amidst the noise of the engines, he didn't make a sound hitting the water, and if he hollered for help, nobody could've heard him. He swam after the ship at first, his powerful arms pumping frantically in the widening wake of the ship. But after a dozen strokes or so, his arms gave out, and then he bobbed up and over a giant swell in the darkness, watching all those hundreds of stern lights getting smaller and smaller, like so many stars in the sky, while high up on the third deck Randy and Rooftop leaned over the rail and watched him disappear into the night.

"Sucks being him," Randy said.

"I guess," Rooftop replied with a heavy wheeze. "But not half as much as it's gonna suck being us."

seven

"I lost the baby, didn't I?"

Ellen was on her feet before she was fully awake, startled by the brightness of the sunlight in the room. She put her hand on Moreen's warm face, the events of the previous day clamoring into her consciousness like jagged shards of a nightmare.

"How do you feel, hon?"

Moreen shrugged, glassy-eyed.

Ellen looked up at the clock. It was eleven. "I guess we both slept late," she said.

Moreen reached a hand up. Ellen took hold.

"You never wanted to be a grandmother anyway," she said, staring up at the ceiling.

"Don't say that," Ellen said, touching Mo's face, trying to make eye contact. "Don't even think that." She took hold of Moreen's hands. The left hand, the one the IV tube was attached to, felt cold.

Tell her.

Ellen hadn't intended to. Not now. But here they were. She took a breath. "Hon, the doctor," she began, and Moreen's eyes met hers, questioning.

"Mo, he had to do a hysterectomy." Right to the point—like a slap. Ellen kept her eyes on her daughter, watching for comprehension.

Moreen scowled slightly. "They did a hysterectomy on me?"

Her dark eyes lost focus for a moment. Ellen nodded, keeping hold of her hands.

"They had to, honey. You would have bled to death."

Moreen swallowed dryly while she processed the information. "So I can never have a baby—?"

Ellen tried to sound optimistic. "They left your ovaries."

She watched for a tear, some sign of emotion, wondering if Mo's complacency was the effect of the painkillers.

"You can always adopt," Ellen said. "When you're ready."

Moreen asked, "Does Randy know?"

"Honey—"

Moreen kept staring off.

"Mo, honey—" She touched her hand lightly to Moreen's brow, and their eyes met again. "Did Randy do this to you?"

Moreen turned her face away.

"Hon, you've got to tell somebody."

"Why are you asking me that?"

Ellen let out a sigh. "The doctor told me it looked like you'd been kicked."

"*I told you,*" Moreen said, her eyes suddenly piercing, her voice lazy and loud. "*Your stupid fucking ram Bucky did it. Just because you hate Randy—*"

"I don't hate Randy—"

"Lie. So now, instead of taking the responsibility for yourself—"

"Mo—"

"Now we can pretend it's Randy's fault!"

The door opened behind them. Ellen stiffened, stared at her daughter. She'd never heard Moreen swear, never heard that kind of anger in her voice.

"You're speaking," the nurse said, the same red-haired woman who had admitted Moreen the day before. "That's a good sign." Mo turned her face to the sunlit wall. "But I think we need to keep the patient quiet today, okay?"

"I feel like sleeping anyway," Moreen muttered.

The nurse checked her IV, felt her cheek, then gave Ellen a wink. "It's the medication," she mouthed, then she left the room.

Ellen took a deep breath of the antiseptic air. She looked down at her daughter, touched her arm. Moreen kept her face to the wall. Maybe it was the medication, Ellen thought. But it felt like the sun had just burned through a fogbank and illuminated the chasm that existed between them. She leaned over the bed and kissed Moreen's head.

Mo sighed sleepily, opening her fingers. "I know Bucky didn't mean it," she said.

Ellen gave her hand a gentle squeeze. "I'll come back and check on you later."

"Love you," Moreen breathed.

"Love you too," Ellen replied.

Randy opened his eyes and looked at the light on the low white ceiling. The ship was moaning and vibrating beneath him, and it took a few seconds to recall where he was. Then he remembered drowning the farmer they were supposed to beat up, and he felt a deep, dull movement in his bowels. Actually, if anyone asked, the dumb bastard jumped overboard when he saw them. They tried to stop him. They would have called for help, but sharks got to the guy the minute he hit water. Yeah, and Ray LaFlamme's dumb enough to believe it.

Randy got out of bed and headed for the toilet with nothing on except his wristwatch, which told him he had slept through docking, the hour when the ship ties up in Yarmouth and the tourists go into town looking for souvenirs. Outside the porthole, the ocean rushed past and the sky shone yellow and gray.

"Hey, Skyscrape," he said, kneeing Rooftop's mattress on the way to the can, but Rooftop wasn't in bed.

He went to the bathroom, then put on his Hawaiian shirt and Dockers, and he slipped his Ray Bans over his eyes, real sharp, in hopes that some single ladies might be aboard. He went up to the restaurant to look for Rooftop, then searched for him near the duty-free shop and in the casinos, finally found him up on the second deck, leaning out over the rail watching all the crooked, colored houses sailing away from them in the distance. The giant was drinking a hurricane, his broken glasses balanced on his nose by one stem.

Randy leaned on the rail next to him, staying a couple feet away. "Been drinkin all night?"

"Fuck you."

"Yup."

In his entire life, Randy had never seen anyone as powerful as Rooftop Paradise, nor as tough, and when Roof started drinking, nobody came anywhere near as mean.

"I thought those glasses was shatterproof," Randy said, noticing that one of Rooftop's lenses was missing.

"Only man I ever killed," Rooftop replied.

"He was still alive last time you saw him," Randy told him, "if you think about it the right way."

Rooftop turned and stared at Randy, the way those wide-set eyes of his could blur over. "You got a dangerous mind," he said.

Randy shrugged. "So what do you got in the bag?"

Rooftop took a deep wheezing breath and let it out, refusing to talk.

"What's the big secret?"

"Something for you to give your wife," Rooftop said.

"What?"

"Thermometer."

"What for?"

Rooftop pushed the bag along the rail and Randy took it, looked inside: a tomahawk made of lacquered pine, with a weather thermometer glued to its handle. The blade said COME TO CANADA.

"Not all that sharp though," Randy said, running his thumb across the wooden blade. "Why would I want to give this to Moreen, so she can scalp me?"

Rooftop gave him an ugly look, then turned his gaze back to the shoreline. "I'm not beatin up any more Mainers," he said.

"Think LaFlamme's gonna let you quit?"

"Ray LaFlamme is an evil man, and I'm not working for him anymore."

"I'm just sayin. I wouldn't be surprised if LaFlamme has Gator-Aid whack the both of us for expiring ol' Humpty, owing him the kind of scratch he did." They stood there in silence for a few moments, then Randy added, "Matter of fact, I had an inspiration last night." In truth, the idea was just occurring to him.

Rooftop took another gulp from his drink then just stood there looking out at the retreating island.

Randy said, "We rummage up the twenty-eight hundred for LaFlamme, you know, like it come from Humpty Dumpty. Then when Humpty turns up missin—and even his own wife can't locate him—Ray and the boys'll figure he absconded with the rest of the money. We had nothing to do with it."

"I'm not lying to Ray LaFlamme," Rooftop said.

Randy gave him a look. "Last night we fed a man to the sharks, but now you don't want to lie."

Rooftop turned toward Randy, stared at his chest. When Rooftop was drunk, you seriously never knew what his mind was up to.

"You know Herbie Handcream? He bodyguards for Ray

LaFlamme," Rooftop said. "He's got one stub of a hand he's always rubbing lotion on, all scarred up and shiny. Ever see him?"

Randy shrugged. "I'm not part of the inner circle."

"He used to do collections, like I do," Rooftop explained. "One time Ray LaFlamme caught Herbie lying about gas mileage or some little thing that didn't amount to twenty-five cents. Next thing you know, a couple of guys deep-fry Herbie's hand. Right there in LaFlamme's restaurant, with the french fries and clam fritters. They stuffed two big biscuits in Herbie's mouth to keep from scaring the customers downstairs." Rooftop peered hard at Randy. "Mr. LaFlamme's been fair to me. I intend to tell him the truth."

"Yeah, you tell LaFlamme we drowned a man that owed him forty grand, and he *will* have Gator whack us. You oughta contemplate on this sober."

"You oughta be nicer to your wife."

"Here we go."

Rooftop kept staring at him. "You need to think about being a better man."

"Yeah, like you, throwin people in the ocean."

"I'm gonna dive for charity," Rooftop said.

"Dive for charity."

Rooftop got that vulture look that made Randy wonder if it was his turn to get thrown overboard.

"So what do you think?" Randy said. "Get LaFlamme the twenty-eight hundred like it come from Humpty, save our asses from the Fryolator—?"

Rooftop knocked his souvenir drinking glass off the rail and let it fall to the lower deck. Even with the sound of the engine and wind, the breaking glass was loud. Then a couple of people started yelling.

"I wouldn't start anything," Randy said. "Nobody knows we're here. They do a head count and find Humpty missing, we probably got his DNA all over us." He looked over the rail and called down to the passengers, "Go on about your business."

Rooftop gave Randy that look again, straight on. "You don't have any goodness in you," he said.

"Me?"

"You treat Moreen like a dog."

"That shit again. Here." Randy handed the bag back to Rooftop. "You give it to Moreen, you want her to have it so bad." He folded his arms and looked off at the bright horizon. "I'd like to see how nice you'd be with a crazy fuckin teenage pregnant wife that's trying to restrict your freedom."

"You're the one that married her," Rooftop said.

"Oh, like I had a choice. When Ray LaFlamme says marry the bitch, what the fuck am I supposed to do? I married the bitch."

Rooftop wheeled drunkenly, and Randy reared back, thinking he was about to get his skull split with the tomahawk. But Rooftop fixed him with a scowl.

"You be good to that girl, I'm telling you right now."

"Fine. I'll be Mr. Jiminy Fuckin Cricket, if it makes you happy. Now are you gonna go along with my plan, or do you want to go to sleep every night wonderin if you're gonna wake up with the Alligator man in your bed?"

"I don't care one little bit."

"Fine, then. Just lend me the twenty-eight hundred to pay LaFlamme off, so we don't get our asses deep-fried."

Rooftop shook his head. "I'm done with this business."

"Fine, then," Randy said. "Maybe I'm done with your diving business."

"Fine with me."

"Fine with me," Randy said, "perfectly fucking A-okay." He walked away from Rooftop, across the sundeck and on down the steel stairway, his boot heels ringing. Two minutes later he came back.

"Okay, I'm gonna ask you one more favor."

Rooftop stared off over the ocean.

Randy said, "Give me three days to procure the money. I've got a plan. Just tell LaFlamme I'm taking over for you—no, I'll tell him, that way you don't have to *lie*. I'll speak to him personally. I'll say you got seasick and slept in the cabin all night, and I collected from Humpty on my own. Understand my thought process here? I'll give LaFlamme the twenty-eight Cs and tell him it's from Humpty. But you gotta give me three days."

Rooftop didn't answer.

"Okay then," Randy said.

When Ellen slid open the glass door that said DESTIN POLICE, Wes Westerback, the chief, was sitting at his desk tying a Gray Ghost. His son Sugar, who was spackling about sixteen feet of newly constructed wallboard behind the desk, glanced back at Ellen, a thick line of joint compound oozing down his thumb.

"Take a load off," Wes said to Ellen. Without looking up, he reached around the side of his desk and shook a sleeping cat out of a chair.

The father and son comprised the entire police force, maintaining their office in the basement of Wes's split-level ranch, which backed up to thousands of acres of woods near the reservoir. A small plastic sign on the desk said PLEASE COOPERATE WITH US. A wooden sign above the front door of the house said HEAVEN.

Wes was sixty-eight, old enough to retire. But in a town like Destin, Maine, the chief of police didn't have a whole lot to do, and the position came with decent benefits, so he kept the job. Wes spent most of his time down here anyway, surrounded by oak display cases that housed one of the finest collections of antique fishing lures anywhere in New England. Fact was, Wes made considerably more money buying and selling lures than he did on police work.

"I'd like to know what the process is for having my son-in-law arrested," Ellen said, still standing.

Wes kept working at the fly, peering through a freestanding magnifying lens that was ringed by a circular fluorescent tube. The top of his pink head, ringed by fine white hair, was perfectly smooth. The intricate wrinkles on his hands glistened under the light, and Ellen could see that his fingers shook a little. "Jeez, for what?" he said.

"He beat up my daughter."

Wes looked up at Ellen for the first time. "That's right, you had a wedding there a week or so ago. I guess I'll hold my congratulations."

"She was pregnant," Ellen said.

Now Sugar looked at her too.

"Mo's in the hospital. She lost the baby and had to have a hysterectomy."

Wes set his pliers on the desk.

"Sounds like a young man with a problem," Wes said.

"Not that young," Ellen said. "He's twenty-seven. Moreen's seventeen."

"So when did this take place, the fight, I mean?"

"What fight? He kicked her. Yesterday afternoon. His name is Randy Cross."

"Want me to take it, Dad?" Sugar said. Sugar himself had just gone through a divorce in which he'd lost the house it had taken him ten years to build. Ellen guessed he was making himself a bedroom down here.

Wes picked up a pencil. The tip was newly sharpened and it snapped when he started writing in his notepad. He opened his desk drawer and took out a small plastic pencil sharpener.

"You were a witness?" he asked, leaning over the wastebasket while the peel of wood curled out of the sharpener in his hand. "You saw it happen?"

"Not the actual beating."

Wes dropped the pencil sharpener in the drawer, kicked the basket back under his desk. Sugar turned and resumed spackling.

"Moreen came to my house afterwards, and we drove her to the hospital," Ellen continued. "She would have died if we hadn't gotten her there when we did."

"You and Scotty drove her?" Wes said.

"Our nephew drove her. I stayed behind to call the hospital and let them know we were coming; then I followed in my truck."

Wes looked up. "Your nephew?"

"Neal," she said. "Jonathan's son."

The older man scowled as he concentrated on his pad. "I remember the boy. His mother and him moved to western Mass, didn't they?"

"Greenfield," Ellen said. "Neal's helping us rebuild our barn."

Wes nodded. "Now, was he a witness to the beating?"

"To the actual beating," Ellen explained, "there were no witnesses. It happened in Moreen's house, in Sanford."

"So she told you about it—your daughter, I mean—she told you that her husband kicked her?"

"She didn't have to tell me. It's obvious he did."

Sugar looked back at Ellen again. " 'Obvious' don't always stand up in court," he said. A former all-state running back at Destin High, he had been given his nickname by his football coach after setting Maine's western division record for running yards. Recruited by the University of Maine, he had broken his leg in three places during a preseason scrimmage and ended up quitting college before the first semester ended.

Ellen appealed to Wes. "Look, I know he kicked her. I also know they're both going to deny it."

Wes put his pencil down. He looked over his notepad, considering what she'd told him. "How did Moreen claim she got the injuries?"

"She said a ram at my farm butted her."

"At your farm. Were there any witnesses to that?"

"To what?" Ellen felt her stomach knot. "It didn't happen."

"Were you home at the time she claims the animal hurt her?"

"I was outside."

Wes looked puzzled.

"She was in the pasture. I was down at our farm pond."

"What about your nephew?"

"He was with me. It was hot. We were swimming."

Wes nodded thoughtfully, then picked up his pencil and started writing again. He tilted the pad away from Ellen. "Then what?"

"I ran up the hill and found her lying there."

"Was the animal out, the one she claimed hurt her?"

"Yes, but that was just her excuse."

"What about her husband? Where was he during all this?"

"I told you, no one saw Randy kick her."

Wes sat back. He took his glasses off and gave Ellen a smile. "Ellie, you're doing your level best to lead this information the way you want it to go. Now I'm trying to determine what the heck happened here. When you found your daughter in your pasture, with her injuries, and the animal was there—at that point in time, where was Randy then?"

"I don't know. Out fishing for stripers. He and his friend Rooftop Paradise."

"Wouldn't be the first fight started over stripers," Sugar said.

Wes cleared his throat. "What does Randy do for a living?"

"He works for Rooftop. Diving."

"Huh," Wes said. "They're not local boys. 'Least I don't recognize the names."

"They live in Sanford," Ellen answered.

"Do you know what time they left yesterday?"

"Obviously after Randy beat up Moreen."

"There's no need to get sarcastic with me," Wes told her.

Behind him, Sugar spoke. "Moreen and him ever have any trouble before, domestic violence, this sort of thing?"

"They only got married a week ago," Ellen said. "She wouldn't have told me anyway."

Sugar scraped his trowel on the rim of the white bucket, then dropped it on the newspapers under his feet.

Ellen said. "She had a bruise on her arm the other day, like she'd been grabbed. I asked what happened, she wouldn't tell me."

"Is that what she said, she refused to tell you?"

"She said she bumped it."

Wes sighed. "Did the doctor say anything about the bruises that might substantiate your claims?"

Ellen closed her eyes.

"Ellie, you got no witnesses," Wes told her. "If your daughter claims an animal gave her the injuries—"

"Forget it, I'll call the state police," Ellen said, standing.

Wes shrugged. "They'll only tell you the same thing. We're all bound by the law, which says we can't make an arrest without sufficient evidence, which, in this case, would be a statement from your daughter, at least. Even then, where it's her word against his, about the best you can hope for is to get Randy into counseling, which is all a judge would probably do if he was found guilty. But with the circumstances here, unless one of them owns up to it, there's not even enough to make a charge. Fact is, if Moreen sticks to her story, they might even have a case against you, for negligence with your animals."

Ellen turned for the door.

"But hold on," Sugar said.

Wes's chair squeaked as he leaned back to look at his son.

Standing behind him, Sugar picked up a rag and wiped his hands. In his T-shirt he displayed a barrel chest and massively muscular arms, but he hadn't grown any taller than he'd been in high school, about five-eight, and he walked with a slight but permanent limp.

"Tell you what," he said to Ellen, scratching his chest. He leaned over his father and tore the sheet of notepaper off the pad. "They've probably had their fill of fishing by now. Lemme go have a talk with Randy, see if I can't get him into counseling myself."

"What if he refuses?" Ellen said.

Sugar gave his father a look. "I can be pretty darn persuasive," he said.

It was a confident gesture that made Ellen feel, for the first time, that she was not alone in this. She turned to go.

"Ellie," Wes said.

Halfway out the door, she turned slightly toward him.

"You're not planning to see Randy yourself, are you?"

"Why?"

"I think it's best you steer clear of him till we get this settled."

"Yeah, just go home and sit tight," Sugar added. "I'll give you a call after I talk to him."

She looked briefly at both men, giving no assent.

"I'd go easy on your daughter too," Wes told her. "If what you say is true, the last thing she needs now is someone else forcing their will on her."

*   *   *

Ellen wasn't in her truck five seconds before she realized that the day had grown even hotter than the day before. Keep busy, she told herself. Heat or no heat, she made up her mind to start working the minute she got home, and keep working. Weed the garden, mow the grass, do the laundry, lift her weights, clean the house, work on her tapestry. Exhaust herself till bedtime and then go to sleep. There was nothing she could do about Moreen, not today anyway. And Randy? She'd give the Westerbacks a day to deal with him, but after that, she knew she'd have to do *something*.

She pulled into her dooryard and stopped beside Neal's truck. The bucket loader was sitting in the spot where she usually parked. Deep, wide pits had been dug alongside the left and right sides of the barn: the foundation holes for the additions, she guessed. And somehow he had moved the silo from the right side of the barn around to the back, where he centered it, making the structure appear pleasingly symmetrical.

She got out of her truck and walked straight to her porch, avoiding the lumber pile and the new cellar holes—avoiding Neal. *Something I'd rather work out myself,* she'd say if he asked.

Her first thought when she got into the kitchen was to pour herself a shot of tequila, to calm her nerves, then take off the skirt she'd slept in and get into some shorts. She opened the liquor cabinet and brought down the tequila, picked a shot glass out of the cupboard and poured it almost full, tossed it down. Turning, looking around the kitchen, she was surprised to see how clean everything was. The floor had even been washed. She capped the bottle and was reaching to put it back, when a noise came from upstairs. She stopped.

"Hello?"

She walked into the living room and started up the stairs, ignoring the pain in her ankle.

"Neal?"

The rustling continued. Reaching the top of the stairs, she turned the corner to her bedroom . . . Pushed open the door. Caught her breath.

Neal's shirt was off, his back to her. He was rummaging through her dresser, her underwear drawer, his back shining with perspiration.

"What are you doing?" she asked.

"Looking for your shells," he answered, turning.

She stared.

"Bullets," he said urgently. "Where do you keep them?"

She noticed her closet door opened and plastic bags of clothes strewn on the floor. In the same moment, she saw the black butt of Scott's revolver stuck in the waistband of Neal's corduroys. Her heart bolted.

"Neal, tell me what you're doing."

He dropped to his knees and felt around under the dresser, seeming to read her mind. Coming up with the small plastic box, he hurried from the room.

She hesitated, afraid to pursue him, but then she thought of Gator, imagining that he'd come looking for her and found Neal instead. Or maybe it was Randy—

"Neal, wait!"

She wheeled out of the room, and pain shot through her ankle. Limping down the stairs as fast as she could, she made her way through the living room and kitchen, banged out the screen door and stopped on the porch, looking out over the pasture for him, her heart pounding.

"Neal?"

She saw her sheep tightly pressed together inside the near fence, trampling their feeding trough, oblivious to her shout. Then a movement to her left—behind the pump house. She hobbled down the steps and hurried over to him, but before she could speak he grabbed her behind the knee and pulled her roughly into the grass. Her ankle shot through with pain.

"Jesus!"

He pulled her down beside him and covered her mouth. "Shh," he whispered.

The elbow of her white blouse ground into the dirt. Her skirt was up to her hips. She raised her head and looked down toward the stream, and she froze. The coyotes were there, three of them in a tight cluster, greedily working at—

"Neal—"

She tried to fight him, but he held her down.

"Ellen."

It was one of her sheep that had gotten outside the pasture fence. The coyotes were tearing at it.

"Don't move," he breathed.

Her blouse had come open, and she could feel the heat of his bare chest radiating through her T-shirt. She could smell his perspiration. Don't move? As he slowly rose off her, his thigh pressed between her legs. Then he went crawling through the high grass along the fence.

She pulled her skirt down and turned onto her side to watch, as he moved along the fence line, working his way downhill until he was even with the ridge, carefully stalking. The feasting coyotes did not see him.

Ellen raised her face high enough to see a pair of curly horns flop up and down, and then she realized: They were feeding on Bucky. She saw the ram's brown leg kick listlessly in the air, and she got to her knees. A coyote turned, his ears perked.

The gun fired. Once, twice.

A coyote screamed. Another collapsed. The third bolted, leaping onto the farm road that ran alongside the stream, racing for the far corner of the pasture. Neal rose out of the grass and fired twice more. The animal screeched and tumbled, then scrambled up again and staggered for the fence.

Ellen pushed to her feet and limped down the farm road after Neal, her chest pounding. In her heart she wanted the animal to escape, wanting to see no more death—despite the way these predators had ravaged her sheep. In fact, the coyote was gaining a fair distance from Neal, who was only walking after it. When it had pulled within twenty paces of the fence, Neal took the pistol in both hands, sighted down the short barrel, and fired one more shot. The coyote leaped off the other side of the road, his tail slipping away into the bright gray and green thicket.

"Neal, just let him go!"

Ellen hobbled down the farm road toward her ravaged ram, not thinking about the dangers of approaching the wounded coyote, the first one Neal had shot. Seeing Ellen closing in, the animal tried to stand and run, but his crippled hindquarter would not comply. He twisted back to look at himself, then bared his teeth at her.

"Stay away from him," Neal called as he came. The coyote turned to face him, attempting a growl that was pitched too high to be taken seriously. Neal walked directly to the animal, straightened his arm, and fired.

"Jesus, would you stop!"

The coyote flattened on the grass, eyes silver-glazed.

Ellen stood there, suffocating in the heat. Two coyotes lay sprawled before her, with her ram at her feet, throat torn, his brown wool matted and shining, his chest heaving sporadically. Ellen bent over her animal. Neal's shadow fell over her.

"How did he get out?" she asked.

"I put him out."

She straightened, turned to face him. This was no accident, no chance encounter. He had sacrificed the ram to bait the coyotes.

He pulled his hunting knife from its sheath, placed the handle in her hand. "You need to do this," he told her.

She stared at the blade and shook her head, but Neal bent behind the ram, got his arms around its hind legs and lifted the animal into the air.

"Ellen, he's suffering," he said quietly.

The knife felt so heavy, her hand so weak, she could hardly lift it. It was as if all the heat and all the tension of the past two days had finally come crushing down around her.

Hoisting the animal under one arm, Neal placed his other hand firmly over hers and directed the knife to the ram's throat. Blood from its wool smeared the underside of her wrist as the blade slipped into the fleece. She felt the stiff wool scrape her knuckles, felt the steel stop against the ram's flesh. She resisted. Her heart pounded in her ears. It was far too hot.

"Ellen—"

She flashed her eyes up at him, squeezed the knife in her hand and plunged. The ram barely flinched as the knife sank into its neck. Ellen's arm hardened. Neal let go of her, and she sliced swiftly across the throat, hot blood throbbing out over her wrist, splattering her ankle. Then it was done. She stepped back, stood there dizzily.

"Did you think I couldn't do it?" she said in a low voice, then flung his knife on the ground.

Neal smiled gently. "I knew you could," he replied as he lowered the animal to the grass. "You needed to." He bent to pick up his knife. "You've protected your flock and made your world a safer place," he said, wiping the bloody blade on the ram's wool. "You've achieved justice." Standing, sheathing the knife, he gave Ellen a look of satisfaction.

Revenge is a dish best served cold. The proverb came to Ellen unsolicited, as she looked down at the dead animals. Indeed, this was no accident of nature, but a meticulously planned execution. In the rising, rippling heat she could smell their fresh blood. Her blouse was covered with it. So were her skirt and legs. Another wave of dizziness hit her, and she took a weak, shaking breath to dispel it.

"Do me a favor," she said to him. "Don't tell me how to live my life."

She turned and started walking back up the farm road toward the house, but as she passed the pump house she staggered and had to stop. The heat wrapped around her like a fat snake, cutting off her oxygen. She leaned on the pump house, then started to kneel, when Neal grabbed her from behind.

"Hold onto me," he said, turning her into his arms.

She did so, helpless to refuse, her hands sliding down his slippery back. "It's okay," he said, supporting her. "Everything's all right."

Ellen hated to cry, but now she seemed utterly helpless to resist. Her body trembled and tears burned from her eyes. She laid her head heavily on his shoulder. "Nothing's right," she whispered angrily, even though she knew they had done what any competent shepherd would have done: killed a pack of predators and culled a bad animal from her flock. But it had been done with such treachery.

"You've got company," he said quietly.

Ellen stepped back and wiped her face with her arm, then turned to see the black Cherokee sliding hard into the dooryard and skidding to a stop, gravel dust rising all around. Incredibly, she felt a fresh wave of anger shoot through her.

"Let me take care of this," Neal told her.

"You stay out of it," she replied, marching up to the dooryard. With the back of her arm she wiped the sweat off her forehead, as she watched Randy get out of the Jeep.

"Do I look like a nigger to you?" he yelled. He was wearing a Hawaiian shirt and a purple bandana around his head.

She continued walking toward him, imagining what she might do if she had a rock in her hand, while Randy came straight at her, his arms bulging out from his shoulders.

"Huh? Do I look like a nigger to you?"

"Did you *kick* Moreen?" Ellen snapped, abandoning whatever control she might have had. They came within three feet of each other, and she would have kept coming, but Neal grabbed her arms.

"Because I ain't no lower class you can throw in jail for something I didn't do."

"Did you kick my daughter?" She pulled against Neal, but he held her tight.

"You got just what you wanted!" Randy snarled in her face. "No baby on the way, you should be happy now."

Ellen's mind stopped.

"Ellen—"

Neal's arms wrapped around her waist and he turned her away, while she threw her elbow at him. "Slow down," he said, grabbing her arms.

Randy, sensing the damage he had inflicted, puffed up his chest. "Fuckin call the cops on me," he said with a sneer, then turned haughtily and went back to his Cherokee.

Ellen spun toward him but Neal held her fast.

"I did you a favor, asshole!" she said. "Because if you ever hurt my daughter again, I won't bother with the police—"

"That's enough," Neal said in her ear.

"You stay out of this!" she snapped, wheeling on him. He took hold of her forearms, pulled her toward him.

"Go cool off," he said firmly. His dark eyes bored into her, making it seem urgent that she do so.

She saw the reason, as Randy turned from his Jeep holding a shotgun in his hands, a frightening thing, black and thick and heavy. However, she stood her ground, bristling beyond fear, knowing enough about Randy to know that he lacked the resolve to shoot either of them. But when he swung around to face the pasture, a chill washed through her.

"Go in the house," Neal said, turning her away from Randy, all the while watching him carefully. "Randy, we already put the ram down."

Randy sighted down the barrel, aiming at a cluster of about twenty lambs in the distance. "I oughta annihilate the whole fuckin herd," he said, his finger sliding into the trigger guard.

Before Ellen could speak, Neal stepped directly in front of the muzzle—

"Neal!"

He deflected the barrel with the back of his hand, and made eye contact with Randy, who said. "Get yourself killed that way, cousin."

Neal wrinkled his nose in a friendly way. "You don't want to start shooting the sheep," he said.

"Fucking moron," Ellen added, which started Randy's head nodding.

Neal kept his hand on the barrel. "Ellen, would you please go inside? Thank you."

She did as he asked, walking within spitting distance of Randy, then across her dooryard in front of the Cherokee, resisting the urge to pick up a rock and smash his polished fender. She climbed the porch steps without looking back, went inside the kitchen, and threw open the liquor cupboard.

★   ★   ★

"I'm no fuckin nigger," Randy said, his shotgun jutting in punctuation.

"She's upset," Neal told him, putting his hand on Randy's shoulder and leading him back to his Jeep. "You can understand that."

"Nobody said I did nothin, except her. Bitch."

"I know," Neal said. "So you're square with the cops now?"

"Oh, fuck them too. They think I'm gonna go to a fucking psycho doctor, 'cause they plant a bag of reefer in my kitchen? Fuck 'em all!"

Neal nudged Randy with his elbow. "You know what the problem is?"

"Fuckin call the cops on me." Randy swung the gun toward the house. *"Bitch!"*

Neal put his hand on the barrel, eased it down. "I don't think she respects you," Neal said.

"Like I give a flyin fuck."

"You know why, don't you?"

Neal stopped walking, and Randy stopped. Neal glanced back at the house, then leaned toward Randy and said quietly, as if confiding, "It's your diving job."

Randy screwed up his face, like he'd chewed on something rotten.

"Six dollars an hour?" Neal said.

"Excuse me, eight plus overtime," Randy told him. "That's cash money."

Neal smiled. "You're still a grunt," he said. "You fetch for the guy making the real money."

Randy went around the passenger side and set his shotgun behind the seat.

"Think about it," Neal told him. "She doesn't think you've got the brains to do the work yourself."

Randy walked around the front of the vehicle and jerked himself up behind the wheel. Neal closed his door for him, then looked right at him. "You know the way a woman's mind works."

"Hey, I *know* the way they work," Randy said, glaring off toward the house as he started the motor. "Take your freedom and all your money, then throw you in fuckin jail. Well, here's a news flash: Not this boy. Not this boy."

Standing at her kitchen sink, Ellen rinsed the blood from her hands, then poured herself a small glass of Cuervo and drank it down. Her hand trembled. Her arms shone with perspiration. She poured another glass, this one fuller than the last, and drank it half down—deep breath in, deep breath out—waiting for her rage to go away.

Noticing the answering machine blinking, she went over and played it back, heard Moreen's voice, distorted with painkilling drugs and volume, slurring, "Why are you doing this? Do you think you're *helping?*"

Ellen stood there as the machine beeped off and the tape rewound, her thoughts as scrambled as the sound of the tape rewinding. She looked out the window and saw Neal talking with Randy, smiling. But why? If Neal had meant to have it out with Randy, why was Neal acting so friendly toward him?

She dialed 911. The phone rang six times before Wes Westerback answered, saying, "What's your emergency?"

"No emergency," Ellen answered, and she identified herself.

"Why don't you hang up," he said, "I'll have Sugar call you right back."

She did as he asked, and in a few seconds the telephone rang.

"Yeah, I caught up with your son-in-law at his house," Sugar said. "Turns out Randy's got a police record. Thought you oughta know in case you didn't. A couple of arrests for assault, and one for drug trafficking, which he did nine months for, back a year or so ago."

"What did he say?"

"Oh, pretty much fussed and fumed, they all do. But I sat right on him there in his kitchen and gave him his choice: either start seeing a counselor or I'd arrest him and haul him into court on other charges."

"What charges?"

"Oh, I used a little professional prerogative—which is to say, I got him to see things my way. I figure a little counselin never hurt anyone. Just some people are afraid of what they might find out about themselves."

In the moment of silence that followed, Ellen wondered if Sugar had just referred to himself, his ex-wife, or her—and she felt a trace of resentment. She looked over at her glass of tequila.

"Anyways," Sugar continued, "I gave him twenty-four hours to get himself a counselor, so I'll check back with him tomorrow."

"He's here now," Ellen said, turning to the window as the black Cherokee pulled out with a screech and a flurry of dust. Neal was standing there waving at him. "Actually, he's leaving."

"You want, I'll come lock him up right now. 'Cause I told him to stay away from you."

"Oh, he threatened to kill my sheep, that's all."

"He threaten you personally in any way, touch you or anything?"

"No."

"Okay, but if he comes back, you call me. Tell Moreen to call, too, if she has any trouble with him. Day or night."

"I don't think Moreen wants me in her life right now," Ellen said.

"Yeah, I think that's one of the syndromes. But nobody should live in fear."

"Yeah, thanks," Ellen said, and she hung up. *Live in fear.*

She finished the glass of tequila, then poured a third. Sufficiently numbed, she went into the bathroom and peeled off her sweaty T-shirt, used it to wipe under her arms, wipe her chest and breasts. She took off her skirt and underpants, then stepped into the bathtub and took a long, hot shower, lathering every inch of herself. For the first time in days, it seemed, she felt her body begin to relax, lulled by the heat. She remained in the flow for fifteen minutes or more. Then she dialed the water cold and rinsed herself.

Wrapping a thick bath towel around herself, she went to the kitchen and drank the tequila she had left. Then she climbed up to her bedroom and dried off. Hearing the backhoe churning outside she looked out her window and saw the gray exhaust rising from down by the dam. A slight breeze came in through the screen, and she dropped her towel to the floor, reached behind her head with both hands and pulled her hair back, let the air cool her. Then she opened her dresser and found a barrette she'd taken in trade at the farmers' market, made of blue sea-glass. She fixed the barrette in her hair then examined herself in the full-length mirror: Tall and tanned, her skin seemed to shine. Her shoulders and biceps were strong, her hips classically rounded, her breasts full, her nipples dark and erect.

She thought of Neal and how, in such a short time, she had come to rely on him so much. In fact, her closeness to him only brought into focus how disconnected she had become from Scott and Moreen.

Pulling a pair of underwear out of her dresser, she stumbled a bit stepping into them, then went to her closet, where Neal had spilled her boxes of old clothes (she wondered what he thought of her stiletto heels), and found her old denim cutoff shorts. She stuck her foot in, barely noticing the pain in her ankle when she balanced on it. Although she suspected the shorts would be ridiculously tight, she pulled them over her hips and zipped them, surprised she was able to do so. In fact, they hugged her perfectly. Then she sat on her bed and pulled on a pair of thick red socks and her leather work boots. She picked through the clothes on the floor and found an old brown tank top. She shook the dust out of it and slipped it down over her shoulders, then walked out of the house and down to the stream, where Neal labored beside the old yellow backhoe, taking apart the old stone wall.

"I took care of the ram and coyotes." he said. "Feel like lugging some rock?"

She looked beyond him, saw the freshly turned soil and realized he had used the machine to bury the animals while she showered. She was amazed by his efficiency.

She began working alongside him, hoisting the heavy rocks one by one off the old wall and carrying them to the bucket, neither of them speaking while the pond water spilled over the dam and raced noisily past. Aware of the silence, Ellen came to appreciate Neal's not intruding on it. She liked working with him, and she liked watching him work. He was sure and strong and absolutely steady. When they filled the bucket with rocks, Neal would drive the machine up to the barn and dump the load, then return to the stream again, where they would load the bucket again.

Although the day still weighed heavily with heat, the pasture fell slowly into shadow as they disassembled the stone wall. Despite her tiredness, the strain on Ellen's biceps and shoulders energized her, and it wasn't long before she worked up a vigorous sweat. Her long legs glistened, the veins stood out on her arms. Her tank top grew wet on her back and chest.

"Set?" Neal said when the bucket was full.

"Set," she replied, and he climbed onto the machine and turned the headlights on.

"Want a lift?" he said.

She climbed onto the loader with him, planted her feet on the grated steel step and bounced along, holding onto the back of his seat as he drove. She liked the exhausted glow in her arms, liked the way Neal looked at her—though she pretended not to notice. She felt her heart beating freely. As the lights of her house rose into view, she suddenly and inexplicably felt a glow of euphoria. In the face of all her troubles, it made no sense. Yet night was falling, frogs were already peeping, the air was perfect. She wondered why Scott was so late getting home.

They pulled up to the dooryard and turned left toward the barn. Neal cut the throttle and braked twenty feet from the new foundation.

"Everybody off," he said, and Ellen climbed down, jumping from the step, feeling no trace of pain in her ankle. In fact she flexed her foot a couple of times, and realized that even her memory of the pain had disappeared. The way Neal watched her, it occurred to her that he may have somehow healed her, and she wondered if he had inherited the gift from his father.

He smiled, then hit a lever and revved the engine, and the hydraulics started. The bucket curled over, dumping the heavy rocks noisily onto the grass. Then he shut off the engine and climbed down, wiping his face with the sleeve of his sweater.

She leaned back against the machine. "Thanks for getting me away from Randy before," she said. She watched while he lifted a heavy rock out of the bucket and dropped it on the ground with a resounding thud. "But when I was in the house, you were out here acting like you were his best friend. What's with that?"

He turned to face her, then wiped his hands vigorously on his corduroys. "Turn around," he told her. She did, and he unfastened her barrette, then gathered her falling hair in his hands.

"Romans twelve, twenty," he said, folding her hair carefully on top of her head. " 'If thine enemy hunger, feed him; if he thirst, give him drink; for in doing so thou shalt heap coals of fire on his head.' "

He slipped the barrette back in, then stepped around in front of her, inspecting his work. His gaze lowered from her hair to her eyes, and her heart surged.

In other circumstances, the look he gave her might have been taken as lustful. Indeed, in the first instant, Ellen felt a stirring and told herself, "He's Scott's nephew, not mine." However, it was not lust he was conveying, not exactly—though it was every bit as fervent. The look in his eye had to do with Randy. Ellen held his gaze long enough to realize this, but she was careful to give nothing in return, not a shadow of affirmation.

"Ellen, you need to drop the charges," he said softly.

"You need to take off your sweater," she answered.

In the brief hesitation that followed, she detected surprise in him. Indeed, she had utterly surprised herself. She had no idea where the words came from.

Neal looked at her darkly as he crossed his arms in front of himself, took hold of the thick wool and pulled it up over his head. His chest was strong, his nipples dark and round. Ellen reached up and pushed the sweater up his thick and slippery arms, breathing in the smell of his perspiration as she pulled it off his hands.

"Give it to me, I'll wipe you off."

Neither had she intended to say that. She felt as if she'd been inhabited by another person who was speaking through her lips. Taking the sweater from him, heavy and moist, she bunched it in her hand.

"I don't know why you wear this thing when it's ninety degrees," she said, raising his arm and running the wool roughly down his underarm and side. "Turn around."

He did and she wiped his back, holding her left hand on his shoulder, suppressing the sudden urge to lay her mouth on him, to lick the salt from his skin.

Once again he turned to face her. Or maybe she turned him. She moved the sweater under his neck and he raised his face, and her free hand slid down his solid arm. Her heart pounded.

Suddenly headlights swung in off the road, the diesel engine.

Ellen backed away from Neal, thrusting his sweater into his hands.

"Does he know?" Neal said, practically in a whisper.

"Know what?" she asked casually, turning.

"About Moreen?"

She turned her head slightly toward him. "Only that she had a miscarriage," she answered.

Ellen walked toward the Mercedes as Scott got out, his Mainely Hardware jacket slung over his shoulder. His tie was undone, his shirt untucked.

"Sorry I'm late," he said. "I went to see Mo."

Ellen stopped. "Scott, I told you—"

"I had to. I brought her some flowers."

She studied him as they walked up the porch steps together. She could smell whiskey.

"She was asleep," Scott said. "They wouldn't let me in." He turned as Neal came through the door. "Hot enough for you, guy?"

"I like the heat," Neal answered.

"Must run in the genes," Ellen said. "You can both have it."

"Better than twenty-below," Scott said. "Who wants a beer?"

So unsuspecting, Ellen thought, so single-mindedly absorbed by his business. Maybe it's what endeared him to her, after all. She leaned to kiss him.

"I'm all sweaty," he said.

"So am I," she answered, and she kissed him on the mouth.

"Mmm," he said, either in enjoyment or protest. "Looks like you started without me."

She gave him a look, feeling the flush of guilt wash over her face, then realized he was alluding to the tequila bottle she'd left on the counter.

"You don't look like you're that far behind," she said, giving him a smile, subtle and seductive.

eight

Scott made them each a margarita before dinner, while Neal cooked
pasta and prepared a rich Alfredo sauce from scratch. Scott opened a
bottle of Merlot for dinner and poured three glasses. While they ate,
Ellen tried repeatedly to catch his eye. When she finally did, she leaned
back in her chair and said, "It's been a long day. After I do the dishes,
I think I'll take a shower and go up to bed."

"Tired?" Scott said.

She didn't answer, waiting for him to catch her eye again.

"I'll do the dishes," Neal said. She saw him suppressing a grin.

Scott looked up. "I miss something?"

Ellen shook her head pitifully at him. "You are getting old."

"Yeah, well, I guess I'm tired too, now that you mention it."

Another smile from Ellen. It was met with a look from Neal, something akin to consolation. Ellen lowered her eyes to her plate.

"I sure miss your dad," she heard Scott say to Neal.

Ellen concentrated on her food. She'd wondered when Scott was
going to get around to it.

"He was a pretty incredible man," Neal said. "Imagine how many
more lives he would have saved if he'd lived."

"Your mom ever say why he did it?" asked Scott. "She have any idea?"

Ellen heard a silence then, and when she looked up, Neal was
looking straight at her, smiling, gesturing that he needed to swallow his
food. She smiled back, not wanting to appear anxious, but her teeth
clenched so hard she could hear a humming in her ears.

Scott raised his wine glass to drink again, but it was empty. He grabbed the bottle and poured himself another glass, then reached to fill Ellen's again. She shook her head.

Finally Neal answered.

"My mother never said," he said. "Although she has suggested on several occasions that it must have been my fault."

"Your fault?" Scott said. "People get depressed, they need to get help. In this town, everyone put your dad up on a pedestal. He was too proud to tell anyone his problems." He took another drink of wine, shooting Ellen a glance over the rim.

"You have to admit, I caused my share of trouble," Neal said.

"It's no wonder. Look who you're related to," Ellen said, with a nod at Scott.

"Ah"—Scott waved off the suggestion—"boys are supposed to cause trouble. Hey, do you remember the time you and Mo found that Indian tunnel in your basement and snuck over to the church? We looked and looked all over for you. We thought you'd been kidnapped. Then the steeple bell started ringing. Jesus Christ, was your father mad. Saturday night—the holy rollers all thought he'd gone Catholic."

"I think Neal was the best friend Mo ever had," Ellen said.

"Hey, is it true that my father healed Grandpa Chambers's bursitis?" Neal asked.

"That is true, sir," Scott said, raising his glass. "It was the same day our parents moved into the house I bought for them up on the hill. Sixty-five thousand bucks I shelled out. Dad said it was the best day of his life, gettin rid of that damn bursitis."

They all laughed, grateful for the relief, then went back to eating quietly for a minute, until Neal broke the silence.

"Oh, by the way," he said, "do your fire insurance rates depend on the farm pond?" It was all very casual.

"Big time," Scott answered, swallowing more wine.

"Because I think the dam's leaking."

Ellen's fork stopped momentarily in her plate. Her heart stopped too.

"It better *not* be leaking," Scott said.

"Ellen, pass the pepper, please," Neal said. She handed the pepper mill to him, eyeing him as he took it. "Have you noticed that the water seems lower?" he asked her.

"Not really."

He turned back to Scott. "When do they usually raise the flash-boards up at the reservoir?"

"Around September, when it starts getting dry," Scott said. "They don't release again till the spring thaw, usually March."

"That's what I was afraid of," Neal said. "When that stream dries up, you might lose your pond."

"Always something," Scott said.

Scott and Ellen made love that night for the first time since before Moreen's wedding. In fact it was two months earlier, on a Sunday morning, and then they'd been interrupted by a phone call from Sugar Westerback who was looking for a sub for his softball team. Even though Scott had declined the invitation, after he hung up he put on his bathrobe and went downstairs to start the day.

All other mornings—Monday through Saturday—he was up and out by dawn. Nights he was usually too tired, or so their routine had developed. Tonight was no different, but Ellen was energized by the tequila and wine, she supposed, and by all the insanity of the past two days. As they made love, she imagined Scott when he was younger and daring and tireless.

Expelled from high school for selling pot he had grown here on his parents' farm, he ended up leasing a small storefront in the village, where he rented videotapes for a dollar-fifty a night, and soon put the town's existing video store out of business. That spring—Ellen's junior year—she started working for Scott after school. One of her jobs was to make copies of the latest movies; Scott would sell them under the counter for ten bucks apiece. He told her it was legal. Ellen didn't believe him, but she didn't care. He was self-assured and cool, and though he was only seventeen, he seemed to be making his way in the adult world.

Scott had a girlfriend, Ingrid, who was twenty-nine, from Long Island. She ran a crafts and clothing boutique in the same building, called Wool 'n' Things. The two shops shared a back room, which quickly became a hangout for a number of Ingrid's friends.

Ingrid was a sort of retrobeatnik who wore black lipstick and spent her days at her spinning wheel, perched in the storefront window. It didn't matter that Scott was a farm boy at heart, Ingrid soon had his black hair tied back in a ponytail and his left ear gleaming with a bright green tourmaline. She called him her country stud.

Most of Ingrid's friends were musicians and artists who would hang out in the back room listening to jazz and reggae, doing cocaine and drinking tequila. For Ellen, it was the first time she had found people who intrigued her, and soon she started working for Ingrid too, stringing necklaces of razor clamshells, painting seagulls on sand dollars, and carding raw wool for Ingrid to spin.

Even when Ellen wasn't working, she'd tell her mother she was, and she'd do her homework in Ingrid's back room. She liked the conversation. She liked the music. More than anything, she liked to watch Scott handle these people who considered themselves his superiors. While they snorted their coke and drank their shots, he smoked his homegrown weed and drank Moxie. They'd listen to jazz; he'd put on George Jones and turn it up loud. They considered themselves artists. But Scott was an artist of commerce. He envisioned money and made it materialize with a creativity and intelligence that Ingrid's friends couldn't begin to understand. Unself-consciously. Unapologetically. Even at seventeen, he seemed to always know exactly what he wanted, and how to get it.

One night that winter, just after Scott's eighteenth birthday, he must have realized he wanted Ellen. She had closed Ingrid's shop and gone to get her coat out of the back room, when she found Scott sitting alone on the couch, with a lone candle burning and Frank Sinatra playing on the stereo. "One for My Baby." Scott told Ellen he had just broken up with Ingrid and asked her if she wanted to go out for a coffee. She was going to say yes. Instead, she dropped her coat and went over and kissed him.

Ellen had made out with boys before, but only ever let one get his hand inside her bra, some college kid from California who was at the beach, an angelic, tanned surfer, and she'd stopped him when he tried to unbutton her shorts. Standing in the back room with the candlelight and the music, Ellen decided then and there to go as far as the feeling took her. In fact, it was Scott who stopped them, and that's when she fell in love.

As it turned out, Scott hadn't actually broken up with Ingrid, not in a way that Ingrid understood. And, as it turned out, Ingrid had been more than a girlfriend—she was also Scott's legal business partner, who held the lease on both shops. By the time Ingrid realized that their relationship was over, Scott had bought the small building from the owners and helped move Ingrid's store to Destin Plaza. Then he sold all his videotapes and proceeded to knock down the walls that had divided the two stores. He was tireless then. He did all his own carpentry, his own wiring, plumbing, and painting, his own accounting. By month's end, he had opened Destin Hardware. Ellen remembered the pride she felt seeing his picture in the newspaper, accepting awards from the Rotary Club, the Chamber of Commerce, the Small Business Association, with his ponytail and earring and the black wool sweater that she had knitted for him, with the green star on the left shoulder.

He was his own man, working on his own terms.

But tonight, while Scott moved lazily inside her, it was the sound of the bucket loader outside her window that spurred Ellen on, churning and growling and shaking the ground—indeed shaking the mattress under her. And it was Neal who occupied her mind: the smell of him, the way his glistening body had felt under her hand, the way the humidity had risen off him. It was his long, muscular stomach; the relaxed way he talked; the way he watched her. It was his competence, his steadiness, his conviction, all the things he had done for her, and the thing he was willing to do . . .

Or perhaps her arousal was simply her way of denying what treachery might be in motion. She was aware of this—even as she made love to her husband—aware not of the treachery itself but of the curious way a person could overlook such a thing.

When Scott was finished, he kissed her and rolled over. In a minute he was snoring, and Ellen realized that the backhoe had stopped too. Through the open windows, she heard the small sound of bells moving lazily through the night, one or two of her ewes up walking, and she suddenly felt more alone and alienated from Scott than she had before they'd made love. It was strange how the act of love sometimes illuminated the distance between them. Lying here now, listening to the steady whisper of water running over the dam, that distance felt to Ellen like an ocean.

Slick with perspiration, she peeled herself off the sheet and took her nightshirt from the clothes tree, pulled it over her head and went downstairs to shower. Leaving the stairway lights off, she made her way through the living room in the dark, went into the bathroom, and closed the door.

Pulling off her shirt, she stepped into the bathtub, twisting the old faucets and pulling the shower valve up, expecting the usual trickle. But the water exploded out of the nozzle full force, and it startled her. Evidently, Neal had climbed down into the pump house and fixed the old water pump, the one Scott had been promising for years to fix. She adjusted the temperature and ducked her head under, luxuriated under the pounding on her back, the sensation flowing down her shoulders and thighs. Turning, she let the water beat against her face, curl down under her chin and run over her breasts. She washed and rinsed her neck, her underarms and breasts, her stomach and abdomen. She ran her hands all over—even massaging herself—but it wasn't enough. She knew she could not adore her own body the way it needed to be touched.

She dried herself with a thick towel, then slid her nightshirt back on, the cotton brushing over her erect nipples. When she opened the door and stepped out of the steam, Neal was there, standing inside the back door, wearing only his black trousers.

Although it was too dark to see his face, Ellen could make out his expression. Or perhaps it was just the attitude of his body, his shoulder slightly cocked, outlined in a faint, glistening light. She felt a bright flutter inside her stomach.

They stood there saying nothing. Despite the noise of the waterfall outside and Scott's loud snoring upstairs, she could hear her own heart beating. She was sure he could hear her too, or that with the bathroom light behind her, he could see the pounding of her chest through the light fabric, and now she became acutely aware of her breasts, her nipples, as if all the nerve endings in her body were focused there. The smell of his fresh perspiration aroused her, and she knew at that moment she should get away from him. But she stayed, opening her mouth so he wouldn't hear how hard she was breathing, and now she was afraid to think that she was breathing his body heat in, but she breathed anyway, deeply, and this rocketed her into a powerful state of arousal. It was astonishing the way she wanted his hands on her, but she knew that if she took a single step toward him right now, what a lifetime of trouble would follow, here in her husband's house *(Scott snoring, snoring)*, here with his nephew . . .

She stepped away from the bathroom door, and now the light fell upon him, the pale ripple of his stomach.

"I thought you were in bed," he said softly.

"It's too hot up there."

A second or two passed, while Ellen felt the sensation growing deeper in her abdomen, the dark and lustful ache.

"It's nice outside," he said.

She looked at him there, imagining how easy it would be to open his jeans and pull them down to the floor. She knew that he was feeling the same thing, she could see the way his chest heaved. She hesitated another moment and then turned away from him and was walking into the living room, back up the stairs, back to the heat of her bedroom, her mind throbbing, wondering how she'd ever let herself get that close. Stripping off her night shirt and dropping it on the floor, she slipped into bed beside Scott and felt a sharp pang of fear. She pulled the sheet up over her shoulder, then rolled toward her husband, took his arm in her hands. He kept snoring, and Ellen lay there quietly breathing the oppressive air, waiting for sleep to overcome her while she listened to the anxious sound of her pond spilling over the broken dam . . . and tried to darken the incessant electric glow in the pit of her stomach; to quiet the warning voices in her head. She pictured Neal in her pond, diving down to the bottom of the dam, and as she wondered what he'd been doing down there, she found herself remembering the day he'd been baptized.

At the time it was unclear what had precipitated Jonathan's decision to anoint his son, since it was customary practice in any charismatic church to baptize only adults, and Neal was only eleven. Scott and Ellen had laughed about it at the time. Although neither April nor Jonathan ever divulged anything about their problems with Neal, Ellen and Scott were aware that the boy was constantly being punished for one offense or another—which meant that whatever Neal enjoyed in life, his father found a way to take it away from him. Because Neal loved books, his library card was revoked. Because Neal loved to swim, he was banned from the parsonage swimming pool. So, when the invitation came announcing Neal's baptism, Ellen and Scott saw it as another of Jonathan's attempts—clearly a desperate one—to discipline his son.

The baptistry was a formidable tank embedded in the back wall of the altar, like a giant aquarium, four feet high and eight feet wide. Stairs descended into the tank from dressing rooms on both the left and right sides.

The ritual had an almost otherworldly feel. As the congregation sang "Nearer My God to Thee," and the parish lights came down, a pair of burgundy curtains parted to reveal the baptistry tank, which fairly glowed in its own blue light. The water was three feet deep.

Ellen remembered the way Neal had stared at his father as he descended the steps into the water, his burgundy robe floating up around his knees. Anyone else might have been moved, mistaking the stare for the fervent look of a boy surrendering to absolution at the hand of his father. Ellen recognized the stare for what it was: staunch defiance.

Moreen, who had been four at the time, reached for Ellen's ear and whispered, "Why is Neal wearing his clothes in the water?" They were sitting in the front pew, along with Scott and his parents and April and her mother, who had driven up from western Massachusetts.

"Uncle Jon is just going to dunk Neal," Ellen whispered.

"God is forgiving Neal for all his sins," April said, leaning over with a strange, wide-eyed smile.

"That's their religion," Ellen explained quietly, and she took Moreen's hand to quiet her.

Jonathan was speaking into a microphone attached to the top of the tank, which broadcast his seemingly disembodied voice throughout the chapel: "Neal Rolley Chambers, have you accepted Jesus Christ as your personal Lord and Savior?"

Standing up to his waist in the water, Neal stared out through the tank. Moreen raised her hand and gave him a timid wave. "Can't he see me?" she asked.

"Shh," Ellen said.

"Neal Rolley Chambers, have you accepted Jesus Christ as your personal Lord and Savior?" Jonathan asked again. "And you say, 'Yes.' "

Neal kept staring.

"You say, 'Yes,' " Jonathan repeated.

Neal said, "Yes."

"And are you trusting in him today for your eternal life?"

Neal kept his eyes on the congregation.

Without waiting for his response, Jonathan took his son's head in one hand, the other holding his nose, and he said, "Upon your confession of faith, I now baptize you in the name of the Father and the Son and the Holy Spirit."

When he tipped Neal's head back under water, Moreen reached for Ellen's arm.

"He's just dunking him, hon," Ellen whispered to her. But they both jumped as the organist struck a chord and the choir stood to sing "Amazing Grace."

Ellen had seen the ritual only once before, when Jonathan baptized his father in the stream behind the farm. The anointing was over in a second. A quick symbolic dip, then out. But this was different. Now savior was father, staring sternly into the water, and sinner was son, staring back, unrepentant.

"He's holding him under," Moreen piped up apprehensively. A few people close enough to hear laughed a little.

By the end of the hymn's first chorus—and what was obviously meant to be the end of the song—Ellen realized that Jonathan was waiting for Neal to close his eyes, and that he wouldn't let his son lift his head out of the water until he did so.

"Mommy?"

"It's okay," Ellen told Mo reassuringly, though she knew it definitely was not okay. Neal was not the kind of boy to give in.

A few of the singers ventured ahead with the hymn's second verse. Others in the choir, looking less confident, nevertheless joined in.

Jonathan's demeanor remained steadfast, with the unshakable faith in his mandate from above. If necessary, he would allow his son to drown—if that was the path that Neal chose.

Ellen did not know how long Jonathan held him under. Thirty seconds may have seemed like five minutes. A minute may have seemed like ten. It was long enough that Scott glanced over at Ellen with an incredulous scowl. And by the time the second verse had ended, the people who had laughed only moments ago were buzzing anxiously. Now Scott looked over at April, and Thelma looked over at April, and the murmur became explicit while Neal stared out of the tank.

"Maybe someone oughta go up there," a man said.

Even the choir members were glancing nervously at one another.

Finally April rose to her feet and called sheepishly, "Let him up?"

Inside the tank, Jonathan could not hear. Neither would he pay attention when April climbed the altar stairs and approached the tank. His eyes remained locked on Neal's.

She rapped on the glass with her rings and said, "Jon, just let him up." In the congregation, people were standing. But Neal would not submit.

In the end, it was Jonathan who gave in. When a gulp of bubbles exploded from Neal's mouth, his father pulled him, choking, out of the water, and Neal's dark eyes swept right to Moreen as he coughed.

"Dry off and go home," Jonathan told him. The small loudspeakers in the church did not miss the anger in his voice.

Neal climbed the stairs out of the water, quietly victorious, while the congregation started singing "Christ the Lord Is Risen Today," and April walked off the altar to her right, the way Neal had gone.

In the dark of dawn, when the clock radio came on, Ellen was already awake. She slid her hand down Scott's stomach and took him warmly in her hand.

"Scott?"

"Hm?"

"Let's go up to Katahdin for our anniversary. Remember the way we used to?" She caressed him. "I'll pack the tent—"

"You're kidding."

"It's a long weekend. I'll get the sleeping bags, the old camp stove—"

"What about the sheep?" he asked, awake now. "Your garden?"

"Neal can take care of it. It's been so long since we've gone away, just the two of us."

"But now?"

She squeezed him playfully and said with a seductive smile, "All by ourselves. Just us, the moose, and the deer."

"Uh." The way his eyes closed, the sound in his voice—

"What?"

He reached down for her hand, held it in his own. "I meant to tell you last night."

She kept her eyes on him.

"I'm not going to manage Mainely Hardware." He watched her closely, while she waited for him to continue. "I'm buying Walter Bolduc's place, on the highway."

"The boarded-up tire place?"

"It's prime location, the perfect size, almost five acres."

Ellen raised herself on her elbow, propped her head in her hand. "You're buying it? You couldn't make ends meet where you were. That's why you were going with the Mainely Hardware franchise—"

"I'm trying to tell you. I'm getting out of the hardware business altogether."

"But where are you going to get the money?" Ellen asked. His brow rose up, as if to explain, but she could see how he was avoiding her eyes. "Scott, you're not mortgaging the farm—?"

"Wait now, let me explain—"

"You didn't—? You mortgaged the farm, the house, and you never talked to me?"

"I'm trying to explain," he said. Then he stopped; sighed. "I had to use the farm as collateral to buy into the Mainely Hardware franchise."

"Jesus, Scott!"

"It's just temporary," he said. "I had to get money somewhere. You know the banks wouldn't do business with me. I went through a private loan company." His fingers pressed up toward the ceiling, then fell back. "I was going to tell you."

"Why didn't you use the store as collateral?"

"Ellie, how do you think I've managed to buy inventory for the past two years? My credit's shot. We were about to lose the store. I had to make a move."

Ellen lay down again, rolled onto her back.

"Don't worry. We've worked out all the details."

"Who's we?"

"Neal helped me."

Now Ellen sat up in bed.

"It's a little complicated."

She waited.

"Like I said," he continued, "I decided against buying into the franchise. Instead, I'm going to use loan number two to pay off loan number one and get the store out of hock."

"And our house and farm in hock—"

"Listen. Then I *sell* the store."

Studying him skeptically, Ellen detected a remnant of his once-confident glint.

"We ran the numbers," he said. "Mainely Hardware is gonna buy me out clean—a hundred twenty thousand for everything, property and inventory." His eyes lingered on her meaningfully. "See? Then I turn around and buy the tire store for eighty, and I've got fifty grand in ready cash to work with."

"Scott, *the farm.*"

"The farm is safe," he said. "This is a sure thing, the chance I've been waiting for."

Ellen closed her eyes, took a deep breath.

"Look, Mainely Hardware can't last in this town, you know it and I know it, I don't care how cheap they can buy their merchandise. They can't compete." Ellen could hear him leading up to something, and it worried her. "These days the only way to stay alive is to specialize, to carry merchandise the big boys don't have."

She looked at him, a heaviness descending in her chest.

He blinked.

"I'm going to sell guns."

Ellen stared as if she hadn't heard him. But she had. The single word hung in the air. *Guns.*

"You're serious."

He was moving his hands like a conductor. "Ellie, it's a great opportunity. I'll have something that nobody can compete with—not Wal-

Mart, not Kmart, not the Trading Post—not any of the other small shops."

"Scott, they all sell guns," Ellen said.

Scott looked straight at her. "But they don't have firing ranges."

Ellen got out of bed, walked to her bureau naked.

"Just listen, El. The garage is a perfect size for an indoor range. Plus there's a four-acre gravel pit out back. This is going to be state-of-the-art: skeet and trap ranges, even sporting clays. We'll take in guns on consignment, used, antiques, small manufacturers. That's another thing you can't get at the big stores. And I don't have to wait for a dealer's license. There's a guy in North Berwick, Jimmy Arthur, who's closing his shop. He's agreed to be my silent partner for a few months, until my license comes through, so I can start buying and selling. I don't even have to pay him. I'll just sell his remaining inventory out of my store and give him half."

Ellen took a pair of black underpants out of her dresser and stepped into them. "I don't believe this."

Scott sighed. "Ellie, come on, you know this is a great idea. It's the break I've been waiting for. Anyway, I already put down earnest money on the tire store. I'm closing with Mainely Hardware tomorrow."

Ellen wouldn't look at him. "You never even talked to me, Scott."

He got out of bed, went to his dresser. "Look, we were going to lose the farm eventually, whether you admit it or not. We're paying property taxes on forty acres that are generating almost no income."

Pulling on a dark blue T-shirt, she opened the closet and snatched her denim shorts off the hook. "So you rebuild the barn to pacify me, while you gamble everything we own on a gun shop?" she asked bitterly.

"That's not the way it happened." He pulled a shirt over his head. "You know, you could be a little more supportive once in a while."

"You want to sell guns, I'm not supporting that. Guns to criminals, guns to fanatics and paranoids, guns to assholes like Randy?"

Selecting a necktie from his closet rack, Scott said, "I'm selling guns to hunters and farmers."

"Oh, *farmers.*"

"While we're at it," he said, "I might as well tell you something else that you're gonna hate. I'm thinking about taking Randy into the business with me."

Ellen stood there, stunned, and barely heard what he said next, something about helping the kids get started in their new life.

Moreen had to have a hysterectomy! Ellen wanted to scream it, but keeping her promise to Mo, she shook her head, speechless.

"Moreen told me what caused the miscarriage," Scott said to her, as though he could read her unspoken words in her accusing look. "Your ram attacked her, that's what she said."

"No!" Ellen snapped. "Randy kicked her."

"Oh, give me a break! Don't you think Moreen would know if Randy kicked her?" His voice was getting louder.

"He hits her. I've seen him."

"You saw him kick her in the stomach—?"

"I've seen him get physical with her."

Scott threw his hands up.

"You don't turn your daughter's husband in to the police!" he said. "They've got enough problems as it is. El, I want you to tell the police you overreacted."

Ellen stared at him with disbelief. A humming filled her head. It astounded her to think of how far apart they'd grown.

"I don't know you anymore," she told him, then walked out of the room, suddenly feeling very unsteady in her bare feet.

"If you think you're helping Moreen by having her husband arrested," he called after her, "you're crazier than I thought!"

Ellen walked down the stairs and through the house in a mindless blur. Banging out the kitchen door, she marched down the porch steps and directly to the new cellar hole at the left of the barn. Neal had dug a square alcove off the new foundation and was troweling cement on the foundation wall around two water pipes that protruded through the rocks.

"How do you like your new root cellar?" he asked, looking up at her.

"Neal, do me a favor," she answered. "If you and Scott plan something that affects *my* life, have the courtesy to let *me* know about it, okay?"

She walked away before he could respond, went off to the toolshed and let her lambs out into the pasture. As she followed them out and overturned the water trough to hose it down, she saw Scott walking down to the pond. A minute later he came up the hill and called to her, "The outlet pipe's leaking, but it's hard to see through the waterfall.

I'm going to call the water district and see if they'll raise the flashboards up at the rez, so we can get it repaired."

She ignored him, and he walked away. Momentarily she heard his car engine start, and she went into the shed for grain. As she scooped her pail into the grain barrel, the door opened behind her.

"Ellen, I'm sorry," Neal said to her, "but I can't tell you something that Scott told me in confidence."

"Fine," she said, kicking open the door to the pasture.

"If I did tell you," he said, "you'd never be able to trust me with your secrets."

She stood in the doorway for a moment. Then, knowing they had nothing more to say to each other, she went outside.

For the rest of the day and all of the next, Ellen and Neal worked together in silence, Neal laying stone on the foundation walls of the root cellar and new additions, Ellen mixing the cement in the wheelbarrow. Emotionally, she was determined to keep her distance from him. If they spoke at all, it was only a word or two about the work they were doing. They did not discuss Ellen's concerns about Moreen, nor did they bring up Scott's gun shop, or Randy, or the leaking dam. Certainly they did not talk about what had almost happened between the two of them the night before.

They worked hard and steadily hour after hour, and gradually the frames of two symmetrical shed-roofed additions, twelve feet wide and running the length of both sides of the barn, rose over the expanded foundation. For the longer beams, Ellen stood in the bucket holding the end of the timber on her shoulder, while Neal carefully raised her into place. He would position the bucket just so, the notch would slide into the groove, and Ellen with her three-pound hammer would drive the wooden pins through the holes. It was dangerous work, and Scott would never have permitted it had he been there, but with Neal at the controls, Ellen never felt at risk.

Finally, late on Thursday afternoon, Neal lowered Ellen to the ground and shut off the bucket loader.

"Right on schedule," he said. "We'll be finished on day twelve, just as I promised."

"You and your twelves," she answered wryly, while she arched her back, stretching.

" 'Twelve Days of Christmas'," he said with a shrug.

Ellen tossed her hammer on the ground. "Twelve-gauge shotgun," she said, playing along.

" 'Twelve Days of Christmas'," Neal repeated.

"You just said that."

He smiled as he climbed off the machine. "Did you know I was born on October second, which is exactly twelve weeks before Christmas?" He grabbed the plastic pitcher of water and took a drink.

She looked at him, saw the glint in his eye. "Is that significant?"

"October second: ten-two," he explained. "Twelve."

"I think maybe that's stretching it, Neal."

"Maybe."

They heard a car engine downshifting out on the road, then the mashing of gravel under wheels, as a glossy black BMW Z3 convertible pulled into the dooryard, sending up a low cloud of dust. Maddy, Ellen thought, happy to see her friend. The car pulled up to the porch and Maddy stepped out, looking over the barn.

Ellen unbuckled her tool belt and let it fall to the ground, then walked across the dooryard to meet her. Neal remained behind, shirtless. Maddy eyed him for a moment, then turned abruptly and walked up the steps. On the porch, she turned back again and stared over the tops of her sunglasses, shielding her eyes with her hand, as Neal started hand-sawing a wide, oak plank.

"You and *him* alone every day while Scott's off at work?" she murmured, as Ellen mounted the steps.

"He's Scott's nephew, remember?" Ellen said quietly.

"Don't give me that. He's not blood-related to you, and you're just as human as I am."

Ellen smiled. "Want a drink?"

"No, I actually came over to tell you that I have a new client."

"Yeah?"

Maddy took off her sunglasses and gave Ellen a long, almost accusatory look. "Mo has a hysterectomy, and you never so much as call?"

Ellen scowled. "You're not counseling Mo—?"

"No, I've been asked to counsel Randy. The police set it up. Mo gave them my name. But I wanted to check with you."

"I wish you'd counsel Mo," Ellen said. "Convince her to have him put away."

"I talked to Mo a little," Maddy replied. "Ellie, what makes you think that Randy beat her up?"

"I know he beat her up."

"I'm not defending him. I just want to know how you're so sure it was Randy and not your ram that hurt Mo."

Ellen looked away.

"El, mother's intuition is one thing. But if Randy didn't do it, this is something they really don't need in their lives right now. If he doesn't show up for his counseling session this afternoon, I'll have to turn him in. He says he's not coming."

"Good."

"But what if you're wrong?"

Ellen felt her stomach twist. She pushed herself off the rail and turned for the door. "I've got to get supper ready."

"You're telling me to leave?"

"I'm telling you that Moreen is my daughter, and I'll do what I need, to help her."

"She's like a daughter to me, Ellie. And I intend to do what *she* needs."

Their eyes locked for a second or two, then Maddy put her sunglasses on.

"And I'm pissed off that I had to find out from the cops," she said, then she left.

Randy pulled his black Cherokee into the woods and drove down the dirt road until he reached the chain barrier and NO TRESPASSING sign, courtesy of the Destin Water District. After looking around, he got out of the vehicle and hid his ignition key under a dusty rock in the grass. He stepped over the chain and started walking, keeping his right hand casually in the pocket of his trousers but tightly on his snubnose .22. When he turned a corner, and the gatehouse and reservoir dam came into view, he stopped. Turned.

Scott was off to his right, thirty feet away, leaning against a white birch, holding a fat, pink Dunkin Donuts bag. The doughnuts weren't what interested Randy, however. It was the way Scott's other hand was stuck in the pocket of his tweed sports coat.

"I didn't touch Moreen," Randy called, his finger slithering inside the trigger guard of his gun. "Thought we'd oughta establish that right off the bat."

"What are you talking about?" Scott said, as he left the tree and started walking over. Randy's pants were loose enough, and his pistol short enough, so he could raise and fire without pulling it out of his pocket. Scott's sports coat pockets were wide, too, certainly wide enough to conceal a handgun. Scott took seven or eight steps toward him, then stopped at the weedy edge of the road, his Dunkin Donuts bag swinging. Randy remained on the grassy hump between the tire tracks, about seven feet away.

"If I don't report to this friggin counselor today for something I didn't do," Randy said, "the cops are gonna be out lookin for me."

Scott shrugged. "Mo says you didn't hurt her," he said. "That's good enough for me."

Randy gave his father-in-law a long, suspicious gaze. He didn't like the look of those doughnuts. Nor did he like the way Scott kept looking over his shoulder.

"Rooftop with you today?" Scott said.

"The Roof's retired from the collection business," Randy answered. "Same as I'm gonna be, just as soon as I can. I'm researching college opportunities—thinkin about it anyway, the art-professor routine. You know, play the game, quote unquote."

Now Randy started looking over his own shoulder, looking all around. He went on. "So, what's with the doughnuts? And how come you wanted to meet me out here instead of at your place of business?"

"I don't own the hardware store anymore."

"You're the manager. Same thing, just about. Got any chocolate-covered in there?"

Scott's hand came out of his jacket pocket, opened the doughnut bag, and reached inside. Randy leaned back, aiming his gun, bulging his trousers. But it was a stack of hundred-dollar bills, not a weapon, that Scott pulled out of the bag, a much thicker stack than Randy might have expected.

"Let's take a ride," Scott said.

"Yeah?" Randy's nervousness tightened his shoulders.

"I want to pay off my debt," Scott told him.

"That's why we're here."

"No offense to you," Scott said, "but I'd just as soon pay LaFlamme personally."

"Can't be done," Randy replied. "Ray LaFlamme don't ever have personal contact with his customers. Like I said when I called you, Ray personally authorized me to give you a 10 percent reduction in interest for an early payment."

"I mean I want to pay all of it," Scott explained.

"All what?"

"A hundred fifty thousand and change, everything I owe—principle, interest, and late fees. I'm done. I'm selling the store to Mainely Hardware."

Randy stared at the Dunkin Donuts bag a moment longer, his synapses beginning to fire. "Wait a minute," Randy said. "You brought all of it?"

"Yeah, minus the 10 percent discount." Scott held out the doughnut bag to him. "Take the money, Randy. I don't need it anymore. I got a bank loan."

Randy reached out skeptically and took the bag in his hand. "I don't know how this is gonna go over," he said.

"Count it up," Scott told him. "I want you to sign a receipt that I paid in full. You can tell LaFlamme for me it's been sweet, but I couldn't see a future in the hardware business."

Randy glanced up at him. There was too much information coming at him, and too fast: bank loan, discount, receipt, a hundred fifty grand. Not to mention he could actually smell the currency through the waxy bag. He opened the top and peeked inside at the stacks of Franklins, and his heart surged.

"So I sign a receipt, then what? You whack me and take the receipt and the money."

Scott reached into his jacket pocket.

Randy dropped the doughnut bag on the road and went for his Dockers. He pulled out his gun. Then, seeing that all Scott held in his hand was a ballpoint pen, he said, "Boy Scout motto: 'Be Prepared.' "

"Yeah, you're a Boy Scout, Randy. For Christ's sake, I'm your father-in-law."

"Don't give me that Mr. Innocent routine," Randy shot back. "I know how you made your money—back when you had it. Wheelin and dealin. I'm married to your daughter, don't forget."

Scott regarded Randy for several seconds.

"Put your gun away, Randy. Even if I thought you hurt Moreen—which I don't—I'd never in a million years make my daughter a widow." Scott handed the receipt and pen to Randy. "Just sign your name and go see your boss."

Randy studied the receipt, studied Scott, then pocketed the revolver. "Just like that, huh?"

Scott eyed him for another second or two, as a smile came over his face. "Just exactly like that."

★   ★   ★

At about seven o'clock, when Neal went down to swim, Ellen called the hospital and was told that Moreen had gone home. She called Mo's house, but no one answered, so she went into the garden to pick greens for a salad. The day was ending with a pleasant calm, swallows darting about in the sky, peepers just beginning their evening song.

As she started picking through a thicket of Swiss chard, she thought of Mo as a little girl and remembered how they would lie together in bed every morning after Scott had left for work. She could almost hear the sound of the little bare feet bounding down the hall, and the way the old bedsprings would bounce when Mo landed, the way the two of them would snuggle under the blankets until their bodies fit perfectly together. Ellen could feel Mo's warm little head nestled in the hollow of her neck. They'd lie together like that for the longest time, making plans for the day. Or just talking about anything that came to mind. Sometimes they'd lie there without saying a word until they both fell asleep again.

Working in her garden, Ellen became aware of an almost perfect silence in the air. At first she equated it with the tranquility of her thoughts. Then she realized why it was so quiet: the waterfall had stopped.

She held her breath to listen, then stepped out of the garden and walked into the pasture with her weeding fork in her hand. Reaching the crest of the hill, she looked down and saw Neal swimming in the pond naked. She also saw the concrete top of the dam, gray and dry.

She heard the diesel engine then and turned to see the old Mercedes pull into the yard. She walked toward the barn as Scott got out of the car. He was dressed in a business suit, and he came toward her with a long, purposeful stride. They met just inside the pasture gate, where he took her in his arms.

"I'm all dirty," she told him, keeping her hands off him.

"I've been a jerk," he said, and he reached inside his jacket and withdrew a banded stack of hundred-dollar bills.

"What's this?"

A slow, beautiful smile came to his face, a look of confidence she hadn't seen on him in years. "First Federal likes my gun shop."

"You got a bank loan? The farm's out of hock?"

"You were right," he said softly. "I've put this family through hell for too long. Now I'm going to start making it up to you." He pulled her close and kissed her on the mouth. It was hard to resist. She dropped her fork and kissed him back, loving the warmth of his lips on hers, his hands on her back.

"The cement around the pipe is all eaten away," Neal said behind them. At the sound of his voice, Ellen broke the kiss.

Neal eyed her cautiously. "We're losing water fast," he said to Scott, "and it's only gonna get worse."

"Got it covered," Scott said.

Ellen looked at him. So did Neal.

"Randy's coming over tomorrow," Scott explained. "He's gonna give us a hand."

Neal shrugged. "Might as well keep it in the family."

Ellen bent for her weeding fork, keeping her objection casual. "Don't you think you should hire someone more experienced?"

"Probably not a bad idea," Neal said.

His remark surprised her, and she turned a glance his way.

Scott shook his head. "It's not like he's gonna be welding down there. All he has to do is take a pipe wrench down and unscrew the cap off the pipe. When the pond drains, we can pack some fresh cement around it, put the cap back on, and we're back in business."

Neal shrugged. "Should be safe enough."

"Besides, the Water District's only gonna give us two days before they lower the flashboards down again. They're afraid the reservoir'll overflow its banks and flood the roads up there."

Neal did not respond. Ellen headed for the house.

"Hey," Scott said, and she turned back, avoiding Neal's eyes. "There's a bottle of good champagne in the car. Any chance I'll be getting out of the doghouse soon?"

She regarded him flatly. "Let's see how good the champagne is."

Ted's Clam Shed was about to close for the night, when the dark green panel truck pulled in: XYZ DIVERS—DIVING IS OUR BUSINESS. Two other vehicles were already parked in the lot, spaced a hundred feet apart, a white Taurus from Quebec and Randy's black Cherokee, which sat off to the right, out of the range of the yellow bug lights.

When Rooftop pulled in beside the Cherokee, Randy looked over, raised a cardboard tray to the window and said, "I didn't think you were gonna show up."

"The heck's that?" Rooftop said out his open window.

"Twin lobster," Randy told him. Motioning with his head for

Rooftop to join him, he leaned over and pushed the passenger door open. He was wearing a bib in the shape of a double-wide lobster.

Rooftop deliberated, then opened his door and came over. Randy held the tray on the dashboard for him, the two red lobsters curled up beside two plastic cups of melted butter. The clawless bodies of two other lobsters lay on another tray in Randy's lap.

Rooftop ducked into the vehicle and Randy handed him the tray, saying, "I see you're drivin again. I thought you lost your license for ten years."

"Special dispensation," Rooftop explained. "To and from work. No night driving."

Randy grinned. "It's nighttime, isn't it? So you're already breakin the law."

Rooftop remained somber.

"Anyways, I haven't talked to you since you moved out. How's life in Destin? Probably never see each other again, now that you're in the same town as my in-laws."

Rooftop shrugged. Randy raised a slender red leg to his mouth and sucked out the meat. "Dig in, man."

"Moreen okay?" Rooftop said. "I went to the hospital to see her, and they said you brought her home."

"She's all right," Randy said. "But that's a whole nother friggin story, which I'm not about to comment on at this point in time."

Rooftop gave him a look. He was wearing his new glasses, which were larger and rounder than his old ones, making his eyes look even bigger, but Randy didn't comment on that either. Instead, he tossed the little hollow leg out his window, then reached in front of Rooftop's knees and popped open the glove compartment. "S'cuse me, big guy."

Rooftop spread his legs, and the glove box fell open. Stuffed inside was the bulging Dunkin Donuts bag and Randy's snub-nosed .22.

"Know what that is?" Randy said with a grin.

Rooftop angled his head to see in. "Dessert?"

Randy shook his head. "Money."

"A good deal of it, by the looks," Rooftop said.

"That's us gettin off the hook," Randy replied, as he closed the glove box again. "That's us not worryin about Ray LaFlamme or Gator or anyone else."

"I wasn't worried in particular."

Randy sat back in his seat. "I just got back from Old Orchard," he said, giving Rooftop a cocky frown. "I took care of things with Ray

LaFlamme. Not LaFlamme personally but one of his bodyguards, some big frog by the name of Marcel something. You know what I mean. Frenchman."

"Marcel Desjardin. Used to be a prison guard." Rooftop cracked a claw in his hand, releasing a small flood of broth into the tray. "You don't want to fool around with Marcel."

"Who's foolin? I gave Marcel the twenty-eight hundred, like it came from Humpty Dumpty, and another four grand off of Scott Chambers's account. And I slipped him a hundred for himself you know, goodwill and all that."

"So what's that in the doughnut bag?" Rooftop asked, gesturing to the glove box.

Randy shrugged. "A little additional something that I didn't turn over at this point in time." He gave Rooftop a look. "What I was wonderin here, you and me with a hundred thousand dollars, huh?"

Rooftop frowned.

"Well," Randy said, getting his attention. "I thought we might go into business for ourselves, you know, buy a little product? Just the once, ba-da-boom, then we get out. I got a couple of assholes I can unload it on, triple the money in a day. Pay LaFlamme the difference next month, and hey. What do you think?"

Rooftop pushed the pink-speckled meat out of the tail and dipped it in the melted butter, then dropped it into his mouth. "I'll stick to my diving," he said.

Randy shrugged. "Three hundred grand, that's a lot of diving."

Rooftop kept chewing.

"Who knows? After I pay off LaFlamme, I'm thinkin about diving school myself. Maybe after I get my certification, the two of us can buy a boat and hunt up some pirate treasure."

"Like I told you," Rooftop said, "I'm figuring on living right for a change."

"I'm definitely down for that," Randy said, tossing an empty claw out his window. "Matter of fact, I'm doin a little diving job for the family tomorrow. Strictly charity work."

Rooftop gave him a look.

"I thought you'd like that. Wanna give me a hand?"

"Can't," Rooftop said. "I joined the volunteer firefighters, and we're taking part in the parade."

"Good ol' Fourth of July on the sixth of July," Randy said. "Only in Destin, Maine. Anyway, best we keep this between the two of us—the cash, I mean."

"Doughnut bag in your glove box isn't the safest place to keep that kind of money, you want my opinion."

"Safer than home, with that friggin wife of mine layin around, kinda mood she's in. Man, I thought fuckin PMS was supposed to be bad."

Rooftop pulverized another claw with a sharp snap.

"Not to mention Gator-Aid," Randy added. "I 'specially don't want Gator to know."

"He's the last person I'd tell anything," Rooftop agreed.

"I mean, like, *Hello!*" Randy laughed. "Anyways"—he wiped his right hand on his pants and stuck it out—"I just want to make sure there's no hard feelings between us. Any man lucky to call someone his best friend ought not screw it up, know?"

Rooftop looked at the hand, looked at Randy, then wiped his own hand on his napkin. "Kinda sticky," he said.

Randy gave a shrug and took the oversized hand anyway. "Good lobster, though."

"Real sweet."

At ten o'clock, when they'd finished eating dinner, Neal went out to work on the barn. Scott poured himself another whiskey and ginger and retired to the living room to watch television. Ellen did the dishes. When she finished in the kitchen, she went into the living room and sat on a corner of the couch still glowing a little from the champagne she'd had. Scott was stretched out in his corduroy recliner, already fast asleep and snoring. An old black-and-white Elvis movie was on TV. Ellen leafed through the papers and magazines on the coffee table and picked up her weaving journal. It had come in the mail back in May and she still hadn't found the time to look at it. She opened it to an article about vegetable dyes, but found when she'd reached the bottom of the page that she couldn't recall a thing she had read. She took the TV remote off the coffee table and hit MUTE, silencing the movie.

"Don't!" Scott blurted, lurching awake. Looking around dazedly, he sat forward in the chair and hunched his shoulders, then sniffed deeply as he struggled off the recliner to his feet. "Goin to bed," he said, climbing up the stairs.

"I'll be up in a while," Ellen said. She started reading again.

Presently Scott began to snore upstairs, a five-drink concerto, by no means his loudest. But with the waterfall stilled, it was loud enough to distract her, to remind her how unwittingly he'd been drawn into Neal's plan—if indeed there was a plan. She wished he'd roll over and stop. Then, apparently, he did.

The back door opened. Ellen listened to Neal's footsteps cross the kitchen floor, then he stuck his head in the doorway. "Night," he said. His hair was tousled and he wore a white T-shirt, his sweater draped over his arm.

"Goodnight," Ellen replied plainly, looking down at her magazine again. She thought of that last remaining coyote—wounded though he was—as she listened to Neal walk back through the kitchen, listened to the door spring stretch and contract, and the door slap shut. If Neal was plotting against Randy somehow, there was no hint of it in his behavior, nothing unusual in his mannerisms.

Ellen made up her mind to stop worrying. The leaking dam was only that: a leaking dam and nothing more—a coincidence. She closed her magazine and turned off the lamp and listened to the night outside, a sheep's bell tinkling, the peeping of tiny tree frogs off in the distance.

Against the silence of the night, now Ellen could hear every detail of sound: the rattle of the clothesline reel against the house as Neal took his sleeping bag down; the squeak of the pasture gate opening and closing.

There hadn't even been a glint in his eye.

nine

Friday morning rose sunny and blue, with barely a breath rustling the trees. It was the third day of a four-day Independence Day celebration that started on July fourth and featured a softball tournament, road race, bike race, pig scramble, pie-eating contest, wood-cutting contest, parade, firefighting demonstration, arts and crafts fair, baked bean dinner, and Casino Night at the fire station, all culminating in the fireworks display at the high school's athletic field on Saturday night.

For the parade, Scott and the other volunteers had polished up the town's two red fire trucks and trained for their annual firemen's muster on the commons. Knowing he'd be home all weekend working on his dam, Scott had agreed to be on call so the other firefighters could attend the celebration.

At eleven-thirty in the morning, Randy arrived, an hour late, having gone to the coast to fill his tanks at Gary Pope's dock. Gary operated the town's marina and owned his own compressor. Randy had told him that the air was for Rooftop. When he got to the farm, he put on his wetsuit in the dooryard, working out of a long black duffel bag in the back of his Cherokee.

Ellen went up to the bedroom so she wouldn't hear the men talking, but when Randy's voice came through the window, she started the vacuum cleaner. She vacuumed the room then put clothes away and made the bed, which she normally did only when she changed the sheets. This morning she even dusted the bureaus. Then she went downstairs to her pantry, where she lay on her bench and started lifting.

She hadn't planned to, so she wasn't dressed properly: barefoot, short-sleeved blouse, khaki shorts. Nevertheless, she did all her reps then repeated them, straining, trying to concentrate on nothing but her breathing, but acutely aware of every minute that passed.

When the footsteps finally came drumming up the porch and the door banged open, Ellen caught her breath, suddenly and chillingly aware that she'd been anticipating this moment for days.

"Ellen!"

She lowered the bar into its cradle and slid out from under it, walked into the kitchen, sweating. Scott was pacing in his bathing suit, puddling the linoleum with water, the portable telephone pressed to his ear. He turned away from her.

"It's Scotty," he gasped into the phone, throwing open the door and heading back outside as he spoke, waving Ellen to follow him. "No, my son-in-law—he's caught in our dam!"

Ellen went along numbly.

"He's stuck, he's running out of air!" Scott yelled as he ran to Randy's Cherokee, a set of keys in his hand. He jammed the key into the liftgate lock, and when he finally got it open he found another scuba tank and diving mask. He thrust the mask into Ellen's hands. "Bring this down to Neal," he told her, "hurry," then continued yelling into the phone as she ran barefoot through the pasture, scattering her sheep, "Well, find somebody! Nothing happens to him!"

Randy was twenty feet down, his right arm sucked into the drain-pipe to the top of his shoulder. As deep as he was, the pressure of twenty feet of water trying to rush through the pipe prevented him from pulling his arm out. So now he sat twisted on the rocky bottom, his head crooked against the concrete, facing the bright, rippling sky. His wetsuit was torn at the top of his shoulder, where the threaded end of the pipe had cut into his flesh, and blood darkened the water around the wound, oozing like smoke out of the tear in the suit. But Randy could no longer feel any sensation in the arm, which had gone from cold to practically numb. His left arm curled around his chest, trying to warm himself. His whole body shivered.

As Neal swam down toward him, Randy gazed up listlessly, his chest rising and falling, bubbles of carbon dioxide breaking quietly from his regulator. He watched Neal stop about three feet above him, hovering there. Randy unfolded his left arm from his body and gave him a thumbs-up sign. You got me, bub. You win.

Neal held up five fingers, then tapped his wrist—five minutes, in diving code—which meant help was on its way.

Randy nodded, gave him another thumbs-up. Hope I can wait five minutes, man. Matterafact, I'm ready to go up now.

Neal turned away and kicked for the surface. Randy watched his dark body grow smaller as it rippled up into the light. Then everything got quiet again. No sound but the cold air coming out of the scuba tank into his lungs, then going out again. In and out. In and out. And the ridiculous fucking cold. Randy rubbed his chest briskly with his free hand. Didn't do much good. He was shivering like crazy.

So, five minutes and they'd get him out. Probably Rooftop was on his way. Randy looked down at his gauge. Five minutes, it said. Cuttin it kinda close, boys. In fact, it was already getting harder to breathe, as if someone was standing behind him, pinching his air hose. He looked at the gauge again, trying to see if it was five minutes or four. Looked more like four. He raised his face to the sky, watching for Rooftop. Then a thought came to him, sudden, uninvited, and entirely unwelcome. More than a thought, it was a feeling, and his entire body jerked with a monstrous jolt of fear.

"He's got five minutes!" Neal shouted when he broke the surface. The water was an inch lower than the top of the dam. The pond was still.

"Maybe we can winch him out," Scott said. "Hook up to one of those trees." He stepped down to the diving rock, beside Ellen, and dropped the scuba tank in the water.

"You'll tear his arm off," Neal told him, swimming over to retrieve the tank. "There's probably five hundred pounds of pressure trying to pull him through the pipe."

"Well, what the hell are we gonna do?" Scott yelled.

"Is it just his arm that's stuck?" Ellen asked.

"Up to his shoulder," Scott answered. "Give Neal the mask."

She dropped the mask into Neal's hands. He spat on the glass and rubbed it around with his fingers, then pulled the strap over his head.

"Pump it out," Ellen said.

Neal stared up at her.

She turned to Scott. "Get the fire trucks down here," she said. "If we can lower the pressure—"

"The trucks are in the parade, they'll never get here in time," Scott told her. He clawed the top of his head with both hands and turned a half circle.

"Can we break through the dam?" Ellen asked him. "From the other side—break through to relieve the pressure?"

Scott looked down at Neal, questioning.

"Rock and concrete," Neal said skeptically.

"It's worth a try," Scott said. "Neal, go down and tell him we're gonna get him out. Ellen, stay by the phone. I'll get the pickaxe." Scott climbed back up the bank then ran off toward the house.

Ellen looked down at Neal in the water, the telephone tight in her hand, her body shivering intensely despite the full sunlight on her back. While birds sang obliviously all around her, she watched a flurry of bubbles break against the dam. She thought of her wounded sheep sprawled in the pasture waiting to die, the way it had breathed.

"Neal, get him out," she said evenly.

"We're doing everything we can."

She stared at him. He gave nothing away. Gulping a quick breath of air, she dived into the water and when she'd surfaced said, "Give me the tank."

"Ellen, don't go down there."

"Give me the tank."

Their eyes met.

"Okay, sit on the rock, I'll help you put it on," he told her. She swam over and hoisted herself up, and Neal handed the heavy tank up to her. She fit her arms through the straps, then pulled the weight belt around her waist, snapped the latch and pulled it tight. Neal stripped the mask off his forehead and handed it to her. She pulled it down over her face. Then she fit the regulator in her mouth.

"Breathe normally," Neal told her.

She slipped off the rock and went under, pulling a deep breath of compressed air into her lungs and blowing it forcefully out, as she turned and kicked for the bottom. At first, she saw Randy only as a vague, black shape in the surrounding darkness, but the deeper she swam, the more acclimated to the darkness she grew, so by the time she was five feet from him, she saw something that made her stop just out of his reach.

He was sitting stiffly on the bottom with his right side pressed tight against the dam and his left fist clenched against his shoulder, facing up at her with his eyes shut and a horrible grimace on his face. Ellen might have thought him dead, were it not for the quick, shallow bubbling from his regulator or the rapid rise and fall of his chest. Then she realized what he was doing. His wetsuit was sliced open in three places at the shoulder, like the gill slits of a shark, and slender threads of blood curled off the blade where he held a knife to his flesh.

She let herself descend another inch, until her shadow darkened Randy's face. His eyes opened. Suddenly the knife blade flashed up at her. She pushed back. But she knew by the sorrowful look in his eyes that he was not attacking her. He was trying to hand her his knife, his eyes desperately pleading. He wanted her to amputate his arm.

She shook her head adamantly.

He waved the knife at her, insistent.

Equally insistent, Ellen refused again.

Behind his mask, his eyes seemed to glaze with sadness. He looked down at his shoulder again, then turned back to Ellen as if to continue the argument. She gestured back at him, that she wanted to give him the tank she was wearing. As she reached to take it off, suddenly his eyes flared and he lashed out, knife flashing.

She kicked back, just as a hand shot past her and captured Randy's wrist. In the flurry of bubbles, Ellen saw Neal pulling Randy's arm upward, while Randy's knife pecked furiously at him. Then Randy swung his legs up, as if trying to wrap them around Neal's neck, but when his right knee kicked up, his knife pierced his own thigh. Ellen saw a burst of bubbles expel from Randy's regulator as the blood inked thickly from his leg.

Clutching Randy's wrist with both hands, Neal pressed his feet against the convex face of the dam and pushed. From above, it might have seemed that he was trying to pull Randy out of the pipe—if the men could have been seen, which they could not, as deep as they were.

Down in the dark, Ellen could see the knife tremble in Randy's hand; she could see the contortion of his face and how his arm actually seemed to stretch as his wetsuit ripped wider, the blood rushing out of his shoulder cut and streaming into the pipe. A sudden pop sounded, then a gurgling scream from Randy, and his wetsuit sleeve snapped free at the shoulder and was sucked into the drain. In the same instant, the knife dropped from his hand and floated to the bottom. Then Neal released his wrist and swam down to retrieve the weapon.

Floating in the fog of stirred-up silt, Ellen could nevertheless see Randy's eyes through his mask, gazing longingly at her, conveying a desperate understanding of his fate. She started removing her tank again, but Neal took hold of her arm. When she wheeled around and shook her head at him, he knocked on the tank, pointed to his wrist, then pointed up. She understood. Maximize both tanks. She kicked for the top.

She broke into open air and pulled the regulator from her mouth as Neal surfaced beside her, looking all around.

"Take this," he said, poking her hand with the handle of Randy's knife. "Hide it."

She scowled at him.

"Ellen, now," he said urgently.

She tore the mask from her face and slapped it on the water between them. "You get him out of there."

"Ellie!" Scott shouted, appearing on the ledge above them with a pickaxe in his hand. "What are you doing?"

She felt the knife handle slide into her palm again, and her heart pounded. She refused to take it.

"What are you doing in the water?" Scott shouted again, his face a bright, burning pink. He slammed the pickaxe onto the abutment under his feet. "I told you to man the phone!"

"We were trying to pull him out," she answered.

"Neal and I already tried. We need to conserve the air in that tank, now get up here."

Treading water, Ellen threw her shoulders back and wriggled out of the diving tank. Neal helped pull it off. Then she took one powerful stroke to the diving rock and pulled herself onto her stomach. Lifting herself to her feet, she couldn't believe the way her legs were shaking.

"How is he?" Scott asked her.

"Cold," Neal answered. "The seal's gone in his wetsuit."

"Don't either of you go down there anymore," Scott told him. "Neal, stay on the surface and watch his bubbles so you'll be ready to change tanks when he runs out of air." He turned back to Ellen as she stepped up onto the bank. "I know it goes against your goddamned nature," he told her, "but right now you've got to do what I say."

Jerking away from her, he marched around the end of the dam and dropped the pickaxe over the side. It rang angrily when it hit the rocky stream bed below. As he started lowering himself down the granite bank, Randy's knife clattered on the rock at Ellen's feet.

She turned back to the pond and glared at Neal, who was floating on the scuba tank.

She wanted to kick the knife back into the water.

"*Ellie, where are you?*" Scott shouted.

"Right here!"

She kicked the knife underneath Randy's duffle bag as she stepped onto the abutment, where she could see Scott on the other side of the dam, pickaxe in hand, balancing over the rocks of the stream bed.

"Can you see Randy's bubbles?" he called up to her.

"Yes," Ellen answered, positioning herself so both Scott and Neal were in her sight. In fact, the curve in the dam allowed Ellen to see part of both faces of the structure: the near half of the pond face and the far half of the dry face, where the outlet pipe was located, a dark, eight-inch hole embedded in the granite blocks about three feet off the ground.

Scott chose a spot about five feet beyond the pipe, secured his footing on the slippery rock, then swung the pickaxe. The impact on the rock did nothing to the dam, but at the same moment, Ellen noticed a movement inside the pipe. She realized, to her horror, that she could see the tips of Randy's fingers beckoning, like pale earthworms, for the light. She visualized the thickness of the dam and imagined how far his arm must have been stretched.

"Ellen," Neal called quietly.

She ignored him.

Scott swung the pickaxe again, with a loud grunt. This time its tip stuck between two keystones and held fast. "Bastard!" he cursed, shaking the handle until the pick came free.

Knowing the way the keystone rocks fit together—the structure was actually strengthened by the force of the water—Ellen wondered how Scott could hope to break through. She looked down to the duffel, saw sunlight flash off the tip of the blade. If Randy died with a wound in his leg, she thought, and the knife were found . . .

Hide it where? She looked back toward the pasture, the house, the barn, the pump house . . .

"Scott?"

He attacked the dam again.

"Scott, I know how we can drain the pond!" she yelled. She bent and grabbed the knife from under the duffel bag, then ran down the bank and on up the farm road.

"Ellie, where are you going?" he shouted.

The pump house was eight-by-eight, windowless, constructed of cinder blocks. Two water fixtures were attached to the side. One fed the garden hose, which stretched across the pasture to the sheep's temporary paddock. The other was a two-inch fire hose fitting, which the family had never needed, until now.

Ellen opened the wooden door, then bent and threw open the hatch. A ladder led ten feet down into the darkness, where the two pumps sat: one tapping the farm pond and providing water for the barn; the other connecting the deep well to the house. She descended to the cold concrete floor, feeling her way between the cold, cobwebbed wall and the two water pumps. Finding the narrow space between the two pumps, she dropped the knife down, heard the incriminating click it made against the floor, then made her way back to the ladder. Climbing out of the dank hole, she shut the hatch behind her then went out in the sunlight, around the side of the pump house, where she opened the ball valve on the fire hose fitting. Instantly a thick jet of water sprayed thirty feet out into the pasture.

Running back to the pond, she climbed the bank and called to Scott, "I turned on the fire hose at the pump house, to draw water out of the pond."

"Ellie, we need you here!" he yelled, his pickaxe ringing hard off the granite. He had taken his shirt off and his arms shone with sweat. "How's Randy?"

Ellen looked over the pond side of the dam, where air bubbles broke alongside the top of the dam. As she turned back to answer, she was distracted by the sight of someone coming around the pump house.

"How is he?" Scott shouted.

"The same," Ellen yelled back, peering up the hill.

It was Maddy, walking down the farm road, wearing a red summer dress and large dark sunglasses. She carried a picnic basket.

"He's going to need more air in a minute," Neal called.

"Are the EMTs here?" Scott shouted, striking the dam again.

"I brought a little peace offering," Maddy called, as she approached the bank, lifting a bottle of red wine out of her basket.

"Mad, we've got an emergency," Ellen replied, hoping to turn her back.

"Who are you talking to?" Scott yelled.

Maddy mounted the bank and looked down one side of the dam, at Neal treading water with the scuba tank strapped to his shoulder, then down the other side, at Scott attacking the rock wall with his pickaxe.

"What is he doing?" she asked with distaste.

"Get her out of here," Scott warned, grunting as he struck the dam again. The impact jolted up through Ellen's legs.

"It's Randy," Ellen explained to her friend. "He's caught in the dam."

Maddy's face changed. "You're serious—?"

"His arm's caught in the outlet pipe."

"God," Maddy breathed. "Wait a minute. How—"

"*Shh—*"

Ellen listened.

"Scott, stop—"

The dam rang with one more blow of his pickaxe, then everything was perfectly quiet. The bubbles had stopped.

"Neal!" Ellen yelled, spinning toward the pond, but Neal was already underwater, his kicking feet darkening to a deeper green-brown. She turned back to Scott. "He's out of air!"

"God," Maddy said again, putting her hands on Ellen's back, as together they watched the unbroken surface.

"*What's going on up there?*" Scott shouted.

"Is his hand still moving?" Ellen called down to him. "Check his hand!"

"His hand?" Maddy breathed.

Scott dropped the pickaxe and fell to his knees in front of the pipe, staring into the dark hole. He raised his face and cried out: "*I cannot do this to my daughter!*"

In the echo of his shout, the silence was pervasive. Even the birds stopped singing. Ellen felt Maddy's grip tighten on her arm.

Then a burst of bubbles broke the surface, quickly followed by more.

Ellen turned toward the pond as Neal splashed into the air with Randy's spent tank in his hands.

"He's only got a few minutes," Neal gasped.

"Five minutes!" Ellen yelled down.

Scott grabbed his pickaxe again and swung it mightily, striking the same bruised keystone again, dead on, the impact staggering him. He regained his footing but his shoulders slumped, and he looked as though he was about to collapse. But he reared back and swung again.

Maddy stared straight at Ellen, her eyes like lights.

Ellen turned toward the pasture. Now someone else was running down the hillside, a short, stocky man in a baseball uniform, no cap, his muscular arms pumping . . . Sugar Westerback, yelling as he charged down the hill, "Rescue units on the way!"

"He needs scuba tanks!" Ellen shouted in reply.

"How much air's he got?" Sugar asked, pounding up the bank.

"Five minutes," Ellen said. "Less than five minutes."

"What, *left?*"

He looked down at Neal treading the water, the empty tank discarded on the rocks.

"What's wrong with that one?" he said.

"Empty," Neal answered.

The pickaxe clanged below them. Scott's grunt sounded like a sob. Sugar stared down. "Scotty, you trying to break him out?"

Ellen looked at the policeman, thinking he might have been drinking. In fact, she could smell beer on him. The words BRISCOE'S MEATS were emblazoned on his softball uniform in deep red lettering.

"He's trying to let water out," Ellen explained. "To relieve the pressure."

"That's not gonna work," Sugar said matter-of-factly, still looking down at Scott. Then his head jerked, and he gaped down at the black pipe, with the white fingertips inside beckoning. "Whoa," he whispered. Behind him, Randy's breath bubbled up.

Sugar lowered his head for a moment, scowling in thought. Then he turned toward the house. "Okay," he said, "bring your truck down. We'll hitch up a chain and haul him out."

"Won't do any good," Neal said. "We've got a winch up in the shed. But you'd only pull his arm off."

"I don't mean *through* the friggin pipe," Sugar told. "I mean haul him out by his feet."

"There's too much pressure," Ellen explained. "You pull on him hard enough, you'll rip his arm off."

Sugar frowned again. "Huh." He looked at his watch and said, "They should be here any minute." He folded his arms, rubbing his biceps with his hands. Then he scowled deeply. "Garden hose!" he blurted, clapping his hands. "He can breathe through a hose."

"He's down twenty feet," Neal said, on the other side. "The pressure'll collapse it."

"I don't hear any better ideas," Sugar said. He pointed at Neal. "You, go get twenty-five feet of garden hose. On the double. Bring that winch down too. What the hell, lose an arm, it's better than losin' your life."

Neal gave Sugar a doubtful look.

"Move it!" Sugar barked. "Splashin around down there sure ain't gonna help."

"Just do it, Neal," Ellen said. Neal swam to the diving rock and climbed up to the bank.

"Hurry up," Sugar told him, as he stepped to the downstream side of the dam. "Scotty, we got a plan up here!"

But Scott did not hear. He was toiling in a panic, sweat pouring off his face as again and again he swung the heavy tool into the granite, not even noticing Maddy climbing down the rocks toward him. But Ellen noticed.

"Maddy, you'd better not," she said, wanting to keep her friend away from Scott.

Maddy was not to be dissuaded. Stepping down into the slippery, puddled rocks, she made her way over to the outlet pipe, where she knelt on the granite bed and reached into the pipe, taking hold of Randy's fingers.

"God, his hand is freezing," Maddy called, and Scott glanced over to her. *Keep working,* Ellen thought.

To her small relief, he said nothing, but reared back with the pickaxe and slammed it into the wall with a terrible grunt. Chips of granite flew. Maddy ducked. Then she whipped her head up at Ellen.

"He's writing something!" she cried.

Ellen looked down, saw the bent finger moving on Maddy's palm.

"He's spelling with his finger?" Sugar asked, leaning over the edge.

"M!" Maddy called up. "He made the letter M."

Behind Ellen, the bubbles breaking on the pond sounded like low, taunting laughter.

"U!" Maddy called.

"M–U," Sugar said.

Scott stopped pounding at the rocks. He looked over, as Maddy gazed into the pipe. Ellen stared down, paralyzed, as the finger continued moving like a planchette over Maddy's palm. She could feel her heart pounding down through her feet.

"That it?" Sugar said. "M–U?"

"R," Maddy said. "M–U–R—" She watched intently, as the white finger continued inscribing on her palm. Suddenly her eyes rose up to Ellen, horrified.

Ellen felt a wave of lightness come over her. "M–O," she said, correcting Maddy. "M–O–R . . . *Moreen.* Is that what he's spelling? *Moreen?*" She stared down at Maddy. And Maddy stared back, speechless, her eyes turning glassy. She nodded.

Scott started bashing the dam again with his pickaxe.

"Moreen?" Sugar said.

Ellen could feel his eyes settle on her. She realized she was holding her breath.

"Wait a minute," Sugar breathed. "That's *Randy* down there? Your daughter's husband?"

Suddenly Maddy's mouth sprang open. If she had meant to scream, her voice was not cooperating.

Ellen watched her, terrified. "Mad?"

"My hand," Maddy gasped.

"I think he's got ahold of her," Sugar suggested.

Ellen turned toward the pond. The bubbles had stopped.

On the other side of the dam, she heard Maddy gasp. "He's breaking my—" Then she fell backward, as if repelled from a shock, landing hard on the rocks. Scott dropped his pickaxe and ran to the outlet pipe, sank to his knees, and thrust his hand in.

Behind Ellen, a great burst of bubbles broke on the pond.

At that moment, Neal came running onto the bank with the winch in his hand and a long section of garden hose coiled around his neck and shoulder. Immediately reading the situation, he dropped the things on the abutment and dived in the water.

"Oh boy," Sugar said, folding his arms, looking up at the sky.

Ellen stared down at Scott holding Randy's hand, his forehead laid against the dam.

Beside him, Maddy numbly raised herself off the rocks.

Scott took a deep breath, then withdrew his hand from the pipe and sat heavily on the basin. He turned his head toward Maddy and Maddy met his eyes.

"You okay?" he asked her.

"Fine," Maddy replied, and she looked up at Ellen, who turned away, to see Neal rise to the surface of the pond.

"We lose him?" Sugar said.

Neal nodded, then climbed onto the rocks, saying to Sugar, "He pulled the regulator out of his mouth."

"What's a regulator?"

"The thing you breathe through."

"What do you mean he pulled it out?"

"There was no air left in the tank," Neal explained and he hauled himself up to the bank. "Probably like trying to breathe through a bent straw. His lungs overruled his brain, told him to breathe. So he breathed water."

Sugar winced.

Neal went over to Ellen, put his cold hand on her arm. "We did everything we could," he said softly. As she withstood his touch, she caught Maddy looking up at them both. Then she heard a siren. Two sirens.

"Here they come," Sugar said. "Right on time."

It was an ambulance and one of the two town fire trucks, trailing red, white, and blue streamers behind. Sugar looked at the truck, then wheeled and stared hard at Ellen. A wave of fear charged through her body, though she tried not to show it.

"*Stupid!*" Sugar cursed himself. "*Pump it out!*"

The state police followed the fire truck in, and a battery of men directed the police down the farm road to the pond, where the fire truck began pumping. As Ellen stood watching, she couldn't stop picturing the knife on the floor of the pump house. Finally she turned away from the pond, picked up the coiled garden hose, and headed for the house.

"You okay?" Scott asked her.

"I need the bathroom," she answered. "Can I turn off the pump now, so the pasture doesn't flood?"

Scott looked at the trooper, who shrugged and said, "I guess it's not really helping."

She walked briskly away from them, followed the gravel road up to the pump house as if she were sleepwalking. She shut off the water at the fixture, then went down inside the pump house and retrieved the knife from the cold floor and stuffed it inside the bundled hose. Climbing back out of the pump house, she carried the concealed weapon up the farm road, walking stiffly past the gathering crowd of police and emergency workers and townspeople, who were just getting the news.

She climbed the porch steps and went inside with the hose, into the pantry, where she opened the freezer and buried the knife under the plastic bags of last year's vegetables. Then she used the bathroom. When she walked out of the house again she saw Rooftop's panel truck parked in the dooryard. Rooftop himself was leaning heavily on the roof of Randy's black Cherokee, his long chin resting on his arms.

He knew. The way he stared at Ellen, she was sure he knew. When he raised his face, the sky flashed off his glasses.

"Your daughter's here," he said to her.

★   ★   ★

Moreen and Scott were together when she reached them, down below the dam, Moreen kneeling on the rocks with her hand inside the drainage pipe, quietly crying, Scott standing at her side, idly stroking her hair. The fire truck's two hoses snaked down the bank beside them, weighted down by blocks of granite, spraying pond water down the gorge.

Ellen stood above Moreen and Scott for a moment, looking down. Loath though she was to admit it, along with the sorrow she felt for her daughter, she also felt pain at seeing the two of them so close, while she was so utterly estranged from them both. It was as though they shared some secret bond that she could not be part of, no matter what she did.

But who had raised Moreen while Scott was away at work, at Rotary, or some other meeting? And where was Scott when Moreen needed rides to Girl Scouts, to 4-H, to softball, hockey, soccer, to school concerts? And all those nights when Moreen was sick, who sat up with her while Scott snored obliviously in his own bed? Who cooked Moreen's meals, bought her clothes, read to her, took her to the beach?

Yes, and who had murdered her husband?

Ellen tingled with awareness of her crime, as she climbed down the bank and balanced over the slippery basin to her daughter. Before she could think of a thing to say, Moreen reached out for her. It was like the pull of gravity, the way they came together, the way Moreen's sobs suddenly made her seem like a little girl again. As much as Ellen's mind stormed with guilt and fear, she relished the privilege of holding Mo while she wept. She sank to her knees and kissed her cheek, while Scott continued stroking her hair.

"I'm so sorry," Ellen whispered. "I'm so sorry."

"It's not your fault," Moreen cried.

When Duane Ramsey, the deputy medical examiner, climbed down to the bottom of the dam, he took Randy's hand from Moreen, felt for a pulse, then climbed back up and signed the death certificate in the presence of Sugar Westerback. Ramsey asked whether Sugar's father, Wes, was on his way, and Sugar told him that his parents had gone up to Lake Winnipesaukee to visit his sister, as they did every Fourth of July. Sugar didn't think they needed to be called home.

Interviews were conducted in the house, away from the noise of the fire truck. While Ellen, Scott, Neal, and Maddy sat around the kitchen table, Sugar leaned against the counter with a pad of paper and pen and he interviewed them together. Scott, speaking for the group, told Sugar that while Ellen was cleaning the house, he, Randy, and Neal had gone down to the dam to drain the pond. While he and Neal stayed on the bank with the equipment, Randy went down to unscrew the cap with a two-foot pipe wrench and three-pound hammer.

"Then he came up and said he got it unscrewed but he needed an axe or a crow bar," Scott explained, "something to knock the cap out of the way."

Sugar said, "Okay."

"So I went up and got the crow bar," Neal said.

"That do the trick?"

"Must've," Scott answered. "The water came gushing out for a second. Then it stopped. We figured Randy capped it again for some reason, and we waited awhile, but he wasn't coming up."

"Did you see what happened?"

Scott shrugged. "He was down too deep to see."

"How you think he got sucked in?" Sugar said.

"The only way I can figure it," Neal said, "he used the crow bar like a lance. Probably when the cap gave way, the momentum carried him forward, "so he held out his arm to stop himself."

Sugar straightened an arm and leaned forward in his chair. "I can picture that," he said.

Ellen studied Neal, thinking the theory plausible. In fact, if Neal had caused Randy's death, she had no idea how.

"Then what?" Sugar said.

"When he didn't come up," Scott said, "I went down to see what happened."

"You went under and found him stuck?"

"I tried to pull him out." Scott shook his head soberly. "We all tried. Even with Neal and me together, we couldn't budge him. So I ran up and called you, got your answering service."

Sugar turned to Maddy, who was once again wearing her sunglasses.

"You have anything to add?" Sugar said to her.

Maddy shook her head. Her tan had given way to a greenish pallor.

"Maddy only got there a minute before you did," Ellen explained. "Are you okay, Mad?"

"I'm fine," Maddy answered.

"You don't look so hot," Sugar said. "Unless you got anything you wanna say, you don't have to stick around."

Maddy stood up and went out the door. Sugar watched her for a moment or two, then turned back to the others, his gaze stopping on Ellen, who was distracted by what she was seeing out the window: Maddy and Moreen huddled beside Randy's Cherokee, quietly conferring.

Sugar leaned forward to see what Ellen was looking at. "Lucky you got a friend who's a psychologist," he said. "Moreen can probably use someone to talk to."

Ellen gave him a sideways glance.

"Almost done," he said, sliding back in his chair and looking over his notes. "Hey, anyway, how do you spell Moreen? M-O?"

"M-O-R-E-E-N," Ellen explained. "It's a type of wool."

"Huh," Sugar said. He scratched the back of his head. "Anyone have anything else to say?"

For a moment, the only sound in the kitchen was that of the fire truck pumping out the pond.

"Good, we're done," said Sugar, closing the pad.

Maddy was gone when Ellen went outside. Moreen was once again down at the dam, holding Randy's hand. For the remainder of the afternoon and well into the evening, Ellen, Scott, and Neal stood vigil on the banks of the pond, silently watching Moreen, while Sugar Westerback and a State Police trooper kept visitors away.

Channel 6 News from Portland had sent a crew to film the recovery of Randy's body—so had a TV station from Boston, along with local reporters and photographers—but the police would not allow the media or anybody else to get close. However, when a neighbor showed up with three pizzas from Rudy's Pizza, Sugar brought the food down to the dam, along with a tray of red, white, and blue Jell-O and a huge bowl of potato salad that other townspeople had dropped off. Chuck Young, who had worked for Scott at the hardware store, sent down a six-pack of Heineken that Scott started drinking immediately.

Eventually a carload of Moreen's friends came to take her away. Moreen declined at first, wanting to see Randy when he was pulled from the water, but after drinking half the thermos of coffee sombrero they'd sent down, Moreen went off with them.

Rooftop came back, too. This time Gator was with him. When Sugar Westerback caught them looking through Randy's Cherokee, he threatened to arrest them. Gator replied that Randy had borrowed some of their diving equipment, which they needed back. Sugar told Gator that unless his name was on the Cherokee's registration, he had no business there. When the state trooper came along, Rooftop convinced Gator to shut up, and they drove away again.

Randy's corpse was not freed from the dam until well after nine that night, when the water level had sunk to seven feet above the drain pipe. By then the crew was working with floodlights. Once the body was removed to the morgue, the fire truck returned to the station and the pond continued draining through its outlet pipe. At ten-thirty, when everyone had finally gone, Ellen and Scott went in the house.

Scott, who had polished off the six-pack, made himself scrambled eggs and toast and downed it with a stiff whiskey-and-ginger, while he watched the reports of Randy's death on the eleven o'clock news. Ellen stayed in the kitchen and poured herself a small bowl of cereal but was unable to eat. She was waiting for Moreen to come home, or at least to call. Eventually she heard Scott begin to snore in front of the TV. Then the screen door closed behind her. She knew it was Neal, but she just sat there, refusing to turn and look at him. After a few seconds, he went outside again. Ellen waited for Moreen until two, but the phone did not ring. Finally she went up to bed.

ten

Scott left the house at five the next morning, to work at his gun shop. Ellen worked in Moreen's room, getting the room ready for Mo's return, all the while listening to Neal outside, hammering in the barn. When she heard the hammering stop, she went into her bedroom and looked out the window, watching him carry Scott's red bucksaw down the farm road toward the pond. Seeing her opportunity, Ellen hurried down to the pantry and retrieved the knife from the freezer, then scrubbed it thoroughly with a soapy sponge while she kept her eye on the window.

She wiped the knife dry with a paper napkin, then tossed the napkin in the cookstove and dropped a match in. While the fire burned, she went out on the porch and looked for Neal again, spotted him moving up in the woods on the other side of the stream. She had no idea what he was up to. No matter. She stuffed the knife upside-down in her back pocket and walked out to the toolshed to get a shovel, then went around to her vegetable garden and dug down between two cucumber hills, as deep as she was able, about sixteen inches—deeper than her tractor's tines would reach. In a couple of weeks, she knew the cucumber vines would cover the spot. When her shovel hit hard clay, she lay flat on the ground and stabbed the knife into the bottom of the hole.

A sudden crunching of gravel alerted her. She turned to see Randy's black Cherokee skid to a stop beside the porch. Rising to her feet, she casually kicked some of the soil back in, as Moreen stepped out of the Jeep. Ellen waved her dirty hand.

"Hello," Mo said with a tired, almost apologetic smile.

"Oh, honey," Ellen said, heading over to her, refraining from asking where she'd spent the night or why she hadn't called, refraining also from giving Mo a hug because of the dirt on her hands. "How are you doing, hon?"

Mo groaned. "We pulled an all-nighter," she answered, giving Ellen a light kiss on the lips. Then she turned back to the Cherokee and opened the liftback. When Ellen saw the cardboard boxes inside, a small wave of relief came over her. Moreen was coming home.

She heard footsteps behind her and turned to see Neal walking up the farm road toward them. He was carrying his boots, his pants rolled up below his knees, his ankles wet. As he passed the garden, he glanced over toward the hole in the ground.

"What were you doing in the woods?" Ellen asked, hoping to distract him from wondering what she'd been up to.

"Cutting some brush," he answered.

When she turned back to the Jeep, Moreen was carrying a box up the porch steps.

"Mo, wait," Ellen said, hurrying up the steps and taking it from her arms. "Honey, you shouldn't be lifting that."

"It's not heavy," Moreen replied, opening the screen door for her.

"Come in and sit down, I'll get the rest," Ellen told her, as she went into the kitchen and set the box on the table. When she turned around, Moreen was back at the Jeep, pulling a bulging trash bag out of the back.

"Mo, be careful, you'll rip your stitches," Ellen called, but Mo hoisted the bag over her shoulder and carried it up the steps, turning her body so Ellen couldn't take the bag from her. Behind her, Neal followed with two more boxes.

"That's everything," he said.

Ellen held the screen door, and they both walked through.

"How are you?" Neal asked as they set the things on the table. His compassion seemed sincere.

"I'm fine," Mo answered brightly, as if nothing in the world were wrong.

Reacting to Ellen's gaze, she repeated, emphatically, "I'm fine." Then she gave Ellen another kiss. "I'll call you later, okay?"

"Wait," Ellen said. "You're not going to work—?"

"I quit," Moreen said, tossing the screen door open. "Either that, or they fired me, I'm not sure which."

Ellen took the door from her. "Mo, we need to make funeral arrangements."

"Oh, can you do it?" Moreen said, giving her a pleading look. "I'll pay you back when I get another job."

"It's not the money," Ellen told her. "We'll pay for it. Hon, if you want, I'll take you shopping so you can find something to wear."

"I've got clothes," Mo sang, laboring down the steps. "Thanks, love you."

"Mo, wait—"

Moreen turned at the bottom of the porch and gave Ellen a look, eyebrows raised.

"Honey, where are you going?"

Mo shrugged her shoulders, as if the answer were obvious. "I've got to find a place to live."

"Here," Ellen said. "You live here."

Moreen steadied herself on the railing post. "Mom, I'm meeting someone for breakfast, and I'm already late," she said, then went to the Cherokee. "I'll call you later."

Ellen stepped to the railing. "You're not even old enough. What are you going to do for money?"

Moreen opened the door without turning back. "I'll sell the Jeep, I don't know. Stop worrying."

"Hey," Neal said.

Moreen turned, gave him the same look she had given Ellen: pleasant smile; beautiful indifference. Ellen saw Neal searching for the right words. Ellen already knew the right words did not exist.

"Your mom wants to know where you're going, that's all," he said, stuffing his hands in his pants pockets. "She loves you, and she's concerned about you."

Mo's smile brightened. "I'm fine," she repeated, pulling herself into the Cherokee. "I'm fine, I'm fine, I'm fine." Then she shut the door and drove away.

Neal stood dumbly, watching the dust settle on the lawn. "I've just decided never to reproduce," he said.

Ellen didn't laugh. "Neal, what are you doing in the woods?"

He glanced back. "Making a road."

She studied him. "A road for what?"

He shrugged. "If you want to lead someone somewhere, make a road." Giving her a parting, cryptic glance, he walked off the porch and headed back down to the pond.

As Ellen watched him, a sudden and profound feeling of regret came over her—or maybe it was fear—that Moreen had told the truth about the ram; and that Neal had made a road for Randy, wide, straight, and paved, that led straight to his death.

. . . and that she had lost Moreen forever.

A perfect peace. Rooftop Paradise soared slowly over a miniature forest of red, green, and brown, while banners of kelp twenty feet long waved in the current. This quaint forest, which teemed with minuscule crabs and sea urchins, grew thickly over a wide, expansive ledge that dropped down over several large steps into darkness.

In his hand, Rooftop held a white plastic quadrat, a one-square-meter outline that he would systematically toss onto the ocean floor and then take a census of the lobsters within its borders—size, sex, and number. He was working off the Cape Neddick lighthouse as a research volunteer for the University of Maine. On his left arm he wore a white plastic cylinder, onto which was taped plastic mechanical drawing paper and a plastic pencil, for recording the information. Having depleted his fourth and final scuba tank—after two hours of diving—he floated up through forty feet of water feeling a fine tranquillity, hearing nothing but his own satisfied breath, while scores of shrimplike amphipods flitted around his mask, and a school of foot-long pollack darted out of his way. As the sun flattened against the ceiling of water, outlining the hull of his Boston Whaler, his quadrat broke the surface, and it was immediately snatched from his hand by Jake, a student from the University of Maine's School of Marine Sciences. Rooftop took hold of the dive ladder then handed up his writing cylinder and weight belt.

"I think somebody's here for you," Jake said, struggling to pull the weight belt from the water.

Rooftop took the regulator out of his mouth, lifted the mask off his face. The kid handed him his glasses, then pointed toward the shore. "Over there on the rocks."

Rooftop pulled himself around the stern and looked. The two men stood above the surf spray: one short, one tall. The shorter man waved his arm over his head, the greasy stump of his right hand glistening in the noonday sun.

An hour later Rooftop was escorted up a set of circular stairs into Ray LaFlamme's private dining room. Rooftop had changed out of his wetsuit in his van and now wore a plain white shirt and black double-knit trousers, along with a stiff pair of black wingtips. His entire wardrobe had been mail-ordered from a supply house for tall men's clothing in the Bronx.

In LaFlamme's rooftop dining room, glass was the prominent feature, covering three walls, floor to ceiling, facing the beach and ocean. The bar, which ran half the length of the fourth wall, was jet black, with a row of mother-of-pearl crucifixes inlaid along its top. The wall behind the bar was red, as was the carpeting. Tablecloths and linens were white, with silver crucifixes embroidered along their borders.

When the men entered the dining room, Ray LaFlamme was eating his lunch, seated alone at one of ten square tables, staring up at a TV beside the bar. *NYPD Blue* was on, dubbed into French. The old man matched the room's decor: red-framed glasses and a red-plaid flannel shirt, white linen slacks, and white suede shoes. His wavy white hair was combed diagonally over the top of his head, his white mustache trimmed square and close to his lip, and his white napkin, spotted with red, was tucked into the collar of his shirt.

"That's okay," he said when the men opened the door. "Come on, in fellas, sit down with me."

LaFlamme ate his lunch out of two cast-iron frying pans. The smaller of the two contained quartered red potatoes with mushrooms and mussels in a cheese sauce; in the larger was half a blackened duck in a red broth, surrounded by mussels. Ray LaFlamme loved mussels with just about anything, and he always ate his meals directly out of frying pans. He considered it his trademark.

Rooftop was led to the table and seated across from the old man, with his back to the bar and kitchen doors. Marcel Desjardin, the larger of LaFlamme's two bodyguards, sat on Rooftop's right. Herbie Handcream sat on his left and leaned his arms on the table. It was hard for Rooftop to understand how Ray LaFlamme could eat with Herbie's greasy stub staring him in the face.

"You hear that?" LaFlamme said. He grinned at the TV with his oversized, overwhite teeth. "I love that Sipowicz," he said. "He's so, you know, sarcastic."

"Sarcastic," Herbie Handcream said. All three men had mustaches.

"He says, 'Hey, it's great to see you,' when what he really means is, 'Hey, seeing you really upsets my stomach,' you know? Sarcastic. Turn it off for a minute."

With his good hand, Herbie grabbed the remote off the table and aimed it at the TV. One click and a boxing match came on.

"Tone it down," LaFlamme said. The TV went silent. He gave Marcel a nod and the big man stood and frisked Rooftop, up the legs and sides, along the arms. Dressed in a brown suit, the big man had a bulldog's face and disposition. He was fifty years old and looked like he could bench 400 pounds.

"New policy," LaFlamme explained to Rooftop after Marcel had sat down. LaFlamme himself was a small man, and a slight tremor shook his hand whenever he raised his silverware. For a few moments, while he tried to sip broth from his teaspoon, nobody watched him and nobody spoke. Rooftop thought of the kitchen behind him, and the Fryolator. He wondered if LaFlamme had someone hiding back there.

LaFlamme set his spoon down and wiped his mustache and chin with a corner of his napkin, then snapped the napkin out of his shirt. He had a silver crucifix pinned to his pocket. "Anyway, you want a nice glass of Merlot, Rupert?"

"No, thank you," Rooftop answered.

"Beer?"

"I quit drinking."

"Soup or something? You like mussels?"

Rooftop shook his head.

"I bet you can put away the mussels."

"He's a big one, ain't he, Ray?" Herbie Handcream said. "Bigger than you, Marcel."

Marcel looked Rooftop over. The man was built like a refrigerator, with a neck as thick as a normal man's thigh.

LaFlamme cleared his throat. "So you're not happy working for me?" he said to Rooftop. "Gonna get a real job, what's the story?"

"I decided to make a career change," Rooftop said.

LaFlamme lifted his place mat and slid out a greeting card. He smiled gently at it. "He sends a thank-you card," the old man said with a big white grin.

"Thank-you card," Herbie Handcream said.

"It was a nice card, nice sentiment," LaFlamme went on. "Of course, most employers require a two-week notice." He set the card down, then picked a mussel out of the broth. Taking the shell between his thumbs, he pulled it apart, spattering broth on his shirt. Then he snatched the meat with his fingers, dunked it in the cheese sauce, and popped it in his mouth. He lifted his napkin as he chewed, wiping his mustache, then his shirt. Outside the windows, the hot sun shone out of a sky that was bluer than possible and glared through the glass onto

Ray LaFlamme's back. The dining room however, was powerfully air-conditioned. When Rooftop took a breath, it shivered leaving his lungs.

"Hey, didn't you make a collection for me last week?" LaFlamme said, tapping his finger on the thank-you card. "You know who I mean—the gentleman with the pickled potatoes." He smiled again.

Rooftop cleared his throat. "We met Mr. Burdock on the gambling ferry."

LaFlamme nodded. "Your assistant, the redhead named Randy, he came by the other day and turned in the payment. Friday—the day before he drowned in that little farm pond. It's in the book."

Rooftop cleared his throat again, his lungs tightening up from the cold. Marcel and Herbie stared relentlessly at him.

"You want some water?" asked LaFlamme.

"I'm okay."

"Here's the funny thing about that. Not ha-ha funny, though. Mr. Burdock's wife—what's her name?"

"Jimmy," Herbie said.

"Jimmy—stupid name for a lady—anyway, she called here looking for her husband yesterday. Marcel, tell him what Humphrey Burdock's wife, Jimmy, told you."

Marcel looked straight at Rooftop and said, "They had a marital dispute. Humphrey left the house and never came home."

"That's what she said, and the night he disappeared was the night we found out he was going out on the ferry boat," LaFlamme said. "So I thought what, maybe he got off the ferry boat in Canada and didn't come back, you know, to avoid paying his debts. What do I know? I'm just a dumb Frenchman."

"I guess we're all dumb Frenchmen, Ray," Herbie said, and he laughed like a woodpecker.

Rooftop didn't like Herbie's giddiness. He pulled his inhaler from his pocket, uncapped it and sucked the medication deep into his lungs.

"But you know what's funny?" LaFlamme continued. "The woman told Marcel that her husband left without, what, shaving kit, clothes, toothbrush—"

"Shaving kit," Herbie echoed.

"Me, if I was leaving home, I'd take my toothbrush. Unless I was planning on returning home the next day."

"I'd take the shaving kit," Herbie said.

"Mr. LaFlamme?" Rooftop began.

The old man leaned on his elbows as if to listen, but he kept talking. "Herbie, clear the table. Marcel, help him. Cold, mussels get tough."

The two men got up and grabbed Ray LaFlamme's frying pans off the table as through they were having a race, wine glass, silverware, napkin, bread basket, wine bottle, clearing the table completely. All the while LaFlamme leaned on his elbows, eyes glinting intently at Rooftop.

Rooftop's heart pounded. "Mr. LaFlamme," he said quietly, "we put him off the boat."

"What, you put Mr. Burdock off the boat in Nova Scotia?"

"No, the ocean."

"What do you mean?"

"We put him over the rail."

The old man studied Rooftop hard.

"How far out?"

"Pretty far."

LaFlamme turned to Marcel as though he was going to start laughing. Then he turned back to Rooftop with a frown. "The man that owed me forty thousand dollars, are you saying he's dead?"

Rooftop nodded, the sun making a blinding halo around the old man's head.

LaFlamme nodded too. "Then you sent me the letter of resignation. And left your friend in charge."

"Randy Cross," Herbie said, "who's now kaput."

Rooftop's chest ballooned with a long, constricted wheeze.

The old man continued nodding as he stared at Rooftop, a slight gleam appearing in his eye. "This is the first time for you, isn't it?"

Rooftop's chest pumped like an overworked bellows.

"First time's always the toughest," Herbie counseled.

"Plus you lost your best friend," the old man said. "See, I think you've got a little case of depression, that's all. But they got drugs now, Rupert, wonderful things, wonderful things."

"Mr. LaFlamme, I won't do your work anymore," Rooftop told him.

The old man suddenly pushed back from the table, as the side of Rooftop's head erupted with a deafening ring.

"*Tabernac!*" the old man cursed.

Rooftop got to his feet, at least he meant to, but the pain radiating through his skull dropped him back in his chair. He saw Herbie Handcream standing beside him, the small frying pan in his hand dripping cheese sauce onto the floor.

"I'm talking to this man!" LaFlamme said to Herbie. "Since when are you so independent?"

"Sorry, Ray."

"Don't apologize to me. It's him you hit."

Herbie looked contritely in Rooftop's direction, his shoulders slumped. "Sorry, Roof. Guess I jumped the gun."

Rooftop raised his arm to his head, and he saw Marcel standing on his other side, holding the larger skillet.

"Rupert, how's your head?" LaFlamme asked, still frowning at Rooftop. He gave Rooftop his napkin.

"Okay, I guess," the giant said, but he felt as though he was going to throw up. He adjusted his glasses.

LaFlamme's wizened smile returned to his face. "People know that I'm not a very religious man," he began.

"Yeah, not much, Ray," Herbie Handcream said.

LaFlamme chuckled. "All right, maybe a little religious."

"Maybe a lot," Herbie said.

"Okay, Herbie," LaFlamme said. "The point I'm making here"— he leaned in closer to Rooftop, his gray eyes crinkling—"I'm not going to heaven when I die. I've done too many wrong things to expect that. But—and this is what I'm saying here—the wrong I've done, I've done for the girls and for Joanne, if you know what I mean, so there'll be a place in heaven for them when they die. I figure, who knows, if I ask God to forgive me when it's my time to go, maybe he'll take that into consideration."

Rooftop's head throbbed, but he shook it resolutely. "I'm sorry, Mr. LaFlamme. I've got to live right from now on."

Ignoring him, the old man reached into his shirt pocket and came out with a folded piece of paper. "Now as far as Humphrey Burdock is concerned, we're covered. Dead or alive, he defaulted on his loan, now I own a potato farm and a tractor and so forth. Big deal. It's not a great location, but we can make something of it, okay? That's not what's upsetting me."

He unfolded the paper. The crackling made Rooftop's head hurt more.

"It's your assistant, the man you put in charge." LaFlamme kept his attention on Rooftop. "When Randy Cross was here Friday he also turned over a monthly payment from another one of your clients, Scott Chambers, the gentleman with the hardware store. Did you know that?"

Rooftop turned and saw that the kitchen door was now opened a crack. Dazed as he was, he didn't hear what LaFlamme said next, until the old man slid the piece of paper across the table to him.

"Saturday's mail," LaFlamme said. "The very next day."

"The day your buddy drowned," Marcel said in Rooftop's ear.

"It's a receipt, signed by your assistant—see, 'Randy Cross'—saying that he received Scott Chambers's balloon payment on Friday. Right here: 'One hundred fifty-and-so-on thousand dollars, paid in full.' But Randy only turned over what?"

"Four thousand," Marcel said.

The old man examined Rooftop for another second, then pushed back from the table as though he was finally through with his dinner. "My men do not deceive me, Mr. Paradise," he said, just as a frying pan slammed against the back of Rooftop's head. Reaching back, the giant grabbed at Herbie's arm, but his greasy stub yanked through Rooftop's palm, and Marcel bounced the large skillet off the side of his head, knocking him to his knees, the floor spinning under his hands.

"I did not lie to you," Rooftop said in a very low voice, crumpling on the carpet.

"In this business, you live by the sword, you die by the sword," Ray LaFlamme said, his own voice distant and shadowy, as another frying pan popped against Rooftop's ear, crushing his face into the carpet. He tried to get up, but more blows fell in quick succession, one on the shoulder blade, one on the hip, another on the back of the head, like a hailstorm, until Rooftop imagined himself lying in a gutter, spinning down the drain.

"Croquet shot," he heard Herbie Handcream say, then the water swallowed him.

"Breathe now."

Rooftop felt the mist rush into his throat. He tasted the vapor and inhaled gratefully, as the old man's face rose to a blur in front of him: the red glasses, the bushy white mustache.

Rooftop took the inhaler into his own hand and pushed the top, sucked deeply, filling his lungs. The adrenaline kick-started his heart, and his head began to throb violently. He felt a knifelike pain in his shoulder when he tried to move. His ear burned. He tasted blood in his mouth. His eyes teared. His glasses were gone.

"On the grave of your mother, Rupert, do you have that money?"

Rooftop snorted, but it was unintentional. He tried to shake his head.

"Do you know who has it?"

"Oh." no. He thought his jawbone was broken.

A raspy Southern drawl rose up behind him. "Hey, how's the young widow? How's Mo-reeen?"

Rooftop angled his head up to see Gator standing in the sunlight behind Ray LaFlamme. Rooftop's head lolled, swimming in pain.

"Hey, I think the big bastard's got a broad," Herbie said with a laugh.

Now Marcel moved in closer. "Yeah, now that her husband went and drowned himself."

Ray LaFlamme sat on the edge of his chair and leaned forward, until all four faces seemed as if they were connected. "Pay attention, Rupert," the old man said.

Rooftop swallowed dryly.

"Number one, you will find the money that Scott Chambers paid to your assistant. It is my money, and you will turn it over to me. Are you listening?"

Rooftop tried to focus his eyes.

"Number two, I'm going to have Gator go with you, to make sure you do the right thing."

Even without his glasses, Rooftop could see the depraved grin on Gator's face. He wheezed a short breath, then shook his head.

"I won't do your work for you," he said, perfectly synchronized with another skillet blow to the ear.

The men behind Rooftop grabbed his arms and pulled him upright. One of them was Gator, with his punch knife, angled at Rooftop's neck.

"No blood, fellas," Ray LaFlamme said, standing up.

Rooftop's shoulders slumped. His head hung down. His big, blurry hands spread before him on the tablecloth like twin skillets. The word *bloodfellas* echoed round his head.

"Rupert, look up here." The old man hovered beside him until finally Rooftop raised his head. Then LaFlamme gave him a warm, sympathetic smile.

"Son, whether you like it or not, you've already chosen your path," he said. "God's got no place in heaven for killers. People like you and me, all we can do is make a better life for our loved ones here on earth." He slipped Rooftop's glasses back on his face and said, "What's her name again?"

"Mo-reeen," Gator breathed.

"Nice name," LaFlamme agreed, and he lined up Rooftop in his vision. "Now, I know you want to make life better for Moreen, and I know you want to keep her from harm. So I'm going to give you three days to get that money."

Gator looked over the old man's shoulder with a grin. "Just remember, we'll all be thinking of Mo-reeen."

eleven

It was an inexpensive funeral. No limousine, no organist, no church. The service was held in the smallest of Chernack's Funeral Home's three chapels. Ellen wore a navy blue suit over a white shirt and sat alone with Scott in the front row of chairs, waiting for Moreen to arrive. Randy's father sat across the aisle from them, looking more uncomfortable than grief-stricken in his short-sleeved shirt and jeans. Gradually the small room filled with many of the same people who had attended the wedding. The only one who seemed particularly distressed was Randy's friend Rooftop Paradise, who sat alone on the right side of the chapel with dark sunglasses on, occasionally blowing his sizable nose.

Moreen arrived five minutes after the service was scheduled to begin. She came in with her friend Keirsted Rawlings, who, last Ellen knew, had been living in the woods by Myers' Pond with some other kids, middle-class and homeless. Apparently, there was an old shack there, or the remains of one, and a junked van that someone had hauled in. Keirsted, whose family owned a hotel in Wells, had supposedly been kicked out of the house after declaring herself a lesbian. She moved in with her girlfriend's family for two weeks, until they broke up. Now she was sleeping wherever she ended up at night. Seeing Moreen with her, Ellen's heart fell.

The two girls came down the aisle together, Keirsted talking loudly, and they sat heavily in the front row, beside Scott.

"Sorry I'm late," Moreen said, as she turned and faced Ellen. Two blue teardrops had been tattooed on her left cheek. Badly drawn, they looked less like teardrops than tiny nooses.

"I told her not to do it," Keirsted said.

Moreen smiled helplessly at her mother as if to say, *Look at what I did now.* She seemed drunk.

Ellen did not respond. "Mo, did you find a place to stay?"

"I'll talk to you later," Moreen whispered, gesturing toward the minister, who had just come to the pulpit.

Ellen traded a glance with Scott, who shrugged helplessly.

Then the music stopped, and the minister asked the assemblage to stand and join him in silent prayer. As Ellen stood, she turned and saw Maddy standing alone four rows behind, her eyes riveted on the closed casket, refusing to acknowledge Ellen. As Ellen started to turn back to the pulpit, she spotted Neal standing in the shadows of the doorway. He caught her eye with a fleeting yet loaded glance, and it made Ellen turn away so fast she grabbed onto Scott to keep from falling.

Scott took hold of her hand, as she stood there tingling.

When the service was over, Ellen took her place in line, dazedly accepting hugs and handshakes and condolences from the assembled mourners. Moreen stood on the other side of Scott, maintaining some degree of decorum through her stupor. A full, hot July sun shone through the open front doors.

The guests moved steadily and Ellen was glad to see they were almost through, although she was disconcerted to see Maddy and Neal at the end of the line. Ellen watched as Maddy embraced Moreen and spoke quietly to her, then moved uncomfortably to Scott. When she got to Ellen, they embraced and Maddy whispered furtively, *"We need to talk."*

Ellen released her while she watched Neal kiss Moreen on the cheek and say something in her ear, to which Moreen blinked her eyes and nodded thoughtfully. Then Neal was shaking Scott's hand. "I'll see you back at the house," Ellen heard Neal say, as he moved on to her. Their eyes met briefly. Neal put his hands on her shoulders and leaned in to kiss her cheek. Ellen closed her eyes to convey her detachment. But then his lips met her mouth. She stiffened, wanting to push him away, but she knew she couldn't. Then the kiss was over and he was holding her and she was holding him. "He'll never hurt her again," he whispered hotly in her ear. Her heart pumped harder as his sweater pulled through her fingers, then someone else was taking his place.

★　　★　　★

The reception was held at the Eagles Club, where Randy's father was a member. The club sprang for a round of drinks and four pepperoni pizzas. Except for Randy's father, nobody stayed once the pizza was gone. Maddy didn't attend the reception at all, nor did Neal. For that matter, Moreen and her friends spent the hour outside in the parking lot.

When most of the funeral guests had left and Ellen was collecting the paper plates and plastic forks, a voice behind her said quietly, "Mrs. Chambers, we need to talk to you." She turned and gasped. It was as though she were looking up at a building with a gargoyle staring down. Below the frames of his sunglasses, Rooftop's cheekbone glowed with an egg-shaped, purple bruise. His forehead appeared swollen and similarly discolored. She looked beyond him and spotted Gator standing in the doorway to the bathrooms, watching her through dark sunglasses.

Abruptly Ellen moved away from them both, wanting to run out of the building.

"Hey, Mr. Bear!"

Moreen's voice startled Ellen. She turned to see her daughter come through the door and wrap her arm around Rooftop's waist. Even as tall as Moreen was, she did not reach his armpit. But she stretched up on her tiptoes to kiss him, saying, "You gonna miss me, Bear?"

Rooftop put his long arm around her shoulder and closed his eyes as he held her there. Moreen flung her other arm around his waist and laid her cheek on his chest. They stood there like that for several seconds. "I can hear you breathe," Moreen said, smiling curiously at the sound. Like a baby, Ellen thought, studying her daughter's tattooed, jeweled face. She almost cried.

Rooftop leaned forward and kissed the top of Moreen's head. She kissed his chest, then pushed away. "Watch out for the sharks," she said, then stepped over to the bar and gave her father a kiss.

"Mo?" Ellen said, coming over to stand beside them while they hugged. "Where can we reach you?"

"I don't know, I'll call you," Mo answered, spinning away and heading back out to the parking lot. "Thanks for the funeral," she called back over her shoulder. "Love you."

"Love you," Scott told her.

Ellen turned. Gator was standing in the same place, outside the women's room, beckoning to her with his index finger. Ellen felt her insides seize. She also felt a sudden urge to pee. Sidling close to Scott, she ran her hand up the back of his thigh and gave his buttock a subtle squeeze. "Let's go home and open a bottle," she said in a low voice.

He gave her a look, almost as subtle. "Now?"

"Right now," she answered, taking his arm and leading him out the door with no backward glance.

When they pulled into the driveway, Sugar Westerback was waiting.

"I just now got here myself," he said, stepping out of the patrol car. He was wearing his softball uniform again and carrying a Polaroid camera by its strap. "You prob'ly heard, our team made it to the tournament finals," he said. As he spoke, he started walking toward the farm road, as if expecting them to follow. "Game starts in a half-hour. I wanted to get a couple of shots of that drainpipe while it's dry."

"Anything wrong?" Scott said, giving Ellen a look of frustration as he reluctantly started walking beside Sugar.

"Aw, the friggin Water District's all over my butt," Sugar told him. "They want to lower the floodgates today. How the hell was I supposed to know we'd make the World Series?" He looked around, then said to Ellen, "Your nephew around? Truck's here, I noticed."

"Must be here somewhere," Ellen answered, and she followed along behind both men, afraid of how it would look if she didn't. She focused on relaxing, trying unsuccessfully to convince herself that nothing was amiss. In fact, she could feel her heart beating hard in her chest.

"I noticed his license plate the other day," Sugar said, as they rounded the pump house at the top of the hill. "From Mass, is he?" He was looking back at Ellen again. "Is that where he lives now?"

"He lives here," Scott said, "for the time being. He's rebuilding our barn."

"Huh," Sugar said again, returning his eyes to Ellen.

"He likes to travel," she said. If this was when she'd have to start lying, she wondered, how far could she take it? Inside her funeral dress, a drop of sweat slithered down her side.

Momentarily they reached the dam, and Sugar suddenly stopped walking. Staring down at the deep, stony gorge, his shoulders sank. "Beautiful," he said sarcastically.

Scott stepped up beside him. "What's up?"

Below them, on the downstream side of the dam, Neal was crouched with a bucket of mortar, striking the area around the outlet pipe with the tip of his trowel.

"Looks good," Scott called.

Neal glanced up, the sun in his eyes. "Let's hope so," he said. "I'm pretty green at this."

"Which way down?" Sugar asked.

Scott walked around the abutment and started climbing down the stony bank, a half-natural and half-constructed staircase of granite blocks. Sugar followed behind, while Ellen remained on the abutment. She looked over the dam to the floor of the pond twenty feet below, where a graceful, serpentine puddle ran along its center.

"This where it was leaking?" she heard Sugar say. She looked over the downstream side again, where Sugar crouched in front of the pipe, running his thumb over the fresh cement.

"I chipped the old cement away and repacked it," Neal told him. "With any luck, it'll hold for another fifty years."

"What do you think?" Scott said to Sugar.

"You know what I think?" Sugar answered. "Kind of pisses me off, that's what I think." He lifted the camera to his face and snapped a picture of the pipe, then turned and made his way to the bank.

Scott looked at Neal and shrugged. Then, together, they climbed up to the bank behind Sugar. "Something wrong?" Scott called.

Sugar didn't answer. Crossing the abutment, then bracing himself on the concrete face of the dam, he took hold of the algae-slick rungs and lowered himself down to the pond bed, then walked directly into about four inches of water, not stopping to take off his softball cleats.

"Only thing wrong is," Sugar said finally, "I already got my ass chewed out once by the old man for not calling him the other day. Now I got to deal with this." He went directly to the pipe, which was similarly mended, and recapped. "You don't remember me sayin don't touch anything here?"

"I thought you meant just for that day," Neal answered, coming closer.

Sugar bent his knees and took a photo of the pipe straight-on, then looked back at Scott. "Scotty, I told you."

Scott scratched his head. "Yes, you did, but you also told us they needed to release water up at the rez. I guess I figured that meant it was okay to repair the dam."

"Yeah, no shit," Sugar said. He looked back at Neal. "What do you do, just ignore the police down in Massachusetts?"

"Come on, Sugar," Scott said, "it was an honest mistake."

Sugar made a throaty noise, a sort of growl, then snapped another picture of the dam. "Yeah, honest mistake, and I'm the one who catches hell for it."

"If you want, I can chip that cement back out so you can get a couple of pictures," Neal told him.

"Ah." Sugar scraped at the cement with his thumbnail. "When did you do this side?"

Neal shrugged. "Last night. I wanted to give it a couple of days to cure."

"Beautiful."

"It's no trouble, I'll chip it out right now," Neal offered again.

Frightened as she was, Ellen marveled at Neal's demeanor. Despite all her own suspicions, he appeared utterly innocent.

Sugar squatted, ran his finger around the inside of the pipe. "Rusty and all," he said, "but not eaten away. See, that's what I mean. Just how the frig was this thing leaking?"

Neal looked at Scott, then Sugar. "It was the cement that was corroded, not the pipe," Neal explained.

"Frost heaves, most likely," Scott suggested. "You know the way old mortar crumbles."

"Huh," Sugar said, and he took another picture. "So what the hell are those things?"

About seven feet high on the dam, three shiny U-bolts protruded from three fresh circles of concrete, spaced evenly across the dam.

"I put them in yesterday," Neal told him, "so next time someone has to release water, they can harness themselves."

Sugar said nothing, but took a picture of the U-bolts, then stood up, fished a pack of Marlboros out of his pants pocket and tapped one out. "You know, I got the authority to stop the Water District from lettin down those floodgates," he said, directing the comment at Scott.

Neal glanced up at Ellen, and she saw a quick but discernible glint of concern in his eyes. But Sugar kept his eyes on Scott, as he flicked his lighter and lit the cigarette, then blew the smoke out. Waiting for one of them to speak, Ellen realized she'd been holding her breath. She let it out.

Sugar looked at his watch. Then he started climbing up the rungs. Scott climbed up behind him.

"See, I wouldna thought anything about anything," Sugar said, "except I got a call from What's-his-name, the medical examiner. Ramsey. He said Randy had a stab wound in his leg, right through his wetsuit."

Pulling himself onto the top of the abutment, Sugar looked straight at Ellen; she refused to meet his eyes.

"The wound wasn't all that deep," Sugar continued, turning back to Scott and Neal, as they mounted the abutment. "But it came from a serrated blade, like a hunting or fishing knife. Divers use them. But Randy didn't have no knife on him when we pulled him up out of there. All he had was that little leather holder there—"

"Sheath," Neal said.

"Yeah, strapped to his leg," Sugar said. "But no knife."

He looked at Scott and said, "You were down there with Randy. You see a knife?"

Scott shook his head. "I never saw a knife." He looked at Neal, who said, "Nope."

Then Sugar turned to Ellen, who shrugged the way she might have if he'd been speaking in another language. But a shivering had started in her stomach, and she was unable to stop it. She felt as if she was going to vomit.

"How about when you both went down?"

"Maybe he cut himself with the crowbar," Neal said, giving Sugar a perplexed frown.

"Maybe," Sugar said. They all walked down the bank and onto the gravel farm road. For a few seconds, no one spoke.

"What time's your game?" Scott said.

"You told me you tried to pull him out by the arm," Sugar answered, to no one in particular. "You dislocated both his shoulders, by the way. That's the other thing they found, pulled right out of the sockets."

Scott raised his hands. "Christ, Sugar, if we didn't, you'd be asking why we didn't pull harder."

"Hey, I'm not trying to give anybody a hard time," Sugar said. "But, Jeez, one day Ellie wants to arrest the kid for assaulting your daughter, next day you go and hire him to fix your dam, day after that he's dead. Don't forget, I got the old man to answer to when he gets back."

"Oh, fuck this," Scott said. "I hired Randy because we needed a diver, because he was our son-in-law."

Sugar looked back at Ellen again.

"And I still think Randy kicked Moreen and put her in the hospital," Ellen said. "Does that make me a murder suspect?"

"Doesn't make anybody a suspect," Sugar said. "Far as I'm concerned, this was an accidental drowning. I guess the question I forgot to ask the other day is how long it was between the time Randy went down with the crowbar and the time that you went down after him?"

He looked over at Scott as they walked, then back at Neal.

Scott shrugged. "I don't know exactly. Ten, fifteen minutes?"

"Give or take," Neal said.

"So you didn't go down there with Randy when he was trying to get the cap off," Sugar said. "I mean, Randy was already stuck when you went down."

"Yeah, all right?" Scott replied, bristling.

Sugar nodded. He looked at his watch and started walking faster. " 'Course, now we got that stab wound—on the dorsal part of his thigh, which the medical examiner says is where you get defense wounds, like if you're fighting somebody. I'm just sayin, you know? Red flags I gotta follow up on. You got this, you got that, you got your daughter's hysterectomy."

Now Scott stopped walking, and he looked back at Ellen with a hard scowl. "What hysterectomy?"

"I'll tell you later," she said, walking past him.

Sugar turned and eyed Scott carefully while he took a final drag on his cigarette. "That's probably best left to the two of you," he said. "Anyway, I gotta boogie. If I'm not on that pitcher's mound in ten minutes, we forfeit the tournament." He flipped his cigarette on the gravel road as he pulled abreast of Neal.

"So, Greenfield, Mass, huh?" Sugar asked Neal.

"Yeah, my mother moved there when I was twelve," Neal replied, "after my father passed away."

"Huh. So what the frig were you doing looking in somebody's window in Virginia Beach?"

Ellen looked at Sugar, then at Neal, wondering what he was talking about.

"I was going to steal a car," Neal answered with a bit of a smile, "but I wasn't too smart about it."

"Yeah, no shit," said Sugar. "Fifteen years old, your family lives in Greenfield, Mass, and you're down in Virginia Beach by yourself?"

"I ran away from home," Neal said. "I was headed for Disney World. Tell you what. You go down to Virginia Beach in the middle of the winter and hold out your thumb for eight hours, you'd commandeer a friggin car at gunpoint—'Step out of the vehicle, Ma'am. Police business.' "

Scott laughed. Even Sugar chuckled a little. "I might just," he said. "I might just."

Ellen thought it was probably the first time in Neal's life he'd used the word friggin.

Sugar got in his cruiser, looked at his watch again, and started the engine. "I don't know what I'm gonna do about the Water District," he said to Scott. "Have to think about it. Maybe I'll have 'em release the water, maybe I'll wait for Dad to get back tomorrow and see what he thinks."

"Do whatever you need to," Scott said. "It's Ellie that's gonna have to haul water for her sheep, not you or me."

"I hear you," Sugar replied, and he sped out of the dooryard with his blue lights flashing.

Scott did not speak to Ellen right away. He opened the liquor cabinet and mixed himself a strong whiskey and ginger ale. By the time Ellen had changed out of her funeral dress and was headed out to do chores, Scott was mixing another one. He caught up to her in the lamb's pasture, where she was filling the trough with grain.

"Moreen asked me not to tell you about the hysterectomy," she said without turning to look at him. "So I didn't."

"Funny that Neal knew about it."

"Neal drove her to the hospital. He was there when they told me." Ellen went into the shed and grabbed two water buckets, which she carried to the faucet on the side of the house. Scott followed, and watched her as she filled the pails. Standing there, not speaking, they could hear hammering: Neal inside the barn, down underneath the new addition, building a set of stairs.

"Husband and wife really shouldn't keep secrets from each other," Scott said.

Ellen turned, saw that he had two drinks in his hands. She gave a short, bitter laugh and carried the full buckets back to the pasture, while Scott walked alongside her. "Ellie, what the hell is going on with you?"

She sighed. "I told you, Moreen didn't want you to know."

"I'm talking about you. You've been hating me ever since Neal showed up here."

"I don't want to talk now," Ellen said, opening the fence and walking through.

"All because of something that happened twelve years ago."

"It has nothing to do with that," she said.

"Twelve goddamn years ago. And I've about killed myself ever since, tryin to make it up to you."

She set one pail on the ground, spilling water over the rim, then splashed the other pail into the water trough. "I forgave you, Scott."

"Then what is it? I'm sorry if the economy went to hell, I'm sorry I lost my business, I'm sorry I can't build you a fucking barn, I'm sorry I didn't finish high school, I'm sorry I'm not twenty-four years old again."

Ellen glared at him as she lifted the other pail. "Neal talks to me," she said.

"I talk to you."

"He *listens* to me."

Scott turned away from her and took a drink, while she poured the other pail into the trough. He looked toward the barn, where Neal was still hammering, then he turned back again and realigned her in his vision. "You never forgave me," he said. "Maybe you told yourself you did, but you never came close. You disappeared is what you did, with all your fuckin sheep and your teaching and weaving. You disappeared from me, and you disappeared from Moreen."

"Get away from me," she said, pushing past him.

"Your precious sheep," he persisted. "Well, it was one of your sheep that hurt Moreen. It wasn't Randy, and you know it."

She wheeled around and stared at him long enough that his face began to disassemble. The dead brown eyes, the pink mounds of his cheeks and receding hair . . . could have belonged to anyone.

Then his chest seemed to collapse in a sigh, and he turned away from her, shaking his head.

"Don't listen to me," he said. "My nerves are shot." He heaved another sigh and turned back to her, holding out a drink. "Here, you want this?"

"I'm not drinking with you anymore," she said, and walked back to the house.

As much as she wanted to go into the barn and tell Neal to pack his things and leave, she knew she needed to cool off. The truth was— and she was dimly conscious of this—she was afraid he'd come out and say he'd been the one who caused Randy's death. She did not want to have a conversation that might illuminate her own complicity.

When she stepped into the kitchen, she saw her answering message blinking. It was Maddy, who had called three times. The first message said, "Call me, please." The second said, "I know you're there. I have to talk to you." The third: "You need to pick up." Then, after a moment's silence, "Goddamn you."

Ellen locked the back door and went upstairs to call Maddy from her bedroom.

"We have to talk," Maddy told her.

"We can talk," Ellen replied, trying to sound innocent.

"Is he there?"

"Is who here?"

"You know what I'm talking about. Does he know?"

"Maddy, what are you talking about?"

"You know goddamned well. I lied to the police for you."

Ellen sat on the bed, telephone to her ear, and she felt a tremor start in her chest.

"Ellie, I'm scared shitless over here. Now you tell me. Does Neal know that Randy wrote on my hand?"

"No."

"What did Scott say?"

"About?"

"About that."

Ellen hesitated. "Nothing."

"Scott doesn't know anything about this, does he?"

Ellen didn't know what to say, so she said nothing, just stood there at the window shaking, watching Neal hammering at her symmetrical new barn.

"You come over here," Maddy said. "So help me God, you come over here. And don't tell him where you're going. *Don't you tell him.*"

Maddy lived in York Harbor, in a cottage that was surrounded on three sides by Victorian mansions. It was dark when Ellen pulled up to the curb in her pickup truck, yet none of Maddy's window lights were lit . . . which was strange, because her new BMW was parked at the foot of her short, hedge-lined driveway. Ellen walked up to the door and knocked softly. She waited, smelling the beach roses that wafted over the salty air. She knocked again, louder, then turned and looked at the inn across the street, where someone was watching her from a second-floor window. She was about to knock one more time when she remembered that Maddy's house key was on her key ring. She pulled the keys out of her jeans pocket and held them up to the moonlit sky until she was able to identify Maddy's.

"Come down to the beach," said the voice beside her.

Ellen jumped. *"Jesus—"*

Maddy stepped around the corner of the cottage. "Come on," she said, heading for the road. At the end of her driveway, she turned left. Ellen followed, neither of them speaking as they walked past the houses to the end of the road and took the flagstone path beside the tennis courts. When they got to Harbor Beach, where waves broke noisily over small, smooth rocks, Maddy stopped.

"I told the police that the word Randy wrote on my hand yesterday was 'Moreen.' "

"Yeah, so?"

"We both know what he wrote, so don't bullshit me," Maddy said. "It was the last thing he said to anybody in this lifetime: *'Murder.'* "

"And you believe him."

"I lied to the police," Maddy hissed. "That makes me an accessory—and in this state, accessory is the same as murder."

They studied one another in the moonlight. Then Maddy broke away from Ellen again and headed to the left, toward the cliff walk, a three-hundred-year-old trail that cut between the old houses and the rocky bluff overlooking the ocean. Ellen caught up to her when the path narrowed and turned uphill.

"Maddy, your imagination's working overtime," Ellen told her. "Randy's death was nothing more than a terrible accident."

"Not according to Randy."

"First of all, you didn't lie to the police. He *did* spell 'Moreen' in your hand. And even if he didn't, you know what a whiner he was. So he screws up, what's he gonna do, take the responsibility himself? No, he's gonna blame somebody. *'They murdered me.'* "

"Ellen, he *died,*" said Maddy. "Listen to yourself."

"Look, Randy was an abusive prick and I'll be honest, I'm glad Moreen is free of him. But he was not murdered. The fact is, he should never have been working on that dam by himself."

As the path led through a thicket of beach roses, Maddy ducked and disappeared amid the bushes. Ellen followed, holding her cap with one hand and protecting her eyes with the other. They emerged on the moonlit face of the bluff, thirty feet off the rocks below, and looked out over the water. Across the cove from them, window lights of a condominium wavered like snakes. Below them, the waves exploded, sending up a bright, steady mist.

Maddy said quietly, "El, you've got to listen to me. You're into something way over your head."

"I don't know what you're talking about," Ellen shot back dismissively.

"I'm talking about your sociopathic nephew."

"Sociopathic? You don't even know him. You've never spoken to him. And by the way, he's Scott's nephew."

The women stared at each other again, until Maddy turned away. "Let's go back down," she said, looking nervously behind her.

Ellen took the lead, bending low into the dark tunnel of roses. Maddy stayed close behind, holding onto the back of Ellen's T-shirt. When they were in the moonlight again, they carefully descended the sharp-edged rocks of the path to the weathered stones of the beach.

"In case you've forgotten," Maddy said, "this is the same young man whose father killed himself the day you caught Scott in bed with his mother."

"That was a lifetime ago," Ellen said. "Besides, Neal doesn't even know about that."

"Oh no? Exactly what do you think brought him back after all these years?"

"Maddy, you're being paranoid."

"And you may be involved in your son-in-law's murder."

Exasperated, Ellen stopped walking. "I keep telling you, no one was murdered."

"Then it's just a coincidence that Neal came to live with you—?"

"What coincidence?" Ellen said. "He knows how to build a barn."

"And I suppose he knows all about sheep."

"He happened to work on a sheep farm when he was younger. What are you saying? He's been planning this elaborate scheme since he was fourteen?"

"Most likely since he was twelve," Maddy said darkly.

Even as Ellen smirked and started walking down to the water, she couldn't help but hear the echo of that number: twelve. Maddy came alongside her and they followed the shoreline for fifty feet or so, staying just back from the waves that chased after their feet.

"I need to ask you something," Ellen said. "You talked to Randy, didn't you?"

"Once. He ended up coming to see me for counseling—"

Ellen took hold of Maddy's arm, stopping her. "Did he tell you?"

"Tell me what?"

"If he kicked Moreen."

"Of course he didn't tell me. He denied it."

"Well, what do you think? Did he do it, or didn't he?"

Maddy shook her head. "Ellie, I just don't know."

They stared at one another, straight-faced, until Maddy sighed and looked around nervously. "I'm going to tell you something because you're my best friend and because, technically, it's not betraying confidentiality."

Ellen waited.

"Moreen's started counseling with me. It's something I wouldn't ordinarily do, get involved with a family member of a friend, but Mo asked for my help. It was the day Randy drowned. She sounded desperate, and she didn't have any money. I didn't feel I could refuse. That's all I'm going to tell you. But you probably knew she was seeing me."

"How would I know that?" Ellen heard her own voice rise in frustration. "Moreen doesn't talk to me, in case you haven't noticed. Oh, she smiles, she kisses me, she says she loves me. But always from ten miles away."

"Kind of the way you were with your mother?" As soon as the words came out, Maddy touched Ellen's wrist. "I didn't say that." She turned, gave Ellen's hand a tug, and they began walking again, along the beach.

"Look," Maddy said, "Mo's a very bright kid."

"Also very self-destructive," Ellen replied.

"When she was six, she walked into your barn and found her uncle hanging from a beam," Maddy said. "A trauma like that is bound to have repercussions. Did you ever talk to her about it?"

"I tried a couple of times, but she didn't seem to ever want to discuss it," Ellen answered, wondering just how true that was. "I didn't think I should push her,"

Maddy hesitated. "Maybe it's something she'll talk to me about."

Ellen felt a hollow pang in her chest, something akin to jealousy. She turned to face the ocean.

Maddy took Ellen's long braid in her hand and stroked it softly. "El, you know she's not coming home," she said. "Even if she wanted to, I'd discourage her."

Ellen bristled and gave her a look. "She's my daughter."

"Ellie, she hates that house."

"She hates *me*. And you're using this!"

Maddy squared herself to Ellen.

Ellen would not meet her eyes.

Maddy took gentle hold of her arms, and it took every ounce of

Ellen's restraint to keep from pulling away. "You know, El, it's possible that the person Moreen hates is herself, not you. You just happen to be the closest thing she's got."

"Hates herself why? Why won't she tell me?"

"Maybe she feels she's protecting you from something."

"Protecting me?" Ellen sneered. "From what?"

"I don't know. Maybe we'll find that out."

Ellen looked out at the ocean again, and let out a voluminous sigh.

"El?"

Ellen turned her head.

"I don't know what happened at the pond the other day," Maddy told her. "And I don't know what's going on between you and Neal—"

"Nothing is going on—"

Maddy squeezed her arms, stopping her. "And I'm not sure I even want to know," she said. "Just promise me you'll be careful."

Ellen met her eyes with brittle defiance.

"I'm serious. We're not sneaking a joint in your bedroom now, we're not climbing out your window to party with the college boys. You're really starting to scare me."

Ellen stiffened, looked off down the beach. "Are we done now?"

Beside them a wave collapsed with a startling roar.

When Ellen got home, Neal was around the right side of the barn, standing in the glare of his truck's headlights, nailing boards to the new addition. The left-hand shed was already sided. Ellen pulled her pickup truck close to the porch and went in the house quickly, avoiding him.

She found Scott asleep on the living room floor, his electric guitar slung across his chest, the old amplifier humming loudly. She flicked the amp off and lifted his guitar off him.

"Where'd you go?" he asked, jerking awake, sitting upright, and looking suspiciously around the living room.

"For a ride," she answered.

He rolled to his knees, picked himself slowly to his feet and started up the stairs. "You coming up?"

"Later," she said.

The knock on Wes Westerback's front door was so timid that Wes didn't hear it over the television until his wife, Polly, came in and tapped the footrest of his recliner. They had driven home from the lake after spending most of the day fishing, and he was dog-tired. Sugar was also asleep, sprawled on the couch in his softball uniform, an empty Budweiser can and bag of potato chips on the carpet in front of him. He hadn't even taken off his cleats.

"Someone's at the door," Polly said. She was a big, friendly woman who enjoyed coffee and cigarettes and usually had one or both in her hand.

Wes levered the recliner upright and fixed the glasses on his face. "Must have closed my eyes," he said.

"Me, too," Sugar said.

"Don't know how anyone could sleep with this TV so loud," Polly said, cigarette smoke exhausting from her mouth. An old John Wayne Western was on, and the Indians were whooping. She turned the volume down a little, then made her way to the front door.

"I can get it," Wes said, pushing himself up. Polly had hip trouble, and he didn't like to see her do any more than she had to. But she was there already, opening the door.

Seeing the small bleach-haired girl with the rings through her eyebrow and nose, and the nervous way she kept checking behind her, Polly turned to Wes.

"I think she wants you," she said.

twelve

Ellen waited until she heard Scott snoring, then she went up and took off her clothes in the dark. She didn't bother closing her eyes. She knew there would be no sleeping for her. The way the moon shone through the window screen onto her white bedspread, like a spotlight, the way the terrible silence outside pressed in around the room, while Scott snored obliviously . . .

She had participated in Randy's death—she could no longer deny this. Even if she hadn't been directly involved, she had encouraged it, and she'd stood by while Neal had set the plan in motion.

No, there would be no sleeping tonight. Not with her secrets.

How long would it be before Sugar Westerback would return with his father, or with other investigators? And how long could Maddy withstand the gnawing guilt of her own involvement?

Scott let out a snort and stopped snoring, and the night became perfectly quiet. And terrifying. To Ellen, the silence was a dry pond bed, a dam laid bare, it was evidence exposed, like old mortar deliberately chiseled away, granite stones gouged, chunks of cement clustered high on a bank downstream where chunks of cement couldn't have ended up unless they'd been carved out of the dam when the stream was still flowing.

A single sheep's bell tinkled as Ellen's thoughts raced on (fiber evidence, flesh under fingernails, DNA in wrong places). Then she heard the jangling of another bell, and another. With a start, she thought of the coyote and sat up in bed. But it was a curious rustling of trees that came through the screen, a strange concentration of wind that grew stronger and stronger until the bells of her sheep became a jubilation and even their drumming hoof beats were overpowered by this incredible rushing of sound.

Ellen got out of bed and went to the window, pulled back the shade. Looking down, she suddenly understood what was causing this tumult: Water. Tons of it, cold and clean, cascading down through the woods, uprooting brush and unseating boulders, demolishing banks, capturing frogs and lizards and chipmunks in its furious mouth. The floodgates had been opened at the reservoir.

In the moonlight she could see the wide contrail of mist charging down through the trees, then all at once the river exploded off the granite chute into the deep gorge of her pond, the roar thundering back off the woods. She saw a wall of mist rising straight in the air above the dam. She saw Neal silhouetted on the crest of the hill, kneeling out of his blanket to witness the flood, his strong shoulders surrounded by the moonlit, rising mist. On and on the water pounded, and Ellen's heart pounded the same way. She could smell the water, she could feel it misting through the screen and brushing over her face and breasts, cooling her, freeing her.

Yes, and freeing Moreen.

She realized this with dazzling clarity: Randy had enslaved Moreen with pregnancy, imprisoned her with marriage. He had beaten her and terrorized her, and he would have continued. But now Moreen was free. That was all that mattered.

Whatever had been done to ensure that, in this long, exuberant moment, Ellen suddenly knew without question that it was precisely the right thing.

She raised her face and breathed deeply. The river roared through the woods, pulsed riotously up the banks, destroying evidence, the moon transforming the rising mist into a fiery opalescence. Ellen stepped to her closet, opened the door, and took her flannel nightshirt off the hook. She slipped it over her head and went quietly downstairs.

She padded through the house in darkness, the squeaking of the floorboards underfoot covered by the surging flood outside. She pushed open the screen door and walked onto the porch. The noise was louder out here, astoundingly so. Mist mounded over the valley. She could feel its wetness in her eyes, on her cheeks and arms, it made her feel gliding like a ghost, and then she was opening the pasture gate and walking through, the grass cool and moist under her feet. She could see Neal plainly at the crest of the hill, up on his knees, staring down at the flood as if transfixed.

She came up behind him and set her hand gently on the muscular space between his neck and shoulder. He took a quick breath as if she'd startled him, then reached his left arm around her legs and drew her against him, laid his cheek on her hip. He took a deep breath, as the river surged into the gorge, pounding against the dam, pounding and pounding.

She looked down at him. His nakedness had not occurred to her until now, that his blanket had fallen down to his thighs. He looked up at her and said, "I killed him, Ellen." His voice, too loud, resonated through her hip.

"Shhh," she said, not necessarily to quiet but to soothe him. He held her with both hands, his face against her stomach, the cool locks of his hair sliding between her fingers, his warm hands rising slowly up the backs of her legs. "It's okay," she said, as his hands slid up the backs of her thighs, onto her buttocks.

She reached to stop him, saying, "Neal." But his hands continued up the small of her back, lifting her nightshirt, the cool air sweeping around her thighs, the water pounding all around them. He raised his face.

"Neal—"

"I killed him," he said again. Then, taking her by the waist, he gently pulled her down to her knees, while her own hands melted down his neck to his chest, meaning to stop this, absolutely to stop, but now with the heat rising off him and the moon in his eyes, his hands, so warm and able, slipped around the front of her and cupped her full breasts, and she lost her breath as she lost her will, and he moved his lips onto hers.

They kissed, and she turned her head away, gasping as quietly as she could, "We can't do this."

"Oh, Ellen, how long," he breathed in her ear, "how long has it been since anyone wanted you this bad?"

And they kissed again, hidden in the mist and roar of the flood, his fingers exploring first her ribs, then her breasts and nipples until she raised her face, raised her arms, and her night shirt pulled into the air and now she was fully naked with him and falling safely into his arms, his hand moving over her hip, inside her thigh—

"Wait," she breathed, pushing him off forcefully enough so that when he fell back he pulled her forward into his lap. "Neal—" She caught her breath, this dark part of him standing thick and urgent only inches from her face, utterly distracted by its size, its hardness, its smoothness. The head was not a mushroom-topped thing like Scott's, but muscular, tapered, rounded. She could almost feel its warmth in her hand, though she was not yet touching it. Nor would she.

She sat up again, and he sat up with her, his fingers lightly tracing her temple to her chin, as if studying her face.

"I've got to go back," she said, holding his hand away from her. "But I need to ask you something."

"Ask me what?" He turned her face and leaned in close, kissing her jaw.

"How you did it," she breathed. "Without Scott knowing."

He kissed her mouth softly, his lips full and warm. Their tongues touched, just barely.

"If I told you that," he said, "you'd no longer be protected."

"I'm not protected now," she told him. "I've already lied to the police."

"Lied how?"

The way his eyes searched hers, or maybe the way his head was angled—

"I feel like I've been lying to everybody," she said, keeping her eyes on his but seeing Randy's finger moving in Maddy's palm. "I feel like I killed him myself."

"Ellen, should I be worried that you'll confess everything in a fit of guilt?"

He kept watching her, and she moved her hand across his thigh, the soft cover of his body hair sliding through her fingers, his heat rising around her wrist.

"Should I be worried that *you* will?" she replied.

Keeping his eyes, her hand descended to the center of his heat, and she closed her fingers firmly around him. She hadn't planned to, so she was startled at the first touch. Closing her eyes, she leaned in closer and kissed his chest, ran her tongue over each of his tender nipples.

She heard his small gasp as she explored him, feeling the heat of his stomach against her ear, breathing him in, his incredible warmth and musk. He made another sound. She squeezed his shaft, milking a bead of oil out of him. She ran her thumb up through the liquid, then ran her thumb back down, lubricating his glans. She heard him sigh deep in his chest. She felt her own nether lips opening, beckoning wetly, hungrily.

She took his solid buttock in her left hand and lowered her mouth to his abdomen, kissing him, tasting him, unbelievably moving her mouth closer until she felt the softness of her lips touch the softness of his head. With her hand she squeezed him, and another drop emerged. She moved her tongue to taste it, and now she was powerless to do anything but suck him softly into her lips.

Her mind was gone. The sound of his low moan spurred her on. She felt his fingers comb lusciously through her hair, then his hands gripped her shoulders, her underarms, while all around them water thundered down the gorge.

Why am I doing this? she thought. He moaned again and she felt him swell inside her mouth. A hot sweetness hit her tongue. It was insane. It was wrong, she knew this without question, so terribly, deliciously wrong, the way she wanted him inside her now, desperately needed him filling her, flooding her. She wanted their minds together, their hearts together, she wanted to be totally consumed—

And she knew she had to stop.

She sat up abruptly, but he captured her again, his left hand going under her arm, his right hand under her buttock, and he lifted her naked into his arms. "Neal," she said with a laugh, and he stopped her protestations with his mouth. Barely aware that he was walking, she tasted his tongue, while she absently watched the gable of her house dip below the hill, then she heard him opening the gate at the bottom of the pasture.

"What are we doing?" she whispered, feeling suddenly confused, with the mist swirling round her head and the flood pounding in her ears, then they were sinking into the wet grass, and they were kissing and she had him in her hand again, her mind flying apart. She couldn't remember the last time Scott had kissed her this passionately. In fact, she knew she'd never kissed anyone like this, and she knew there was no longer any question about stopping, no possibility. She guided him, and she gaped up at him as she felt him move inside her.

Her mouth opened in disbelief at what she was feeling. He seemed to grow larger as he went deeper, and he kept going in, slowly, incredibly, until it seemed she could feel him moving up her spine. He took her breasts in his hands, tenderly squeezed her nipples between his fingers and thumbs. She felt strangled, staring up at the mindless moon, as if she'd lost her own mind to anything but this one enormous, magnificent sensation of their union. Then, incredibly, he was moving out.

"Ohhh!" she yelled and immediately buried her shout in his shoulder, biting his solid, slippery arm, clutching his hard buttocks and pulling him into her again, taking him in until their bodies molded perfectly together. She strained, she ground her pelvis into him. She arched her back. "Oh *God,* this is wrong," she whispered, and she reached for his shoulders, to stop him, but his hands moved under her hips and he lifted her, sliding, along his hard stomach and lowered her again, filling her so effortlessly, so completely, again and again and again.

The two of them moved like that, brilliance upon brilliance, their overheated bodies emerging as a glowing image through seventy-five feet of cold vegetation. The indistinct lines and shadows that clouded the sight were typical of older night-vision scopes.

Up on the wooded hill the pair looked down. One wore goggles strapped to his head, a binocular eyepiece that transformed to a telescope. The other, the larger of the two, watched through more traditional Nite Site binoculars.

"I say we do it now," Gator murmured.

"Later," Rooftop replied firmly, "when he's alone."

Gator started to stand, but Rooftop stood first and grabbed the smaller man's neck, his thumb hooked around the larynx. It was clear to Gator that if he went for his pocket, he'd end up swallowing his Adam's apple.

"*I said wait,*" Rooftop told him.

"*God!*" Ellen cried. She gripped his buttocks, dug her fingernails in, as every muscle in his body turned rigid and huge. She felt him expand inside her, she felt an astonishing heat. His mouth opened at her ear. She heard him strain for a breath.

Mindlessly full of him, it was impossible for Ellen to stop. His breath in her ear drove her on. Her own muscles surging, she pulled him into her as deep as he'd go. A shout caught in her throat. He covered her open mouth with his hand, and she tasted him, the salt of his skin, and that's where her mind stopped, at one with his taste, with her flooding, the flooding of the river, everything gushing out of control. Her teeth bore down on his palm, and all at once the massing of energy exploded inside her, like a deluge of sparks, a swarming of ice crystals. She rose over him, gazing down, transfixed, unable to breathe, this orgasm going on endlessly, deliciously, as if they were creatures made entirely of raging muscle who needed no oxygen, no light, no sustenance. Mindless, sightless, they stared into one another, deeply, endlessly—

Suddenly he froze.

"Oh, don't stop," she breathed.

He cocked his head as if he'd heard something in the woods. *"Don't be frightened,"* he whispered.

"What?"

"Shh—"

She sprang off him, rolled onto the grass, realizing for the first time that they were on the bank above the pond. She looked back toward the house, afraid Scott was coming down. "What is it?" she whispered, shaking.

Neal was up on his knees, alert, staring up into the woods across the pond. "Probably the rogue," he said softly. "The coyote. We must've spooked him. I don't think animals have ever seen behavior like that."

Soberly, Ellen rose to her feet. Her breasts were engorged, electric. "God," she said, her legs trembling beneath her. "I must be out of my mind."

Behind her, the pond was already full and flooding noisily over the dam. Tree branches and whole bushes clung to the safety cable. Others continued washing over. She was astounded by what she had done, and, suddenly conscious of her nudity, she felt a riveting bolt of fear, sensing the enormity of her sins. She folded her arms tightly across her breasts.

Neal touched her thigh; he was still peering off into the dark woods. "Ellen, walk back to the house," he said quietly.

Heart thumping, she looked down at him. He returned an urgent nod, and she did as he instructed, walked down off the bank and across the farm road to the pasture gate, completely naked, feeling as though hundreds of hidden eyes were suddenly following her, but refusing to give in to the fear. When she turned back, Neal was nowhere in sight.

She started to run.

thirteen

Ellen locked the back door when she got inside. She took a quick shower with the bathroom door also locked, then wrapped herself in a bath towel and tiptoed upstairs, terrified. She slipped into bed naked and closed her eyes, but she did not sleep. She didn't dare, although her conscious thoughts were more nightmarish than anything sleep might concoct.

Murder.

Adultery.

Incest.

The reality stared down on her starkly. There were clues, there were witnesses, and now, apparently, there were watchers.

She thought of the woods above the pond, where she had seen Neal working. If you want to lead someone, make a road, he had said.

Actually, the road was little more than a trail, and the way the trail wound through the woods, it looked no different than any other animal path, taking seemingly random turns around trees and brush and rocks, as if generations of coyote and fox and raccoons had worn the route to the stream above the gorge.

In fact, with the night fully penetrating the woods, there was no other way for the men to come. And they came eagerly, the bed of pine needles softening their footsteps—not that they were in danger of being heard, anyway, over the noise of the waterfall. The path led them downhill at an advantageous angle, permitting advance behind a cover of foliage while allowing a constant view of the pasture from between branches. Through their night scopes, they could see the green shimmer of someone sleeping on the pasture hill, tucked inside his blankets.

The plan was simple: Recover the money stolen from Ray LaFlamme and make the guilty parties wish they'd never been born. In case things got out of hand, Gator had secreted a silenced .22 Ruger Mark II in the back of his jeans.

The one complication with this plan was that Rooftop, suspecting Ray LaFlamme had ordered Gator to kill him and everyone else in the house, had slipped a bullet-proof vest under his hooded sweatshirt and a .45 Smith and Wesson in the rear pocket of his work pants—

—both of which, to Gator's Nite Sites, appeared as stark black impressions against the warmth of Rooftop's body.

So, as the pair made their quiet way through the woods and down to the stream, they never lost sight of each other for more than a second or two, nor did their right hands ever stray far from their weapons. Gator didn't know exactly what Rooftop had in mind, but the concealed piece didn't bother him half as much as the flask of rum the giant kept raising to his mouth.

When Rooftop made his final approach down to the granite bank of the stream, the path dumped him directly behind a large block of ledge with a V-shaped top—perfect for surveillance. However, even as he crouched behind the ledge, Rooftop kept his head turned back and his Nite Sites trained on Gator, who snickered like a chipmunk as he made his way down the path. As soon as he ducked beside Rooftop, the giant rose up and moved around the ledge, stepping down into the black current, continually looking back at Gator's grinning face as he slogged on, knee-deep, five paces to the middle of the stream, where the rounded top of a huge boulder rose out of the water.

Working carefully around to the left, upstream side of the boulder, Rooftop stumbled and caught the top of the rock to keep from falling. As soon as he regained his balance, he looked back at Gator, whose right hand was suddenly hidden behind his leg. Gator grinned. "You be careful out there," he called in a whispered drawl.

Holding the boulder with his left hand, Rooftop came back around the front of the rock, all the while keeping his eye on his partner. Now, moving around to the pond side of the boulder, he stumbled again, feeling a drop-off in the stream bed under his feet. He leaned in closer to the rock and sidled steadily around it, until finally the boulder separated the two men. Then he quickly navigated the remaining ten feet to the opposite bank and backed himself up onto the rocks, aiming his long green face at Gator.

As the kid furtively tucked his pistol back in his pocket, through his goggles, he watched Rooftop's green hand move down to his hip then bring the flask up to his mouth. The giant's fingers were shaking.

Gator snickered, then slipped into the current and plodded through the water. Reaching the boulder that split the stream, a thrill of goose-bumps raced up his lean sides. Not only was he protected by the rock, but he knew Rooftop well enough to know that, even rummed up, the giant would never fire first, never risk murdering Ray LaFlamme's rela-tive—especially since it was Rooftop who was responsible for the miss-ing money in the first place. And there he was, sitting up bigger than life on the open bank.

Gator pulled the .22 into the night, kept it hidden behind the boulder. He almost laughed, thinking about what Rooftop apparently didn't know: that .22 shells are small enough to penetrate the fabric of a bulletproof vest.

He touched the silencer to the right side of the rock. If he was lucky, the size of his shells wouldn't matter. He'd place his first shot straight into that big target of a face and prevent Rooftop from firing the .45 and alerting anyone else. He raised his eye slowly from behind the rock, looking for the edge of Rooftop's green aura . . . and there it was: the bony top of Rooftop's crown, shining like the moon.

Gator felt a jerk of adrenaline and he stepped out to the side ready to fire. But then Rooftop wasn't even looking at him. He was twisted around on the bank, training his Nite Sites on the pasture. Gator low-ered the .22 behind his knee. Fine. He'd get even closer—close enough to drill one clean through the giant's eye as soon as he turned around.

Holding his left hand on the pond side of the rock, he stepped ahead, finding the granite bed solid and free from obstruction. Except that halfway around, the bottom suddenly dropped steeply into the pond, and Gator stumbled, his right arm rising for balance, his .22 out in the open.

Rooftop swung the .45 around, aimed dead at Gator's heart.

Gator fell against the boulder and aimed at Rooftop's face.

Rooftop stretched his arm as far as he could, as if his bullet might reach Gator's chest before Gator's bullet perforated his own forehead.

Gator grinned.

They stood in that position for a number of seconds, without speaking, until Gator said, quietly, "Man, you should see the look on your face."

Neither of them budged. Several more seconds passed. Then Gator slowly spread both arms out to the sides, his .22 aimed out over the dam.

"You drunk enough to drop me in cold blood, Jackson? I seriously don't think so."

Rooftop kept his weapon trained on Gator's chest.

Finally, Gator shoved the .22 into the pocket behind his hip. When he brought his hands around in front of him again, he showed Rooftop his unoccupied fingers.

"You gonna let me cross over now?"

Rooftop took a big breath. Let it out. Then he nodded his head. But he did not lower his .45.

Gator snickered as he proceeded ahead, keeping his left leg pressed against the base of the rock—and his eyes riveted on Rooftop's shining hand, watching for the slightest twitch. When he felt a sudden tug at his right boot, he figured he'd been snagged by a submerged branch carried in by the flood. But then he went to move his foot and found himself firmly caught. And the instant he reached his hand underwater, his leg was yanked violently from under him and he plunged feetfirst down into the pond, propelled fast and deep.

Submerged, and going deeper, he drew his gun, ready to fire. But without a good breath in his lungs he also pulled hard for the surface with his free hand—to no avail. Something was hauling him down. Then his foot hit something hard, and his motion stopped. He lashed out with the pistol, and his silencer struck concrete—the dam, he realized. His ankle was twisted hard against it.

The pressure in his ears told him he was down deep. His lungs cried for oxygen. He reached for his trouser cuff and found that what had snared him was a steel cable, maybe a quarter inch in diameter. The cable ended in a tuna hook that had pierced both his cuff and the top of his leather boot. The cable led through a steel U-bolt in the face of the dam and then back out again, pulling in the direction from which he'd come, the U-bolt acting as a pulley. His attacker could have been twenty feet away.

With complete and sudden terror, Gator understood his predicament. He dropped his gun and grabbed onto the tuna hook with both hands. He pulled up on it, trying to tear it out of his boot, but the barb would not let go, no matter which way he pushed or pulled. Now his lungs shrieked for oxygen.

He unbuckled his belt, tore open his trousers and pulled them down. Logic failing him, he turned the pants leg inside out over the tops of his boots and tried to swim out of them, but his right boot was married fast to the U-bolt. It didn't matter. All he could do, all he could think to do, was to break for the surface. Bright lights were flashing behind his eyes, his head spinning crazily. With his free foot he stood on top of the U-bolt and stretched every muscle, stretched every inch of his strong young bones, pulling higher and higher, until finally his fingertips broke into the air. He felt the water dancing past his knuckles on its way over the dam. He reached higher, he dug his fingers into the concrete, watching his bright green hands through the Nite Sites as if they belonged to someone else, someone groping for life. He felt a rush of excitement. He felt air on his fingernails and thought wildly that air on his fingers was enough. Then he saw another flash behind his eyes, an expanding, blinding orb, and his mind gave over to instinct. He opened his mouth and let the water fall in. It felt so cool and light at first, like a bright summer wind. With great relief, he breathed it in.

In Ellen's dream, she is in her garden, picking cucumbers. The day has ended with a pleasant calm, swallows darting about in the sky, peepers just beginning their evening song. She is making a salad for Scott and Neal. As she steps through her thicket of cucumbers, her foot sinks into a soft depression in the soil. She parts the fat cucumber leaves to get a better look, when she's startled by a most unusual frog, big and brown and bulbous-eyed. In fact, he looks startled himself, as if she's caught him doing something wrong, basking on the edge of this cool dark hole. His wide mouth clamps down tight, his eyes stare up at her like two black pearls. Ellen makes a kissing sound and reaches her thumb to pat his head, but he darts away—and this is the strange thing. He doesn't jump. He glides, almost as if he's on wheels, *gliding* around the rim of the hole and then down in. When Ellen parts the cucumber leaves for a closer look, she is the one who jumps, repulsed at her discovery. This is not a gliding frog at all, but a coarse, black snake. The frog is in its mouth, half swallowed.

"Jesus Christ," Scott mutters in his sleep, and Ellen, waking, realizes she has kicked him.

Outside, bells were ringing.

She turned her head, squinted at the clock, and saw that it was ten past two. Scott snored once, loudly, sleeping again. She could tell by the depth of his snoring that he had taken his sleeping pills. She remembered seeing the bottle on the bathroom sink.

She stepped out of bed and went to the window. She pulled back the shade and looked for Neal down in the pasture, but couldn't see a thing outside except the black wooded hill standing up against the night sky. But the bells kept ringing. She thought of the trail he had made up in the woods. *If you want to lead someone somewhere . . .*

She leaned over Scott and took the flashlight off his nightstand, took her bathrobe off the bedpost and went out the door, headed down the stairs, through the dark living room and kitchen. She was afraid to turn on the lights, she didn't know why. Her whole body shivered.

In the dark, she went out onto the porch and across the dooryard. The night was quiet, except for her sheep. Even the waterfall had settled to its normal whisper. Leaving her flashlight off, she opened the pasture gate and wove her way silently through the agitated sheep. As she approached his sleeping form at the crest of the hill, she knew something was wrong. Catching her breath, she crouched down and gently laid her hand on the blanket. The body was soft, but lifeless. Simultaneously, a hand clamped down on her mouth.

"Go back to the house," the voice whispered close in her ear.

She knew it was Neal. His grip was gentle, but his arm against her cheek was soaking wet.

She turned to him and saw what looked like a pair of goggles over his eyes. He was also bare-chested, and he held a long pistol in his hand. Her stomach dropped. He laid his finger on her lips, then leaned in to her and whispered again. *"Lock the doors when you get inside. Go."*

She left him there, padding back across the pasture in the dark, wondering who else was here, who was watching her tripping past her sheep. Opening the gate, she ran barefoot across the gravel to the porch and up into the kitchen, where she locked the door and pulled the windows shut and locked them. She left the lights off. Her chest pounded. Her mind raced with options: Wake Scott. Call the police. Get Scott's gun and go back out to help Neal. Lock the front door.

She felt her way past the cookstove and stepped into the living room, a sweet, fresh breeze blowing the scent of roses through. She realized too late: The front door was open—

She turned to run, and an arm clamped around her chest, under her arms, yanking her powerfully off her feet.

"Don't say anything," the voice whispered. With both hands, she took hold of his massive, hairless forearm, and he carried her back into the kitchen. She could barely breathe.

"I don't mean to hurt you, Mrs. Chambers," he said, releasing some pressure.

Ellen knew who it was. "Rooftop?"

"The devil's out there," he answered. "You've got to call him off."

Above the sound of his wheezing, she could hear Scott snoring upstairs. She thought about yelling for him but was afraid of what would happen if he came charging down.

"What do you want?" she gasped.

"I got nothing against you," Rooftop said. "I got nothing against anyone. I just need to get back to my van."

She could smell alcohol on his breath. She could feel him shaking. In fact, they were both shaking.

"Rooftop, I don't know what you think I did—or what any of us did."

Something dug into her ribs. "Just go to the window and call to him, tell him I want to leave." He turned her around and together they shuffled toward the window.

"Don't call." Neal's voice rose quietly from the darkness behind them, the living room.

Rooftop's arm hardened around Ellen's throat. "I've got a gun," he said. The pistol lay cold against her cheek.

"As do I," Neal said. "So be careful, Mr. Paradise. What you feel against your kidney might be a little wet, but it's perfectly functional. With one twitch of my finger, I can paralyze you faster than you can blink—and I will. You're an intruder, which makes you fair game."

Ellen heard Rooftop's wheezing intensify.

"Now I'm going to take the gun from your hand. I don't want to startle you."

Ellen felt the cold steel lifted from her face, then she ducked out from under Rooftop's arm and backed to the counter.

"Are you okay?" Neal said.

"I guess," she answered. "Can I turn on the light?"

"No, I can see. Rooftop, I can see like a cat with these goggles your buddy gave me. I can see that little tic on your temple."

"Should I call the police?" Ellen said.

"Hold on," Neal told her. Then, to Rooftop, he said softly, "Put your hands on the table." With his foot, he slid a chair back. Against the relative lightness of the window, Ellen could see him run his hand down Rooftop's hip. "That's quite a little militia you had there," Neal said as he frisked the giant. "Hands behind your head."

Rooftop complied, and Neal, a full head shorter and a hundred pounds lighter, pulled something from Rooftop's pocket.

"What's this?" he said.

"Rum," Rooftop answered.

"Rum, you say." Neal tossed the flask on the table. "I'm going to ask you some questions now, and the Geneva convention does not apply. You lie to me, I'll take you outside and shoot you. Understand?"

"Neal—"

"I wasn't going to hurt anyone here," Rooftop said.

"What did I say about lying to me?"

"I don't lie," Rooftop said. "There's money missing."

"What money?" Ellen said.

"The money that was in Randy's Jeep."

"What's he talking about?" she said to Neal.

"You think I stole that money, or somebody here stole it," Neal said. "Is that why you and your buddy came in the night with loaded weapons?"

Ellen's heart dropped. Gator had been here.

"It's a bad situation," Rooftop said.

"I don't particularly like the insinuation that we're thieves."

"Neal, you've made your point. Let him go," said Ellen.

Neal sighed. "See, this is something my aunt and I disagree on. My aunt believes in turning the other cheek. I'm just the opposite—sort of the New Testament-Old Testament dichotomy. Do you know what I mean?"

Rooftop breathed in and out.

"There were just the two of you, right?" Ellen said. "You and Gator?"

"Yes," Rooftop said. "But now I need to go."

"From what I saw out there tonight," Neal said, "there didn't seem to be a whole lot of trust between you and Gator."

Rooftop did not answer.

"Does Gator have a wife?" Neal asked. "Girlfriend somewhere?"

"He's got people down in Louisiana," said Rooftop. "They think he's dead."

"Maybe Gator took the money, and he's gone back to convince them otherwise. You think so?"

Rooftop wheezed, in and out.

"How about you? You got anyone expecting you home tonight?"

"My family's passed on," Rooftop said.

Neal reached around Rooftop's body and picked up the flask from the table, swished it around.

"I thought you gave this stuff up," Neal said.

The giant stood there quietly with his hands behind his neck, his head near the ceiling.

"Proverbs," Neal said. " 'Give strong drink unto him that is ready to perish.' "

Ellen placed her hand on Neal's sopping shoulder. "Neal, I mean it. Let him go."

"Mr. Paradise," Neal said, "are you ready to perish?"

"You need to know that Mr. LaFlamme isn't going to give up on this," Rooftop told them. "He's bound to get his money back, and he doesn't care who gets hurt. For my own self, I'm bound to protect certain people."

"Certain people . . . you mean Moreen?"

Once again, the only sound in the house was Scott's deep snoring.

"Neal," Ellen said softly.

"Okay, I'm going to set you free," Neal said to Rooftop. "You've been good to Moreen, and I know that you intend to do the right thing. But first"—with his teeth he unscrewed the cap of the flask—"I want you to finish this." He reached the flask up to Rooftop's hands. "Take it and drink it down," he said. "Ellen, do you have any more rum in the house?"

"Just whiskey and tequila," she answered.

"Would you get him the whiskey, please?"

She hesitated.

"I'm letting him go," Neal told her. "Just get it."

"Excuse me," Rooftop said.

"Down the hatch," Neal said. "Do you think I'm playing games?"

While Rooftop drank, Ellen went to the cupboard and lifted the heavy bottle down, then brought it over. "Neal, I want to know what's going on," she said.

"Take the cap off, please," he said to her. She did as he asked, then set the bottle on the table. "Pick up the bottle, Mr. Paradise."

Rooftop stood stiffly. Neal slid the silencer underneath his sweatshirt.

"Pick it up," he said again. "I want to hear you swallow."

In the darkness, Ellen could make out Rooftop raising the whiskey bottle to his mouth. She heard the bubbling of liquid as it ran down his throat.

"More," Neal said.

Rooftop took several more gulps, his Adam's apple pumping loudly, until finally he sputtered and coughed.

Neal took the bottle from him and set it on the table. "Where's your van?"

"Up on the fire road, other side of the hill."

"Let's go, I'll walk you down to the stream."

"I'm coming with you," Ellen said.

Neal turned toward her. She thought he was going to argue, but he didn't. She stepped past him and unlocked the door, and Rooftop and Neal went out. Ellen followed with the flashlight.

"You gonna give me back my gun?" Rooftop said, as he stumbled down the porch steps. "I need my gun."

"You'll be better off without it," Neal told him, keeping his own gun aimed at the giant's lower back.

Ellen pulled up beside them and shone the flashlight beam in front of Rooftop's feet.

"Next time I see Moreen, I'll tell her you were asking about her," Neal told him as they walked past the pump house.

"Yeah, big damn joke," Rooftop muttered. By the time they reached the dam, his boots were slapping drunkenly at the gravel road. "You see Moreen, tell her you stole my damn gun," he said. "That's what you can tell her."

"Forget your gun," Neal told him. "Man your size doesn't need a gun."

"Little prick."

They took a few more steps, until Rooftop tripped over his feet and almost fell. Then he stopped and turned toward Neal, his long chin seeming to melt to his chest. "I'd like to know what the hell you're doing here," he said.

Ellen moved in between them, to head off another confrontation. "Neal, where do you want to cross?"

"Shut the hell up while I'm making a point," Rooftop slurred.

"I might as well shoot him right here," Neal said.

"Here," Rooftop turned around. "Here's my damn back."

"Rooftop, just go home," Ellen told him.

Rooftop snorted groggily. To Ellen's relief, then he turned and resumed walking, following the farm road alongside the water until they reached the end of the pond, where the stream entered.

"This is where you cross over," Neal told him.

Rooftop stopped. He turned, stumbling again as he did so, then glared down at Neal, his big head bobbing. Ellen could hear his labored breathing.

"I'm gonna tell you for the last time," he said. "I need my gun. I do not intend any harm to the good people."

"I'm going to shoot you if you don't leave," Neal said.

The giant stared drunkenly through the darkness.

"You can sleep in your van if you can't drive," Ellen told him.

"Yeah, sleep," he said with a sneer, then he stumbled up the rocks to the top of the bank. "You tell Moreen for me—" As he slowly turned his body to face her his knees collapsed beneath him, and he fell down the other side. Ellen heard the shallow splash and climbed up the bank to help him. Neal climbed with her but held her back.

"He's going to drown," she said.

"He's a professional diver," Neal said. "Isn't that right, Roof?"

Rooftop staggered up out of the current only to fall a second time. He caught hold of the boulder in the middle of the stream and pulled himself up, then turned and peered straight into Ellen's flashlight beam, his thick lenses reflecting the light like twin mirrors. It made Ellen think of a crocodile deciding whether or not to attack. She was glad that Neal was beside her, glad he had the gun.

"Just tell her for me," Rooftop said. "Tell Moreen."

"Tell her what?"

Rooftop stared some more, then he scowled painfully, as if he wanted to cry. Ellen kept her light on him until finally he turned and slogged away from them. Reaching the opposite bank, he pulled himself up by a birch sapling, gave one more look back at the light, then turned and started trudging up the hill.

"He can't drive like that," Ellen said, as they listened to footsteps crashing through the woods.

"He'll be fine."

Soon the rustle of his uneven footsteps diminished, lost in the noise of the waterfall. Ellen shut off the flashlight.

"Look up," Neal said, touching her back. "You can see the stars."

Indeed, the mist had subsided, and a black, glittering sky shone down on them.

"The stars have nothing to do with me," she said. "Neal, you need to answer some questions."

"I'll try."

"What did you do to Gator?"

"I let him go," he told her.

"Was that him in the pasture, under the blanket?" she asked calmly. She didn't want to know, but she needed to.

"It was one of the lambs," Neal answered. "A decoy. I knew they'd be coming."

She stood there, unable to absorb all this. "Neal, what money was he talking about?"

He looked toward the house. "Don't ever tell Scott I told you this."

She waited for him to continue.

"They worked for the loan shark—Randy, Rooftop, and Gator."

"Randy?" She stared at Neal through the darkness, her mind grasping at bits of memory, trying to piece them together.

"The bank loan Scott got last week, he owed most of it to the shark," Neal continued.

"I knew that."

"Well, he gave the money to Randy, and apparently Randy never delivered it to the boss. Now it's missing."

Ellen felt a low rumble in her stomach. "So Scott knew that Randy worked for this criminal?"

"Randy and Rooftop were the collection men. Which is how Randy first met Mo, when they came here looking for a late payment."

Ellen turned away from him and started walking toward the house. Neal caught the sleeve of her bathrobe, gently stopping her.

"Ellen, you don't know any of this."

"Why?"

"Because it would give you motivation."

"For what?"

"Randy's death."

Ellen stood there stunned. Her mind refused to work.

"Neal, did you take that money?"

He shook his head, looking into her eyes. "No," he said, and she believed him.

The clock radio turned silently, from 2:48 to 2:49. Sugar Westerback rolled from his right side to his left, scratching at a fierce itching in his palm as he drifted out of a dream. He heard the mosquito pass close to his ear and he swiped it away. But in a few seconds it was back again, and when it landed on his cheek, he slapped himself.

Awake now, he turned onto his back, fluffed up his pillow, and tucked the sheet under his chin. He could hear an army of other mosquitoes bumping up against his window screen, whining crazily, trying to get in at him. He scratched and scratched at his palm, as he listened to the peepers singing off in the woods. He wondered what they were saying to each other.

"Hey, these mosquitoes taste good."

"Yeah, I've had a dozen already."

He wondered if the mosquitoes could hear the frogs, if that's why they were so desperate to get through the window screen. *"Come on, buddy, open up. The frogs are murdering us."*

He scratched at his palm some more.

Outside, some distance in the woods, an owl hooted into the night.

Sugar stopped scratching.

His fingernail remained in place, poised in his hand, as he whispered the word in quiet amazement.

"Murder."

fourteen

Rooftop Paradise fell to his knees again as the doors came open. He freed his hands from the handles and reached inside the panel truck. There was a long, plywood box built inside the left rear quarter. He threw open the lid, and his hand dropped into the box. Pulled out his weight belt with a loud clatter, as each eight-pound lead weight followed the previous one out of the box and onto the floor of the van. When the entire length of belt was free, Rooftop dragged it across the bumper and it fell heavily onto his hip. Eyes closed, he gathered the whole belt in his arms and pulled himself to his feet. He fell backwards. As much as his body cried out for sleep, he refused to submit. Not tonight.

He got up again and made his way to his door, then climbed onto the soft vinyl seat, hitting his chin on the steering wheel and his head on the ceiling. He felt for the ignition key, pushed in the clutch and started the van.

He pulled his headlights on. The woods lit up a bright, sleeping green. Staring at it all, he realized he'd never really seen the beauty of the woods before. He started to sleep, but he revved the engine to wake himself, and the wheels rolled out of their mossy ruts. He'd forgotten how far he had backed in—with his boat attached. Maybe a quarter-mile, maybe more. Didn't matter. The gas tank was full, and he had a few hours before morning light. In fact, he was already moving, hauling his big Boston Whaler down that beautiful green

tunnel toward the end of his life, watching tree after tree turn grace-
fully past him, saluting him, scratching at his roof to keep him awake,
white and black birches, white pine, red oak, rock maple, red maple,
red pine . . .

Just after one o'clock the bartender of the Belle Atlantic Restaurant
served last call. The kitchen had closed at midnight and only one waitress and a busboy remained, waiting for a party of four to leave. Upstairs,
in Ray LaFlamme's money room, the dining room manager had just
finished the day's receipts and stood by the door while LaFlamme put
half the cash in his safe. On his way home the manager would deposit
the rest of the cash, plus the credit receipts and checks, in the night
deposit box at Saco First Federal. When the safe was closed, LaFlamme
and the manager rode the elevator down to the ground-floor office. In
the meantime, the bartender went out to the parking lot and started
LaFlamme's bulletproof Eldorado, then drove it around to the kitchen
door. He did so every night, armed with a .377. At that point the
manager, who was also armed, escorted the boss out to his car. Both
men would remain in the parking lot until LaFlamme was on his way
home. Then they would go back inside, get rid of the stragglers and
lock the restaurant for the night.

Ray LaFlamme lived four miles from his restaurant. His home, a
nineteenth-century captain's mansion, sat on a gently sloping hill overlooking Saco Bay. These days the place looked more like a fortress than
a captain's home, protected by an eight-foot-high stone wall and inner
steel fence that was wired to alarm systems in both the master bedroom
and the guardhouse. By land, the only way into the property was through
the front gate that stood at the end of a quarter-mile private road. The
gate was made of two eight-feet-high wrought-iron sections that slid open
from the center, each section rolling on tracks behind the stone wall. The
brick guardhouse, which sat directly behind the gate, had three small bedrooms, a bathroom, kitchen, living room, and armory.

When Ray LaFlamme arrived home, Herbie Handcream was on
watch. From his window, Herbie opened the gate and gave LaFlamme
a fingerless wave as the old man drove past. LaFlamme continued up
the drive and pulled his Cadillac into his garage. The door closed behind
him. When he walked into his kitchen he found that his wife, Cather-
ine, had left a cheese croissant and a cup of mussel stew on the counter.
He heated the stew in the microwave and ate at the kitchen table while

he watched the end of a Ray Milland movie on a fourteen-inch television. After he'd finished his food, he lost interest in the movie, so he turned off the TV and went to bed.

The Boston Whaler sailed due north on Route 1, tacking left, tacking right, as Rooftop fluttered from dream to wakefulness and back again, the rain blowing lightly past his ear, wetting the left lens of his glasses. The towns were sound asleep, which was good. His windshield wipers clocked hypnotically, while Rooftop stretched his eyes wide open, then squeezed them shut. He banged the graduation march on his steering wheel and chewed on coffee beans to stay awake. The taste was terribly bitter but strong enough to do the job—some gourmet brand, rainforest mocha nut, something that cost ten dollars a bag. Rooftop hadn't realized the coffee wasn't ground until he'd pulled back on the road. So now he chewed on the beans while he drove, handfuls at a time, and it wasn't long before he found himself pulling into Biddeford.

With his gun, he wouldn't have had to be so sneaky. Herbie Handcream would be in the guardhouse. Seeing Rooftop driving in at this hour—hauling his Boston Whaler, no less—Herbie wouldn't know what to think, but he'd open the gate, thinking Rooftop had brought him LaFlamme's money; of course, never suspecting that Rooftop would shoot him. Then the giant would go inside the guardhouse and kill Marcel. He'd grab the keys to the mansion and go kill the old man. After that, he'd throw all three guys in his boat and head out of Kennebunkport five or six miles, where the Army kept an undersea dump in 150 feet of water, and he'd weight the bodies down and toss them overboard. Then who knows? If he had a shell left for himself, maybe he'd lash himself to his motor—125-horse Johnson—unclamp it from the transom and blow his own big head off, give the fish a real feast.

Only thing was, now without a gun, he'd have to improvise. Not that easy when you're drunk as a skunk. He turned off Route 1 onto a side road, hauling his boat under a canopy of oaks and maples, until he came to a fruit stand, then he turned right then left and left again, negotiating the panel truck along a narrow, winding road until he came to LaFlamme's sign, PRIVATE—ABSOLUTELY NO TRESPASSING, and there, at the gate, he stopped. The rain falling on his roof sounded like applause.

The guardhouse was positioned to the left of the wide drive. A bay window jutted out a foot from the side of the building, with a small counter positioned below the window and a pair of floodlights above, much like a bank's drive-up window.

Rooftop flashed his high beams, then saw Herbie Handcream's head jerk up behind the glass. He saw Herbie stare out at him, then heard the snap of a loudspeaker embedded in the stone wall.

"What the fuck do you want?" Herbie said.

"I got Mr. LaFlamme's money," Rooftop answered.

" 'Wha-wha-wha,' " Herbie mimicked. "Speak up, moron."

Rooftop stared back at him through the rain until his eyes started to cross. "I brought the damn money," he enunciated.

The gate slid open, and Rooftop drove in until Herbie held up his good hand. Rooftop slammed on the brakes and the Boston Whaler slammed against its trailer hitch. Herbie slid the glass aside, slid the screen aside and stuck his head through the window, looking back. "You gotta pull up. You got your boat on, and I can't close the gates."

Rooftop kept staring.

"You're stickin out, asshole. Pull up."

"I need to see the boss," Rooftop said.

Herbie squinted past Rooftop, into the empty front seat. "Where's fuckin Gator? He's supposed to relieve me in two hours."

"He's on his way," Rooftop answered. "Tell Mr. LaFlamme to come out so I can give him his money."

Herbie peered through Rooftop's thick lenses. "Whaddaya, tanked? Just give me the fuckin money."

Rooftop leaned across the front seat and opened his glove box. He reached in and pulled out a fat pink Dunkin Donuts bag, held it up for Herbie to see.

"Yeah, good," Herbie said. "Put it up here and go home. I'll have Ray call you in the morning."

"I want to give the money to Mr. LaFlamme personally," Rooftop insisted. "I don't trust you minor bums."

Herbie smirked. He bent down, out of sight, then appeared at the window again, his good hand down where Rooftop couldn't see it.. "Big boy, put the money on the counter and back on outta here."

"Go ahead and shoot me," Rooftop said. "You don't even know what's in the bag. Yeah, kill me. Then go explain a bag of doughnuts to Mr. LaFlamme."

He tossed the bag on the floor of the van, then grabbed another fistful of coffee beans and tossed them in his mouth, started chewing. A gust of rain washed his windshield.

Herbie expanded his chest, blew a big sigh. Then he swung away from the window. At the same time, Rooftop stepped out of the panel truck. His legs stiffened underneath him, and he almost fell, but he made his way around to the guardhouse door.

Inside the house he heard Herbie say, "Hey." Rooftop imagined the little man thumping on Marcel's bedroom door with his elbow. "Hey, Sleepin Beauty."

Rooftop stepped in front of the guardhouse window, where he saw a telephone sitting on Herbie's desk, a large bottle of Rolaids, and a couple of Maine State Lottery tickets. Herbie came back over, pushed the leather desk chair aside, and picked up the telephone. "Ray ain't gonna like this one friggin bit," he warned. "If you got the money, just bring it inside."

Rooftop leaned heavily on the counter. Fat raindrops patted the top of his head.

Herbie pushed a button on the phone then grabbed a pen and started tapping it on the desk. "Marcel, don't go back to sleep in there," he hollered, and was answered by a low, muffled curse.

Something Herbie heard on the telephone made him wince. He listened for a second, then said, "Yeah, Ray, we got some money here. I know, it's . . . No, Rooftop. No, he's here now. He says he has to give it to you in person."

"Outside," Rooftop said.

Herbie looked at him.

"I give it to him outside," Rooftop clarified. "Out in the open, not in the house."

"Ray says just give us the money here. We'll bring it to him in the morning."

"To heck with him," Rooftop said. "I'll buy myself a plane ticket to Argentina and spend the money myself."

"You hear that?" Herbie said in the phone, then he hung up and looked up at Rooftop. "Ray says okay. Just hold your fuckin horses. We'll drive you up to the house."

"Nope. We walk."

"You on drugs? It's a fuckin typhoon out there!"

Rooftop turned carefully and stepped to the corner of the building, where he watched the screen door bang open. Herbie stepped out, wearing a green rubbery poncho and yellow leather moccasins.

"Big man, big balls," he said. "I'd watch your mouth around Ray LaFlamme, or you'll be eatin those balls for breakfast."

"Where's the other bum?" Rooftop said.

Herbie turned and yelled at the door, "It ain't exactly dry out here!"

Marcel grumbled something in response.

Now Rooftop stepped out from the corner, spreading his black, knee-high fishing boots carefully on the flagstone walkway.

Herbie, seeing the weight belt he wore loosely around his waist, and the way Rooftop held his big hands around the buckle, said, "What the fuck are you supposed to be, some kinda fuckin Argentina cowboy, with the fuckin kangaroos?"

Then the door swung open and Marcel emerged, wearing a white T-shirt and jockeys, and a dark felt hat on his head. A small, bright pistol in his hand was aimed in the vicinity of Rooftop's knees. "Okay, Fuckinsky, what?" he said, raindrops pelting off his brim.

Evidently, the rather slow turn of Rooftop's shoulders did not alert him until the weight belt snapped out of the darkness six inches from his ear. Then it was too late. The square-cornered slab of lead at the end of the belt weighed only eight pounds, but it was propelled by a whipping force of nine identical weights distributed along a nylon belt sixty inches long—not to mention the 300 pounds of drunken rage driving it home.

The lead hit the back of Marcel's head with enough force to launch the big man clear off his toes and out of his hat. The weight belt never stopped in its trajectory, but kept whistling around Rooftop's head.

"Hey, Roofy!" Herbie said, and his arm shot up to protect his face, but the belt passed through his phantom hand and knocked him in a wild backward flip. Sprawled in the grass with the weapon still in his hand, Marcel drew his muscular arms alongside his ribs, wanting to push himself up. But the weight belt continued in its orbit and drove straight down, no fewer than six lead weights smashing down the length of Marcel's spine to the back of his skull. The big bodyguard flattened in the wet grass, one last ripple of energy traveling down the fat of his back. Herbie was already dead, a two-inch-wide fissure cracked in the center of his forehead like a third thick eyebrow, but Rooftop clobbered him once more, straight down over the top of his head, as though he were swinging a splitting maul.

Fastening the belt around his waist again, Rooftop picked up both bodies and dumped them in his boat, then opened the panel-truck door and took out the Dunkin Donuts bag. He turned.

Out in front of Ray LaFlamme's mansion stood a life-sized statue of Jesus Christ absolving the property. The statue was brightly lit by a pair of in-ground floodlights. Rain hitting the lights danced like sparks. Lining up Jesus in his vision, Rooftop marched up the rain-soaked asphalt and across the lawn. When he reached the statue, he stepped beside it and turned toward the house, the rain beating off his forehead and glasses. The floodlights blinded him, so he closed his eyes. When he opened them again, Ray LaFlamme was standing on the other side of his screen door in a red satin robe.

"I've got your money," Rooftop called, raising the dripping doughnut bag.

"Where are my boys?"

"Back there."

The old man stuck his hand in the pocket of his robe. "Rupert, be good and bring me the money."

"You'll have to come out and get it, Ray LaFlamme."

The old man blinked his eyes a few times. Raindrops jumped up and down off the roof above his head. "So they stayed back there, did they?"

"They don't like the rain."

"Neither do I," LaFlamme said. He stared intently through the screen. "How much is there?"

"I didn't count it up," Rooftop replied.

"Okay, open the bag and let me see the money, so I know you're not up to any sort of trick."

Rooftop set the doughnut bag in the palm of his hand and unfolded the top. LaFlamme opened the screen door and stepped halfway out, keeping his hand in his pocket. Rooftop stuck his hand in the bag and pulled out three bills, tossing them into a rain-filled sea breeze. The currency flipped and tumbled over the wet grass.

"Roofy, don't let it blow to the neighbors," LaFlamme said.

Rooftop folded the top of the bag down and tossed it toward the veranda, but only halfway. It landed on the lawn with a wet splat.

LaFlamme drew his pistol, gave the giant a long look, then stepped down into the rain, the slender, silvery barrel in his hand sparkling with the rain and reflections. "I know you're a good boy," he said, as he walked out on the lawn, "but you're acting too funny." Keeping the pistol aimed at Rooftop, he picked up the doughnut bag and hesitated curiously, bouncing the bag to gauge its weight. Then he unrolled the top and took his eyes off Rooftop, as he let the bag open.

The curse caught in his throat as the first swipe of Rooftop's weight belt flew diagonally through the rain and shattered his ribs, the whip-end cracking against the middle of his back, sending him and three jelly doughnuts tumbling onto the wet lawn. The old man flopped over on his side underneath the Christ statue, one arm crossed over his chest, as though protecting himself. His other arm lay beneath him. His knees twisted uselessly to the side.

Rooftop came and stood over him, his weight belt slung to the ground. "I did not choose this path," he said, and he was about to say more, but he saw the silver barrel under LaFlamme's arm, aimed point-blank at his long, flat face. He stared into it, waiting to be shot.

"Oh, God bless," the old man gasped, "I'm all numb." His head was shaking, yet he seemed to be smiling. "Rupert," he breathed.

Rooftop leaned in closer, until he could see right down inside the small barrel.

"Rupert," LaFlamme whispered again.

Rooftop looked directly into the old man's eyes.

"I'm talking to God now, Rupert."

Then, slowly, Rooftop straightened. He lifted the end of his weight belt in two hands. Then he stepped back, swung his arms in a powerful arc, swiping the belt over his head like a bullwhip. The ground shook at the impact, and water splashed up from under LaFlamme's body.

Then Rooftop was driving on Route 1, the rain blowing in his windows, warm and salt-smelling, buffeting the panel truck, shaking the boat behind him. He dozed as he drove, eating jelly doughnuts and chewing coffee beans by the mouthful, his body pleading for sleep. He dozed even as he stood in the rain, winching his boat down the trailer at the public landing. He brought the bag of coffee beans into the boat with him and kept eating them as he plowed through three-foot stand-ing waves at the mouth of the river, bounding headlong into a rose-colored horizon, feeling the black land backing away from him for the last time.

The motor sang, despite the weight: three dead bodies and a cement statue of Jesus Christ sprawled on deck. Rooftop stood at the console staring at his compass, but it made no sense. He set his course and closed his eyes.

When he heard a car horn, he grabbed the wheel, expecting to be on the highway, but it was a lobster boat flashing its running lights, some father and son trading time for distance, out to beat the dawn. Rooftop turned on his lights in response, then fell asleep again.

When he awoke, the rain had stopped. The low horizon glowed brightly, gray pink-streaked. The ocean rolled big and dark.

Realizing he had missed the dump, probably by miles, Rooftop cut the engine to an idle and sat there quietly, bobbing in the swells. The Christ statue rocked on the deck, from elbow to elbow. With a length of yellow nylon rope, Rooftop tied Herbie Handcream to Marcel, then tied Marcel to Mr. LaFlamme, then tied Mr. LaFlamme to the 200-pound concrete block he used as a mooring. He removed the pistol from LaFlamme's pocket and tossed it overboard. Then he went to the console and opened the side door, took out the bag of doughnuts. He pulled out the last one, a honey-glazed, and stuffed the bag in the pocket of LaFlamme's robe. Then he ate the doughnut.

Next he removed the hatch door from the left side of the boat, leaving the deck level with the ocean's surface—his diving platform—and he heaved the concrete mooring over the side. The three bodies jumped in after it, one by one.

Rooftop stepped over the statue and returned to the cockpit, opened the throttle, and headed farther out to sea. Seawater splashed in the open hatch, lapping up the blood. As the boat bounded over the swells, Rooftop dozed again and dreamt that he was swimming with giant sea turtles.

When he woke up, he cut the throttle and turned the key, stopping the engine. He went back to the stern and cut another length of nylon rope then threw his fishing knife into the ocean. He lifted the Jesus statue upright and walked it to the very edge of the diving platform. Then he tied one end of the rope around its outstretched arm. He picked up his weight belt from the deck and buckled it around his waist. Returning to the console, he took out Marcel's handgun, a .380. He checked the clip as he returned to his diving platform, where he sat beside the statue, facing out to sea. Waves rocked the boat. The statue wobbled heavily beside him. Rooftop set the gun in his lap while he tied the other end of the rope around his weight belt, imagining those great slow turtles again.

Then he picked up the pistol and leaned his long body over his knees, taking up the slack in the rope between himself and Jesus. The boat splashed up and down. He took a deep breath of the cool, salty air, then blew it out, then pressed the muzzle to his forehead. As he slid his thumb inside the trigger guard, he looked into the water one last time.

Then he closed his eyes and asked Jesus to forgive him.

fifteen

When the window blinds began to gray with the dawn, the clock radio came on. Ellen kept her eyes closed and listened to Scott slap the clock quiet then get out of bed. Hearing the sound of his bureau drawer opening and closing, the simple jingling of his belt buckle, she wondered if he knew, or even suspected, everything she was guilty of. She listened to him go downstairs and eat breakfast, same as he did any other day. She heard the back door close; then his voice outside.

"Jesus, man, don't you ever sleep?"

" 'He that will not work,' " Neal recited in response, " 'neither let him eat.' Thessalonians three, verse ten."

"Yeah, well, 'All work and no play kinda sucks.' Scott Chambers, chapter one, verse one."

Ellen stepped out of bed and looked through the screen, saw Neal walking around the front of the barn in his black sweater and corduroys, carrying a small, fixed-pane window in his arms.

"Looks like it's gonna be a wet one," he said. "I want to get these windows in."

Hearing his voice, Ellen felt a stirring deep in her abdomen, but resisted it, disgusted with herself. She watched Scott slide into his old Mercedes and drive off. She watched Neal fit the window into the wall of the addition.

In ten days he had refashioned the barn into a beautiful thing. Its front doors were slightly narrower than they had been but arched at the top, lending the building a sense of grace and symmetry, as did the

attachment of the two additions and the centering of the silo, which
rose off the roof's peak. Ten days. If Neal was serious about finishing
the job in twelve—and she knew he was—by tomorrow night he would
be done and gone. As far as she knew, the only thing left to do was
install the windows in both additions, twenty-four in all.

Imagining his absence, a keen sense of relief washed over Ellen, yet
standing there naked, watching him work, Ellen felt the stirring grow
inside her again, a low, tantalizing hum. She turned away from the
window. Opening her dresser drawer, she took out a pair of cotton
underpants and stepped into them. No more french-cuts. No more tank
tops, halter tops. She found a clean gray sports bra and put it on. Nor
would she swim with him anymore. She put on a black T-shirt and a
green muslin skirt, slipped on her clogs, and went downstairs.

She started the coffeemaker, then went into the bathroom to wash
her face and brush her teeth. She heard the scream of the circular saw
outside. The sky looked darker. She was sure it would rain. So she'd
stay inside and wash the kitchen floor. Maybe she'd finish her tapestry
today. She heard hammering again and pulled the bathroom window
down, left it open an inch or two. She watched a pair of raindrops
paint diagonal lines on the window glass, as a low black sky moved
over the pond, sealing off three beams of sunlight, one by one. Then
more lines graced the window, as the smell of rain came richly through
the screen.

She couldn't believe what she had done.

With both hands, she gathered her hair behind her ears, then opened
the vanity drawer, where she kept her barrettes and elastics. Instead of
an elastic, she took out a pair of scissors. As long and thick as her hair
was, it took her ten minutes to cut it all within an inch of her skull.
With the summer rain falling down her window, great warm sheets of
auburn hair slid down her arms and mounded around her ankles. When
she was done, feeling amazingly lighter, Ellen went into the kitchen
and got a trash bag, then came back and stuffed the hair inside.

Then she went back to the kitchen and took a coffee mug down
from the cupboard. All at once the rain hitting the porch roof sounded
like a stampede. She looked out the window and saw Neal's shadowy
form come running toward her, his footsteps pounding on the porch.
When he came in the door, she went to the counter and poured her
coffee, keeping her back to him.

"Looks like rain," he said wryly.

She didn't respond. Against her wishes, her heart was hammering.

He walked closer to her and said, "I've read that after a good person commits a crime of passion, often they disfigure themselves somehow. It's one of the signs of guilt that investigators look for." He stepped closer. "But you've done exactly the opposite."

She raised a hand to deflect him and said, "You need to get out of here." Although it wasn't how she'd intended to tell him, it was exactly what she meant to say.

"One more day, and I'll be through," he replied quietly.

Ellen turned, saw how the rain had wet his hair and face. He pulled his wet sweater off over his head and tossed it across the room, onto the washing machine. She turned away.

"I've never hated myself before," she said. "I don't want to give myself any more reasons to start."

His hand touched the cool back of her neck, brushed a severed strand of hair away. "You are so incredibly beautiful," he said, standing so close she could smell the rain on his arm. "Ellen, do you have any idea what it's like to kiss you? Just to kiss you?"

She pushed his hand away. "For God's sake, Neal, you're my nephew."

"You know that's not true," he replied. He laid his warm hands on her shoulders, and the rain beat harder on the roof, mimicking her heart. It was like sorcery, the way his touch seduced her.

"Remember the picture of the barn I showed you when I first came here?" he asked.

She sighed.

"There's also a house. And sixty acres of the greenest farmland you've ever seen. It belongs to me."

She looked out the window, the gray rain streaking down the eaves, splashing off the gravel dooryard. What was he saying to her?

"I invested my inheritance," he continued. "I have all the money we'd ever need. You wouldn't have to teach unless you wanted to."

She stared down at the water on the floor, his boot prints. She took a halting breath, hesitated a second, then said, "Neal, how did you know Mo was getting married?"

"Why is that important?"

"How did you know?" she persisted, looking back at him.

A playful glint crossed his eyes. "I've been stalking you," he said.

She waited.

"You're serious?"

He shrugged. "I was feeling nostalgic one day. Lonely, I guess. I called the hardware store to talk to Scott. Somebody there answered the phone and said he was out making wedding arrangements. It was a week away, so I decided to surprise you. Why?"

She closed her eyes, massaged her brow. "You need to leave," she said, stepping away from him.

"Ellen, if I left the barn without windows, people would wonder—especially this soon after Randy's death."

She shook her head, refusing to meet his gaze. "Just go outside," she told him. "Work in the barn. I've got to think."

He sighed. "Okay if I take a cold shower first?"

"Take whatever kind of shower you want."

She could feel him standing behind her, could feel the change in air pressure when he finally turned and walked into the bathroom. She brushed her fingers across her skull, feeling the cool bristle of hair snap through her fingers. She retrieved her mug of coffee from the counter and brought it to the table, where she sat and looked out the window. While the rain trampled the roof and washed down the eaves in sheets, she heard the clink of Neal's belt buckle hit the bathroom floor. Then the shower came on.

Against her will, she pictured him lathering his arms and chest. She put it out of her mind but couldn't quite suppress the memory of his warmth the night before, the incredible solid, thickness of him. She breathed deeply to regain control of her mind, and she recalled the precise smell of him, so she leaned toward the window to breathe in the scent of the rain. She heard the water pump shut off. As she sipped her coffee, she imagined herself living with him hidden in the hills of Vermont, where no one knew anything about them or the things they had done. It was ridiculous, the way her mind worked against her. When she heard the bathroom door open she said, "Neal, I'm scared."

"Scared of what?"

"Everything. You, me, the money that's missing. What if Mo's got the money, or Scott?"

She turned, saw him standing outside the bathroom door, holding a brown bath towel around his waist.

She turned away, then listened to him walk softly across the room and stand beside her chair. She could feel the heat coming off his body. She looked up at him, and he leveled his dark eyes at her.

"Ellen, I promise you," he said. "There is nothing to worry about." He made it so easy to believe him. She felt his hand brush softly over her head then move down the back of her neck. She took a deep breath and let it out in a sigh, radiating in his tender touch, as the rain continued drumming on the roof.

"What worries me," he said, "is how I'm going to live without you."

Under the slightest pressure of his hand, she let her cheek lay against his warm side, and they stayed like that for a number of seconds, not speaking, while she watched his chest expand and contract with his breathing, and water droplets roll down the rippled muscles of his stomach and through the fine black hair under his navel. She could feel the humidity rising off him. She could hear herself breathing harder, could hear the drumming of his heart. All the while she told herself to get up, get away from him, but this other notion was already in her head, deep in her gut and gnawing at her resolve: the two of them alone all day, closed inside the house, warm and dry and out of the rain.

How had she allowed this to happen? she wondered. It was as if another person lived inside her, with powerful needs and a will not her own. As she watched, her hand left her coffee mug and came to rest on his stomach, firm, wet, and warm. She watched herself brush the water slowly down his abdomen, breathing huskily at the sight of him rising beneath the terrycloth. She squeezed her thighs together, feeling a wetness starting, as his rough hand began caressing her cheek. While a distant voice screamed at her to stop, her fingers tucked quietly under the towel, into that rich black jungle of hair—

The telephone rang, and she jumped out of her chair, almost knocking him over.

"Ellen, let it ring," he said, moving in front of her.

Her heart pounded. Everything inside her trembled. They watched each other fervently, while the telephone kept ringing. Then her answering machine picked up.

"Go get dressed," she said, pushing off him. "Finish my barn."

She went around him to the counter and grabbed the phone from its cradle. The machine cut off. She took a breath, tried to stop her trembling as she said Hello.

"They know," Maddy told her.

Ellen's heart thumped against her chest.

"What are you talking about?"

"The police know what Randy wrote in my hand. They just left here."

She felt Neal come up behind her, press his hardness against her, his rough hand sliding around her hip, up under her T-shirt, electrifying her.

"Wait," Ellen said, turning away from him, holding up her hand to keep him back. "Did you tell them?"

"Tell them what he wrote? El, they already knew. One of them was there when it happened."

Ellen heard a car slowing down out at the road. She walked to the doorway of the living room, ducked her head and saw the blue police light on a car roof gliding past the window. She wheeled back into the kitchen and pushed Neal toward the bathroom, staring hard at him.

"They're here, Maddy. Jesus, what did you say to them?"

"I told them I *thought* Randy wrote 'Moreen' in my hand. And they patronized me. But they know what he wrote."

Ellen grabbed Neal's wet sweater off the washing machine, opened the bathroom door and threw it in. Her legs were shaking.

"Ellie, they're not interested in you," Maddy told her.

"Is that what they said?" Ellen was practically yelling now. She returned to the table and sat down in front of her coffee mug, trying to appear as if nothing were wrong. She smoothed her skirt with her hand.

"It's Neal they want," Maddy said. "Stop protecting him."

Ellen took a deep breath, reached across the table, and shut the window. Her whole body tingled.

"Listen to me," Maddy said, "I'm risking my goddamned life while I'm waiting for you to come to your senses. I'm terrified. Do you know what it's like to be here alone every night, waiting for that doorknob to turn?" Maddy's voice dropped suddenly. "You told him, didn't you?"

"What?"

"You told Neal that Randy wrote in my hand, I know you did."

"Maddy, you need to get a grip—"

"Don't you fucking tell me to get a grip. Neal has already made it impossible for you to go to the police without implicating yourself. Ellen Chambers, don't let him get you in any deeper. He needs to be put away."

The cruiser pulled up to the porch. Sugar Westerback was driving, his father, Wes, riding shotgun. Their side windows were rolled up and rain-spattered, and she was sure they couldn't see her inside. The wipers and headlights went off, then the engine.

"I've got to go," Ellen said, her voice shivering. "But it's important that I find Moreen."

Maddy said nothing.

"Maddy, just tell me where she is. I'm afraid someone might be after her."

"Jesus Christ, don't you get it?"

"What?"

"You're living with him."

Ellen slammed the phone on the table, and watched out the window as the car doors opened and the men stepped out, Sugar wearing his police uniform, Wes dressed in a khaki shirt and trousers, an outfit a game warden might wear. Ellen raised her coffee mug to her mouth. "The police are here," she called casually.

Inside the bathroom, the shower came on, as outside, footsteps clomped up the porch steps. Ellen tried to slow her breathing as she got up from her chair. She wondered how flushed her face looked. She scratched her fingers roughly across her scalp as she opened the screened door. Then she stood in the doorway so as not to invite them in.

The men climbed the steps slowly, despite the rain. Sugar stayed close behind his father.

"Hi," Ellen said as innocently as she could. She felt as if she had a light bulb glowing between her legs.

"Hope it's not too early," Wes told her.

"Just watching the rain," she said. "What's up?"

The two men stopped on the porch where the roof protected them from the deluge, both staring unabashedly at her shorn skull.

"Not a whole lot," Wes said. "I heard about the trouble this weekend. Sorry I was away."

"I don't begrudge you a break, Wes."

"We just need to tie a couple of things down," he said. "I wondered if I could talk to your nephew, ask him a thing or two about the incident. Inside, is he?"

Ellen knew she couldn't hesitate, yet in the moment she couldn't think of a way to deflect them.

"He's taking a shower," she said. "Want to come in?" She offered the door.

"If it's no trouble," Wes said, stepping inside on the throw rug. Sugar squeezed in behind him, although he was looking back at the barn.

Ellen walked to the cupboards, pretending nothing was wrong. "Can I get you coffee?"

"None for me," Wes replied.

"I wouldn't mind," Sugar said.

"Just made it," Ellen told them, taking a mug down, wondering if she was seeming too hospitable. Skirting the counter, she knocked at the bathroom door. "Neal, are you almost done? The Westerbacks are here, and they want to talk to you."

"Be right out," he said.

"He got caught in the rain," Ellen explained as she poured Sugar's coffee.

"A couple of questions," Wes said, looking up from the floor, where a pair of small puddles faced the kitchen chair she'd been sitting in. The telephone was there on the table, beside her coffee mug.

"Milk and sugar?" she said, wondering if they could hear the pounding of her heart.

"Yes, please," Sugar answered.

"Have a seat," Ellen told them as she opened the cupboard and took down the sugar bowl, along with a box of shortbread cookies. When she turned back, both men were looking down at the puddles.

"Neal?" she called.

"Coming," he said.

She brought the mug of coffee and sugar bowl to the table and set them down, then sat in a different chair, away from the puddles.

"Watch out for the water," Wes said, as Sugar sat in Ellen's chair, his shoes spreading the puddles around. The older man pulled a small notepad from his shirt pocket, the one Sugar had used during his interview, and he put it on the table along with two pencils. "You'd better get that ear looked at," he said to his son, whose lobe was inflamed around his silver stud. Sugar's eyebrows went up, wearily protesting the fatherly advice.

The bathroom door opened, and Neal came out wearing only his jeans, his wet sweater bunched in his hand.

"I don't have anything dry," he said to Ellen. He glanced up at the policemen. "I was trying to put in the last few windows before the rain."

"Quite a project out there," Sugar told him.

"I'll get you something of Scott's," Ellen said, taking the sweater from him. She went upstairs where she hung the heavy wool across the footboard of the bed, then found a Patriots sweatshirt in Scott's bureau.

When she came back down, the three men were talking about Neal's father, a subject Ellen had always steered clear of. It amazed her, how casually Neal could converse, leaning back against the counter, bare-chested, sipping a cup of black coffee, smiling and agreeing, while Wes went on about how much Jonathan had done for the community. Neither of them mentioned the fact that Wes had been the one who responded to Moreen's 911 call twelve years earlier and found Jonathan's body hanging from the barn's center beam—nor that it had taken him twenty minutes to reach the farm because he'd been casting for stripers down at Cape Neddick. She gave Neal the sweatshirt and he pulled it over his head.

"Now, I read your statements at the time of the accident," Wes began, thumbing back through the pages of the notebook.

"I should've done separate interviews," Sugar explained contritely.

"Next time you'll know," Wes told him. As Ellen sat down again, Wes pulled a small tape recorder out of his shirt pocket and set it on the table. "You mind if I use this?" he asked. "Saves a lot of writing."

Ellen shrugged. "Of course not."

He switched on the machine and faced it toward Ellen, then looked up at Neal. "We had a visitor last night."

"Out of her mind on something," Sugar interjected.

Wes turned his attention to Neal. "She told us that you had a little altercation with Randy a while back, at the wedding."

Hearing this for the first time, Ellen looked over at Neal as nonchalantly as she could manage.

"Hardly an altercation," he said, sipping his coffee. "We were drinking, words were exchanged, you know how it goes."

"You and Randy and that other one," Sugar said, sliding his finger across the table toward his notepad. "The Southern kid."

"I remember talking to Randy, can't say I remember anyone else," Neal told him with a perplexed frown. "You did say this girl was out of her mind."

Ellen glanced at Neal, misgivings flooding through her. She sipped her coffee so the Westerbacks wouldn't see her agitation.

"What was your trouble with Randy?" Wes said.

Neal smiled at the older man's persistence. "I don't know what the girl told you," he said. "I suggested to Randy that he start showing a little more respect for the family."

Sugar nodded. "That checks with her story. But she said you were all set to get physical. Matter of fact, I myself saw Randy coming out of the barn. He had a bloody finger, which he said he got from the barn, old nail or something."

Neal laughed a bit. "We shook hands. That's as physical as it got. I don't know how Randy cut himself."

The older man turned to Ellen. "You didn't see the altercation, did you?"

Ellen took a chance. "Neal told me he had a discussion with Randy at the wedding," she lied. "From everything I saw, they got along fine afterward."

Wes nodded thoughtfully, studying her. "You still believe Randy was the cause of Moreen's injuries?"

"I know he was the cause," she told him. "I hope that doesn't make you think that it was anything more than Randy's own carelessness that got him killed."

"I don't make you out to be a killer," Wes told her. "It sounds like you did everything you could to get Randy free once he was stuck."

"We all did," Ellen said.

Neal put his coffee mug down on the counter. "What we needed was a fire truck to pump out the pond," he said. "But the trucks were all at the parade."

Wes looked over at Neal. Ellen stared straight ahead, afraid to move her eyes, wondering why he had said that.

"I know you probably went over this already, but maybe you could tell me one more time," the old man said to Neal. "How long was it before you went down to check on Randy?"

Neal shook his head. "Scott went down to check, I'd say fifteen or twenty minutes after Randy went down with the crowbar. When he came up and said Randy was in trouble, we both went down and tried to pull him out, but we couldn't budge him. That's when Scott ran up to the house to call for help."

"And you don't have any idea how Randy's leg got cut?" asked Wes.

"Thigh," Sugar said, pointing to a spot on his own leg.

"Maybe when he was trying to pry the cover off the pipe?" Neal suggested.

Ellen felt Wes's eyes on her. She glanced over at him, and he gave her a fatherly smile. "Did your friend call you this morning?" His eyes dropped to the telephone on the table.

"Madeleine Sterling," Sugar said. "She was down at the pond that day."

"We asked her not to call you," Wes said, "but she wouldn't be much of a friend if she didn't."

"I guess she's not much of a friend," Ellen lied, trying to seem unconcerned. "I haven't heard from Maddy in a day or two."

"So you don't know what she told us, about Randy—?"

Sugar picked a cookie out of the box and started toward his mouth, then he stopped and balanced it on the rim of his coffee mug. "You know how Randy was writing in her hand," he said, "just before he drowned there? Remember how you said he probably wrote the word 'Moreen?' "

Ellen lifted her mug and sipped casually, though she knew that Neal's eyes, and probably Wes's too, were probing her.

"Well, I got a little different theory," Sugar said. He leaned his elbows on the table. "It didn't kick in at the time. He starts writing, and your friend says 'M,' then 'U,' then 'R'—then you told her it must've been an O—for Moreen—and I figured, 'Yeah, that makes sense,' you know?" He sounded as if he'd had too much caffeine.

"I don't understand," Ellen asked them. "Maddy said he wrote Moreen's name."

Sugar pretended to write in his palm. "'Moreen?' 'Murder?' Big difference." He looked over at Neal, who shrugged.

"First I've heard of it," said Neal.

Wes kept his eyes on Ellen. "Probably we ought to talk to Ellie alone," he said, glancing over at Neal. "Mind?"

"Not at all," Neal replied, pushing back from the table. "You need me, I'll be out in the barn." He made fleeting eye contact with Ellen, a slight, reassuring glance, then walked out the door.

Wes turned in his chair and watched him as he walked down the steps and headed toward the barn. "Building's comin along," he said.

"Neal's done a good job," Ellen replied.

"Interesting look to it," Sugar said.

Wes returned his attention to Ellen again. "You know, I can't honestly say what I'd do if I thought my daughter was living with someone who was a danger, and the law wasn't protecting her. Maybe resort to my own devices."

Ellen looked at him. "You might. I didn't. And I don't like your insinuation."

Wes gave her a patient smile. "We're not looking at you," he said. "But what do you think of the chances that Neal had it in for Randy?"

"Zero."

"Except that Randy and Neal already had words," Sugar said.

"We told you there was no problem between them," Ellen said, showing some impatience. "Besides, Scott and Neal were together the whole time at the dam. There's no way Neal could have done anything to Randy without Scott knowing."

"Didn't you say Scott came up to the house to get you?"

"Randy was already caught in the pipe then. Obviously." It struck Ellen how serious the conversation had become all of a sudden. Wes was studying her, the paternal sparkle gone from his eye.

"They could've been in on it together," Sugar said, popping another cookie into his mouth. "I mean Scott and Neal."

Ellen kept her eyes on Wes. "Scott liked Randy," she said. "When I wanted Randy arrested, Scott defended him. As a matter of fact, he was just about to take Randy in as a business partner."

"Coulda been a setup," Sugar said, chewing.

"Wes, that's ridiculous and you know it," Ellen said to the older man.

Wes shrugged. "People oftentimes don't want to believe anything bad about someone they love," he said. He watched Ellen while he drummed his fingers on the table for a second or two. Then he stopped and folded his hands around the tape recorder. "I've known Scotty since he was a youngster," he said. "I've seen him get into scrapes, and I've seen him get out of 'em. I watched him build up his business, and I watched him lose it. And you're right. I don't see him doing anything like this. How well do you know your nephew?"

"Well enough to know that he's not a murderer."

Wes sat back, examining his thumbnail. "He did have some trouble when he was a boy. Not only here, but over in Mass. I talked to the Greenfield police this morning." His voice had quieted somewhat.

"Oh, come on," Ellen said. "Who didn't get into trouble when they were young?" She tried to sound confident, but now she wondered what kind of trouble the old man was referring to.

Wes let out a troubled sigh, and Ellen thought he was going to stand. Instead, he clicked the tape recorder off. He leaned his arms on the table and looked over at her.

"I don't mean to scare you, Ellie, and God knows you folks don't need another expense. But I've got to say, I think Scotty might think about hiring himself a lawyer on this."

Ellen felt her stomach tighten.

Wes took a deep breath, let out a sigh, then put his hands on the table and pushed himself to his feet. "Is he at the gun shop today?"

"As far as I know."

"Okay if I take a couple for the road?" Sugar said, standing, stuffing his hand in the cookie box.

"Help yourself," Ellen answered. "Wes, I need to ask you a favor."

"We'll do what we can."

"Does Moreen need to know about this?"

"About—"

"That you're asking questions about Randy's drowning."

Wes took a breath and let it out reflectively. "Sooner or later somebody might need to talk to her, Ellie."

"Listen, if Moreen even thought there was a chance that Randy's death was anything but an accident, she'd never forgive us. I'm serious. I don't know what's going on with her, but she's finally getting some help. Wes, I don't want to lose her."

The old man nodded. "We'll do what we can," he said again. "But we may end up shooting this whole thing over to the state police, and you know I can't speak for them."

Sugar slipped in the water getting up. He caught the edge of the table to keep from falling.

"Careful," his father told him.

"Kill myself one of these days," Sugar said, and the men left the house.

When the policemen drove away, Ellen watched Neal come across the dooryard, wanting to see some sign of awareness that he'd just implicated Scott—or that he'd kept his altercation with Randy from her. But all she saw was Neal's confident stare as he climbed the stairs.

"What are you doing?" she demanded, suddenly feeling terribly vulnerable.

"Making a road for them."

"Yeah, that leads straight to Scott. That comment about the fire trucks being at the parade, which of course Scott knew perfectly well, since he's a firefighter—"

"I'm leading them away from us," Neal said calmly. "Scott's innocent. He's believable."

Above their heads, the rain slammed down on the porch roof. Neal smiled at her. "Ellen, stop torturing yourself. There's not a trace of evidence that can possibly implicate us."

She kept her eyes on him. "But now I have to wonder," she said, "if Randy's death had more to do with your getting revenge than protecting Moreen."

"Does it matter? Moreen is safe. Randy is out of her life."

Ellen stared at him, struggling to keep her composure.

"I did what I did for you," Neal said calmly. "I have no remorse about Randy."

"Maybe that's the difference between you and me," she replied.

He gave her a look long with skepticism. "Tell me honestly, Ellen: You didn't get the slightest bit of satisfaction watching him die?"

"It made me sick," she said quietly.

He kept her eyes for another second or two, then turned and walked back out into the rain. She pursued him, banging the door open, wanting to finish this, but words wouldn't come.

sixteen

Mainely Hardware came into town with a flourish: mass mailings, radio commercials, and a full-page newspaper ad in every newspaper within thirty miles. GRAND OPENING SALE, announced the orange banner that stretched across the quiet village street. A new electric sign jutted out from the old brick building where the wooden DESTIN HARDWARE sign had hung for fifteen years. The new sign shone garishly, even in the daytime, the little dancing handyman smiling down on the sidewalk, which was crammed with merchandise: wheelbarrows, riding lawn-mowers, gas grills, plastic trellises.

"Times are changing," Wes said as they drove by.

"Scotty don't care," Sugar said. "Bound to get more business out on the highway."

"Just what the world needs, more guns," Wes said. "Let's go have a chat with him."

Sugar glanced over at his father. "You told the wife Scotty ought to get a lawyer."

Wes smiled. "See, police work's like a game of poker sometimes. Little bluff here, little bluff there. You never want to show what you're up to."

Sugar looked over at his father. "If we're talkin murder, maybe we oughta turn it over to the big-hats."

"Keep your eye on the road," Wes replied.

Transforming the tire store into a gun shop took longer and cost more money than Scott had anticipated. It took a week to clean up the tires, oil drums, and assorted brake parts that had been stored in the building. The landfill fee came to almost two thousand dollars.

Then, while he had the showroom painted and carpeting laid, he began hauling over the contents of Jimmy Arthur's shop—unsold weapons and ammunition, an assortment of oak cabinets, shotgun racks, and glass display cases. On Wednesday Scott paid a couple of carpenters to build plywood counters and shelves. And he hired a bulldozer to start building his skeet and trap ranges outside. On Thursday and Friday the carpenters turned the garage into a shooting range. First they built a long plywood counter, three feet high, and separated it into six four-foot bays, with plywood dividers between each to deflect ejected casings. Above each bay they hung simple pulley clotheslines from which targets hung at the end of the range. To prevent ricochets, Scott had taken up the steel floor plates from around the garage and propped them up near the back wall, angled down forty-five degrees to deflect rounds into the mechanics' pits, which he'd half-filled with sand.

On Friday the first shipment of guns arrived, thirty-thousand-dollars' worth, and Scott bought a half-page ad in the Portland and Portsmouth Sunday papers.

NOW OPEN FOR BUSINESS

30% OFF ALL FIREARMS

CHAMBERS AND SON

GUN AND FIRING RANGE

When Scott saw the Westerbacks walk in, he was arranging boxes of shells in a display case.

"Nice-looking store," Wes said.

"It's gettin there," Scott said. Off to the right, behind a heavy door, came the muffled sound of gunshots. "Guy tryin out a forty-five back there."

Wes walked over to the counter. "You got somewhere quiet we can talk?"

"Now what?" Scott said, staying put. "Come on, Wes, you busted me over twenty years ago for growing a little weed. You think that qualifies me for murder?"

"I think you'd protect your daughter," Wes replied. "Father's bound to protect his child."

"Maybe I would have, if I thought Randy hurt her."

A rapid seven-shot volley interrupted them.

Sugar said, "Scotty, you know that friend of Ellie's, Madeleine Sterling?"

Scott swiped the air.

"She told us that Randy wrote something in her hand when he was stuck in the drain pipe."

"He wrote Moreen's name," Scott said, contorting his face. "Sugar, you were there."

"Except 'Moreen' don't start with M-U," Sugar said. "Not when I went to school."

"The way we spell it, Moreen starts with M-O. It's a type of wool."

"Scotty, the woman said 'M-U,' not 'M-O.' You know what I think? I think what Randy wrote was 'murder,' and Madeleine Sterling is covering up for somebody."

Scott shook his head. "That woman is crazy as a shithouse rat, just like she's always been."

"Believe me, Scotty, I'd like to put this one right to bed," Wes said. "But we got other problems too."

"Red flags," Sugar said.

"Ellie's claim that Randy kicked Moreen."

"That'd be motive," Sugar said.

"Which never happened," replied Scott.

"Not to mention the stab wound in Randy's leg."

"What, we stabbed him in the leg now? It's not enough we drowned him, now we stabbed him in the leg?"

"Never mind that the fire trucks that could've saved him were all off at the parade," Sugar continued.

"Oh, bullshit!" Scott yelled. "Those trucks are in the parade every goddamned year!"

"Now there's no need—"

"Ah, fuck you."

"Hey, hey! Don't be—"

"It's all bullshit—"

"Hey, Scotty—"

Wes turned to Sugar, holding his hand down to keep him cool.

"Scotty, just don't swear at him," Sugar said.

"Fuck you too, Sugar. You know me better than that."

"Just watch your language, that's all I'm saying." Sugar's glance met with his father's, then separated. "Anyway, I was there," he said to Scott. "I know *you* probably weren't involved."

"Hey, thanks a shitload."

"Fact of the matter is," Wes said, "it's your nephew Neal we're looking at."

"I was with Neal right from the start," Scott told them both. "We stayed together up top while Randy went down. When he didn't come up after ten minutes, I'm the one who went down after him. Then Neal came down with me and we tried to pull him out."

"But you don't know how he got stabbed? I can understand the cut on his shoulder—hesitation wound, it's called. You see them in suicides. But the cut in the thigh, that sure looks like a defensive wound, like he'd been in a fight."

Scott shrugged. "I told you what I know. Hey, the guy's drowning, he's got a knife in his hand, the way they flail around—?"

"I can see that," Sugar allowed. "But where's the knife?"

"Scotty, we're probably gonna have to drain the pond again," Wes said.

"Drain the fucking pond," Scott told them. "Do whatever you want to do. Just don't talk to my daughter about this. You make her think we had anything to do with Randy drowning, I'll have the both of you in court so fast it'll make your heads spin. I mean it."

"Like I told Ellie, we've got no plans to question Moreen right now," the older man said. He glanced over at Sugar, then lowered his head, rubbing his palms together nervously as if he had something more to say.

"Scotty, I don't really know a gentle way to put this," he began, looking up again.

"You're worried about upsetting me?"

Wes pressed his lips together. "You think there's any chance that Ellie and Neal—"

"What, Ellie killed Randy?" Scott smirked. "You guys really are fishing."

"I didn't mean that exactly," Wes said.

Sugar gave his father a curious look as the old man scratched at the back of his head.

"Scotty, do you have any idea why both Neal and Ellie would make it a point to tell me that both your fire trucks were busy at the parade?"

"What are you talking about?"

"Well, where you're in charge of the fire trucks—"

Scott cut in. "What do you mean, 'they made it a point'?"

"Trying to be delicate here," Wes said. He lowered his voice to a croak. "You ever hear of something called 'female midlife crisis'?"

The lines on Scott's forehead deepened.

Sugar's eyes held fast on his father.

"Let's put it this way," Wes said. "Suppose the tables were turned, and every day of the week Ellie left you at home with a pretty young woman, say, twenty-five or so. You work together hand-in-hand, you talk together, you swim in the pond when it gets hot, maybe have a drink or two in the afternoon. What time do you usually get home at night?"

"Wes, she's his friggin aunt." Scott spread his arms in disbelief. "Wes!"

The old man held up his hand. "I don't mean to offend, embarrass, whatever, but oftentimes a husband's the last to know."

Scott held his head. "He's our nephew. Jesus, Wes, what kind of people do you think we are?"

"Well, I'm sure you're right, Scotty. It's just funny that both of 'em made it a point to tell us that you were the first one to go down after Randy, and then, like I said, about the fire trucks." The old man shrugged his shoulders.

For a second or two, while gunshots knocked at the side doors, Scott just shook his head adamantly.

Wes turned to his son. "You got anything else you wanted to add?"

Sugar looked at him, dumbfounded. "Not to that."

"You guys," Scott said, still shaking his head. "I think you both need a long vacation."

"You got that right," Sugar said.

"You know us old cops," Wes added. "We see trouble around every corner."

"I guess," Scott said. "Ellie and Neal?" He waved off the idea with both hands.

Driving away in the cruiser, Sugar said to his father, "You really think there's something goin on there?"

Wes shrugged. "Who knows? Sometimes this work is a little like a game of solitaire."

"Always some card game."

Wes chuckled. "You know how it is when you get stuck and no matter how hard you stare at that deck you just can't make a play—?"

"I bin there."

"Well, best thing to do at that point is shuffle up the deck once or twice, then deal again. See if those cards look any different to you."

"Yeah, that's called cheatin'."

"It is indeed. In cards."

Sugar thought for a minute. Then he chuckled too. "I guess we just shuffled 'em up pretty good."

"Yes, we did."

Ellen stood under the clothesline, facing the barn, white bed sheets flapping around her shoulders in the clearing breeze. Several minutes earlier, when she had come outside with the laundry, the hammering in the barn had stopped. She had ignored the silence then, but now as she looked for Neal inside the long, shed-roofed addition, eleven brand-new windows winked back at her. The twelfth window opening gaped darkly, the last unfinished piece of the barn, and that's where she focused her gaze.

"I know where she is," the voice said.

Ellen jumped. Behind her, Neal pushed between the sheets and bath towels.

"Moreen?" she asked, bending nonchalantly for her laundry basket. "Where?"

He waited until she straightened and turned to look at him. Then he held her eyes intently with his own.

"My father's house."

They drove up Main Street, along the east side of the commons, then turned down Oak Street, where Ellen pulled over at the entrance of the deserted cemetery. They got out of her truck and walked through the iron gate, where weathered gravestones rose out of lush, wet grass that looked as if it hadn't been mown in weeks. Neal led the way alongside the whitewashed stockade fence until they were behind the church and their feet were soaked. Then he lifted up on the door in the fence and pulled it back on its one remaining hinge. The door croaked as it opened.

"Go ahead," Neal told her.

Ellen looked into the church grounds, to make sure they weren't being watched from the parsonage, the rear corner of which was visible to the right of the church—the downstairs living room and an upstairs bedroom. The Wings lived there now, Al and Louise and three of their five children. Al, a former church deacon, had taken residence in the parsonage in exchange for maintaining the property after Jonathan's death. Judging by the condition of the buildings and grounds, it was an arrangement that benefitted the Wings much more than the church. Neglected clapboards on both buildings showed graying grain beneath the scant film of paint. Roofs needed repair. Two window panes were broken and patched with cardboard and duct tape.

"Go on," Neal said, ushering Ellen through the stockade door and following close behind. As soon as they'd gone five or six steps across the deep lawn, the parsonage was obscured by the corner of the steeple.

Centered at the rear of the church, three stone steps led down to a black wooden door set in the foundation. Neal went down the steps past Ellen, taking a screwdriver out of his back pocket.

"Mo and I used to do this all the time," he said quietly, sticking the screwdriver between the jamb and the latch. "We'd sneak in for the communion grape juice."

He looked back with a glint as the door swung open. Ellen glanced nervously over her shoulder, then followed him in. He closed the door behind them, and they stood together in the darkness at the head of a long corridor. Ellen heard him sniff. At the same time, she detected the faint smell of smoke—cigarettes, candles. Then a small penlight came on in Neal's hand. He wrapped his hand gently around her shoulder, as he directed the beam to the gritty floor. "Go ahead," he told her.

"I'll follow you," she whispered.

He stepped out ahead of her, and they went creeping along behind the light beam, opening doors on both sides of the corridor, until they came to an interior room where the smoke smelled stronger. They went in, Neal shining his penlight at a long, rectangular table that had a mound of melted wax in its center. In a corner of the room, an empty potato chip bag lay on the floor beside an overturned, mostly empty liter bottle of Coke and another puddle of candle wax.

"Coke and potato chips. It's her," Ellen said. She lifted the bottle but was unable to detect the warmth of a recent hand. When she pushed her thumb into the soft candle wax, however, she felt heat.

Neal touched her shoulder, then gestured with the penlight to the door. She followed him out into the corridor where, a few feet ahead, he turned right into an intersecting corridor.

"Moreen?" Ellen called as they walked on, bypassing other rooms. At the very end of the corridor, Neal opened a blue door and stepped down a step to a concrete floor. Ellen waited nervously in the doorway while he shone the light around the small, dingy room.

To his immediate right, a wooden bin holding between two and three feet of coal stretched about twelve feet to the back wall. In the rear-left corner stood a black furnace, separated from the coal bin by a massive brick chimney.

"She's not in here," Ellen said quietly, but Neal went farther into the room and shone his light on the narrow, soot-gray plaster wall between the chimney and the coal bin. "What are you doing?" she asked, but when she saw him reach his hand up into the dark bay between two floor joists, she knew. It was the Indian tunnel, the secret, underground passage that connected the cellars of the church and par-sonage. Ellen stepped down into the room just as Neal tugged at some-thing with his finger, and the narrow wall jumped a bit. Now he squeezed his fingers between the chimney and the exposed edge of the wall and swung the wall out, revealing an arched, brick opening that reminded Ellen more of an oven than a passageway. Holding the wall open, he looked back at her, as if expecting her to step inside.

"I'm not going in there," she told him. He didn't argue. He simply turned away from her, ducked his head and stepped into the tunnel, taking the light with him.

"Neal?"

The wall swung shut. He stopped it with his heel. Ellen came closer and got her fingers inside, pulled it open again. The entire tunnel was arched and very small, two feet wide and only five feet high, if that. Because the floor was natural bedrock, it rose in places, lowering the ceiling even more.

"She's not in here," Ellen said, hanging back.

In response, Neal aimed the light at a loosely rolled sleeping bag just ahead of him. Ellen felt a weakness in her legs, a slight shivering.

"Christ, Mo," she said, and she ducked in, pushing her hip against the door to keep it from swinging shut.

"Is it hers?" Neal asked.

Ellen turned her head toward the opening and took a deep breath, preferring the ashen air of the boiler room to the sour, under-earth chill inside the tunnel.

"Wait a minute," she said, taking another breath to calm herself. Then she hunched her shoulders and moved in. When the wall shut behind her, she closed her eyes for a second, to stop the slight panic from muddling her mind. Then, taking the penlight from Neal, she stooped and picked up the sleeping bag, uncovering Mo's backpack and boom box.

She shook her head, exasperated, then raised the light and saw that fifteen feet ahead of them the tunnel bent to the right.

"Maybe she's up around the corner," Neal suggested.

"She's not," Ellen replied, wanting only to get out of there.

"She could be hiding in my cellar," Neal said.

Ellen looked back at him in the darkness. It was the second time he'd referred to the buildings as his or his father's.

"Only one way to find out," Neal said.

Aware that he was goading her, Ellen stepped over the sleeping bag and moved along, tossing the light beam out ahead of her while she did her best to ignore the spider webs that collected on the bill of her cap. Coming to the bend, she ducked around the corner and saw that the tunnel stretched out another forty feet, to the end. Here, underground between the church and parsonage, she suddenly felt as if she couldn't breathe. She started to turn back, but Neal was right behind her.

"Don't stop," he said.

"Neal—"

"We're almost there."

"Are you enjoying this?" she snapped, swinging away from him and proceeding on. At the tunnel's end, a single, wide pine board, she reached up into the cobwebs and found a small iron ring lying flat on the sill. She managed to stick her thumb into the ring and pull up on it. The door popped open on the right, only an inch, but the bright daylight angling in startled her. Ellen peered out into the cellar of the parsonage, the dusty casement window shining at her from the top of a stone foundation. She heard a noise above them: the ring of silverware against dinner plates.

Neal laid a hand on her shoulder, reached around her, and pushed the door open wider, exposing the black oil tank on their left, the wooden stairs off to the right, the spider webs that stretched between ceiling timbers.

"Are you claustrophobic?" he said quietly.

She grabbed his arm, squeezed it to quiet him. "I don't like to be closed in," she whispered.

"That's often called claustrophobia," he teased.

"She's not here," Ellen whispered. "Let's go."

"Hey!" a sudden voice called. "Didn't you make a pie this afternoon?"

Ellen jumped. Neal wrapped his arm around her chest to steady her. "Shh," he said in her ear. His hand dropped down to her breast. She grabbed his wrist, moved his hand back up.

"I thought you were gonna make a strawberry pie." It was Al Wing, up in the kitchen. They heard a chair scrape overhead, then a woman's muffled voice. Ellen could feel her heart pounding against Neal's forearm. He took the penlight from her hand, then stepped around her, out into the cellar.

She grabbed the back of his sweatshirt. "Mo's not here," she whispered. "Let's go."

"Well, Jeez, Louise," Al Wing said, raising his voice. "If I'da known I was supposed to get the strawberries, somebody should've told me. I'm not a mind reader, you know."

Neal reached back and took hold of Ellen's hand. He pulled her arm gently, but she twisted out of his grasp, remaining in the mouth of the tunnel. "Neal, I mean it."

"I want to make love to you here," he said softly. He stared at her, as footsteps crossed overhead.

"A simple matter of communication," Al Wing yelled, his voice much clearer.

"I'm going," Ellen whispered. "Give me the light."

He shook his head at her as he backed toward the stairway.

"Neal, I want the light," she said, stepping down onto the hard-packed cellar floor.

He held her eyes with a dark, seductive look, and the voice above them shouted, "Well, excuse me for trying to catch a little friggin fish to put in the freezer!" Neal blurted a laugh, shattering the silence.

Now they stood perfectly still, eyeing one another as the house hovered silently around them. Ellen looked up the stairs, listening for the latch of the door at the top, prepared to turn and run back into the tunnel, light or no light. The sudden bang of a cupboard door shot goosebumps down her arms.

"Great!" Al Wing shouted. "Now we're out of Oreos?"

Neal smiled at her, though the darkness in his eyes hadn't changed a bit. "Tell me what's the matter," he said.

"Just give me the light."

He held the penlight away from her, teasing, but the grin had left his face. "Tell me."

"I said no!" She pushed him hard enough to make his eyes flash with anger. Then she spun away and ducked into the tunnel without the penlight, rushing off into the darkness.

★   ★   ★

They didn't speak on the drive home, until Ellen pulled into Destin Plaza, saying, "I've got to drop off some work at Wool 'n' Things." Because it was after five and the store was closed, she drove around the rear of the plaza and parked beside the dumpster.

"I'll be out in a minute," she said, stepping out of the truck and lifting the bag of wall-hangings from the back, five small seascape tapestries for which Ingrid would pay her twenty dollars apiece. Ellen unlocked the back door with the key Ingrid had given her when she'd relocated to the Plaza twenty years earlier.

Returning to the truck, Ellen shifted into gear and pulled around the front of the building, then drove across the parking lot, trying to ignore the fact that Neal was sitting with his back against the passenger door, staring at her.

"Can you not do that?" she said finally.

"Do what?"

"Leering. I teach school in this town."

"I'm not leering. I'm admiring your haircut."

"I'm wearing a hat."

"Okay, I lied. Actually, I'm thinking that this is my last night with you and wondering if you're even going to kiss me goodbye when I leave."

"No, I'm not," Ellen said. "But since it is your last night, I thought we'd pick up some tuna steaks to barbecue for dinner."

"Tuna steaks."

"Yeah." She gave him a firm look.

"I'll continue leering, if you don't mind."

Without humoring him, Ellen stopped the truck near the Beecham Supermarket on the other side of the plaza, far enough away from the other parked cars to avoid running into anyone she might know. She turned off the key and pulled three twenty-dollar bills from her pocket. "Would you get the fish?" she asked. "I need to pick something up at the drugstore. And buy a couple of lemons and some barbecue sauce. We also need paper towels and a jug of milk. And Scott's out of pickles—kosher dills. Spears, not whole."

Neal kept staring.

"No?" she said.

"Put your money away," he told her, and he popped open the door. "Fish, lemon, barbecue sauce, milk, and paper towels, right?"

"And kosher dills, for Scott."

As soon as he got out of the truck and started walking to the store, Ellen pulled the truck over to the pharmacy. She hurried inside and bought the first thing she saw—Rolaids—then hurried back outside.

Keeping her eye on the supermarket next door, she went to the public telephone in front of the pharmacy. She used her calling card and dialed Massachusetts directory assistance, asked for the Greenfield Police Department. When a Corporal Philbrook answered the phone, Ellen identified herself as Sergeant Beecham, with the Destin Police. "Chief Westerback called you a day or two ago, asking about a Neal Chambers," she said.

"I remember," the corporal told her. "I spoke with your chief."

"He wanted me to follow up," Ellen said. Shielding her eyes from the lowering sun, she watched the people entering and leaving the supermarket. "What we're interested in," she continued, "is any anec-dotal information you might have on Mr. Chambers. Maybe incidents you remember, or crimes where he might've been a suspect—?"

"That's your boy," the corporal said. "He was only in town for a couple of years, you understand. Then he went away to school and never came back—someplace in Maine, I believe—after DYS cut him loose."

"DYS?"

"Department of Youth Services," he said, as if Ellen should have known. "They had him in Springfield, locked up in a twenty-day assess-ment unit."

"For what?"

"Jeez, you name it. Fires mostly. Trouble is, we could never make any of the charges stick. When his mother lawyered up, like I said, DYS had to cut him loose. At least they convinced her to send him out of town. I think it was Maine he went, maybe Vermont."

"We were led to believe the state placed him in a boarding school after his mother was hospitalized with a nervous condition."

"Best of my knowledge, the mother was never hospitalized. Even if she had been, the state wouldn't have had the authority to send him out of state. Technically, the boy never did a thing wrong. But I'll tell you this, if you could build a case against someone on the basis of how much quieter things got after he left—"

"All set?"

Ellen turned. Neal was standing behind her, holding two grocery bags in his arms.

"Okay," she said in the phone. "I'll see you when you get home."

She hung up and tried to read Neal's face in the fleeting glance they exchanged, as she took one of his bags and started walking to the truck. "I didn't see you come out of the store."

"I went through to the pharmacy," he explained. "Who was that?"

"Scott," she said, walking around to the driver's side, to avoid his eyes. "I called him at the shop. He loves tuna."

"Is he going to join us?"

"He said he's busy, but he'll try."

When Ellen pulled into the dooryard, Scott's Mercedes was already there. Her heart fell.

"Wow, he really does love tuna," Neal said, giving her a look.

It was the way the car was angled toward the corner of the barn, as though he'd almost run into it. Ellen knew he'd been drinking; she also knew the Westerbacks had been to see him. Before she turned off the engine, she heard a volley of gunshots. She gave Neal a quick, ominous look.

He shrugged and opened his door. The gunfire stopped. "Over there," he said.

Standing beside the pump house, Scott appeared to be loading a handgun. When he spotted them, he turned away, raised his arm and fired six rounds toward the pond. With each shot, Ellen could see flames spewing from the muzzle. She got out of the truck.

"Thirty-eight special," Neal said.

Scott he turned back and stared at them.

"How's it going?" Neal called.

Scott bent down and grabbed a handful of shells, popped open the cylinder and began feeding the revolver.

Ellen looked at Neal. *Something's wrong.* The look Neal returned was thick with arousal. He started walking toward Scott.

"Neal?" she warned softly, but he kept walking. Ellen followed, trying to clear her face of emotion.

While Scott watched them coming toward him, he raised a half-liter bottle of whiskey to his lips and drank, then set the bottle down beside his feet. Then he turned and fired another volley, each shot churning Ellen's stomach. She blocked her ears as she got closer, trying to read meaning in Scott's actions, at the same time deflecting Neal's backward glance with a look of her own: *He knows.*

"That for me?" Scott said to her when he stopped shooting. She realized he was talking about her haircut.

"No, me," she answered. "I couldn't stand it long anymore. Ready for grilled tuna?" Even her tone of voice was a lie. "We've been out looking for Mo."

"I liked it long," Scott said as he bent and picked through the spilled box of shells at his feet, then reloaded the small revolver. Off beyond the pump house, about a hundred feet away, he had propped an eight-foot sheet of plywood and drawn a figure of a man in black marker.

"We think she's been camping out in the old church," Neal said.

Scott turned to him, snapping the cylinder back in place. "Hey, you wanna knock off a few rounds?"

Neal regarded the gun for a moment and, with a shrug, took it into his hands. "Colt Detective Special," he said, obviously feigning admiration. But perhaps it wasn't obvious to Scott. The way Ellen felt, everything was obvious, every gesture transparent. "We shooting any-one in particular?"

Scott looked off at the target with a murderous smile and said, "I haven't decided yet."

The revolver was black, with a blue sheen, and no bigger than Neal's hand, from hammer to muzzle. He wrapped his palm around the grip, gave Ellen a reckless grin. "Block your ears," he said as he straightened his arm.

Scott turned his back on him, bent for his bottle, and brought it to his mouth, all the while studying Ellen fatefully. He didn't flinch when Neal started firing the handgun. Neither did Ellen shrink from his gaze, although she pressed the heels of her hands against her ears and winced with each shot.

When Neal had emptied the cylinder, Scott held out his hand and Neal dropped the revolver in it.

"Your turn, El." Scott's stare on her intensified. "Can I still call you El? I mean, you haven't changed your name, have you?"

She stared back at him, bright with anger.

"No?" he persisted.

"I'm going to light the grill. I'll let you know when dinner's ready," she said, leaving them both, walking up the gravel drive but wanting to run to her truck and drive out to the highway and keep driving. As she reached the porch, the sound of pistol shots pounded like fists on her back, and she could no longer resist the fear. She ran up the steps, tore open the screen door. The telephone was ringing. She picked it up.

"*Asphyxia,*" said Maddy, over the line.

Ellen walked away from the window.

"Did you hear me?" Maddy asked.

"Maddy, I can't talk to you now." Unnerved at how dark the kitchen was, nevertheless, Ellen left the light off, not wanting the house to seem inviting.

"How did Randy die?" her friend demanded.

"You know how." Ellen paced across the floor, legs weak and trembling. Six rapid gunshots slapped off the clapboards. Then it was silent.

"He drowned," Maddy said. *"Asphyxia."*

Footsteps clomped up the steps. Ellen felt the kitchen shake. Neal opened the door and stepped inside, giving her a long, fervent look.

"Hold on a minute," she said to Maddy, and covered the phone with her hand, waiting for Neal to leave. But he remained at the door, staring seductively, while outside the windows another volley of shots pounded a rhythm in sync with her heart.

She waited for him to leave. Finally he crossed the kitchen to the refrigerator, opened the door, and grabbed a bottle of Pabst, held it up to Ellen as if offering it—or maybe he was toasting her. She turned away and heard the screen door slam. When she saw him walk down the porch steps, Ellen carried the phone through the living room. "Tell Mo I need to talk to her," she said to Maddy as she climbed the stairs.

"Moreen's fine. Listen to me—"

"Don't tell me Moreen is fine. She's my daughter, and I want to talk to her."

"What about your mother?" Maddy persisted.

"What about her?"

"How did she die?"

"You know how."

"She choked to death on a piece of candy," Maddy said. "That's called 'asphyxia.' "

Ellen went into her bedroom and shut the door, pulled the shade down over the window, then peeked through the side to watch Neal walking toward the pump house. She turned away from the window.

"And Scott's parents went through the ice in Carrier Pond. They drowned."

"Maddy, some drunk ran them off the road."

"Some drunk who was never caught. The car was stolen, with no fingerprints but the owner's. They were robbed of their breath—all of them—just like Neal's father."

Three gunshots rang out. The bedroom reverberated.

"Even his own mother—"

"Neal's mother committed suicide!" Ellen interrupted. "Jesus, Maddy, she stuck her head in the oven and gassed herself."

"Right. Also called asphyxiation."

Ellen scratched her fingers across her short hair. "Look, I can't talk now."

"I just talked to Jeff Hamill," Maddy said. "He was the school psychologist when Neal went to grammar school here."

"I know who he is."

"He hasn't seen Neal in fifteen years or more, but he said the kid was a textbook example of severe conduct disorder."

"Which is?"

"No. Which *does*."

The window shade jumped with a puff of wind. Ellen's heart hammered.

"Ellen, he's a born sociopath."

"Those were Hamill's words?"

"His words? He said he'd never met a ten-year-old who scared the shit out of him the way Neal Chambers did."

Ellen breathed a loud, exasperated sigh.

"Ellen Chambers, listen to me. You might think this is just some kind of kinky affair—"

"Maddy, you're obsessing about this. You're paranoid—"

She heard a click in the phone and thought Maddy had hung up on her. "Christ," she breathed, knowing she'd have to call back and apologize to her friend.

"Just tell your house guest this paranoid lady's bought herself a gun," Maddy said, still on the line. "Drop it in a conversation where it seems appropriate."

Ellen frowned.

"El, are you there?"

"Hold on."

Ellen returned to the window, pulled back the shade and looked out over the pump house, the pasture and barn. Neither Scott nor Neal was anywhere in sight—and the shooting had stopped some time ago.

"Ellie, what's the matter?"

"Hold on."

She took the phone with her and went out the bedroom door. The hallway seemed much darker than it had only minutes before.

She stopped at the head of the stairs and called down softly. "Hello?"

"You're scaring me," Maddy said. "What's going on?"

"I'll call you back."

Ellen switched off the phone and started down the stairs.

"Scott?" she called, a tremor tightening her voice. "Neal?"

She walked through the living room and was about to enter the kitchen, when her heart jumped. She turned.

Scott was sitting on his desk, the bottle of whiskey in his hand, the telephone and revolver sitting side-by-side at his elbow.

"The cops stopped by my shop a while ago," he told her. "Wes and Sugar Westerback." He nodded his head as he watched her, dangerously passive.

"Is Neal outside?" she asked.

Scott laughed quietly. "Don't you want to know what they wanted?"

She looked at him fearfully as he raised the whiskey bottle to his lips again. She turned and hurried through the kitchen, threw open the screen door, looked left and right, then spotted Neal walking out of the barn with his sleeping bag rolled under his arm, his tool belt flung over his shoulder. He pitched the things in the back of his truck, as though he were leaving, but then he went around to his passenger door and opened it. "You'd better come with me," he said to Ellen.

She heard Scott's footsteps behind her. Her heart pounded.

"Ellen, come on," Neal told her.

The screen door banged open behind her. Ellen turned, saw Scott standing crookedly with the .38 in one hand, his whiskey bottle in the other. She felt the railing post dig into her back. Scott took a step forward, and the door slammed shut behind him. He chuckled a little.

"This been going on awhile?" he asked.

"Scott, you need to put that away," Ellen told him, trying to make eye contact. "You've had too much to drink."

He glared at her, then he looked out at Neal. "So, did I tell you two about the cops coming by the shop today?"

"Scott, please, would you give me the gun?" She moved cautiously toward him.

"Somehow," he said. "Somehow—" He waved the gun out toward Neal and fired a deafening blast.

"Stop it!" Ellen cried, as a chip flew from a barn board two feet above Neal's head. Seeing that Neal was unhurt, she turned back to

Scott and stepped in front of him, in front of his gun, her chest pounding crazily.

Scott's eyes brightened. "Somehow," he said, "the cops think that I had something to do with Randy drowning."

"They were here," Ellen told him. "They questioned us too."

"Us, huh?" He started nodding again.

"Ellen, come with me," Neal called to her. He was standing against his truck with his arms folded, in full view of Scott, who walked past Ellen to the head of the steps.

"Don't do this," Ellen said to Scott, reaching again for the revolver, but he pulled it away from her and laid it up beside his ear.

"Neal, just go," she said.

"I'm not leaving you here with him."

"That's good," Scott said. "Because before anyone goes anywhere, we've got a number of things to talk about, the three of us."

Ellen looked back, saw Neal stick his hands in his pockets and start walking toward them. "Neal, get out of here!" She stepped in front of Scott again, ready to grab the pistol if he moved it off his shoulder.

Neal stopped within spitting distance of the porch, staring at Scott with a sharp glint in his eye. "You have something to say to me, Uncle?"

Scott glared down at his nephew. Ellen could hear him breathing.

"Neal, I want you to go," she said, as calmly as she could. "Please."

"Oh, turn my back on him?"

"I took you in," Scott said to Neal. "You ate my food, you slept in my house—"

"I wouldn't sleep under the same roof as you," Neal replied with a satisfied smile.

A chill of nausea swept through Ellen. She looked at Scott and saw apprehension tug at his drunkenness.

"Scott, please," she said, "let me talk to him."

"Talk all you want. Go with him, for all I care. Ellie, what the Christ are you doing to me?"

"Give me the gun." She held out her hand.

"You want the gun?" He shouted at Neal. "*You* want the gun?"

He dropped his arm, aiming straight at Neal's chest.

"Scott, don't!"

She saw Scott's eyes glaze over, as he breathed noisily through his nose. Then he stepped back, found the deck chair with his leg and sat down hard. He tossed the revolver on the glass tabletop, slammed the bottle down beside it. "Go talk."

Ellen checked him for a second, then turned back toward Neal.

"I'm staying here with Scott," she told him. "You need to leave."

"Is that really the way you feel?" asked Neal.

She looked back at Scott again, who seemed to be chuckling to himself. Then she walked down the steps, passing Neal and going to his pickup truck, where she got in the open passenger door. Neal kept his eyes on Scott for another few seconds, then turned and walked around to the driver's side. When he got in and shut the door, Ellen looked straight at him.

"You want to know how I feel?" she said. "I'm scared to death."

"Scared of what?"

"Why did you pretend you didn't know about what happened between your mother and Scott?"

Neal stared straight out the windshield. "Why bring up the past?"

"Because I think you're obsessed with revenge, that's why. And I want to know why you ever came here."

Neal turned to Ellen, his dark eyes gleaming. " 'Obsessed with revenge.' Interesting choice of words. To be honest, I never knew exactly what happened the day my father died—until now." For the moment, Neal's eyes left hers. Then they returned. "Tell me this: Did you ever forgive my mother?"

Ellen watched him adamantly. "Yes, I did."

"And you forgave Scott?"

She looked off toward her house, where Scott was slumped in the deck chair, sullenly watching them. "It took a long time," she said, "but, yeah, I forgave him."

Neal laughed. "If that were true, *Aunt Ellen,* we wouldn't be sitting here having this conversation."

Her stomach clenched. She wanted to lash at him with her fist. Instead, she pushed the door open and got out of the truck.

He started the engine. She closed the door, then looked in his open window.

"When does it stop, Neal?"

"When does what stop?"

"Your *justice!* When does it stop?"

The way he smiled, she could tell he'd been waiting a long time for that question.

"When all the twelves are in line," he said, and backed his truck away from her.

She kept her eyes on him while he stopped and shifted, then started to drive away. "That's childish, cryptic bullshit!" she yelled.

He gave her a smile as he drove slowly out of the yard. Then he pulled out on the road and was gone. Through the dust of his departure, Ellen turned back to the barn, all the bright new windows gazing blindly out at the pasture.

"How does it feel, Ellie?" said Scott, sitting on the porch. "Feel pretty good, turnin the tables on me? I've got to admit, I never saw it coming."

Bristling Ellen came toward him, climbed the steps and went into the kitchen. She threw open the cupboard, pulled down her bottle of tequila, and spun the cap off . . . then stopped. She bowed her head and heaved a deep, shivering sigh. She shoved the bottle to the back of the counter, then went to the table and leaned on it with both hands, feeling the heat from her chest rising up over her face. *When all the twelves are in line.* Neal's words came back to her. She looked out the window at Scott sitting with his back to her, his arms folded, the bottle of whiskey and revolver standing in front of him. Her heart would not stop pounding.

She spun off the table, punched out the door, and grabbed his .38 off the table, taking the box of shells too.

"Honeymoon over?" Scott said.

She went down the steps and marched to her truck, intending to leave, go anywhere, maybe to Maddy's, just leave. She threw the door open and slid inside, then leaned across the seat and popped open the glove compartment, stuffed the revolver and shells in.

That's when she heard the cars turn in, and she watched in her rearview mirror as they passed behind her—the blue Destin Police cruiser in front, followed by a dull black Dodge Colt.

"Here it comes," she heard Scott say. "Here comes the knife in the back."

Stealthily, she closed the glove box, then sat up and checked her face in the mirror, her jagged hair, her wild, dilated eyes. She took as deep a breath as she could manage and stepped out of the truck. The Westerbacks got out of their cruiser at the same time.

"Comin or goin?" Wes said to her. He seemed slower and heavier than he had in the morning, but no less animated, as he approached the porch.

Caught without an answer, Ellen pretended not to hear. "I didn't expect you back so soon," she said, falling into step beside him while she glanced back at the man in the station wagon.

"Business must be good," Wes said to Scott as they climbed onto the porch. "You look like a man of leisure sitting there."

"I figured if you guys were gonna be throwin my butt in jail, I might as well enjoy a couple of hours of freedom," Scott answered.

"Actually," Sugar said, "this visit doesn't have anything to do with what we talked about before."

While they spoke, Ellen watched a man get out of the Dodge Colt. He was maybe five-nine, dressed in a wrinkled tan suit over a white shirt and black tie, and he approached the porch in a distinctly business-like way. He looked to be forty, his face was round and his brow and beard heavy, his lips wide and pulled down in a permanent frown. He reminded Ellen of a Neanderthal.

"Detective Dave Gallagher," Wes said, introducing the man. "Dave's with the state police."

"Beautiful farm," the detective said, his frown unchanged.

"This is a personal call?" Scott remarked. "If so, beer's in the fridge."

Gallagher rested his shoe on the bottom step of the porch, a brown wingtip, impeccably polished. "I'd like to ask you some questions, if you've got a minute or two."

"Fire away," Scott told him. "Whatever's wrong, we must be responsible."

Ellen noticed the worried glance Wes cast toward Scott. As much as the old man liked to play close to the vest, his feelings for Scott showed through.

Gallagher checked a small notepad in his hand. "Mr. Chambers, could you account for your whereabouts, say, from one until seven o'clock this morning?"

"At one this morning I was in bed," Scott replied.

"And you have someone who can verify that—?"

Scott looked at Ellen and said, "Would you like to verify that, dear?"

Ellen looked at the detective. "We were in bed. Why?"

"Is there anybody else who can vouch for your whereabouts?"

"Neal around?" Wes asked Scott. "I don't see his truck."

"Neal is your nephew?" Gallagher consulted his notepad.

"Scott's nephew," Ellen said. She saw Sugar's less-than-furtive glance at his father. "He's been staying with us for a few days, rebuilding our barn."

"Sleeping here?"

"That's right."

"And he slept here last night?"

"Yeah."

The detective wrote in the notepad. "Mr. Chambers, could you describe your relationship with a man named Raymond LaFlamme?"

Scott looked at Ellen as if she had asked the question. "I borrowed money from him, and I paid him back. Why?"

"How about Randy Cross?"

Scott lounged deeper in his chair. "These guys didn't tell you?"

"I'm conducting a separate investigation," Gallagher said pleasantly.

"Randy Cross was married to our daughter," Scott said. "He drowned in our pond. He caught his arm in the drain pipe and we couldn't get him out."

Gallagher kept his pen moving. "You had a business relationship with Randy, as well?"

"He was coming to work for me in my gun shop. I was going to make him a partner eventually."

"I was referring to your relationship with him in his capacity as Ray LaFlamme's employee."

Scott looked at Wes again. "Am I permitted to ask what the hell he's doing here?"

"I don't see why not."

"Address your comments to me, please, Mr. Chambers," Gallagher said.

"Okay." Scott stared over the table at him. "What the hell are you doing here?"

Gallagher nodded without a trace of emotion. "If you'll answer a couple more questions, I'll tell you what you need to know, okay?"

Wes gave Ellen a cautious peek. His meaning was clear.

"Detective, should we have a lawyer present?" she asked.

"That's up to you and your husband," Gallagher answered cordially, with a glance at Wes. "I like to keep things informal. However, if you'd like, we can drive to the police station and continue our discussion there. You could have your attorney meet us."

"I don't need a goddamn lawyer," Scott said. "Randy was one of LaFlamme's part-timers. I gave Randy the money I owed the old man."

"How much was that?"

"A lot."

Gallagher's pen waited on his notepad.

"Around a hundred fifty thousand."

"And Randy drowned here the day after you paid him the money, is that correct?"

"Exactly," Scott intoned.

"Your son-in-law drove a Jeep Cherokee, is that also correct?" Gallagher said.

"That is also correct, sir."

Wes interrupted. "You folks expect Neal back anytime soon?"

"Was the Jeep parked here during the time Randy was caught in the dam, as well as afterwards, while the pond was being drained?" said Gallagher, precisely.

"Hey, last I knew, there was nothing illegal about borrowing money from a man and paying him back," Scott said, his voice growing louder.

"Yeah, but Scotty, they're all missing, LaFlamme and his bodyguards," Sugar said. "So's the money."

Scott stared at Sugar. As did Gallagher. "Excuse me," the detective said, "could I have a word with the two officers?"

The Westerbacks walked off the porch, and Gallagher accompanied them to their police car. After a minute of tense conversation, Wes and Sugar got in the cruiser and drove off, and the detective returned to the porch, where he stood a few feet away from the rail with his arms folded.

"Mr. Chambers," he said, "Ray LaFlamme and some of his employees turned up missing this morning. Your name is on a receipt that was discovered in Mr. LaFlamme's office. The receipt was signed by Randy Cross, but it looks like Randy never delivered the money to LaFlamme."

"Okay, Lieutenant, Sergeant, whoever you are," Scott said, pulling himself upright in his chair. "You want to know if I drowned my daughter's husband and took my money back, right? The answer is, 'A, I love my daughter, and B, I'm not a goddamned murderer *or* an idiot.' If you're asking whether I had anything to do with LaFlamme and his people disappearing, I already told you: I was in bed all night."

Gallagher's mouth widened, from jaw to jaw. "How about your nephew, Neal?"

Scott looked over at Ellen.

"He was here all night," she said flatly.

"If both of you were in bed all night, how do you know for certain what Neal did after you fell asleep?"

Ellen felt her husband's eyes linger.

"Scott goes to bed before I do," she said, the heat rising to her face. "Neal and I stayed up until two o'clock, talking. When I got up at six, he was already working on the barn."

"So who's to say he didn't go out for a drive between two and six in the morning?"

"I would've heard him leave," Ellen said. "I didn't sleep very well."

Gallagher looked over his notes again.

"I've read the police report, including the complaint that Randy physically abused your daughter—"

"Which he did not," Scott interjected.

"Together with the knife wound and certain other information," Gallagher continued, "I wanted you to know that we'll be opening our own investigation into your son-in-law's drowning."

He stuck his hand inside his lapel, then approached the porch and set two business cards on the rail. "I'd like you to stay in touch with me if you hear anything or maybe think of anything that might help. I'd also like to ask that, until the investigation's over, you'll notify me before going out of state."

Scott snorted. "I'll tell you right now, if I'm your chief suspect, your investigation's a long way from over."

Gallagher gave a nod. "I'll be in touch," he said.

The knocking was incessant—knock and scrape, knock and scrape, knock and scrape—as slowly the tops of two scrawny pine trees came into focus, outlined by a flat, slate-blue sky and three dim stars winking down.

Rooftop shivered with the cold. He rolled to his left and saw Jesus lying beside him, one-armed. The absolving limb lay on the deck between the console and the pilot seat, attached by a long yellow rope to Rooftop's weight belt.

Rooftop sat up slowly and looked around, saw that his boat had run aground in a wooded cove, although he had no idea where he was or how long he had slept. He realized that the pistol was no longer in his hand, which was crinkled, cold, and pink. He looked around the cove for houses but saw only rocks and bristly evergreens, a low, dark ocean, and high, darkening sky.

He wasn't totally sure if he was alive, indeed, if this was the same earth he had intended to leave. If it was, he knew that he was not the same man who had left it.

He eased his body to the edge of the platform and lowered himself down onto the rocks. Then he swung the boat around and pushed it out till he was waist-deep. He pulled himself back onto the deck, raised himself to his feet, and walked quietly to the console. He started the motor, then shifted into gear, heading out for deeper water, to get his bearings.

seventeen

Ellen drove straight to the church, barely able to think. She parked her truck behind the high school and walked briskly across the green commons, keeping her head down, lifting it only to keep an eye out for Mo's black Cherokee. It was just after eight, and overcast; street lights on both sides of the commons cast Ellen's faint shadow left and right in the grass. She carried a small disposable flashlight and flathead screwdriver in her hand, and a scrap of grocery receipt and a pen in the pockets of her jeans. If Moreen wasn't in the church, Ellen would leave a note, warning her that the police and apparently some other people were looking for Randy's missing money—and that Neal knew her whereabouts.

As she turned down Oak Street, outside the range of the streetlights, she tried to assure herself that if Neal had been responsible for the disappearance of Ray LaFlamme and his men, it was because he was protecting Moreen, as he had been when he killed Randy.

But if she believed that, Ellen wondered, why was she running through the cemetery?

Pushing through the stockade gate, she hurried across the overgrown church grounds and down the cement steps, then jammed her screwdriver in the door jamb and pried open the door, the way Neal had shown her. Closing the door behind her, she flicked on her flashlight in the darkness, illuminating the long corridor. The church hovered over her in a deep silence.

"Mo?" she called quietly. Her echo made the damp walls shimmer with life. "Honey, I have to talk to you."

She stood and listened but heard nothing, so she walked briskly down the corridor, then turned right at the main intersection and continued to the end. Inside the boiler room, she walked past the coal bin, squeezed in beside the huge chimney, reached up and pulled back the iron ring. She felt the latch give, and the right side of the wall swung out an inch from the bin. She pulled it open and ducked into the arched brick tunnel, shining the light out ahead of her, at Moreen's things—sleeping bag, backpack, boom box.

Kneeling, Ellen gathered up the sleeping bag and backpack, but gave up on the boom box when she found the handle was broken. She turned back to the tunnel door, reached for the latch and pulled, then ducked out of the tunnel, into a pair of open arms.

"What are you doing?" cried Moreen.

Ellen gasped, chest pounding.

"Mom, I don't want you here!"

"Come on, we're going home," Ellen said, walking ahead.

"Mom," Moreen cried, pursuing her. "I need my things."

"You can't stay here," Ellen said. "Neal knows where you are, and I don't trust him."

Reaching the back entrance, she slapped the thumb-latch with the flashlight, pulled open the door, and walked up the steps, grateful for the open air.

"Would you stop?" Moreen persisted, following her outside. "I'm not going with you."

Ellen pushed through the stockade gate and turned, Mo's backpack and sleeping bag stuffed in her arms. "Listen to me," she said quietly. "The police came to our house. Did you take some money from Randy's Jeep?"

"Why are you asking me that?"

"Because the men who were looking for the money are missing. The police think they were murdered."

"I don't know anything about any money."

"Then what are you hiding from?"

"You!" Moreen glared wildly, then ripped the backpack from Ellen's hands and headed off through the cemetery.

"Mo, wait," Ellen called, but Moreen started to run, quickly dissolving into the shadows of gravestones and oak trees. A dog started barking. Then another. Ellen lowered her head and walked to her truck with Mo's sleeping bag, never once looking back to see if she was being followed.

*   *   *

Maple trees turned fat green circles in her headlights, two boys labored to peddle their mountain bikes up Ramsey Hill, a white Corvette squealed out of the convenience store in front of her, but Ellen barely noticed any of it. She was thinking of a Saturday morning a long time ago, trying to remember exactly when Moreen had stopped coming into her bedroom in the mornings. She wondered if it was a gradual thing, or if it had happened suddenly at about the time of Jonathan's suicide. Surely if it had been an abrupt change, Ellen told herself, she would have noticed.

This particular morning must have been a Saturday, she realized, because Scott had gotten up early for work, but she hadn't had to. Nevertheless, she got out of bed as soon as Scott left the house and started stripping the sheets off the bed—when she felt someone's eyes on her. She turned and saw Mo standing in her doorway wearing her plastic Dracula teeth, which means it would've been around Halloween of that year, a week or two after Scott's affair—and Jonathan's death.

"Oo, you scared me," Ellen said. "Coming in?"

But Mo just stood there sleepily. Her hair was redder then, as Ellen remembered. In fact, she could even recall that Mo had on her purple flannel nightie.

"Did you have a nightmare?" Ellen asked her.

Moreen continued looking in. It wasn't exactly a sleepy stare; it was more a scowl, a sober, worried look, and Ellen was afraid it was the emotional fallout from finding Jonathan's body that she was seeing on her little girl's face.

"Mo, lamb, is everything okay?"

Now Ellen remembered the way they stood there watching each other; the way Moreen's vampire teeth clicked, the intensity of her eyes; finally the way Mo sighed, as though she'd just figured something out for herself.

"You sure?" asked Ellen. What she remembered most clearly was the great relief she felt when Mo turned out of her doorway and went quietly away.

When Ellen got home, the empty bottle of Harwood's was on the kitchen counter, along with two empty bottles of ginger ale. She stepped into the living room, where Scott sat in his recliner, the remote control in his right hand. Television channels blinked rapidly by.

"Can we talk?" she said.

His eyes didn't leave the television. "Not a whole lot to say," he told her. "I guess I got what I deserved. It took you a bunch of years, but you got even with me. I hope you're satisfied."

She walked past him and sat on the couch, so she could at least see his face. "I found Mo," she said, wanting to allay any suspicions that she'd gone after Neal. "She won't come home. She won't even talk to me."

Scott ignored her.

"The only one she'll talk to is Maddy, apparently."

The channel-surfing stopped. Scott muted the volume and looked straight at Ellen.

"Mo's in therapy," Ellen explained.

With a sour laugh, Scott turned his head, glaring at the dark window.

Ellen leaned forward on the couch. "Scott, I have to tell you something."

"Hey, load it on."

"When Randy got caught in the dam—"

"Yup."

"—I don't think it was an accident."

Scott chuckled to himself.

Ellen sighed, annoyed with his drunkenness. "Scott, Neal told me he was going to do it."

Scott turned slowly toward her, a deep scowl on his brow, while a Pepsi commercial played silently between them.

Ellen shook her head helplessly. "When he told you the dam was leaking, it wasn't. Neal was setting the whole thing up. To kill Randy."

Scott sat back in the recliner. Slowly, a broad, closed-mouth smile dawned on his face, and his eyes shut. "Ellie, why are you telling me this?"

"Because I'm going to turn him in," she said. She realized her intention almost simultaneously with hearing the words tumble from her mouth. A tingling rose up the back of her neck.

Scott's eyes opened again, gravely. "You're planning to tell the cops you knew what Neal was up to all along? Do you want Moreen to find out?"

"Of course not. But I'm afraid, Scott. I think Neal set everything up—to get back at us."

Scott paused and was quiet for what seemed like a full minute. Then he grinned again, broadly dismissive. "I think maybe you're right," he said. "But you can't go to the cops."

"I don't know how else to stop him."

Scott chuckled again, a soft, bitter sound. He paused thoughtfully, then shook his head with a bright look of defeat.

"You can't go to the cops," he explained, "because I'm the one who pushed Randy's arm in the pipe."

Instantly silence settled over the room, broken only by the whisper of the waterfall and the hum of the television. Ellen stared at her husband, desperately looking for a sign that he was lying. To scare her? Perhaps to taste a little revenge of his own?

"Neal told me all about Randy kicking Mo," Scott continued. "He told me about the hysterectomy and he said that I wasn't supposed to know. He told me not to let on. With you ranting and raving, if there was any suspicion, the cops would look at you. When they saw you were innocent, they'd write it off as an accident."

"Neal said the same thing about you," Ellen said.

"That's why I stuck up for Randy," Scott said. "That's the only reason I offered to take him into the business with me, to erase any suspicion."

The amount of information coming at Ellen was overwhelming, and her mind reeled. Even as she marveled at the precision with which Neal had manipulated them, she felt a wave of sickness engulf her. She held her breath until it passed. "Scott, did you take the money?"

"Now don't you think that would've been a little obvious, dear?" Scott said, his voice weighted with rancor. "Yeah, I gave Randy a bag full of money and had him sign a receipt. But I did not murder him and take my money back. Ellie, just how dumb do you think I am?"

She stared at him, feeling her rising blood color her face.

"Nope, Neal got his revenge, all right. A few days' work, a little slap and tickle, and he drives into the sunset with a cool one-fifty. And we go away for murder." Scott laughed again, as if he admired Neal's cunning. "See now? That's why you can't go to the cops."

Ellen could barely say what she was thinking. She forced her mouth open, heard the words come out. "Scott, what if Neal's not finished with us?"

Scott turned back to the television, hiked up the volume, and resumed changing channels. "Believe me, Neal won't be back," he said with fierce satisfaction. "He got everything he came for."

Ellen took a quick breath to respond, but held the poisoned air in her lungs.

Scott reclined his corduroy chair almost flat. The channels kept changing.

"Scott—" she began.

"Just don't tell me you're sorry," he told her.

The next day Ellen tended her sheep and gardens and worked on her tapestries. Scott went to work early in the morning without saying goodbye and he came home well after midnight, smelling of whiskey. In bed they lay side by side like mannequins, staring up at the darkness until Scott started to snore. Finally, when it was well past four o'clock, Ellen rose from the bed, electric with energy.

She gathered her sweatshirt and jeans off the floor, went down to the bathroom to put them on. When she was dressed, she started the coffeemaker and wrote a note to Scott. *I'll be gone for a day or two. Please try to find Mo and feed and water the sheep. Be careful.* She brushed her teeth, washed her face, and filled her thermos with coffee. Then she fit her cap on her head, grabbed a box of Cheerios from the pantry, snatched the photo of Neal's barn off the refrigerator, and went out to her truck. Up above the hill, the sky was already glowing yellow behind the treetops. She opened the glove compartment, reached her hand inside to feel the cold steel of Scott's .38, then she started the engine.

Before she drove away, she went back in the kitchen, picked up a pen and added to her note: *Love, Ellen.* She wondered if her handwriting looked forced.

eighteen

Ellen got into St. Johnsbury at three in the afternoon, by which time she was hungry and deeply tired. She stopped at a McDonald's, where she used the bathroom and washed her face with cold water, then she pulled up to the drive-through, ordered a salad and a large black coffee. While she waited for her food, she studied the map the helicopter pilot had drawn for her, and she ate while she drove, continuing north on Route 91 until she left the highway in Barton, heading west. According to the pilot, who sprayed for farmers all over the state and had recognized the unusually shaped barn, she was looking for Route 14. In ten minutes she found it and turned south.

Of course Neal knew she was coming. Where else would she go? The road he'd made for her led directly to this place. She thought of the revolver in her glove compartment and felt a weak jolt of dread.

When the blacktop narrowed, crowded in by thick woods on either side, she drove for another five minutes until she crossed over a bridge. A sign on the abutment said BLACK RIVER. She checked her odometer and went another half mile, then she saw a mostly hidden dirt road that rose straight into the woods on her right. It felt right. She turned in, and the road curved around a gigantic boulder, then pitched uphill. As she shifted into low and started up, the gravel giving way to shale, she wondered why she had come in the first place.

Did she expect an explanation at gunpoint? A confession? An apology? Yes, all of that, though she knew she'd never get it.

So could she shoot him?

Before she had time to answer herself, the vista yawned open before her. She hit the brakes.

It was a painting, a dreamer's farm, cradled in a basin of the richest greens and surrounded by ancient, round-topped hills that seemed to pile one on top of the next, far into the graying distance. By the looks of the pasture, the farm had been unattended for years. Unmown grass, three feet high, waved gently in the cool of the afternoon, spotted with buttercups. Small yellow butterflies hopped along the tops of the flowers all the way to the tree line, where birch and pine saplings crept in from the woods.

Nestled in the center of the basin, the white farmhouse and barn stood side by side facing east, seeming to pay tribute to the hills. The barn was identical to Ellen's, with its arched windows and high white silo rising off the peak. In fact, from her vantage point, Ellen could easily see the resemblance to a church.

There was no truck in the dooryard nor any sign of human habitation. No highway sounds, no planes passing overhead. Except for the ubiquitous chirring of insects, everything was perfectly quiet.

Ellen lifted off the brake and let the white truck roll quietly down the hill, her approach seemingly unnoticed amidst the elaborate workings of the field. When she stopped her truck in front of the house, the sun was already down behind the barn. She could feel a bright chill in the air, a harbinger of clear August nights, wide open windows. But the thought of sleeping in Neal's house made her shudder.

Opening her door and stepping out of the truck, four dark windows stared out of the house at her, each one hung with lace curtains. She considered taking her revolver with her, but decided against that. In a way, she wished Neal would just open the door and come out, so they could have the conversation. In another, she prayed he wasn't there.

"Neal?"

The old shingles absorbed her voice like rainwater. She looked for footprints in the gravel but saw no clear impressions. Nor was there any sign that anyone had been there recently. A pair of power lines came down the drive attached to old leaning poles, but no phone line accompanied them.

Ellen walked to the porch, climbed the three stairs and pulled the screen door open. She peered through the glass into the kitchen then turned the doorknob.

"Okay, I'm here," she called as the door opened. But the building hovered in silence.

Almost certain that she was alone, Ellen let the screen door close quietly behind her. The house smelled as if it had been left to itself for a long time, the scent of unused cupboards, of a damp cellar penetrating the floorboards. Yet the kitchen looked perfectly clean, and this made Ellen nervous. Corners of the ceiling were free of cobwebs; the old pine floor looked freshly waxed.

If Neal wasn't here now, it was clear that he'd been here recently— and he'd be back. The only question was how long he'd make her wait.

She opened the refrigerator, found it empty. She opened a cupboard and saw a stack of white china plates on the bottom shelf, cups and saucers on top, all neatly arranged. In the cupboard beside it, juice glasses and drinking glasses stood in perfectly aligned rows. She ran her finger over the counter, picked up no dust. She bent and threw the lower cupboard doors open, one after the other, each one empty.

"Neal?"

Her shout raced through the empty house. She walked into the next room, a small parlor that contained an overstuffed sofa and a Boston rocker. On the opposite wall was a stairway, painted salmon pink. She turned on the lamp and walked up, each tread creaking underfoot. As she suspected, she found two neat bedrooms upstairs, each with beds made.

She walked down to the kitchen again and opened a white door over a set of brown cellar stairs, old but freshly painted. She flipped the light switch and the red dirt floor lit up below. She refused to be afraid. Hiding in a cellar like some troll was not Neal's style. If he was here on the farm, Ellen knew he would have already made his presence known. Then what was the point in going down? None, she told herself, but what was the point in not? She descended the stairs as casually as if the cellar were her own, and when she reached the floor she saw the furnace, the water heater and pump, exactly as she'd expected. But when she turned to go back upstairs, the door above her moved. Her chest clenched with fear and she ran, taking the stairs in a blinding panic and throwing doors open, practically running down the porch steps. Light was dying outside, the surrounding greenery darkening. She ran to her pickup truck, intending to leave. But the barn . . .

Stepping away from her truck, she wandered to the arched front doors, curious about how exactly he had replicated the barn where his father had died. She pulled the doors open and caught her breath.

Not a speck of sawdust, no sprig of hay, not even a boot print. Yet everything was exact, from the roof rafters to the hayloft to the twelve stalls that lined the left and right shed walls, even to the heavy, hooked chain hanging from the low center beam. The lumber was as crisp and sweet-smelling as the day it had been milled.

"Neal, if you're here, we have to talk!"

The barn swallowed her shout. Once again Ellen's rational voice told her to get in her truck and drive away as fast as she could. But she listened to the voice of her heart, which told her that a connection had been forged between them. Even if their love-making had been pretense, she knew they'd been joined at the heart the day Neal's father had killed himself.

She walked out of the barn and gently latched the doors, then went back inside the farmhouse, stopping first at her truck to get the box of Cheerios she'd brought along. Inside the kitchen she set a chair against the door, facing the rest of the house, and ate the dry cereal with her hand until the room darkened.

Then she waited. She set her sneakers flat on the floor. She leaned her elbows on her knees, rested her cheeks in her hands. Above the somnolent buzzing of insects in the field, she listened to a lone cricket chirping. Too early for crickets, she thought sleepily, as she closed her eyes and followed its sound down a warm, inviting river . . .

. . . She gasped and jumped to her feet, pacing the floor before she was fully awake. The night pressed against the windows, throbbing and chirring as if the entire farm had conspired to make her sleep. She looked at the wall clock, saw that it was twenty past ten. She went to the sink and splashed cold water on her face.

Determined to wait him out, she climbed the stairs and tore the blankets off the bed, then took them outside and crawled into her truck. She locked both doors, then cranked the windows down a half-inch. Took her pistol out of the glove compartment. Laid it on the floor. Curled up under the blankets. Closed her eyes.

Madeleine Sterling kept her pistol under her pillow—not the pillow she slept on but the one beside it—the one her eight-year-old Siamese, Cleo, slept on. The weapon was a Wilkinson Sherry, a demure, nine-ounce automatic with a blue trigger and slide, and a black cross-hatched stock. The remainder of the pistol was bright, gold-framed steel that reminded Maddy more of an elegant cigarette lighter than a firearm.

They had gone to bed at eleven-fifteen, she and Cleo, but only after Maddy had performed her nightly ritual: checking the locks on her windows and doors, and looking through closets and under her bed.

Finally she'd slid between the satin sheets, placed her pistol under Cleo's pillow, and turned off the lamp. Although the room was stuffy with the windows closed, and the ocean sounds muted, she was lulled to sleep by the cat's steady purring.

The instant Cleo stopped purring, Maddy opened her eyes. The room was dark, but she could tell the Siamese was sitting upright; she could see the cat's eyes like twin black pearls collecting the gloomy light from the venetian blinds. Maddy lay there, all heart. She did not breathe. As quietly as she could, she slid her hand under the pillow, under Cleo's weight, until she found her pistol. Ordinarily, the cat would have thought it an invitation to play, but Cleo remained intent.

Maddy wrapped her hand around the stock, but she was afraid to take the gun out from under the pillow. Everything inside the room was so incredibly still. She moved her eyes, not her head. But without her contacts or glasses, all she could see were shadows upon shadows and the dark glow of her window blinds across the room. When she saw a blacker shadow move across the blinds, she tried to convince herself it was only the hawthorn branch waving outside. But the longer Maddy stared, the more she saw.

In the corner of the room, her clothes tree came to life—as if a human figure were separating from the jerseys and jeans: legs from legs, arms from sleeves. Cleo sat rigidly on the pillow, her weight pressing heavily on the back of Maddy's hand, while the pistol in Maddy's palm grew clammy. Suddenly the cat sprang from the pillow. Maddy heard her paws hit the carpet. She felt the small vibration through the mattress, of the cat moving under the bed.

Now Maddy watched the human shape step in front of the window. And she watched it come closer.

This is real, Maddy told herself, her hand frozen on the pistol. *It's finally, truly happening.*

A gunshot awoke Ellen, and her revolver was in her hand before she opened her eyes. Chest pounding, she raised her head just enough to see out her side window. The sky was solid white. A gust of wind shook her truck, and Ellen heard the bang again: not a gunshot, but the screen door slapping against the jamb.

She set the revolver on the seat and pulled herself upright by the steering wheel. Judging by the activity of the swallows that flitted about

the silo, she guessed it was around seven in the morning. But was it
Friday or Saturday? The screen door banged again, and she looked over
at the porch, half-expecting Neal to come walking outside. It was Saturday; she'd driven all day yesterday, which had been Friday. And she
was alone here. She stepped out of the truck and stretched her long
bones, feeling surprisingly well rested.

     She went into the house and used the bathroom. Washing her face,
she peeked out at her truck through the lace curtain. Swallows continued to dart about the barn roof, undisturbed. She came back into the
kitchen and opened the cupboard to get a glass of water. The glasses—

She stepped back.

—had been rearranged.

Both drinking glasses and the smaller juice glasses were now assembled in two uneven rows—six on the left; five on the right.

The meaning was clear. Neal had left her house on Thursday, his
eleventh day, without finishing the windows in the addition—

—*which meant he had returned on Friday.*

Ellen swung down from the porch and ran to her truck, started the
engine and fishtailed in his dooryard, speeding up the drive, retracing
the country roads on instinct. In less than five minutes, just outside of
Barton, she pulled up to the gas pumps at a country store and ran inside.

"Do you have a phone?" she asked the elderly man at the cash
register.

He raised his brow in a bemused sort of way and, without hurrying,
reached below the counter and set an old black telephone in front
of her.

"It's long distance, I'll pay you," Ellen said. "It's an emergency."
She dialed her house, desperate to hear Scott answer, but after four
rings the message machine came on.

"Could I get a large black coffee to go?" she said to the man who
sat watching her. He turned on his stool and pulled a Styrofoam cup
out of a slender plastic bag. When Ellen heard the beep on the telephone, she said, "Scott, if you're there, pick up."

Her flesh tingled, imagining Neal sitting in her empty kitchen listening to her frightened voice. The old man poured coffee in the cup
and snapped a plastic lid on the top, watching her all the time.

"Scott, find Moreen and keep her away from the house. I'm on
my way."

She pushed down on the cradle, lifted up again, dialed Maine directory assistance and asked for the number of Chambers and Son Gun Shop. The old man slid a pad of paper to her, set a freshly sharpened pencil on top. "I need gas," she told the man. "Would you fill it?"

While she dialed, he lifted himself off his stool and walked around the counter. To her great relief, Scott answered the phone at his shop. "Did you find Mo?" she blurted after his hello.

"How the hell would I have found her?" He sounded as though he'd been drinking already.

"Scott, Neal's after us," she said. "He knew that Mo was hiding in the church. He'll find her again."

"And if Neal is after us, that would be my fault, right?"

"Jesus, I don't care whose fault it is. This is serious!"

"Like I told you, Neal got exactly what he came for," Scott replied. Then he hung up the phone.

"Scott!" Ellen yelled. She pushed down the cradle and dialed Maddy's number, but got the machine.

"Mad, you've got to find Mo," Ellen said. "Tell her not to come to your house, not to go anywhere. Then call the police and have them pick her up. I'll get there as fast as I can. Maddy, you've got to do this."

Ellen took her coffee off the counter and went outside. The store owner had pumped eleven dollars' worth of gas in her tank. She reached in her jeans pocket, pulled out some bills.

"This should cover everything," she said, giving him an extra five.

The man moved slowly, pulled the nozzle from her truck and shut off the pump, while Ellen screwed her gas cap back on. Then she got in her truck and peeled away.

The owner of the inn across from Maddy's house stared down from his ladder as the old maroon Bonneville pulled up to the curb. It was dented along the right side, as though the car had been rolled; two rear windows were covered with duct-taped plastic wrap. "Great for business, really improves the neighborhood," the man muttered, dipping his paintbrush in the can. The girl stepped out of the car, the same young, sloppy broad who'd been coming every other day for the past week.

"She's got a driveway, use it!" he yelled. Never mind that the woman's own little howdy-mister sports car was blocking it for some stupid reason. The girl glanced back, then turned away as though she'd never heard him and walked across the street to the cottage.

"Fine, ignore me, I'll have you towed." Though best not push it, he thought, she might turn on him. You never knew with these people. In fact, it was hard to tell who was crazier, the nuts who came here all the time or the so-called psychologist they came to see. It wasn't bad enough that his guests had to look at her dark little cottage with so much ivy crawling over it you could barely see the windows, but now the loonies were parking on his curb. He heard the girl knock at the front door of the cottage. And knock. And knock.

"Oh, for God's sake," he said. When she knocked again, he laid his paint brush on top of the can and turned around to yell, but now she was at the side of the cottage with her face pressed against the window glass, moving her head up and down like a cat.

"That's it," he said, climbing down. But as he stepped off the ladder, he turned to see the girl racing right past her car and on up the middle of the street, like a wild woman. "Goddamned lunatics," he muttered, and ambled off to call the police.

The long bands of yellow tape danced in the sea breeze. Ellen sat on the curb across from Maddy's cottage with her cap pulled down, watching the men entering and leaving through the front door, feeling as if she might never be able to stand again. She could not come close to fathoming the depth of her guilt.

Down at the bottom of the street, the ocean hummed restlessly, as official-looking vehicles came and went. Already, police cars lined both sides of the street. Two cruisers from the York Police Department, one from the York County Sheriff's Department, two from the Maine State Police, as well as three or four unmarked wagons and SUVs that belonged to the lab men. Mostly Ellen kept her eye on the dull black Dodge Colt that was parked two houses up from Maddy's cottage—beyond sight of even the police tape. The detective sat inside with his back to his door. Moreen sat opposite him, her arms folded.

"Twelve, in what sense?" Wes Westerback asked again. He was sitting on the curb beside Ellen, his notepad balanced on his knee, while Sugar stood facing them both, leaning against the cruiser with his arms folded.

"I don't know, twelve everything," she explained. "Twelve-volt battery, twelve-gauge shotgun, twelve months in a year . . ."

"Twelve men on a football team," Sugar added.

"The dimensions of the barn are in multiples of twelve; he put

twelve windows in each side," she explained. "He told me he was
going to do this."

"Kill your friend?"

"Not in those words. But I should have known. I *did* know."

"Ellie, what words did he use?" Wes asked gently. The smell of
his spicy aftershave was an odd comfort to her.

"I don't know exactly. He said he was going to finish the barn in
twelve days."

"I wouldn't have taken that as a threat."

"He talks in code. He teaches you the code." She thought of the
drinking glasses.

Wes nodded in a kind way, keeping his eyes on her.

"I think he killed my mother and Scott's parents," she continued.
"They all died the same way his father did. His mother too.
Asphyxiation."

Sugar pushed himself off the car, giving his father an urgent look.
"Want this on tape?"

Wes shook his head.

"Asphyxiation," he repeated, nodding thoughtfully. "I handled your
mother's death—and I was first on the scene when Scott's folks'
drowned, but I never made anything of the coincidence. As far as I
recall, nothing appeared suspicious. Just terrible accidents. But you're
saying he's taking revenge for his father's hanging himself by asphyxiat-
ing the people closest to you and Scotty?"

His tone of voice said he didn't necessarily share her suspicion.

Ellen sighed wearily. "Neal holds Scott responsible for destroying
his family, so he's destroying our family. Is that so hard to believe?"

"Well," Wes said patiently, gesturing toward Maddy's cottage,
"Madeleine Sterling wasn't family. And she wasn't asphyxiated. She
died of a bullet wound, which right now looks like it was self-
inflicted."

Ellen turned away in frustration.

Wes leaned forward on the curb. "Ellie, did Neal have anything to
do with Randy drowning in your pond?"

"No." She refused to meet the old man's stare, knowing that she
couldn't tell him what she knew about Randy's drowning without
implicating Scott in the murder. She pictured Neal and imagined a
coyote picking off a flock, working systematically, patiently, from the
outside in to the center.

"What worries me," she said, "is that Neal has finally shown his hand. Now he's committed. Now he's going to show us how smart he is."

"How smart is he?" Sugar asked, but before she could answer, Detective Gallagher approached.

"Thank you, officers," he said to Wes and Sugar. "I'd like to ask Mrs. Chambers a couple of questions now, if you don't mind." He patted the trunk of the Westerbacks' cruiser, signaling them to leave.

Behind him, Moreen's Bonneville turned out of the road, and Ellen jumped to her feet. "I told you I wanted to see Moreen when you finished with her."

"Your daughter's headed home, you can talk to her there," the detective replied.

Ellen laced him with a glare. "Moreen doesn't live at home. You just let her get away—and her life is in danger."

The detective gave her a patronizing, seemingly disinterested frown. "Who is it you believe is endangering her?"

"The same person who murdered Maddy."

Showing no emotion, he pulled a notepad from his suit coat pocket. "From the evidence collected so far, we believe that your friend took her own life."

"If you're so sure it's suicide," Ellen replied, "why send a homicide detective?"

"I recognized your daughter's name when the call came through," he explained. "The decedent was present at the death of your son-in-law—who is also peripherally connected with the missing men from Old Orchard Beach. And now there's your message on Miss Sterling's answering machine this morning. That's a lot of connections."

"Detective, I think we've got a serial killer on our hands," Sugar said.

Gallagher ignored him, keeping his eyes on Ellen. "I assume you're referring to Neal Chambers, your nephew."

"Neal Chambers killed Maddy," Ellen told him.

Gallagher nodded thoughtfully. "Before we get off on a tangent, let's operate under the assumption of available facts and see if we can rule out the possibility of suicide. Tell me about your friend Madeleine. Are you aware of any previous suicide attempts?"

"None," Ellen said. "Even if Maddy wanted to kill herself, which she did not, she would never have shot herself in the head. She was particular about her appearance."

"I see."

"Besides, if she wanted to kill herself, she had a small pharmacy in her medicine cabinet."

"Oh? Any illness that you know of?"

"No."

"Financial difficulties?"

"Maddy had more money than God."

"Issues of guilt?"

"None." The way Gallagher glanced up at her, Ellen wondered if she had answered too quickly.

"How about problems with men?" he went on.

"Yeah, she was terrified of Neal Chambers."

"Did he give her some reason to be afraid?"

Now Ellen could feel Wes's eyes on her, too.

"Maddy knew what Neal was up to," she said.

"What did she know, exactly?"

"That he was here to destroy my family."

"And how was he doing that?"

"He murdered my mother. He murdered Scott's parents. He wants to kill everyone we love. And you just let our daughter get away."

Gallagher glanced at Wes, who shrugged slightly.

Ellen expanded her chest. "Look, is it that hard to make a murder look like suicide?"

"To experienced investigators, frankly, yes," Gallagher said. "In this case, the decedent has a single bullet wound to the side of her head. The bullet is the same caliber as her weapon, her weapon is found in her hand, with her prints and no others. There's no sign of a struggle, either on the body, her clothing, or the bed covers. There's nothing disturbed anywhere in the house, although she had cash in plain sight and a significant amount of jewelry in unlocked boxes."

"Neal Chambers is certainly intelligent enough to place the gun in her hand and clean up after himself. He's not stupid."

"Okay," Gallagher said. He paused a moment, as if reluctant to continue, but he went ahead just the same. "Without getting into details, we can be certain that the decedent was sitting upright in her bed at the time of death, with her reading lamp on. That much we know; it could not have been staged after the fact."

"He could have killed her, then propped her up."

Gallagher shook his head. "Blood dispersion. Your friend was alive and sitting up in bed when the bullet entered her skull."

Ellen turned away.

"We also know that she kept the firearm under her pillow," the detective continued. "And because we can fairly accurately pinpoint the time of death at three-fifteen in the morning—two independent reports from neighbors who were awakened by the gunshot—we're able to put together a scenario."

He paused, as if to give Ellen a chance to stop him; she didn't.

"In order for this to have been a homicide, we'd have to assume that Madeleine was sitting up in bed—not trying to defend herself—while this man, whom you say she found terrifying, talked her into handing him her pistol, which he then held an inch from her head and fired." The detective stopped, as if the unlikeliness of the scenario spoke for itself, while Ellen sat numbly, trying to force the picture from her mind. "We have no evidence of a struggle."

"Neal Chambers killed Maddy," Ellen maintained.

Gallagher shrugged. "How did he get in? There's no sign of forced entry. The doors and windows were all securely locked. The only way anyone could have gotten into that house is if she let him in herself. You tell me: Would Madeleine have let Neal Chambers in?"

Ellen's hands tented around her mouth, the sudden realization numbing her. Tears distorted her vision, but she could see Wes scowling, as though waiting for her to speak. She knelt up and dug her hand into her jeans pocket, pulled out her key ring. Her voice barely escaped from her mouth.

"I let him in," she said to Wes.

Gallagher gave the older man a look.

"I have Maddy's house key," Ellen explained. "He must have taken it and copied it."

"Bingo," said Sugar.

Gallagher folded his lips inward, a speculative expression. He turned to the younger Westerback. "Excuse me, gentlemen, but at this point, all we have on our hands is a suicide. As such, the York Police are handling it. If it rises to a homicide investigation, then it falls under state auspices, in which case I will conduct the investigation. Is there a reason the Destin police force is present?"

"We're not here in official capacity," Wes said.

"Exactly," Gallagher replied.

"But because Ellen and her family live in our town, we need to learn whatever we can, so we can provide protection if we have to," continued Wes.

Gallagher furrowed his brow, then turned back to Ellen.

"You and your husband have both told me that on Wednesday morning, between one o'clock and six, when Ray LaFlamme and his bodyguards disappeared, no one left your house and no one came to your house. There were just you, your husband, and Neal on the premises, is that right?"

"Yes," Ellen replied, without hesitation.

"And you and Scott stayed in bed together until morning."

"That's right."

"Where did Neal sleep?"

"Neal always slept outside, either in the pasture or in his truck, if it rained."

"So it's conceivable that he could have left for an hour or two and come back, and you wouldn't have known?"

"It's possible," Ellen acknowledged.

"And you also feel that Neal was responsible for your friend Madeleine's death."

"I know he did it."

"As well as the deaths of other relatives."

"That's right."

Gallagher nodded. "So how is it you're so sure that Neal had nothing to do with your son-in-law's drowning?"

Ellen sat like a stone under the eyes of the men. Gallagher didn't make her answer. He closed his notepad and stuck it in his pocket. "Is your husband at his shop?"

"This has nothing to do with Scott," Ellen said.

"Oh, I'm going to talk to your nephew too," he said. "I'm going to keep talking to all of you. Because no matter how your friend died, I think there's a definite connection here to your son-in-law's death. And I believe that when we find the missing money, most of our questions will be answered."

"This is *not* about money," Ellen said.

"Rule of thumb," the detective replied. "Murder's almost always about money, or it's about sex."

From the corner of her eye, Ellen saw Sugar look in her direction. Gallagher waited, giving her a long invitation to reply. She didn't.

"Make sure you let me know next time you decide to go out of state," he said, then turned and walked across the street, to the cottage where Maddy had died.

Early the next morning Ellen was awakened by the sound of the Boston Whaler rolling into the driveway. She stepped out of bed and looked out the window, realizing by the silence that the waterfall had stopped again. She got dressed and went downstairs, opening her door as Rooftop Paradise ducked around the back of his van with a blue dive bag slung over his shoulder.

"I've been asked by the state police to drain your pond," he said, glancing at the porch but not meeting Ellen's eye. Despite the way he hunched, he looked enormous in his wet suit.

"It's almost dry season," she said. "If you drain the pond now, they'll leave the floodgates open for the rest of the year, and the pond won't have a chance to fill up again. I'll be hauling water till next April."

"Wasn't my decision," Rooftop said, hoisting his bag on his shoulder. "It's a small pipe—take a couple of days to drain. Maybe you got some barrels you want to fill now."

Ellen sighed. What bothered her more than the thought of hauling water all winter was the way he avoided looking at her. No mention of his recent late-night visit, no acknowledgment that anything unusual had happened between them.

"Rooftop," she said—feeling slightly ridiculous saying his name—"do you have any idea where I can find Mo? I've called anyone who might know, but no one's seen her. Either that or they're just not telling me."

For a moment he didn't speak. Then he said, "Moreen doesn't seem to want me in her life."

"Then you've seen her—?"

Obviously uncomfortable with the conversation, he started walking toward the farm road.

"Can you at least tell me if she's okay?"

"Just fine, according to her," he replied, continuing on.

"Please?"

He stopped.

"If you see her again," Ellen implored, "would you please tell her that it's very important that she call me?"

The giant turned and peered at her through his magnifying lenses. "I don't mean to sound uncaring, Mrs. Chambers," he said, "but I'd just as soon not have any more to do with this family."

nineteen

The remaining days of the week passed slowly, with a kind of silence that seemed to be fed by the drought that had settled over the Northeast. Ellen tried to fill the cavernous void of Maddy's death by staying as busy as she could, but hard as she tried, she could not keep the awful thoughts away. Maddy's attempts to warn Ellen about Neal—and Ellen's refusal to heed her warnings—had created a tension-filled gulf between the two women just before Maddy's death that stood out in bitter contrast to their many years of friendship. It was almost unbearable for Ellen to think that Maddy had died before they'd had a chance to reconcile their love for each other.

Meanwhile, Detective Gallagher came and went, asking endless questions about Randy's death, and detectives in blue lab coats crawled all over the dam and stream bed. Ellen worked in the pastures alone, mowing, baling, gathering, and stacking the hay in the barn. She weeded her garden and planted fall spinach; she froze peas and broccoli. Without the pond to water her sheep, she had to fill four barrels from the reservoir every other day, but other than that, the animals required little of her time. She wormed them, as she did every summer, and she trimmed their hooves.

When she wasn't busy at home, she searched for Moreen. From various sources she heard various stories: Mo was bumming around Portland, living on the streets in Cambridge, she'd been seen at a punk club in Portsmouth. But the sightings were always secondhand or thirdhand. The only thing clear was that Mo seemed to be avoiding her.

At home with Scott, the silence was deadening. When they did speak, words were strange, tones indifferent. He told her that Detective Gallagher came to the gun shop every day but all they talked about was baseball. Although Ellen and Scott continued sleeping in the same bed, they retired and rose at different times. Scott left in the morning without saying goodbye, and he spent his evenings at Stan's, the local sports bar, rarely returning home before midnight.

She spent her own evenings in her spinning room, her revolver on the floor beside her, working on several small pieces for Wool 'n' Things. On Friday afternoon, when she dropped the tapestries off at the shop, she thought it unusual that Ingrid was so quiet while she stood at the cash register, figuring Ellen's commission. Then Ingrid looked up and curtly addressed a woman who had been dawdling over the racks of wool. "Dolores, do you have everything you need?"

Dolores Packard, Destin's PTA head and self-appointed town gossip, approached the register, smiling pleasantly, and paid for the things in her basket while she talked to Ingrid about the gorgeous weather. She completely ignored Ellen, although Ellen had taught both her sons in high school. When the woman left the store, Ingrid shook her head in disgust.

"This can be a miserable little town," she said. Nine years earlier, Ingrid had abandoned a ten-year marriage for a relationship with another woman. Ellen remembered the unofficial boycott of the store that had followed. Ingrid punched the cash register and the drawer rang open. She counted out thirty-eight dollars and placed it in Ellen's hand.

"You hold your head up," she said, keeping her hand on Ellen's. "Don't let the fuckers wear you down."

Ellen studied her friend's face, feeling an abrupt chill of reality, realizing that Neal's careful work was only beginning to bear fruit. When she returned home and found a message from Brian Quinn, asking her to come to his real estate office the following Monday, she began to glimpse the size of the orchard he had sown. Quinn was not only a realtor, he was head of the Destin School Board.

The second she sat down in his office, he got up and closed the door, then returned to his chair. "I wanted to let you know in advance of official notice," he told her, "the board is going to recommend suspension pending outcome of the police investigation."

He had obviously spoken to the school board's lawyer; she had never heard anyone use the word "pending" in a normal conversation.

Not that Quinn was a bad person, in fact he was an old friend of Scott's, notwithstanding his history of flirting with Ellen.

"You will continue to be paid until either you return to the classroom or you're terminated. Although officially we need to wait for the investigation to conclude, I believe I speak for all the board members when I say I feel strongly that it's in the very best interest of the town if you'd tender your resignation at this time."

She stared at him without emotion. "On what grounds?"

Quinn hesitated, as if contemplating what to say, but Ellen knew the gesture was rehearsed. "Ellie, officially speaking, you're a public school teacher who's involved in a criminal investigation. Of course, this is America, and you're innocent until proven guilty." He made eye contact for the first time, and she knew what was coming.

"Unofficially," he went on, "it's the extenuating circumstances that pose the real problem."

She squinted at him, wondering if this was going to be as bad as she suspected. Quinn sighed heavily, and she knew it was. "You know what a small town this is. Even if the rumors going around are totally without merit—"

She felt a trembling in her gut and stood up, pushing her chair back with such force that it slammed against his computer desk. "Who have you been talking to?"

"Oh, come on, Ellie. Look, gossip is gossip and it doesn't amount to so much smoke, but that's not the point. You know how much newspapers love a story like this, a school teacher involved in a sex scandal—"

"Tell me who you've been talking to," she insisted.

"We both know that you can't begin to function as a teacher without the respect of your students."

Ellen gave him another searing look, then turned and threw open the door.

Quinn stood up, hands open. "Ellie, this was not my decision. You know I'd do anything in my power to help you."

Ellen paused, feeling suddenly lightheaded. All she could think of was Moreen—keeping Moreen from hearing the rumors—but she was afraid it was too late.

"You're a fucking weasel, Brian," she said in a low voice, and she left his office. She did not slam his door. She simply walked out of the building and across the parking lot, feeling as though she was being watched by every window in the village as she stepped into her rusted white pickup truck. She waited until she had pulled out of the parking lot and was beyond sight of Quinn's windows before she started to cry.

The last load of sheep pulled out of the dooryard just as Scott drove in. Through the stakes of the truck Ellen could see her ewe Helga huddled with her lambs. She saw Scott watching the truck pull away as he opened his car door. She wondered why he was home early and realized someone must have told him what was going on. As he surveyed the scene over the top of his Mercedes door, his gaze settled on the cardboard boxes stacked in the back of her truck. Ellen's head began humming in anticipation of what she had to tell him.

"I rented an apartment," she told him. "Above Nielsen Ford."

"Yup," Scott replied, the sum total of his emotional response.

"I'm going to start working part-time for Ingrid."

"Hey, you're going to live in a car lot, maybe you can get me a deal." He closed his door and leaned back against the fender with his arms folded. She could tell that he'd had a couple of drinks with lunch. He shook his head with a regretful laugh. "Funny thing is, I thought we'd make the perfect match," he said, "now that you're no better than I am anymore."

Ellen got into her truck, closed the door, and gave him one last look out her open window.

"Maybe that's why I'm leaving."

twenty

Gradually, as September came and went, and Ellen got used to her apartment and job—and Detective Gallagher finally stopped calling with questions—she began to consider the possibility that Maddy may indeed have taken her own life; that the deaths of her mother and Scott's parents had been accidents; that Neal had built their barn and rid them of Randy because of family loyalty; and that his leaving had been out of indignation that she'd mistrusted him, rather than any sinister plan.

Even Ingrid tried to convince her that the stresses of Mo's hysterectomy—then Randy's drowning and Maddy's suicide—could have triggered paranoia in anyone. Furthermore, Ingrid tried to persuade her that Moreen was an intelligent, independent young woman who had been the real victim of the tragedies—and for the moment, at least, had simply chosen to sort out her life without help from her mother.

Ellen's apartment was roomy for a single person, with a kitchen, living room, bath, and two bedrooms, one of which Ellen used as her spinning room. Her entrance was a covered staircase in the rear of the automobile showroom, where the mechanics parked cars waiting to be serviced. She tried to time her comings and goings when the lot was closed, to avoid the stares of the mechanics and the car dealers.

In the same way, when she returned to the farm to harvest vegetables and put them up for winter, she always went when Scott was at work. One such morning, the first day of October, Ellen dug the last of her potatoes and wheeled them down the barn's bulkhead and into the root cellar Neal had built. The room was deep and narrow, six by twelve, with rock walls and three wooden bins on the back wall. An insulated steel door, wide enough to accommodate Ellen's wheelbarrow, kept the room dry and constantly cool. Because the root cellar was underground and situated on the side of the barn facing the pump house, Neal had run new water pipes through the wall just above the center bin, then elbowed the pipes up the wall and along the ceiling, and on through the wall into the cellar of the barn.

The digging and storing took Ellen most of the morning. When she was finished, she lifted the planks off the bulkhead stairs and returned to the root cellar to close the door. That's when she saw the calendar.

DESTIN HARDWARE

ALL YOUR HARDWARE NEEDS

Scott had given out the calendars every December. At first, Ellen thought it was just another sign of Neal's efficiency: hanging a calendar in a root cellar to record harvest dates . . . but Ellen had been in the root cellar several times before today, storing carrots, turnips, and early potatoes. Why hadn't she noticed the calendar before? Of course Scott might have hung it in the past few days . . . but why? Then she noticed the photo of the man fly-fishing in a river and realized it was last year's calendar. Yet none of the pages had been removed.

She pulled the calendar off the door and held it under the single ceiling light, becoming increasingly aware of the silence around her. If Neal had hung it, what did it mean? Certainly that he had visited Scott's store long before Moreen's wedding. Ellen started folding back the months, expecting to see some cryptic message, but the pages were all unmarked—

—until she came to October. And there it was: a thick red circle around October 2.

"It's his birthday," Ellen said, slapping at the calendar. "It's the anniversary of his father's hanging. It's tomorrow, and he's coming. He told us he's coming."

Detective Gallagher leaned his elbows on his municipal gray desk, pressed his folded hands to his spacious mouth in a show of rumination.

"Just playing devil's advocate," he said, "let's say you're right about your mother and your in-laws, and let's say Neal Chambers has this thing with twelves. The twelfth anniversary was last year. This will be the thirteenth anniversary." He shrugged his shoulders. "Why now?"

"I don't know—I can't read his mind—but I do know he's planning something."

"I'm not unconvinced," Gallagher said, turning the calendar toward himself. "I just like to talk things through. Now, how many of the other deaths in your family occurred on October second?"

Ellen sighed. "Look, if you're not going to help, just say so."

Gallagher paused. "Ellen, you're demanding that we find this man in the next twenty-four hours—"

"Fourteen hours," she said. "October second starts in fourteen hours."

Gallagher sighed, conceding the distinction. "You're talking about a full-bore search, and right now I'm not armed with enough evidence to convince my lieutenant that such a search is warranted." He looked up at her with a furrowed brow. "That is, unless you or your husband know something about your son-in-law's drowning that might incriminate Neal."

"Great, play games," Ellen said, flipping her hand at him. "Neal Chambers killed my mother and my in-laws. He killed his own mother. He killed my best friend. He's taken everyone Scott and I love, except our daughter—and I'm trying to tell you she's going to be next."

"Again," Gallagher said, "I don't want to seem disparaging, but we still have nothing concrete—I'm saying concrete—that links Neal Chambers to a single death."

"Me. They're linked to me."

The detective leaned way back in his desk chair, his hairy fingers raised off the arms. "Even if your friend Madeleine was murdered—and in three months of investigation, we haven't found a single thing to support that theory—she died in the middle of July from a bullet wound, not October, not asphyxiation." He lifted his shoulders and brow simultaneously. "The fact is, and I say this hoping to give you some peace of mind, none of your friends or relatives has died on October second." He reached forward and placed his hands on the edge of his desk, as if to tell Ellen that their meeting was through.

Ellen breathed deeply, pretending she hadn't read the gesture. She looked down at the calendar, the bright red circle around October 2. The calendar stared back at her.

"Three months," she said, giving Gallagher an obvious look.

She swung the calendar toward herself and flipped back three pages, then grabbed a black marker off his desk and marked a thick black **X** through July 14. "This is when Maddy was murdered," she said.

He gave her a patronizing look.

She placed the marker on the X and counted six weeks forward, through July and August, then began counting aloud as she rapped the marker against the calendar page, "Seven, eight, nine, ten, eleven . . . "

Flipping the page, her marker landed with a slap . . . on October sixth. Four days past Neal's red circle. Her shoulders fell.

The detective gave Ellen a sympathetic shrug. "Close," he said. "If your friend's death had been four days earlier"—he flipped the pages back to July, put his finger on the tenth—"exactly twelve weeks from Neal's birthday, well, maybe I could do some convincing. But from everything you've told me about your nephew—"

"Neal Chambers is my *husband's* nephew."

Gallagher gave her a look. "Do you really think Neal Chambers would be four days off?"

Ellen stared at the date. July 10 was the night that she and Neal made love, she thought—but she didn't say that.

Gallagher got up from his chair and came around to the front of his desk, where he sat on the corner, somehow managing to squeeze one of his large hands in his pocket. The more casual he tried to act, the more awkward he appeared.

"Ellen, I'm not trying to dismiss your fears," he said. "Judging from the evidence we've gathered, there's more than a good chance that Neal knows something about your son-in-law's drowning, as well as the disappearance of the men who loaned money to your husband."

"Look," Ellen said. "I'm here. And I'm warning you. My family is in danger."

Gallagher slid off his desk and went to the door. "Let me talk to my lieutenant. Maybe we can arrange to put you folks under surveillance for the next day or two, until you feel the threat has passed."

Ellen slapped his desk. "You *cannot* protect my family," she said. "Neal Chambers has systematically picked off everyone close to us, and he is not going to stop until he's destroyed us all."

The detective looked down at the floor and let out a tired, contemplative sigh. Then he looked back at Ellen. "Would you wait here for a minute?" he said, and he walked out of the small office, closing the door behind him.

Ellen stared down at the ink-stained desk. Like the rust from the window bars that stained the sill, the office had the appearance of having been worked too hard for too long. The only sign of life in the room was the pair of small, framed photos on the heater, one of a gangly, blond-haired boy around ten years old, holding a baseball glove beside his head; the other of a smaller boy holding a fat fish in his hands. The smaller boy had a squat build and the dark, heavy brow of his father. Ellen looked closer and saw a white prosthetic thigh showing under his bathing suit. She wondered how the boy had lost his leg. She wondered why Gallagher had no photo of the boys' mother.

She looked back at his desk, the calendar. She turned the pages ahead to October again and stared at Neal's red-circled birthday—Tuesday, October 2—then she counted ahead by Tuesdays, flipping the pages through November and into December . . . her finger suddenly stiffening on the twelfth week, the shiver climbing her arms.

"Christmas," she whispered. The day Scott's parents drove into the river and drowned. Twelve weeks, exactly. She rose from her chair. Hearing Gallagher's muffled voice from the next room, she pounded the wall with the side of her fist. "Christmas!" she yelled.

She sat down in Gallagher's chair, snatched the black marker and scratched an X through the date. Then she returned to October 2, and she counted backward twelve days. Now the shiver took her entire body. September 20, the date her mother choked to death. Another X.

When all the twelves are in line. Neal's words dropped into her mind as though he were standing right beside her.

She opened the manila folder marked CHAMBERS and looked at Gallagher's scribbled notes, until she found the name of Neal's mother, April Chambers, and the date of her death: October 14. Twelve days after October 2. Twelve upon twelve upon twelve.

Ellen heard the door open behind her and turned to see Gallagher standing there. She stared up at him, almost afraid to speak. The detective blinked his eyes.

The small green ranch house had been built in 1955, the last property on a dead-end lane that was surrounded by boarded-up summer cottages and separated from the rest of the neighborhood by about five acres of wooded marshland. The home's owner, a widow who wintered in Florida, left her house vacant nine months of the year, with shades drawn and a timer set to turn lights on at dusk and off again at dawn, to convince prowlers that someone was home.

In fact, someone was. Inside the steam-filled bathroom, Moreen sat naked in the bathtub with her eyes closed, singing, "Oh-ay-oh-ay-o," while water poured into the tub and The Automatics wailed in her ears:

They're just wasting away,
Hanging out at EJ's,
Living their life day by day by day,
Hoping everything will be okay.
Oh-ay-oh-ay-oh,
Oh-ay-oh-ay-oh,

When the door opened, Moreen kept singing at first—until she saw her mother standing there. Then she threw her walkman headphones into the water "Why are *you* here?" she cried.

A policeman pushed past Ellen in the doorway. "Cover up," he told Moreen, averting his eyes. "You're coming with us."

When Moreen was dressed they hustled her into the living room, where her friends—three guys and her friend Keirsted—sat lined up on the couch. Another cop was telling them they were free to get out of town and stay out. Then they were herded outside, where Rooftop Paradise waited, slouched in the dark against the side of his panel truck.

Seeing him, Moreen screamed, "Bear, what are you doing to me? Did you tell them where I was?"

The officer hustled her toward the patrol car and seated her inside. "Don't hurt her," Ellen said, getting in beside her daughter.

"Do you actually think you're *helping* me?" Moreen demanded.

Ellen closed the door, and they were whisked away.

By midnight, everyone was protected. Down in the car lot that surrounded Ellen's apartment, two pairs of men kept watch from inside smoked-glass vans that were parked strategically among the cars for sale. Motion sensors had been set up around the perimeter of the lot. Inside the showroom, where security lights routinely burned through the night, nothing stirred. But two men waited behind the counter and another pair sat quietly inside the dark garage. Upstairs, in the kitchen of Ellen's apartment, an officer sat in the dimly lit living room, peeking out the window; another sat in the kitchen, doing the same.

It was Neal Chambers's twenty-fifth birthday, the thirteenth anniversary of his mother's infidelity, his father's suicide. For the next twenty-four hours, the decoys and guards would remain in place, while Moreen and Ellen shared the holding cell in the York Beach Police Station, and Scott stayed in a sixth-floor Holiday Inn suite in Portsmouth.

Scott made the most of the situation, playing nickel-dime poker with the cops and eating room-service steaks. While the cops drank coffee, Scott drank highballs until the whiskey was gone, then he went to bed and slept until eleven, at which point he had a huge breakfast sent up, along with another bottle of Crown Royal. Although there was almost no chance that Neal would know Scott was here, let alone infiltrate the security, Detective Gallagher was taking no chances. Outside of the lieutenant and the officers assigned to the detail, nobody knew about the operation, neither the officers' families nor the local police departments.

Internment in the York Beach holding cell was not so pleasant. Ellen and Moreen were locked together in the windowless, cinder block cell, with a twelve-inch television sitting on a wooden chair and two cots on either side of the room. An armed woman was stationed just outside their door, while another policeman guarded the corridor. Police had instructions that no one arrested in the next 24 hours was to be brought to the station but taken either straight to the county jail in Alfred or released. Drunk drivers and casual drug users were to be driven home; dealers, burglars, and wife abusers handed over to the State Police.

Everything in the cell was painted light green, from the cinder-block walls and iron bars to the small wooden table and chair, even the iron frames of the two cots. For the first two hours in the cell, Moreen refused to speak. She stalked the floor of the tiny room, drinking cup after cup of black coffee, while Ellen lay on the cot in her jeans and jersey, trying to read a *People* magazine by the light of a small desk lamp, wondering if the words existed by which she could ever get close to Moreen again. For now, with Mo pacing, Ellen knew enough not to try.

As far as Ellen could tell, the rumors about her affair with Neal or the investigation into Randy's death hadn't reached Moreen. She ached with love for her daughter and fear for her safety. And she ached with the knowledge of her own complicity in Randy's death, even if she was still convinced that his death may have ultimately saved Moreen's life. But no matter how hard she tried, she could not understand Moreen's remoteness or her grim determination to push her out of her life.

"I can't believe you called the police on me," Moreen said, finally.

"It was the only way to protect you," Ellen replied, lowering her magazine.

"Mom, I keep telling you, I don't need your help," Moreen said firmly, stopping to look down at Ellen. "I have *never* needed your help."

"Hey!" the policewoman yelled in. "You start showing your mother some respect, young lady."

"Mo, *why?*" Ellen whispered, desperate to know. "What did I do to make you feel like this?"

Moreen's brown eyes remained on Ellen, seeming to shine with anger. But, saying no more, she turned away and lay down on her cot, pulling the covers over her head.

Ellen let her magazine drop to the floor—not that she had read a bit of it—then she reached up and shut off the lamp.

The farmhouse was the most heavily guarded site, not only because of the number of ways in, but because of the likelihood that Neal would strike here. Pairs of armed personnel were stationed in the pantry of the house and in the barn's hayloft. Detective Gallagher sat at the top of the stairs with his police radio turned on, keeping an eye on Scott's and Moreen's bedrooms, inside which lay decoys under the covers, each armed with a five-shot .38 Special, in the unlikely event that Neal Chambers might somehow materialize in the room.

At the bottom of the pasture and across the stream, up through the woods at the beginning of a fire-access road, two other detectives sat in the back of an unmarked panel truck, their radio left open between the farmhouse, the car lot, the York Beach Police Station, and Detective Gallagher at the farmhouse, so all parties could hear each other's conversations. One of the detectives in the van wore headphones. The other sat in a low-slung beach chair eating a tuna sandwich and listening to the perking of the 12-volt coffee pot he'd brought along.

Neither of them heard the shifting of rock dust or saw the black figure stalking their vehicle. In fact, the detective wearing the headphones was just beginning to nod off, and the one eating the sandwich was just pouring coffee into his thermos cup when the light burst through the window.

The man dropped the cup and coffee pot and dived behind the seat, pulling his piece from his shoulder holster in the same move.

The sleeper, pinned by the light beam, raised his hands in front of his eyes, half in surrender, half in an attempt to block the light or gunshot, if it came next. But instead of the gunshot, the men heard a voice outside their van.

"Hold on, you fellas on the job?"

"No, we're rabbit hunters," said the man with the headphones. "Who the hell are you?"

In the distance, a siren sang a winding solo.

"Identify yourself," said the cop behind the seat, "or I'm gonna shoot right through that fucking light!"

"Whoa! I'm on the job too."

The inside of the truck darkened as, outside, the flashlight beam lit up a silver shield. "Destin Police," Sugar Westerback said. "I've got the farmhouse under surveillance."

The man with the headphones reached for the radio, pressed a switch. "It's okay," he said into the mike. "Some local cowboy action."

"Excuse me?" Sugar said.

"You want to come around to the back," the detective replied. "I've got someone on the radio who'd love to speak to you."

In the York Beach holding cell, Moreen slept until four in the afternoon, while Ellen lay on her cot reading a worn copy of *To Kill a Mockingbird* that the dispatcher's son had left in her car.

When Moreen woke up, Ellen handed her a Styrofoam cup of coffee.

"Are you okay?" Ellen asked, noticing how Mo was slightly hunched over, with an arm wrapped around herself as if she were cold.

"I just need to get out of here," Moreen answered, sitting up and taking a sip of coffee.

"Mo, I explained it to you," Ellen told her. "Tomorrow morning we can leave, but until Neal is in custody—"

"Mom, why can't you understand?" Moreen interrupted, giving her mother a smile fraught with helplessness. *"I don't need your help."*

She threw her blankets off and started to stand. Then she doubled over.

Ellen dropped her book. "Call a doctor, please," she yelled out to the guard, who came immediately to the door.

"I'm just dizzy," Moreen said, trying to straighten. "I don't need a doctor, I need to leave." She sank back onto the bed, shivering and hugging herself. She looked pale.

"Where did you get the coffee?" Ellen snapped at the guard.

"I opened a can and made it myself," the woman answered. "It's the same coffee you're drinking. We've been drinking it all day. I feel fine. You're all right."

"Get a doctor!" Ellen shouted at her.

Fifteen minutes later a young man came into the cell and took Moreen's temperature and pulse and looked in her eyes, ears, and throat. He told Ellen that Moreen had simply come down with a stomach virus.

"Is something going around?" Ellen asked.

The doctor smiled as he packed his bag. "Looks like it will be."

Six hours later and six hundred miles down the coast, in Virginia Beach, a handsome woman opened her front door.

The black-bearded young man in a red chef's hat smiled. "Medium combo," he said, opening the lid of the flat box and displaying his creation. The smell wafted through the screen door.

The woman looked past him at the van parked on the curb. "I'm afraid you might have the wrong address," she said apologetically.

The delivery man looked at the slip of paper in his hand. "416 Shore Road?"

"That's our address," the woman said, perplexed. "Drew, you didn't order a pizza, did you?"

Her husband, a fit, white-haired man of sixty-two, came up behind her. "Not me."

The pizza man eyed the husband curiously.

"Care to use the phone?" the husband said. He was dressed in a blue sweat suit.

"Wouldn't do much good," the delivery man answered. "I own the business, and I'm on my way home. You were my last stop." He gave the husband another protracted scowl, then said, "Excuse me, but aren't you"—he snapped his fingers—"I'm terrible with history."

The woman smiled. "Oh, boy, you just made his day."

"The astronaut, right?"

"Drew McDermott," the man said, folding his arms.

"Drew McDermott, unbelievable." He gazed through the screen, admiring the older man. Then he said, "Hey," and held the box up to the door. "I'm only gonna throw it away when I get home."

The woman turned to her husband. "Want to go off your diet?"

The astronaut rocked his head, deliberating. "It smells great," he admitted. "Okay, let me get my wallet."

"Don't move a muscle," the pizza man said, opening the door. "You sign your autograph on my slip, and we'll call it even."

While the astronaut and his wife spent the next fifteen minutes— the last of their lives—jerking and gasping and crying for breath on their living room carpet, the pizza man got in his van and headed north.

At seven-thirty in the morning, Ellen turned on the television, keeping the sound down to avoid waking Mo. The first image she saw was a cartoon man lying prostrate, panting like a dog, while a voice-over explained how cyanide poisoning prevents the oxygen in a person's lungs from bonding with his blood. The image cut to the network's medical expert, who had been providing the voice-over.

"And so," he continued grimly, "while the victim can respire up to two hundred fifty times a minute—and this can take fifteen minutes or more of pure agony—he slowly suffocates."

Cut to the show's somber host, who thanked the man.

Dissolve to an image of earth as seen from space, then a face superimposed. A name. A date.

"But you're not even sure that this man—Drew McDermott—was your father," the detective said, his eyes glassy from sleeplessness, his face black with whiskers.

"It doesn't matter. Neal Chambers *believed* he was my father. And he died, *he suffocated*, on October second."

"I want to go," Moreen said weakly, sitting on the edge of her cot with her backpack in her lap. Gallagher held up his hand, quieting her.

"Neal Chambers was arrested in Virginia Beach when he was fifteen years old," Ellen told him. "The police caught him looking in someone's window. Call them, check the records—see whose house it was."

"You can't keep me here," Moreen told them.

"Mo, please," Ellen said, then addressed Gallagher again. "Call Walpole State Prison, in Massachusetts. There's an inmate there named Michael Landry."

The detective gave her a questioning frown.

"He's the other man who might be my father," she explained.

Gallagher held up his hand again.

"Believe me," he told her, "it's only a matter of time before Neal Chambers ends up in an interrogation room with me. We've added his name to a long list of people wanted for questioning, and every major police department in North America has his profile. However"—the detective moved a bit closer to Ellen's cot—"as I explained to you, 'Wanted for questioning' doesn't carry the same weight as 'Wanted for murder.' " He shrugged his heavy shoulders. "So until somebody comes forward with something incriminating, 'wanted for questioning' is about as much as we can do. That is, unless you or your husband has thought

of anything about your son-in-law's drowning that may have slipped
your minds—?"

Ellen heard a squawk from the springs of Moreen's cot, and glared
at Gallagher in disbelief at what he'd said in front of Moreen. He stared
back at her, with absolute deadness in his eyes. "No?"

Ellen continued to glare. Gallagher reached back for the door.

"I'll be right back," he said. "I'm going to check on that prison
for you." He turned and left the cell.

When he closed the door behind him, the silence that remained
was suffocating. Ellen sat perfectly still, keeping her eyes on the door
as she listened to Moreen's breathing. They remained like that for what
seemed to Ellen like several minutes. Finally Moreen sniffed—or she
laughed. Ellen turned, saw her lying on the cot, staring at the ceiling,
her eyes tearing, her mouth curved in a sort of smile.

"Hon, it's because I went to the police about Randy, that's all.
They'd have to wonder about something like that. It's their job."

Moreen closed her eyes. Another minute crawled along in tortured
silence, until they heard the sound of footsteps outside the door, then
the hollow clatter of the lock as the door opened and shut, and Gallagher came in. Moreen got up, threw her backpack over her shoulder.

"Michael Landry died a year ago in prison," the detective announced. "He was in the weight room, and his barbell fell on his
windpipe. The prison physician's report called his death accidental."

Ellen kept her eyes on the green bars. "What date?"

"A year ago last night."

"October second," Ellen said, fixing her glare at him. "Is Neal
wanted for murder now?"

Moreen walked to the barred door, tried to open it.

Gallagher eyed Moreen for a moment, then he turned back to Ellen.
"We're going to find your nephew," he said assuredly. "Until we do,
we'll have people watching your family at all times."

"You mean you'll use us as bait."

He gave her a stern look. "If you'd rather, we can relocate the
three of you to another state until your nephew's in custody."

"We have lives," Ellen said, keeping her eye on Moreen. "How
long?"

Gallagher shook his head. "You know I can't answer that. If you
choose to remain in town, we'll give you as much privacy as possible.
But you can be assured we'll be protecting all of you."

"Please unlock the door," Moreen said.

"Moreen, you can go home with your mother, or you can go with your father," Gallagher said. "Your choice."

Moreen glared at the wall outside the cell. "I'm eighteen," she said.

"She's seventeen," Ellen said.

"Moreen, we can keep you in protective custody until your cousin is apprehended," Gallagher said. "Is that what you want?" He tried to make eye contact.

"Fine." She slung her pack over her other shoulder and waited.

"Which?"

"Either."

Gallagher looked at Ellen. "Do you want her?"

Ellen glared at him. "Are you ignorant or just totally insensitive? You just insinuated that my husband and I had something to do with the death of my daughter's husband. Of course I want her! But do you think she's going to stay with either of us?"

Gallagher studied Ellen for a moment. He turned to Moreen, who stood at the door, looking at the ceiling. The detective stepped up beside her.

"Moreen, are you going to stay with your mother?"

"Yes," Moreen said, staring through the bars.

"This isn't the time to be difficult," he said. "Until we find your cousin, we need to know where you're going to be at all times, or we'll lock you up for your own protection. Do you understand me?"

"I understand you."

He turned to Ellen. "If she runs off, give a call, and we'll grab her up."

Ellen looked away.

"Door, please," Gallagher said, and the policewoman came with the key.

Ellen drove inland, toward Destin, with her daughter beside her and an unmarked car following a hundred feet behind. Afraid that Moreen would bolt the first time the truck slowed down, Ellen drove through stop signs. She took a roundabout, wooded route to her apartment, trying to buy time, though she knew how pointless these maneuvers were.

"Mo, I know you're angry at me—"

"I'm not angry."

Ellen sighed. "Honey, just tell me you understand the danger."

"I understand. I just feel sick to my stomach." Moreen slouched in the seat, shivering and pale.

"Do you want to stop somewhere for breakfast?"

Moreen lurched up. "Pull over," she gasped, holding her mouth.

Ellen kept her foot on the accelerator.

"Pull over!" Moreen cried, grabbing the steering wheel as she spread her legs and gagged painfully, as if she were going to throw up on the floor.

Ellen hit the brake. "Please don't do this, Mo."

But Ellen stopped the truck on the shoulder, and when Moreen opened the door, she grabbed her backpack that lay between them. Ellen popped the clutch, hit the gas. The truck shot forward, and Moreen tumbled out of the truck.

"Mo!" Ellen cried, stomping the brake. She turned and saw her daughter pick herself off the roadside and stagger down the embankment into the woods, her pack wrapped around her shoulder. Behind them the gray sedan came up fast. While Ellen watched, paralyzed, Moreen started to run.

Ellen jumped from the truck. "Moreen, don't!" she cried, but her daughter was already swallowed by the foliage.

The gray sedan chirped to a stop. Both men jumped out. One ran to Ellen, the other took off after Moreen.

"Don't chase her!" Ellen yelled, knowing it was futile to bring Moreen back. She also knew that they'd never find her.

She prayed that Neal wouldn't, either.

twenty-one

Ellen returned to her life alone, though she felt as if she lived in a bell
jar. For the first week, every time she passed a window she was aware
of binoculars on her, men in vans with smoked windows, detectives
pretending to be car salesmen. When she drove to work, cars pulled
out of side streets behind her. Men followed her into the drugstore,
they followed her around the supermarket. Even the Westerbacks, although they'd been officially barred from the case, drove past Wool 'n'
Things several times a day when Ellen was working, and they drove
through the car lot while she was home.

Slowly, as the days turned to weeks and the nights grew long and
cold, with no sign of Moreen, no sign of Neal, Ellen found herself
getting used to living her life on the brink of disaster. Although she
knew without doubt that the day would come, that one fiery moment
when all their lives would finally be ripped apart—and she always kept
her revolver close at hand—eventually she was able to shut the lights
off when she went to bed.

As intrusive as the surveillance might have felt, the scrutiny from
townspeople was far worse—the cautious glances of the customers who
came into the store, the awkward, truncated conversations with old
friends and ex-coworkers.

On November 15, Detective Gallagher called to tell Ellen what she
already suspected. Although the search for Neal had been given top
priority all over the country, the surveillance team protecting Scott and
her would have to be scaled back slightly. He went on to explain that

they would bolster security on certain "target dates," such as Christmas, but otherwise they'd begin coordinating with the county sheriff's department.

"Are you giving up on Moreen too?" Ellen asked.

"We're not giving up on any of you," Gallagher answered. "Fact is, we've talked to a couple of people in Portsmouth who heard she was in the Boston area recently, and we have people there as we speak, following up."

"What if Neal's already found her?"

The detective shook his head. "We're doing all we can."

The next day three inches of snow fell. Two days later a cold, two-day rain dissolved the snow and ushered in a stretch of thirty-degree, sunless days, leaving little doubt that a long gray winter was on its way. A week before Thanksgiving, Ingrid began playing Christmas music in the store and staying open till nine. Ellen was glad for the extra hours, not only because she needed the money, but because working kept her away from her empty apartment. She also found comfort in Ingrid's company.

"My first Thanksgiving alone wasn't exactly a picnic," Ingrid said one night.

"I haven't thought much about it," Ellen answered, as she finished a piece on the tapestry loom, though she knew it was obvious that she was dreading the holiday.

"Some friends and I get together every year, " Ingrid told her. "We eat like pigs and drink like fish, and we're all very thankful for the opportunity. Why don't you come with me?"

Ellen smiled as she snugged the shed rod down. "Thanks. But I don't think I'd be much fun."

A moment of silence followed, after which Ingrid asked, in a kind way, "Ellie, why do you stay in Destin?"

Ellen kept working, though she lost her smile. Not that she minded Ingrid's prodding. Indeed, she felt a kinship with the woman, who reminded her of her mother in the way she prized her independence. Unlike Ellen's mother, however, Ingrid was also practical and present and strong.

"Where am I supposed to go?" Ellen replied.

"It's your map," Ingrid answered simply, then went on with her work.

At 5:30 the next morning, when only the milk trucks and bread trucks were out, the blue Taurus wobbled down the back streets of

Hampton Beach, then pulled into an alley beside a darkened tenement building. In a minute the driver emerged from the alley wearing an oversized black sweatshirt, her face hidden deep inside its hood. She turned the corner onto a deserted boulevard of boarded-up T-shirt and pizza shops.

There were no other cars, no people, no sounds except for the murmur of ocean waves breaking in the distance. Half a block down the street, she came to a door that opened on a narrow set of stairs. She looked behind her, then rang the bell. In a minute a man came down and let her in. He was startlingly thin and wore a short-sleeved terry-cloth bathrobe. Celtic designs were crudely tattooed all over his arms, from his wrists up. Moreen didn't know his age. Some days he looked fifty, some days older. This morning he seemed to have developed some kind of twitch in his eye.

"Come on up," he said, "you're gonna love this stuff, which is why I got in touch with you. I mean, you're really gonna dig it."

He was called Speedo not because he took amphetamines—in fact he was a heroin addict—but because he talked so fast, which was usually a sign that he hadn't fixed in too long. Moreen followed him up the stairs, into his apartment. Empty Pepsi cans were strewn everywhere, candy bar wrappers, chewing gum wrappers. A box of Sugar Smacks sat on the table, beside a small white candle that smelled of vanilla.

"Same weight, is that what you want, same weight?" Speedo asked.

"Yeah," Moreen answered.

He turned his back on her, undid his bathrobe tie, and reached into his money belt, pulled out a small plastic bag with a quarter-inch of cream-colored powder in the bottom.

Moreen reached in her jeans pocket, came out with her money

Speedo sat down at the table. "Got time for a little sample? On me, I'm not gonna charge you, I want to see the look on your face, you know what I mean? That's my enjoyment."

Moreen said, "Whatever."

He grinned at her with small gray teeth, then stuffed his thin hand down inside the Sugar Smacks box and came out with his works, along with a short length of brown rubber tubing. "I only use brand-new, disposable syringes, you know, medical supply, quality control—which is why Randy always came to me. He knew I could be trusted, know what I'm saying? Why take chances?"

He kicked the chair back for her. "Go 'head, tie off and I'll do you, I already did myself before, just a little before you came, I'll probably do some more later, but first I wanna see the look on your face, go on, tie off."

Moreen pulled her sweatshirt over her head and dropped it on the floor, then sat in the chair. She unbuttoned her flannel shirt and pulled her arm out. Underneath, she wore a black T-shirt. She picked up the tubing and tied it around her right arm, pulled the end tight with her teeth as she made a fist, flexed it, and squeezed, then watched the hungry veins rise to the surface, big and dark. Her eyes watered while Speedo studied the road map with his finger.

"Like I said, this is top-shelf, only the best, only the best," he said, tapping the vein and watching it swell even more. He held her wrist with his free hand, but he never looked at her face when he sank the needle in. Didn't look at her when he pulled her blood into the solution or pushed it back into her bloodstream. He did peek, however, when she unlooped the tubing and the drug rushed into her brain.

At first, her head went slowly back, a lazy smile taking her lips. In the next instant she met his eyes with her own, stark and protesting. Before Speedo could slide the syringe out of her arm, she tried to stand but her chair kicked out from under her. Attempting to catch her in his arms, Speedo ended up falling to his knees with her head in his lap.

"Okay, man, I don't need this," he said, speaking to the other man in his apartment, the stranger who had been waiting silently in the bathroom. Speedo pushed up on Moreen's shoulder, searching down her arm for his works. He ran his hand under her back. "You said you weren't a cop," he said quietly, "and once you say that, I have immunity from prosecution under the Constitution, that's in the Bill of Rights, check it out, man."

He found the syringe under his own leg and examined it, grateful that the needle hadn't broken off in her arm. He turned Moreen's face toward him.

"Whatever that was you had me give her, she's under, man. I mean you could fuck her six ways to Sunday and she'd never know what hit her." He heard the young man's footsteps move out of the darkened hall and into the kitchen. He glanced back over his shoulder.

The stranger slid a wooden chair over behind Speedo. "Sit down," he said.

"It's none of my business, like I told you, I don't know nothin about nothin, but if you want my opinion, this girl doesn't have that missing money, either, just my impression, my general overall impression based on lifestyle, etcetera, etcetera."

"Sit."

Speedo did as he was told.

"Not to be uncooperative but, I mean, just what are we doing here?"

The stranger stripped a length of duct tape from a roll. "Give me your leg."

"Okay, this is totally unnecessary," Speedo objected, starting to stand, but the stranger flashed him a quick, dark look.

"I don't want to be followed," he said. "Leg."

Something in his voice told Speedo that the next few minutes of his life would go a lot easier if he didn't argue. So he sat down again and watched while the stranger bound one leg, then the other, to the front legs of the chair.

"Oh, yeah, like I want any more to do with this happy horseshit, which I know nothin about," Speedo grumbled.

When the stranger finished with Speedo's legs, he said, "Hands behind you."

"Follow you for what?"

"Put your hands behind you."

"Seriously, do I look like a hero to you?"

"Hands."

"Fuck." Speedo took a big impatient breath, wrapped his arms behind the chair.

"Lean forward," the stranger said, and Speedo complied, immediately feeling the tape securing his skinny arm to the wooden stile, winding after winding around his forearm, wrist, and hand.

"There's such a thing as overdoing it," Speedo complained, as his other arm was bound. "You know? I'd like to get up sometime this century—"

His voice was cut off as the stranger reached over his head and stuck a length of tape over his mouth. Speedo grunted an objection when the tape wound around the back of his head and over his mouth again. And he objected strenuously when the third winding covered his nose. In fact he threw his head back, as if to shake the duct tape free, and he made a loud sound in his throat, but the stranger grabbed his hair and went once more around, this time sealing his nose completely.

Then the stranger stepped back and watched.

Speedo stared up in wild indignation. His chair jumped off the floor and fell on its side with a crash. He flipped the chair onto its front and began knocking his forehead on the floor, like someone hammering.

He polished the linoleum with his knees, with his shoulder, with his cheek, trying to peel the duct tape away, while the noises from his throat began sounding like the cries of a far-off whale. When he rolled the chair onto its back, his eyes bulged, sprouting tiny red veins. His chest and stomach heaved rapidly. Suddenly his eyes closed in a tight grimace, and his chair began rapping at the floor like a jackhammer. When the convulsions stopped, Speedo's eyes opened again, cherry red. That's the way they stayed.

"Come on, I haven't been drunk in years," Ingrid said, counting the money in her cash register drawer. "What the hell, we're halfway there now. I'll call a taxi, we'll get chauffeured."

It was five minutes to five, the day before Thanksgiving, and they were closing early. For lunch, Ingrid had surprised Ellen with a turkey dinner and a bottle of Chardonnay that they'd shared while they worked.

"Actually, I was looking forward to going home and taking a long, hot bath," Ellen answered, as she lowered the quilted shade on the storefront window. In fact, she was picturing the telephone, not the tub, and wondering if Ingrid had any idea how much she was hoping Moreen—or even Scott—would call.

She opened the door to the small back room, went in and turned off the cassette player, turned off the coffeemaker, and brought the coffee pot into the bathroom to wash it out.

"I talked to Priscilla Clancy last night," Ingrid called. "Remember her, from the Guild? She moved out to Oregon."

Ellen flushed the toilet then turned off the bathroom light. She could hear the wind outside, whipping the dead leaves up against the back door. She checked the back door, to make sure it was locked, then took her jean jacket off the coatrack and walked back into the store.

"Priscilla's in wine country," Ingrid said, "raising llamas and sheep— prize Rambouillets. She said she's got too much farm and too much house to manage alone."

Ellen smiled. "Not that there's any particular point in telling me this."

Ingrid shrugged, while she wrote in her accounting book. "I figured I'd give you something to think about so you're not sitting by the phone for the next two days."

Ellen laughed a little. Being around Ingrid gave her hope that she might be happy again someday, although on days like this it wasn't always easy to believe.

As if on cue, the telephone rang. Both women looked over at it, as though Ingrid had somehow willed it to happen.

"Can you get it?" the older woman asked, pretending she couldn't be bothered. But Ellen knew they were both thinking the same thing. She went to the phone casually and let it ring a third time, so as not to seem anxious. Ingrid looked up at her. Ellen picked up. The phone beeped at her.

"Fax," she said, and pressed the START button. The paper curled out of the back of the machine. Not that it would be unlike Scott to fax her a dinner invitation. Avoid the chance of rejection. The machine beeped off, then cut the paper.

"If it's not obscene, we don't want it," Ingrid said.

Ellen pulled the paper from the tray, turned it over, saw the dark photo centered on the page. She pulled the paper out and turned it right-side-up. She stared.

"What is it?" Ingrid said.

The ransom is you.

Ellen's legs weakened. She backed against the wall. In the photo, Moreen was sitting on a wooden floor with a blanket wrapped around her shoulders, her eyes downcast.

"Ellie, what?" Although Ingrid was coming closer, her voice sounded miles away.

Pay phone, 12 minutes. Do not betray me.

Ellen crumpled the paper in her hand, stuffed it in her pocket.

"It's him, isn't it?" Ingrid whispered, coming toward the phone. "Ellie, call the police."

"Don't." Ellen's scowl stopped the older woman. She bunched her jacket in her hand, felt for her keys in the pocket. "It's nothing," she said, wondering if Neal was watching her right now. "I'm going home, and you're closing the store."

"What's going on?" Ingrid demanded.

"Please. Smile and say goodbye," Ellen said, heading for the front door. "Keep cleaning up. I'll call you in an hour."

"I'm smiling," Ingrid said, following her. "But your truck's out back. Ellie, just tell me where you're going."

"I'll call you," Ellen told her, throwing the door open and walking off into the darkness.

★   ★   ★

Ingrid locked the door then stood there, vibrating with anxiety. She watched Ellen walk across the parking lot of the plaza toward the pharmacy, illuminated briefly by a car's headlights. Then Ingrid turned and went back to her telephone. She did not lift the receiver, but she angled her trifocals to read the buttons on the front panel, then pushed the one that said FAX MEMORY. Immediately she heard the paper roller shift into gear.

Sugar Westerback had just stepped out of his new shower when the 911 call came through from Ingrid. "Hold on, wait," he said. "What pay phone?"

"The only one in Destin Plaza," the woman told him. "Outside the drugstore."

"Okay. He's calling her when?"

"Ten minutes. But no one's supposed to know."

"Right." Sugar stared at his naked reflection in the window, wondering if he should call his father at the Lobster Palace.

"What about the FBI or the state police, shouldn't we notify them?" Ingrid said. "She's in danger. Her daughter's in danger."

"I'll take it from here," Sugar told her. "You stay put. If you hear anything else, call me on my car phone."

He gave her the number, then hung up and called Stan's Sports Tavern and asked to speak to Chuck Lyon. Chuck was the right fielder on Sugar's softball team. He was also a cable splicer for the phone company.

"I need a favor quick," Sugar told him, and explained what he wanted.

"You got a warrant?" Chuck said. "You need a warrant."

"You got a driver's license?" Sugar shot back. "You and I both know I could take that license from you any night of the week, and I will. Now get your ass in gear!"

He hung up and got dressed as fast as he could, finished with a bulletproof vest, then strapped on his shoulder holster, his Desert Eagle .357 magnum. He folded down the visor of his Patriots cap, then walked out to his Bronco, where he dialed the number Chuck had given him. While he waited for his friend to answer, he pulled the Bronco to the head of the driveway, facing the road. The phone kept ringing. He drummed on the steering wheel until he heard it pick up.

"Sugar?" Chuck asked, sounding out of breath.

"Ten-two."

"Hold on, they're already connected. I'm gonna patch us in. What's that motor noise?"

"My vehicle."

"Shut it off. Keep quiet."

Sugar turned the key. In the phone he heard a click, then silence. Then Ellen's voice: "Neal, please tell me."

There was a pause.

"Ellen, is anyone else on the line?"

Sugar recognized the male voice as Neal's. He felt his heart accelerate. He looked down the dark country road, first left, then right, all the bare branches clicking at the clouds.

"Just tell me what you did to her," Ellen persisted, although she sounded timid, as if she were afraid to hear his answer.

"What *I* did?" Neal replied calmly. "Moreen sold a brand-new Jeep. A month later she's living on the street. Her arms are bruised, her friends are junkies, and her husband was a dealer. What *I* did? I may have saved her life. But that's up to you."

"Don't play games with me, Neal. Where is she?"

"Somewhere she can't stick a needle in her arm. I left her enough blankets to keep from freezing and a couple days' supply of food and water."

"It's Scott you want to hurt," Ellen told him. "Scott and me. Not Moreen."

" 'Shall I give my firstborn for my transgression, the fruit of my body for the sin of my soul?' " Neal recited, his voice radiating a warmth that sent a chill down Sugar's back. "Ellen, you know I don't want to hurt Moreen. All I want is a chance to see you one last time, so I can ask your forgiveness."

"I *forgive* you," Ellen pleaded.

"See me," Neal told her. "Grant me your forgiveness, and I'll return Moreen to you and be out of your lives forever."

Silence took over the line.

"Will you deny me three times?" came Neal's voice.

Sugar squeezed the steering wheel, his forearms pumped and ready.

"Where do you want me?" Ellen demanded.

"Scott won't be home for another hour or two."

"I'm not meeting you in the house."

"Of course not. The barn is far more appropriate."

Silence.

"When?"

"If you don't mind my overworking a theme—"

"*When?*"

"Twelve minutes."

"Don't hurt Moreen, Neal. Please. You know she doesn't deserve it. I'll get there as fast as I can."

"Alone."

"I won't tell anyone. Please, Neal."

Sugar heard the click of the phones disconnecting.

"Still there?" Chuck croaked.

"Ten-four."

"I recorded the conversation for you," Chuck told him. "Maybe it'll help you find the girl. You can't use it for evidence, though, or I'm screwed. Okay?"

Sugar started the Bronco and swung out on the blacktop, pounding through the gears, racing toward the River Road, less than a mile away. "Chuck, where'd he call from?" he said, switching the phone to SPEAKER.

"Hold it, I'm in the database now."

"Just tell me where he called from." Sugar's headlights illuminated the back of a jogger on the road, dressed in red. Bad night to be running, he thought, with a storm coming in.

"Tell you one thing, your guy wasn't too bright staying on the line so long," Chuck said.

"Oh, he's plenty bright enough," Sugar replied. "But he's definitely a doughnut shy of a dozen."

Suddenly the jogger stopped running and turned slowly into the Bronco's headlights. Sugar eased up on the accelerator and peered through the windshield until the face came into focus . . . Theresa Arnold, he had dated her in high school. As he pressed the gas pedal and blew past her, he thought maybe he'd give her a call this weekend, see what she was up to.

"Got it," Chuck said. "Cell phone."

"Just my luck," Sugar said, downshifting to second and swerving onto River Road with a long fanfare of burning rubber.

Approaching the top of the hill, he punched off his headlights and rolled to a stop overlooking the farm. "Well, well," Sugar said quietly, peering down at the light coming from the arched hayloft window. "Looks like you got company, kid."

He backed the Bronco about 50 feet, until a stand of white pines

obscured the farm below. Then he pulled the vehicle head-on into the
brush between the trees.

"Hey, Champ, you want me to call the staties?"

"Negative," Sugar answered. "Big-hats'll screw things up. Just give
me two or three minutes, then page my dad with my 10–20."

"Say it in English."

"My location. Just tell him 'Code 33.' You don't have to understand
shit, okay? Dad'll know what to do."

Then Sugar was out the door, darting downhill from tree to tree,
his big Desert Eagle tight in his hand. When the trees gave way to
open hayfield, he kept his body low and ran as hard as he could. The
rising wind helped cover the sound of his uneven footfalls.

Vaulting across the farm road, Sugar pulled up behind the pump
house and drew his pistol. His chest heaved, his heart pounded. Steam
huffed from his mouth into the raw November night, as he assessed
the situation. The light in the barn was the kid's second mistake. The
phone call was definitely his first. Raising the pistol beside his ear, Sugar
peeked around the side. He scanned the twelve windows of the shed,
from back to front, hoping to see movement inside, and that's when
he saw the open bulkhead. He pulled his head back. Strike three.

Right about now, his father would be throwing his lobster bib on
the table and marching out of the Lobster Palace, elbows pumping out
from his sides the way they did when he hurried. Sugar pictured Detective Gallagher and the rest of the staties speeding into the dooryard
from all directions, jumping out of their cars with their guns drawn,
only to see Sugar Westerback emerge from the barn, pushing the pris-
oner along before him. "Someone lookin for this guy?" he'd say.

He took his small flashlight from his vest pocket and swung out
from the pump house, then ran low across the hardpacked paddock and
pivoted beside the bulkhead, so that his back pressed against the barn
between windows, his Desert Eagle ready. Stooping down beside the
raised bulkhead door, he moved around to the entrance and peered
down into the cellar. He could make out a dim yellowish light coming
from the right, but couldn't hear a sound except the wind behind him.
Flicking on his flashlight, he shone it on the wooden steps, as he ducked
low and started down.

The steps were made of new planking, solid and silent under his
feet. Reaching the concrete floor, he looked toward the source of yellowish light and saw a stairway coming down from above. The light
was upstairs. Sugar swept his flashlight to his left, the beam fluttering

along the new wooden posts until it illuminated the tractor and hay baler that were parked at the rear of the barn. Satisfied that he was alone in the cellar, he decided to wait there until Ellen showed up. Once he heard them talking upstairs, he could make his way up while the kid was distracted.

Then Sugar smelled the kerosene.

At least he thought it was kerosene. He sniffed the air attentively, thinking maybe it was diesel fuel from the tractor. Whatever it was, it had an odd tinge to it, like maybe a note of turpentine. Or pine pitch. And, actually, it seemed to be coming from the right, not from the tractor.

Holding his pistol and flashlight out in front of his chest, Sugar crept over to the stairway, circling around behind the stairs, out of the light. He held his breath and listened for footsteps above him, but the barn remained completely silent, strangely so, which meant either the kid wasn't there yet . . . or else he was waiting at the top of the stairwell.

Sugar braced himself. With both hands, he held the .357 and flashlight together in front of his face. Took a breath. One . . . two . . .

He wheeled around the corner post, aiming up. Strange, now the smell seemed to come from above.

He placed his foot on the first step and pushed himself up. The wood squeaked. Goosebumps broke out all over his arms—seemed to freeze on his flesh. He waved the big Desert Eagle out in front of him, keeping his eye at the top of the stairwell. He waited another moment, listening. But nothing stirred. Nothing but the smell wafting down, now more intense than before. He lifted himself to the next step, then climbed two more, feeling his leg shiver each time he set his foot down.

He could see by the low wooden ceiling at the top of the stairwell that the stairs emerged in the barn's new shed-roofed addition, and he knew the kid could be hiding in any one of the stalls that stretched to the back of the barn. In fact, he might be anywhere. Imagining suddenly that Neal was below him, Sugar swung his pistol down at the darkness behind him, and his flashlight whacked off the railing and jumped out of his hand. He watched helplessly as it banged off one step, then hit each successive step in its clamorous descent, until finally it smacked the concrete floor and rolled away from the stairs, glazing the dusty floor with its long, narrow beam.

Sugar stood suspended in the echo of the racket he'd made, tingling with goosebumps. In fact, he was beginning to regret having come by himself. Then he noticed that the railing under his hand was wet—no, oily. He lifted his fingers to his nose and smelled. Diesel fuel. His belly fluttered.

He concentrated on the .357 in his hand, the trigger under his index finger, and he turned to face the top of the stairs again. Point of no return. Quietly as possible, he resumed climbing. When his head was almost level with the floor joists, he lowered his back and crawled up one more step. Now, with his face close to the oil-soaked treads, he could detect other smells: alcohol, maybe gasoline, maybe paint thinner, a conglomeration of fumes that burned his eyes and told him he really had to get out of there. But he also had to protect Ellen Chambers.

He readied himself, knowing that when he raised his head above the floor, he'd have a clear shot down the shed's walkway and into the top of the first stall, possibly into the open barn. He gripped the ten-inch magnum with both hands. He took a breath . . .

No guts, no glory.

He sprang up—

Then lowered himself again.

Kneeling on the step, heart pounding, he replayed what he'd seen: wires everywhere, buckets and crates and wax-paper milk cartons lined up along the wall. Sugar crouched there as he puzzled it out, ears pricked for any speck of sound around him. Then, very slowly, he raised his head again. He stared.

The tops had been cut off the milk cartons. Stretching down the length of the wall that divided the shed from the open barn, there were probably fifty or sixty of them, and he was sure they were filled with fuel. The goose bumps went down his body in a flood. He looked over his right shoulder, at the door to the paddock. A tenpenny nail protruded from the top corner of the door, positioned to connect with a long strand of copper wire if the door opened an inch. Attached to the nail was a shorter length of wire that was buried in the glazing that surrounded the door's window. Not glazing, Sugar realized. Plastique, enough to perforate someone with glass shrapnel, head to waist, if the explosion didn't blow their head right off.

Another copper wire followed the low ceiling in two directions: over Sugar's head into the main section of the barn; and over the stalls to the rear wall. That's when Neal Chambers's plan became clear to Sugar: total destruction—and escape during the chaos.

Sugar lowered himself down three steps and unclipped his radio from his belt. He flicked it on and whispered: "Dad? Over." He released the microphone button and waited for a response.

"Where the hell are you?" Wes replied in a whisper, which either meant he was acknowledging Sugar's code 33, or he was close to the barn himself and afraid to raise his voice.

Sugar continued backing down the stairs, keeping his eyes peeled on the ceiling above the stairwell, watching for any hint of movement. "Dad, stay away," he said in a barely audible croak. "Everything's booby-trapped."

"Are you in the barn?" his father asked, exasperated.

"That's affirmative," Sugar answered, glancing over his shoulder into the darkness below him.

"Okay, get out of there."

"Ten-four that." As if he needed to be told. In fact, the second his foot hit that cellar floor he was going to bolt for the bulkhead and shoot anyone who tried to stop him. But first: "Dad, you've got to stop Ellen Chambers from coming."

"Just get the hell out of there. I'm a few minutes away. Backup's coming."

"Ten-four."

Reaching the bottom step, Sugar released his mike button and clipped the radio to his belt. He eyed his flashlight lying halfway to the bulkhead—the red glow of its lens cover—and he planned his move. He took a shallow breath of the deadly air, then made his break, running full tilt, snatching the flashlight on the fly, then veering left—

—and stopping quick, spinning around, waving his light at the darkness, as if he were fencing. Then he swiped the light back around to the bulkhead, which was now closed, copper wire and gray plastique affixed to the aluminum frame.

He shuddered with unspent adrenaline, then turned in a circle, painting his meager light beam across the kerosene-soaked posts. Then his light landed on a gray door built into the stone wall, no more than ten feet from the bulkhead. In fact, the door appeared to be another way out. Either that, or a trap.

"Come on, asshole." He spoke aloud to the darkness. "But you better be good."

Sugar approached the door cautiously, examining the jamb for wires, studying the hinges. It could be the kid's escape route, he thought, which would explain the reason why it didn't appear to be booby-trapped.

" 'Cause I got a nine-shot .357 magnum in my hand," he continued. "Fully loaded."

He reached out and touched the door with the back of his flashlight hand. It felt cold, probably made of steel. He hooked his finger under the latch, snapped it up. "Yup, you better be real, real good," he said, easing the door open so gently that a thread could have stopped it.

Now the cold, sweet stench hit him hard: as if he had popped the lid on a giant can of turpentine. He shone his light through the crack between the door and the jamb and peeked in at a pile of potatoes in a wooden bin. He pushed the door another inch and got a much stronger smell of turpentine, along with a slightly rotten whiff, heavier than bad potatoes should be, more like a huge dead rat in a wall. He opened the door wider, and that's when he saw the body.

The flashlight stared, along with the magnum.

Encased in a plastic bag, the young man was sprawled facedown, dressed all in black: black sweater, black corduroys, black boots, hands by his sides. Sugar could make out the ear and cheekbone, and he knew without question that the kid was dead. No mistaking death, once you've seen it. But he kept his pistol aimed at the body, just in case.

The words THIS SIDE UP and a bold red arrow were printed on the plastic—probably a refrigerator bag, Sugar guessed—and the opening was folded up at the bottom and sealed with duct tape. What was weird was the way the bag stuck to the side of the corpse's ear with a strange, reddish translucence. The hand was similarly colored, as though an inch deep in shellac.

Sugar recalled the Californians who killed themselves with bags over their heads and new sneakers, believing they were going to hitch a ride to heaven on the tail of a comet. By the looks of things, with the kerosene and booby traps, this kid had booked himself a one-way ticket to hell and was looking for fellow passengers.

"Sorry, my friend, not this time," Sugar said, raising his radio to his mouth and pushing the button down. "Hey, Dad," he said. "Elvis has left the building. Over."

The radio clicked, and his father said urgently, "What the hell are you talking about? Are you outta there yet?"

Sugar pressed the button to respond, but his voice was abruptly cut off.

Her mind swimming with trepidation, Ellen drove down the hill to her farm. She pulled into the dooryard unceremoniously, the same way she'd pulled in thousands of times when she had lived here, as if nothing were wrong. Indeed, no other vehicle was parked there—but she guarded against taking any relief from that.

She had known this day would come eventually, and now that it was here, she felt utterly helpless to do anything other than follow the path Neal had prepared for her. She pictured herself wandering through the barn door and seeing Moreen hanging from the beam.

She should have called the police, that's what she kept telling herself, while another voice kept warning her of what Neal had intimated, that any police involvement would cost Moreen her life. Neal didn't lie. Ellen knew that much about him. He considered lying beneath his dignity. But his particular brand of truth was always riddled with layers, his self-righteous sleight of hand. Another thing she knew: No matter what words he used, he was not about to abandon his vendetta at this stage.

But what could she do?

Forgive him? Of course she could say the words. But she'd be lying, and they both knew that, without going through the ceremony. Somehow this little drama didn't seem symbolic enough or brilliant enough for Neal's *coup de grâce*. And if there were some significance to the date—the day before Thanksgiving?—Ellen couldn't figure it out.

She stepped out of her truck and walked cautiously to the barn. The front doors were opened maybe two inches, wide enough so she could see a vertical line of light in the opening, and, as she got closer, wide enough so she could smell the kerosene. As soon as she pushed the door open another inch, she saw the glint of Neal's eye less than two feet from her face. Startled as she was, she almost didn't recognize him. He'd grown a beard and his hair was long.

"Ellen, don't be afraid," he said, smiling softly. He opened the door another inch and peered out at the night. A fine, icy mist hung in the air.

She looked past him into the barn and saw the milk cartons, the rags piled around posts. Now the smell of kerosene was overpowering, and she knew he was planning to destroy the building.

"Come in," he said, opening the door wider. Now she could see the centerpiece of this passion play: a thick rope hanging from the low beam, ending in a noose. Her heart stopped. One of her kitchen chairs stood below the noose, surrounded by a frightening pile of two-by-fours and oak timbers, stuffed with oil-soaked hay.

Reacting to Ellen's expression, Neal's smile turned beatific. "This is the cup my father has given me," he said. "Shall I not drink it?"

Suddenly she wondered: Was he planning to kill himself?

"Neal," she began, then didn't know how to continue. *He thinks he's Jesus Christ.* His eyes shone fiercely, as though daring her to say he was insane. "Neal, please tell me what you did with Mo."

As though he'd been waiting for that question, he lifted a hand in front of his face. A small leather pouch tied by rawhide dangled from his thumb. Then he turned away from her and walked into the center of the barn. She opened the door wider.

"Neal, you don't have to do this."

She held the door, terrified to go in after him. But having no choice, she stepped inside, and once she did, the door swung shut behind her. She heard a clunk above her and looked up, saw a pair of ropes on pulleys attached to the doors, with plastic pails tied to the ends of the ropes—counterweights, to keep the doors closed. She also saw copper wires and rags and milk cartons attached to the door's frame, and she realized that the hanging pails were probably filled with gasoline. She moved farther into the barn, out from under the gently swaying pails.

"Neal, I understand how you feel," she said. "And I forgive you."

As she approached his funeral pyre he turned his head and gave her a placid smile, teeming with contempt. "You forgive me? For what?"

"I know you murdered my mother," Ellen continued. "You killed Scott's parents too. I know the things you've done, and I know why."

" 'Breach for breach,' " he said calmly. " 'Eye for eye, tooth for tooth.' "

"Neal, I forgive you."

He stared at her darkly.

"Is Moreen here?" Ellen said. "Is she in the barn?"

Holding the pouch by its rawhide tie, he held it out to her again.

Ellen stopped breathing. Did his gesture mean the pouch held the answer to Moreen's whereabouts—or was it her remains? She did not try for surprise, nor was she coy. She reached into her jacket pocket and withdrew the revolver, aimed at the center of his chest.

"I'm not playing this game with you," she said. "Tell me what you did with my daughter."

"Or you'll kill me?" He shook his head at her, the pouch still dangling from his thumb.

She lowered her aim to his stomach. "You know I'm capable."

Even as she thumbed the hammer back, his expression did not flag. Rather, he held out his other hand, then spread both his arms wide, offering himself as if he were Jesus on the cross. Then his other hand opened, revealing what might have been a pager. But it wasn't.

"My twelve legions," he explained. "Also called a dead man's switch, for the benefit of the Pharisees listening in. Meaning if I drop it, or if my thumb somehow releases this button—"

Ellen narrowed her eyes at him, refusing to avert her aim. "Nobody is listening in, Neal. No one is here but you and me."

His smile disappeared. He turned his back on her and climbed up the oil-soaked pyre onto the chair, saying, " 'And ye shall know the truth, and the truth shall make you free.' "

"I have told you the truth!"

Balancing himself precariously on the chair, he turned to face her again, and the noose brushed his hair. Even though Ellen matched his persistent stare with her own and kept her .38 trained on his stomach, they both knew he held the upper hand: He had Moreen. When her vision twisted with tears, she lowered the gun.

"Neal, don't you think I know how much you were hurt?" she said, exasperated. "I was hurt too. We've all been hurt. But Moreen had nothing to do with it."

"Colossians three," he said. " 'The wrath of God cometh on the children of disobedience.' "

"Neal, you're not God. You could at least give her a chance."

He studied her again, and she hoped he was considering what she had said. Then he tossed the pouch to her feet. The sound of it striking the floor convinced her it was not filled with ashes. When she came forward and picked it up, its contents jangled like heavy coins.

"You don't have time to open it," he said. "You need to leave."

She looked up, saw him pulling the noose down over his head, raising his face to fit the rope under his beard, all the while holding his dead man's switch close to his face. As he pulled the noose tight around his neck, Ellen straightened and raised her revolver again, aiming at his thigh, prepared to fire. "I've forgiven you, Neal. I've done everything you asked. Now tell me what you did with Moreen."

He raised a boot on the chair's top, coaxing the chair to wobble, and Ellen started backing away from him. "I'm not going to watch you, Neal. You're not going to leave me with that."

"You know this cannot be stopped," he said, "or how else could the prophecy be fulfilled, which says this has to be?" He fixed his dark eyes on her, long and sorrowful. "Ellen?"

Her boot heel hit the door. She reached behind her, found the latch. "Neal, I need my daughter."

"Don't forget me."

"Neal—"

Suddenly her arm was caught from behind and she was yanked out the door. In the same instant, an explosion sent her hurtling to the ground. Another explosion shook the earth, and she heard the horrible din of men shouting and screaming. Then she was hauled roughly to her feet and dragged along, as the explosions continued clocking off behind her, one after another, while someone chanted, "Keep going, keep going, keep going." Ellen couldn't tell how many men were pulling her while she resisted, trying to get back to the barn.

"*Let me go!*"

"Mrs. Chambers—"

It was Gallagher, by himself. He pulled Ellen down to the gravel road behind the pump house, while she threw her elbow at him, trying to escape.

"You're okay," he said, capturing her arms.

"*He's got Moreen!*"

"I know. Stay down!"

He pulled her back against the pump house door and held her tightly. With each small explosion, lines of fire radiating from the barn raced serpentine paths across the hayfield and pastures, until the entire farm was networked in flame lines. Ellen saw a man running a crazy path away from the barn, holding his face, and another man, his back and shoulder on fire, writhing in the muddy paddock, while flames crackled out of all twelve shed windows, and flashlights fluttered like moths around the burning farm, silhouettes of men racing in confusion. Ellen watched one of them running toward her, vaulting line after line of flames, scattering the smoke. Wearing a dark windbreaker, he fell to his knees beside Gallagher, barking into a handheld radio, "Stand by!" Then he looked wildly at the detective. "We've got to pull back, we're gettin hammered up there." In the flickering firelight, Ellen could see blood stringing down his cheek from a gash under his eye. Suddenly sirens rose up amidst the chaos, and the blowing smoke started flashing red, as a fire truck pulled into the yard.

"Keep everybody back, firefighters, everybody," Gallagher told him. "But watch the windows and doors—this may be a smokescreen for his escape."

The officer sprang to his feet and took off running, shouting into his radio. As dozens of men retreated from the barn in what looked like military maneuvers, a floodlight lit up on the farm road about thirty feet in front of Ellen, and another came on beside the house, both aimed through the smoke at the barn.

"Get those vehicles out to the road!" someone shouted. Someone else called out, *"Save the house!"*

Huddled against the safe side of the pump house, Ellen realized that the explosions had stopped. Now she could hear the busy murmuring of the fires inside the barn, like elders in conference, and she could hear the droning and shouting of men's voices, the drumming of fire-fighters' boots as they ran through the burning field with Indian pumps strapped to their backs. Underneath all the commotion, she realized with amazement that Neal was dead.

Suddenly a firefighter burst through the smoke, his boots and trouser cuffs steaming. "Detective, you need to move!" His voice was nearly obscured by the rushing of grass fires that threatened to close in on them.

"Come on," Gallagher said, grabbing Ellen's arm. The firefighter took her other arm and, pulling her to her feet, they ran farther down the farm road, maybe fifty feet, to the crest of the hill, where they dropped to their knees and turned back. Now the pasture on one side and the hayfield on the other were lit in smoking, flickering yellow-gray.

"There it goes," Gallagher said, watching the barn.

The fire did not climb the side of the building but seemed to materialize through the walls in a solid sheet, like some brilliant, shimmering ghost.

"Rainstorm or no rain," someone said, a firefighter in a long, black coat, "there won't be nothing but a pile of ash by the time we can get to it. That's one hot son of a gun."

Even from this safe distance, Ellen felt the incredible heat of the fire. Holding the pouch toward the light, she tugged at the rawhide drawstring.

"Don't open that!" Gallagher snapped, ripping the pouch from her hand. A bright jangle flew from the opening.

"He's got Moreen!" Ellen shot back, lunging at the ground to find what had spilled. Twin flashlight beams cut through the yellow smoke, shining on two silver dollars in the wet hay. She grabbed for them, just as a black shoe came down beside her hand.

"Move!" she snapped, pushing at the leg.

A hand gripped her shoulder. "Did you see my boy in there?"

"You're in my light!" Ellen yelled.

"Look," said Gallagher, "I need everyone to shut up for a minute. Chief Westerback—"

"My son was in that barn!"

Ellen looked up, saw that it was Wes Westerback standing over her, his face streaked black and red in the firelight, his eyes stark.

"My boy Sugar was inside," he said to her, his voice forced and trembling. "Did you see him?"

Horrified, she stared back at him and shook her head, at the same time understanding the meaning of the pouch: pieces of silver, blood money. Moreen was lost. She rose to her feet and looked recklessly at the barn. Gallagher positioned himself in front of her, as though to keep her from running back to the burning building.

"Why did you come?" she asked Gallagher.

"Look," he said, spilling silver dollars from the pouch into his open hand. "Silver dollars, that's all—"

Gallagher jumped back, emptying his hand, and the coins and pouch hit the ground with a deadening smack. The flashlight beams intersected, then illuminated the fleshy ringlet that had been tucked inside the pouch with the silver: a severed ear, decorated with a single silver stud.

Ellen's heart stopped.

"Jesus," Gallagher said softly, while Ellen stood there shaking, desperately telling herself that the ear could not be her daughter's. She tried to remember what Moreen's ear looked like, and with a flash of relief, recalled its multiple rings and studs. Beside her, Wes sank to one knee and reached for the ear, his hand shivering.

"Probably best if we brought that to the lab," Gallagher said, trying to sound sympathetic even as he wiped his bloody fingers on his handkerchief.

Wes rose again, almost summarily, and peered off at the raging barn, already radiating so much heat that the firefighters and equipment had given up on it and were focusing all their water on the house, which sent thick clouds of steam up its clapboards.

"He's gonna want that sewed back on," Wes said, setting the ear gently in the handkerchief in Gallagher's hands, then turned toward the valley, where dozens of volunteer firefighters roamed amongst the flames, pumping water at the grass fires. "Any of you men check down by the pond? Cripes, injury like that could turn anyone around."

Gallagher wrapped the ear in the handkerchief, then put his hand on the old man's shoulder. "Chief Westerback, you understand we've got to keep moving on this——?"

Although their eyes did not meet, Ellen could see that a certain understanding passed between the two men. Gallagher looked over his shoulder and said to someone, "Officer, help Chief Westerback home, please."

Wes looked toward the barn once more, his eyes glimmering. "I'll be in my car," he said. "Take care of that ear. His mother's gonna want that sewed back on." Then he expanded his chest, turned and started walking up the gravel road.

Gallagher turned back to Ellen, who crouched with a trooper on the ground, collecting the spilled contents of the pouch. "Thirty dollars," the trooper said with his hands full.

Ellen narrowed her eyes at Gallagher. "He told me to come alone! Didn't you know that?"

"It doesn't matter. This is all he gave you," the detective answered calmly, indicating the coins. "It's all he ever intended to give you. But we have certain information——"

"Oh, *information!*" Ellen snapped.

Gallagher stepped away from her.

Ellen heard a commotion and spotted three men marching around the pump house, arguing. She recognized Scott's voice. The other two men were state troopers. Gallagher stepped toward them and barked, "Let him through!" The men separated, and Scott came running across the blackened, smoldering field, his eyes raging.

"What the hell's going on?"

"Neal's got Mo," Ellen said. "He told me to come alone."

"Is she okay?"

"I don't know." she said desperately. "Neal's dead. In the barn."

"Jesus," Scott breathed, looking off toward the inferno.

"We found the car your daughter was driving," Gallagher said.

Ellen wheeled. "Her car? Where?"

Gallagher ignored her. "The Hampton police tagged it this morning," he explained to Scott, "parked in an alley by the beach. It belongs to a girl who admitted she loaned it to Moreen. We're also investigating a homicide that occurred in the vicinity of the car. There's a possible connection. If so, then Neal could have kidnapped Moreen two days ago."

Ellen sucked in a rigid breath. "You said we'd be protected," she said. "So how does he manage to come here and fill that barn full of explosives? How does he get to Moreen before you do?"

"I told you, we identified certain target dates, based on our profile," Gallagher said, not looking at her. "November 22 wasn't one of them."

"It should have been," Scott said.

Ellen stood stiffly, while the others turned to Scott.

"November 22 was my brother Jonathan's birthday," he explained.

"Oh, yeah, *target dates,*" Ellen said to Gallagher.

She felt a hand on her arm. The female trooper moved her a couple of steps back. "I know you're upset," she said quietly, "but the detective's got a little boy in the hospital, and he's not doing too good. Why don't you lighten up a little."

"Our tech people are analyzing the document your nephew faxed," Gallagher said to Scott, unaware of the trooper's intercession. He turned to Ellen. "They're listening to tapes of your telephone conversation with Neal, as well as your conversation inside the barn. What I need to know is if he said anything that we missed, maybe in a whispered voice. Or if he made any gestures or facial expressions that might be meaningful."

Ellen stared at the detective, trying to think. She felt rain hitting her face, or maybe it was spray blowing over from the fire hose. She shook her head helplessly.

"You must have some idea where she is," Scott said to Gallagher.

"Somewhere she can't stick a needle in her arm," Ellen answered, with an accusatory ring that she did not intend.

"What's that supposed to mean?"

Ellen turned away from him, as the image of Mo's bruised arm came to her unbidden—the sight of which, a week after Mo's wedding, had convinced Ellen that Randy was manhandling her daughter. The truth was worse: The bruise had been needle marks. Randy had made Moreen an addict.

"What's she talking about?" Scott said to Gallagher.

"It fits," Gallagher said. "The victim in Hampton Beach was a heroin dealer. We're canvassing the neighborhood and checking the vacant cottages and shops. There's a possibility Neal locked her up somewhere in the neighborhood."

"But where?"

"Any of hundreds of cottages," Gallagher said. "It's a beach town, most everything's closed up for the season."

Ellen took the fax out of her jacket pocket and unfolded it. The female trooper shone her flashlight on it: Moreen sitting sullenly in the corner of the room. A heroin addict.

Scott lowered his face toward the paper. "She's not tied up. Why wouldn't she leave?"

"It's possible he's got the doors and windows booby-trapped, like he did here."

"More likely she's out in the water," a deeper voice said.

Ellen turned, saw Rooftop Paradise towering over them all, dressed in a black firefighter's coat that was open down the front and much too short in the sleeves. The Indian tank strapped over his shoulder looked like a thermos.

"Keep on with your work and let us do our job," one of the policemen said to him, but Rooftop didn't move.

Gallagher ran his finger across the photo. "See the construction of the wall behind her—no wallboard, no insulation? That's either a cottage or a hunting camp in some remote location."

"You don't get light like that in the woods," Rooftop said. "That's under the open sky."

Gallagher turned and looked up at the giant.

"Besides, any beach cottage with an ocean view isn't likely to be this ramshackle," Rooftop added.

A loud cracking started, then a barrage of shouting, and they turned to see the barn collapsing, its roof parachuting down with a fierce crunch, blowing flames and sparks in all directions. An almost visible wave of heat rolled over them. Ellen thought of Neal with amazement, killing himself that way, but her thoughts quickly returned to Mo.

"How many islands are off the coast?" she asked.

Gallagher hesitated, then said to Scott, "I just don't know how he'd get her out there."

"Boat," Rooftop said.

Ellen turned to Rooftop. "Are there any islands twelve miles out?"

"For Christ sakes, El, let the men do their job," Scott told her, then he turned to Gallagher.

"Okay, look, what I can do is notify the Coast Guard," the detective said. "I'll have them call around to the marinas, see if anyone's seen anything unusual. For now, we'll focus our resources on the more plausible scenarios."

Ellen glanced toward the burning barn and her chest hardened. She turned back to Rooftop. "Where's your boat?"

"El, don't start," Scott said.

She started walking away, then turned back to the giant. "Are you coming?"

"Twelve miles or twelve nautical miles?" Gary Pope asked, his eyes never leaving the television. "And twelve miles from where? Shit, my own dock's twelve miles from Ogunquit, Kittery, Berwick, you name it. Everything's twelve miles from lots of places."

The fisherman was small and wiry, probably in his fifties, with wire-rim bifocals and a thick growth of neatly parted gray hair. Dressed in his green work clothes and black rubber boots, he sank deeper in his leather recliner, eating a boiled hot dog with his fingers. His television sat on top of the refrigerator, tuned to *Wheel of Fortune*. The room smelled strongly of cigarettes. The kitchen table, where Rooftop and Ellen hovered over the nautical chart, was given to piles of bills and receipts, an adding machine, a set of scales, and a boxy two-way radio whose dial danced with silently blinking red lights.

Rooftop placed a transparent plastic ruler on the chart, with the zero line approximately centered in the clustered Isles of Shoals, and he swung an arc westward over the shore, tracing the twelve-mile mark with his finger.

"Rye Beach, that's next to Hampton," Rooftop said, then he turned. "Hey, Gary, we need to know if anyone had a boat stolen in the past couple of days."

The fisherman let out a sigh. He levered his La-Z-Boy forward and sprang to his feet, walked over to his radio and flipped a switch.

"Rye Harbor Marina, Rye Harbor Marina, Urchin Matters, switch and answer, channel sixty-eight, over." He listened for a moment, then flipped the switch again. "Rye Harbormaster, Urchin Matters, switch and answer, sixty-eight, over."

"Okay, Urchin Matters," the radio squawked.

"Just checkin on something," Gary continued. "Anyone down there have their boat stole, past few days? Over."

"Hold on. Over."

Ellen and Rooftop exchanged a look, while the radio hissed. Then the squawking resumed.

"Yeah, Urchin Matters, fella named Hughes came in two mornings ago and said his cabin lock was cut. No damage, nothing missing except for a half-tank of fuel. Figured some kids took it out for a joyride. Over."

Gary looked over at Rooftop, who nodded.

"Gotta be some unfulfilled to go joyridin in a lobster boat," the harbormaster said. "Over."

"I guess prob'ly," Gary said into the radio. "That's it then. Over and out." He pushed the toggle switch, silencing the radio.

Rooftop eyed Ellen solemnly. "Just about exact," he said, holding his ruler on the chart.

A charge of apprehension started Ellen's heart beating.

"Gary, I need you to gas me up," Rooftop said.

The gray-haired man stared hard at him. "In this weather, mister, you ain't gonna do a thing but radio the Coast Guard. Besides which, they're not about to go out in a storm themselves, where you don't even know for sure if the girl's out there."

"I know she's out there," Ellen said to Gary, pulling a slicker off a coat hook. "I need to borrow your rain gear."

Rooftop gave her a look, then turned back to Gary. "You mind if she keeps you company while I go look?"

"I'm coming with you," Ellen told him.

"Too dangerous," Rooftop said, not even looking at her. "Gary, gas me up."

"Do you have some gloves?" Ellen said, pushing her arms into the rubber sleeves.

"You can't come," Rooftop told her.

"It's my daughter out there," she said, pulling the zipper to her neck. "Now hurry up."

Gary showed her an indulgent frown. "Well, yes, ma'am."

Rooftop stood at the console and steered the Boston Whaler out of the York River, his red and green bow lights making haloes in the rain. Ellen sat on the pilot seat to his right, holding tight to the side rail. Despite the rain slicker and layers of clothing underneath, the cold spray from the waves and riotous beating of near-frozen rain on her hood made her realize just how much they were at the mercy of the elements.

As they left the safety of the harbor, Rooftop yelled over the howling motor, "It could get rough," and they hit the first wave of the open ocean with a startling crunch. With its characteristic tub-shaped design, the seventeen-foot boat lifted its bow and slapped the water again and again, harder every time, until Ellen felt each impact jar the base of her spine. Soon a green bell buoy rose out of the gray like a foreboding angel, bobbing and clanging as it passed on their right. Behind them, far back to the left, she heard the owlish hoot of the Cape Neddick foghorn.

She peeked up at Rooftop hunched behind the short windscreen, saw the water blowing off his face as though he were taking a shower.

"How can you see?" she yelled.

"Half hour!" he yelled back, obviously misunderstanding her.

He wore a miner's lamp strapped around his watch cap, and he angled the beam at the chart that was clamped between the windscreen and wheel. Incredibly, the rain began blowing harder and the waves grew larger, lifting and lowering the boat in an endless, nauseating rhythm. Despite the windscreen, every time the boat climbed, the waters found their way into Ellen's hood, working a deep chill into her shoulders. Her shivering was more from fear, however, than the cold.

As the boat fought its way farther from land, she clutched the side rail and tried to envision Moreen waiting safely indoors, while her uncooperative mind whirled with images of the barn fire, of Sugar's ear, of Neal's spectacular suicide, until she realized that she had lost the sounds of bell buoys clanging, and the foghorn had disappeared far behind them. Now there was only the wind, the rain, and this small boat churning laboriously up the sides of mountainous waves, then plummeting down the other. The way the motor screamed to make it to the top, it almost seemed that they were making no forward progress but just fighting to keep from being driven back to land.

Once when they descended into a trough Ellen felt water slosh against the backs of her boots, about a foot deep. Terrified, she looked up at Rooftop.

"The bilge pump's working as hard as it can," he shouted.

As they rode up and over the next wave crest and descended to the bottom, the water piled over her calves, knocking her into the console.

Rooftop lifted her by the elbow. "She's unsinkable!" he yelled, with more confidence than was his nature, as a wall of water slammed against Ellen's side.

"Hold on, we're turning south," he yelled. "It's gonna get a little rough."

Ellen gave him a look, aghast, as the motor churned valiantly, pushing the whaler up toward the black rain. This time, when they started to fall, she felt a weightless chill take her stomach, and she fell back heavily in her seat. Feeling as if she was about to vomit, she tried to put it out of her mind.

"How much longer?" she yelled, her stomach swelling like the waves.

"Stay up," Rooftop yelled back at her.

She pulled herself to her feet, clutching the console rail with her left hand and the grab rail with her right, and she realized she had lost her left glove. Another wave hit the corner of the bow and blew past her shoulder. She sank dizzily in her seat, lowered her face and stuffed her cold hand in her pocket. When they plunged into the next trough, the flood splashed full against her chest, knocking her to her knees.

Rooftop raised his fingers to his teeth and pulled his glove off his hand.

"I don't want that," Ellen shouted at him.

He slapped the glove against her arm. "Put it on, my hands are protected!"

Not stopping to figure out what he meant, she took the giant glove and slid her hand inside, grateful for the warmth. The boat fell. Her stomach leaped. She caught the grab rail and threw up over her arm, holding on for dear life the whole time.

"I'm sorry," she moaned.

"You get *me* throwing up, you'll know what sorry is," he replied. "Hold tight."

He wrapped a long arm around her just as a hard, cold spray hit her face. Then he reached his other arm in front of her and cut the motor. A jolt of panic shot through Ellen, thinking he was going to throw her overboard. She grabbed for the rail.

"Listen," he said.

The wind whipped across the froth, as a wave lifted the boat high, then dropped them back down. Ellen felt her stomach roll.

"Waves," he said.

"Yeah, no kidding," she answered.

"Listen," he said again.

But all she could hear was the hum of the bilge pump laboring and the rain slapping off her hood. However, as the next swell passed under them, she heard the whisper of a distant surf crashing against a shore. She looked off toward the sound and thought she saw a small haze of light winking through the fog.

"The White Island lighthouse," Rooftop said, slowing the motor even more. He switched on his miner's lamp and pressed his face close to the chart, then looked over at the compass. In the light, Ellen could see raindrops the size of dimes hitting the windscreen.

"Five minutes," he encouraged, opening the throttle and turning the wheel fully to the left. As they surged ahead, he said, "Only a couple of islands are isolated. One of them has a shack on it."

Ellen pulled herself to her feet. "That's the one."

Amidst her fear and nausea, Ellen was able to clear her mind just enough to say a short prayer that they would find Moreen on the island and that she'd be alive. That was all Ellen dared to ask for, certainly more than she felt she deserved.

Rooftop peered out over the windscreen, his glasses spilling the rain. "We want to head for the lee side," he said. "There used to be a dock."

Five minutes later, they found the dock standing in water that was incredibly calm, despite the fury of the storm. Rooftop tied the boat to the posts, and they followed his flashlight beam along the slippery wood and up a trail to puddled bedrock, then to moss. On the island, the fog was every bit as thick as it had been at sea, and Rooftop's flashlight beam did not reach even ten feet in front of them. Luckily, a slight path was worn in the sea grass.

"Mo?" Ellen yelled into the wind. "Moreen?" She stopped walking for a moment, to listen for a response.

"Just ahead," Rooftop told her, and they continued for twenty feet or so, before his light landed on a gray-shingled wall. The shack looked to be about ten feet from corner to corner, and the single window was hung with burlap.

"Mo?"

"Here," Rooftop said.

The door was solid wood, chipped green paint. Ellen pushed in front of him and took the doorknob in her hand.

"Maybe you should let me go in first," Rooftop suggested.

"No," she said, and she shoved the door open. The wind blew in, and a foul smell blew out. Rooftop moved the flashlight across the floor to a pile of blankets in the corner, with dark hair flowing out of the top and a single black boot sticking out the bottom. Ellen shivered in the doorway. Rooftop steadied her with a hand on her shoulder.

"Mo?" she said, her voice shaking.

The moan she heard might have been the wind.

"Mo?"

The blanket twitched.

"Oh, God." Ellen threw herself across the floor and pulled the blanket away from her face. In the light beam, she saw the closed eyes, the tattooed tears. In Ellen's frozen hand, Mo's cheek felt hot.

"Don't touch me," Moreen complained, jerking the blanket over her head.

"Oh, God, Mo," Ellen breathed, clutching her daughter tightly. "Oh, God, you're safe—"

"Get *off!*" Moreen said, thrashing out of the blankets so that the back of her hand caught Ellen's frozen cheek and sat her back, momentarily stunned.

Mo squinted against Rooftop's miner's lamp. Her peacoat was buttoned wrong, her jeans were wet and stank of urine. Her cheeks looked horribly gaunt, her eyes sunken. "You woke me up," she said, then crawled back inside her blankets.

Ellen heard Rooftop's sigh. "I'll radio the Coast Guard," he said quietly, and walked out into the rain.

twenty-two

Moreen spent the next thirty-six hours in the Portsmouth hospital, refusing to speak, refusing to eat the hospital food, even refusing the pecan pie Ellen had baked her for Thanksgiving. Her weight had dropped twenty pounds, but other than exhaustion and an overall listlessness, doctors found no reason to keep her hospitalized longer. On Friday evening, at 6:30, while Ellen dozed in the waiting room, she was awakened to the sound of Scott's voice.

"We're going home," Scott said to her. "Mo's coming with me."

Ellen took a deep breath, a sort of yawn, wondering how long she'd been asleep. Then Mo appeared in the corridor, behind her father. She glanced in at Ellen, her beautiful brown eyes conveying nothing, then walked out of sight, while the facts assembled in Ellen's mind—Moreen going to live with Scott?

"I'll see you," he said, and he turned for the door.

Ellen drove home, tense with the chill inside her truck, trying to convince herself that, under the circumstances, things had worked out for the best. Certainly, having Mo living at home with Scott was an improvement on wherever she had been staying. Indeed, if she'd been hooked on heroin, maybe the ordeal had scared some sense into her.

Ellen turned up the heater in the truck and lifted the collar of her jean jacket, but still she could not shake the feeling, this anxiety, that things were profoundly unresolved. Yes, Neal was gone, and that was a relief, but his death did little to balance what he had taken from her.

And how was it that Neal, who'd been so calculating, had extracted his vengeance on everyone *except* Scott?

The car lot was closed when she pulled in. The showroom lights glared, and orange-tinged security lights projected hazy rings on hundreds of windshields and hoods. But Ellen's apartment was dark, and she couldn't help feeling nervous. Pulling around the back of the building, she shut off the truck, took her keys from the ignition, then reached in the glove box and took out her revolver. Slipping the gun into her jacket pocket, she got out of her truck and walked quickly to the stairs.

Inside the enclosure that protected her stairway from the elements, she climbed into darkness, keeping her hand on her revolver, wishing she had left the stair light on. Reaching the door, she scratched her key over the lock until it found home. She pushed the door open, but didn't go in. Instead, she turned her head and looked down.

"Mrs. Chambers?"

"*Jesus—*"

"Ellen, it's Dave Gallagher," the detective said from the bottom of the stairs. "Sorry to startle you. Can I come up for a sec?"

Her hand came out of her pocket. She reached into her kitchen and snapped on the overhead fluorescent light, then went to the gas space heater and dialed up the thermostat. When she turned back, Gallagher was there rapping lightly on the door jamb. She didn't tell him to come in. He did anyway, carrying two manila envelopes in one of his hands. He was wearing a dark trench coat and a fedora pulled down to his brow. He looked freshly shaven. The combination enhanced his appearance immeasurably.

"I wanted to apprise you of the results of our investigation," he said.

"Close the door, please," she told him, and he did. Then he turned to face her, holding the envelopes in front of him, and told her that although police and fire investigators were still sorting through the ashes of her burned-out barn, their investigation confirmed what they already knew, that Neal had rigged the barn with enough fuel to practically vaporize the building and everything in it, including himself.

Gallagher's cheeks were pink, making Ellen think he'd been waiting in the cold for some time. Either that, or he was embarrassed that she had found Moreen and gotten her to a hospital while he and his troops were still breaking into summer cottages in Hampton Beach. For her part, Ellen felt a little remorse at her impatience with him, especially in light of his son's medical problems. She wondered if the boy had cancer.

He told her that Sugar Westerback's remains had been found in the root cellar, which, although protected from the flames by its steel door, had acted like a giant roasting oven. Nicks on the front of Sugar's spine indicated that his throat had been cut.

"I don't need any more details," Ellen told him finally. She left her jacket and cap on while the room warmed up.

"We also found your nephew's van," Gallagher said.

"He was my husband's nephew," Ellen told him, not for the first time.

"The van had been stolen in Pennsylvania four years ago, probably kept in his barn till he needed it. He got the license plates in June, off a car in Portland."

"How do you know the van was his?"

"He left a couple of detonators behind, his sleeping bag, some carpenter's tools . . . and this." The detective tried to hand Ellen one of the envelopes. She refused to take it.

"It's a deed to his Vermont property," Gallagher explained, "notarized and signed over to you before his death."

"I don't want it."

Gallagher tossed the envelope on the table. "You're free to sell it. You don't need to decide now." He set the other envelope on the table, too, this one heavy and bulging. "This is also yours."

Hearing the sound it made when he set it down, Ellen didn't need to ask what was inside. "Keep the money," she said. "Don't you have a policemen's ball or something?"

"I'm not allowed to take donations."

"Take it home and give it to your little boy," she said. "How is he?"

Gallagher held up a finger, declining the distraction. "Mrs. Chambers, did Neal ever talk about religion?"

"You mean, did he believe he was Jesus Christ? I think that's obvious."

Gallagher folded his arms. "Judas was paid thirty silver coins to betray Jesus," he explained. "And when the Pharisees came to arrest him, his disciple Peter cut off one of their ears—"

Ellen turned away from him and leaned heavily on the small kitchen table, her wayward worries suddenly crystalizing.

"Is something wrong?" the detective asked.

Ellen turned back to him. "Doesn't it make you wonder?" she said. The coldness of her apartment seemed to have found its way into her bones.

"Wonder about what?"

"That maybe Neal also planned for his resurrection—?"

The detective frowned, and he shook his head slowly from side to side. Although his eyes were dead-on reassuring, he fell short of convincing her.

"How do you know that was him you found?" she asked. "Did you do DNA tests? Dental matches? What exactly did you find?"

"We were present when he died," the detective said. "You were there. There's no way he got out of that barn."

"He could have dressed as a fireman and jumped out a window during the explosions."

The detective shook his head again. "We had men videotaping that building the entire time. We've reviewed those tapes over and over. You've seen the damage. Even in the cellar, the tractor melted. Nobody—not even Jesus Christ himself—could have survived that fire."

"Neal Chambers began planning his revenge when he was twelve years old," Ellen said. "That has been his sole purpose in life. Not love, not friends, not money . . . but revenge against Scott and everyone close to him. Can you give me one reason I should believe Neal would spare the life of the one person he holds most responsible for his father's death?"

"Moreen."

"What?"

"I think he had feelings for her."

Ellen shook her head, refusing to be swayed.

"Look, I'm no psychiatrist," Gallagher said, "but I do have a master's degree in criminal psychology, and I've been in this business a long time. I believe Neal planned to execute all three of you on his father's birthday. I also think when he got close enough to your family, when he made real human contact, he saw that Moreen had problems of her own—as did you all."

"You mean he figured we'd kill each other if he gave us enough time?"

The detective leveled his eyes at her. "I think he lost the will."

Ellen shook her head adamantly.

"With what you've been through," he continued, "frankly I'd be very surprised if you didn't have feelings of anxiety. But I want you to be assured that, as far as Neal Chambers is concerned, you have nothing more to worry about."

"As far as *Neal* is concerned?"

Gallagher tightened his lips. "Your son-in-law's drowning," he said. "I'm afraid that case remains open."

Ellen blinked her eyes once, while she waited for him to continue.

He lifted a sealed plastic bag from his trench coat pocket. Inside was a blackened, serrated knife blade. "This is most likely the knife that Neal used to murder Sergeant Westerback. It was found in the root cellar, beside the officer's body."

Ellen kept blinking, but now her heart was pounding. She recognized the blade—Neal must have dug it out of her cucumber patch.

"We're pretty sure it's the same knife that caused the wounds to Randy's thigh and shoulder," Gallagher said, studying Ellen for a moment.

"And?"

"I never believed Randy's death was accidental," he explained. "Too many coincidences, not the least of which being that his death occurred twelve days after he married your daughter . . . all of which points to Neal." He raised his hat to his hairline. "Trouble is, Neal couldn't have pulled it off without an accomplice. Maybe two."

"In other words, Scott and me—?"

"My personal opinion? Society is better off without Randy Cross. And I have no doubt that your daughter is better off without him."

"So if I ever feel compelled to confess—?"

Gallagher eyed her without humor. "I take my job very seriously, Mrs. Chambers; it's not up to me to dispense mercy. I investigate, I apprehend, I deliver criminal suspects into the justice system."

She unzipped her jacket, went to the stove and turned the heat down a little.

"With what your family's been through, I could almost guarantee immunity for voluntary information. And considering all the extenuating circumstances, along with Randy's criminal record, I don't know anyone at the DA's office who'd be ambitious about prosecuting an accomplice."

"Don't they take their jobs seriously?" she asked pointedly.

"They have discretion. I don't."

She gave the detective a look, wanting him to leave. He took the hint and reached behind him for the doorknob. "You're here alone, aren't you?" he said, opening the door.

"I can take care of myself."

"I was just going to say, maybe you've got a friend you could stay with for a few days, until you feel better about things."

"Thanks, but a few days isn't going to change much."

Gallagher smiled slightly. "You have a license for that—?" He nodded to the bulge in her pocket.

Ellen waited.

"Just"—he raised his hand—"get one when you have a chance. Or give the weapon back to your husband. Believe me, you'd be a lot safer without it." He stepped out on the landing. "Ellen, if you'd care to call me tomorrow, I'll be happy to put you in touch with someone you could talk to. She works with trauma victims."

Ellen stepped into the doorway. "Detective, do you know how sheep defend themselves?" she asked.

Gallagher gave her a puzzled look.

"Individually, they don't," she explained. "They can't. They're not strong enough or smart enough." Ellen took the door from him. "So they flock. Which means they bunch up. The strongest and fittest of them manage to push their way into the center of the flock, which leaves the oldest and youngest and weakest on the outside, vulnerable to attack." She ran her hand down the outside of her jacket pocket until she felt the revolver hard against her palm. "That's how I've lost the rest of my family. I'm not going to lose any more."

He hesitated outside the shreshold, as though to reply, but she shut the door before he had a chance. Then she locked it.

She kept her jacket on, feeling the weight in her pocket as she walked through the apartment turning on lights. She looked inside her bedroom closet. She looked under her bed. She returned to her kitchen and poured a shot's worth of tequila in a coffee mug and drank it down. Then she called home. The answering machine came on. When she began to speak into the machine, Scott picked up and said, "Yup."

"How's Mo?" Ellen asked.

"In bed."

"Has she eaten anything?"

"Sugar Pops."

"Can I talk to her?"

"I want to let her sleep."

The flatness of his voice seemed an accusation. Ellen was tempted to tell him she was sorry—but why? It was Scott, not she, who had put them in this position.

"Detective Gallagher just left," she said.

"Yup. He's been over here for three days, him and the rest of 'em."

She considered telling him what Gallagher had said about the investigation into Randy's drowning, but she didn't feel safe having the conversation over the phone.

"He told me they have a counselor Moreen can talk to," she said. "It won't cost anything."

"Mo's all right," Scott said. "She just needs to get on with her life."

Ellen resisted getting into an argument, knowing it was time to hang up.

"Tell her I'll come over in the morning," she said.

"Maybe you should give her a few days."

"No, I'll be over to see her. If you want, I'll come while you're at work."

"It's not me," Scott said.

"What do you mean?"

"It's Mo," he said. "She'd rather not see you right now."

Ellen's chest tightened. "What did you tell her about me?"

"Nothing," Scott said. "Maybe Neal talked to her when he took her out to the island."

Ellen's heart kicked. "What did he say?"

"I don't know. Mo asked me if I had anything to do with Randy's drowning. I said no."

"Then she's talking to you."

"Not a whole lot."

"So it's only me she wants out of her life. It doesn't matter that I saved her, or that I was the one who tried to save Randy."

"Look, I don't know what she's thinking."

Ellen paced to the limit of the phone cord, then stopped. "Scott, do you think this is fair?"

"What?"

"That she's chosen you."

"Fair's got nothing to do with it," he replied. "Like I said, give her a few days."

Ellen stood there staring at the side of her gas stove, the blue flames flickering behind the heater grate. She felt the scowl hardening on her brow.

"Tell Mo I won't bother her," she said, and she hung up the phone, then turned back to her quiet apartment, feeling more alone than she'd ever felt in her life.

twenty-three

The next day, Ellen walked into Brian Quinn's real estate office and set the deed on his desk. "Can you sell this?"

He gave the document a quick look, then regarded her with a curious scowl. "In Vermont?"

"Can you?"

He shrugged. "I can contact a realtor up there and get it on the multiple listings."

"Good. Take your commission and give the rest to Sugar Westerback's parents."

"No reason I can't do that," Quinn said amiably, pulling a padded chair close to his desk, not acknowledging that the last time they'd spoken, he'd blackmailed Ellen into resigning. Gossip was gossip. Business was business.

"Thank you," she said, and left.

November turned to December, unnoticed. With Christmas season coming on, Ellen started working seven days a week in the store, sitting at the store's tapestry loom from ten in the morning till nine at night, while endless streams of faces passed by, some asking questions about her craft, most just staring. Through it all, Ellen concentrated on her work, certain that many townspeople blamed her for Sugar Westerback's death; just as certain that they'd all heard about her affair with her nephew and his subsequent, fiery suicide. In fact, she suspected that her notoriety may have had something to do with the boom in business.

As fast as Ellen could turn out her handicrafts, customers would carry them out of the store—linen hand towels and aprons imported from China, onto which Ellen would embroider a tiny image of Nubble Lighthouse, or a lone pine tree under a full moon, or a bright red lobster. It didn't matter. Her two inches of hand-stitching brought thousands of dollars into the store every week. Although Ellen's own share of the proceeds amounted to far less, she was grateful for the occupation. On these busy days, it was often close to ten when she got home. She liked it that way. She would read or watch TV for a half-hour, until she got drowsy, then she'd go to bed and fall painlessly to sleep.

For most of the month, Ellen kept her word about Moreen. She neither telephoned her daughter nor visited the farmhouse. Sometimes she did stop at the gun shop during her lunch break, to pick up her mail from Scott. On these occasions, she asked about Moreen, but Scott was stingy with information.

"She's okay," he'd say.

"Has she decided to go back to school?"

"Not that I know of."

"Is she looking for a job?"

"Not yet. She pretty much stays in her room."

While Ellen drove back to work one day sorting through her mail, she came upon an envelope from Quinn Real Estate. Parking her truck behind the store, she opened the envelope and found a clipping advertising Neal's farm. It was from a Vermont regional newspaper called the *Cold Hollow Express*. The photo showed snow surrounding the house and barn, and bare trees in the background—the same silent place she had visited. With one exception.

Ellen took her keys from the truck, went to the back door and unlocked it, letting herself in. She heard Ingrid in the front of the store, thanking a customer. She came through the door, saw a number of shoppers wandering the aisles.

Ingrid looked at her and rolled her eyes. "Two more days of this," she said.

Ellen walked over to the register. "Look at this picture," she said. "Tell me if you see anything strange."

Ingrid peered through her trifocals. "The cross on the silo?" She turned to Ellen, raising her brow. "Are you thinking of buying it?"

"I need to use the phone," Ellen answered.

"Help yourself," Ingrid said, with a curious glance.

Ellen brought the telephone in the back room and dialed Quinn's office. "The clipping you sent me," she began.

"Place looks great," the realtor said. "We've had some bites."

"Who took the picture?"

"Of the farm? The listing agent, I imagine."

"When?"

He paused. "I can find out for you."

"Did you notice a cross on the silo?"

"I guess I didn't look that close," Quinn said. "Ellie, is there something I can help you with?"

"I'll let you know," Ellen said, and she hung up, then returned the phone to the front. Judging from the way Ingrid examined her, Ellen knew she must have looked terrified.

"Give me another half-hour?" Ellen asked.

"Ellie, are you okay?"

"I'll be back as soon as I can."

Under the cold sunlight, the place where Ellen's barn had once stood was nothing but a black, stony cellar hole filled with crystalized mounds of ash and melted machinery. The temperature outside struggled to reach five degrees Fahrenheit, and the forecast predicted minus five by the end of the day. Despite the frozen air, Ellen could smell the destruction the minute she stepped from her truck.

Even the porch railing of the house had been scorched from the heat of the barn fire. Paint on the clapboards had blistered; soffits had blackened. Ellen climbed the steps and discovered a small, freshly cut spruce lying on the porch, a Christmas tree that Scott had evidently dragged in from the woods but hadn't yet brought inside. She tried the door and found it unlocked.

She went in, saw a couple of Christmas cards on the table. Hers was on top, the one she'd sent to Mo, the envelope unopened. Other than that, no sign of the holiday. Dishes were piled in the sink and on the counter, a pile of dirty clothes dumped on the floor in front of the washing machine.

Besides the hum of the furnace in the cellar, the house sat quietly. Ellen walked through the kitchen into the living room. Shades were drawn. Two empty plates sat on the coffee table, an empty popcorn bowl on the floor. She crossed the room and started up the stairs.

"Mo, it's me," she called. She climbed to the hallway upstairs and turned on the light. More clothes on the floor. "I need to talk to you," she said, taking hold of Mo's doorknob. She waited for a response but got none, so she opened the door.

It took a couple of moments for Ellen to understand what she was seeing: Moreen sitting at a low table made of plywood set on cinder blocks. Her back to the door, Mo worked closely on a reddish-brown hunk of clay with a sculpting knife.

"Mo?"

"Hi," Mo sang lightly, not turning around.

Lined up on the plywood were figures of humans, most with women's features, no larger than fifteen inches tall, each of them grotesquely deformed . . . but every one teeming with life: arms and legs twisting painfully, heads thrown back in agony, eyes staring outward.

"Moreen, did you do these?"

"Mm-hm."

Ellen stepped closer, stunned, while Mo worked her knife delicately, her fingers white from squeezing the tool.

"Do you like them?"

The sculpted girl stared up accusingly at Ellen, her womb scraped out like the inside of a melon, revealing another face growing out of the empty abdominal wall: It was Randy, Ellen realized, his goatee softened, a limpid smile on his closed lips. She scanned the other figures on the table—there were nine or ten of them, each missing body parts, each with extra faces. They were horrifying—but undeniably brilliant.

"Mo?" Ellen searched for words. "Do you understand how good these are?"

Moreen smiled.

"You have every bit of your grandmother's talent," Ellen said.

Looking closer at the figures, Ellen could see that all the bodies were Moreen's, hollowed out, ravaged. All seemed terribly confined, too, entwined with extra arms and legs not her own, while heads and anguished faces tried to push out of her body, as if other people were imprisoned inside her. In fact, now Ellen thought she recognized Maddy's features in one of the trapped faces. She saw Randy in others. A face that might have been Scott's brother, Jonathan, stared up sternly from a womb. Yet these faces of death were soft and membranous, their noses small and round: they were the faces of infants, stillborn.

The moment paralyzed Ellen. It was as though she were in the company of a woman with years and experiences far beyond her own. Although Moreen was not yet eighteen, she had lived through widowhood, a hysterectomy, she had survived a kidnapping, she'd been addicted to heroin and beaten back the addiction. The elementary task of living on her own—which Ellen was now struggling with—even that, Moreen had already done. Ellen felt almost childish in her presence.

"Mo," Ellen began, "I need to talk to you. Honey, there's a chance that Neal might be alive."

Moreen turned her face to the side, still smiling. "Really?" she said, then she returned to her sculpting, her long black hair covering her like a shawl.

Ellen's head throbbed. "I'd like you to go someplace with me," she said. "Just for Christmas."

"Where?"

"It doesn't matter. We'll get in the truck and go find a hotel, just for a day or two."

Moreen kept working at her clay. "I'd love to," she said, "but I don't want to leave Daddy alone on Christmas."

He's the one who murdered your husband! Ellen almost screamed. *And he's the reason Neal is hunting us down!*

"Moreen, would you stop that, please, and talk to me? Just stop for a second."

Mo laid her knife on the table and turned to face Ellen, her eyes lit pleasantly but her face otherwise devoid of emotion. She placed her hands in her lap.

"Jesus Christ, don't look at me like that," Ellen said, the words tumbling recklessly from her mouth. "And don't tell me you *love* me and you'd *love* to go with me, when you make it clear with everything you do that you only want me out of your life!"

Mo gazed at her mother for a moment, her expression unchanged.

Ellen stepped closer, resisting the urge to touch her. "Mo, just talk to me, can't you? Tell me what I did that makes you so angry at me."

Moreen gave her a bewildered smile. "I'm not *angry* at you," she replied, with a shrug that suggested Ellen must have been hysterical to imagine such a thing. Then she turned and leaned close to her work, her knife ticking like a clock at the small clay mouth.

Turn around, Ellen told herself. *Turn around and leave.*

In the gun shop, she slid the newspaper clipping across the glass case, the neat display of handguns and leather holsters.

"The cross is new," she said, pulling her hand out of the wool mitten. Her ears stung from the cold outside.

On the other side of the counter, Scott flicked the clipping back at her, refusing the conversation.

"Scott, I think he's still alive," Ellen said.

"Think what you want," he replied.

"It's not what I *want* to think."

He leveled his eyes over the counter. "I watched them pick through the ashes for two solid days," he said quietly. "I saw them take out Sugar Westerback, wrapped up like a mummy so he wouldn't fall apart. They took Neal out in a shoe box. What gives you the idea that he's not dead?"

"You," she said, gathering up her newspaper clipping and stuffing it in her jacket pocket. "You're still alive."

Ellen felt his stunned silence as she turned and put her mitten back on, then went out the door. She imagined his bowels slackening, and it gave her a small degree of pleasure; her Christmas gift to herself.

When Polly Westerback opened her door, her eyes seemed to fill with worry.

"I'm very sorry to bother you," Ellen told her. "I called but no one answered, and no one's in the office. Is Wes here?"

"He's in having a nap," the older woman said. "There's a new man in training, but he's out on a call. When he comes back, I can have him get in touch." She looked as though she hadn't slept herself.

"It can wait," Ellen said. "I'm sorry to bother you." She tried to let the door shut, but the older woman put her hand on the glass, keeping it open. "What with the holidays, Wes isn't having an easy time of it." she said. "Just as soon as they find another office space, he's going to retire. This is too much."

"I'm sorry," Ellen said again.

"Should I have the new man contact you when he gets back?"

Ellen shook her head. "That's okay."

Ellen returned to Wool 'n' Things, sat down at her tapestry loom, and continued turning out gifts. Christmas music played incessantly, customers came and went, talking with Ingrid about the frigid weather and the prices of things. She heard the noises their children made, but everything stayed in the back of her mind. White yarn, red yarn, blue yarn, gray. Another lighthouse, another solitary seagull, another lobster.

At six o'clock, as soon as Ingrid went to dinner, Ellen picked up the phone and called the state police, asking for Gallagher.

"I'm sorry, Detective Gallagher is not available," the dispatcher told her. "Is there anyone else who could help you?"

"No, just contact the detective, please, and tell him Ellen Chambers needs to speak with him."

"Mrs. Chambers, I'll put you through to the shift commander. Just a moment."

"I don't want to talk to anyone but Gallagher," Ellen began, when another voice cut in.

"This is Sergeant Anderson," the man announced with military crispness. "I'm familiar with the case. Why don't you tell me the nature of your problem and we'll see what we can do."

"I need to speak with Detective Gallagher," Ellen said as calmly as she knew how, though she was pacing behind the checkout counter.

"Detective Gallagher has been out on personal leave for most of the week," the sergeant replied.

Ellen stopped. "Is it his son?"

"We're not at liberty to divulge that information. If it'll make you feel better, Mrs. Chambers, we can send another detective by."

She stretched the telephone into the back room and shut the door on the cord, holding the newspaper clipping in her hand. "Could you just get a message to Detective Gallagher for me? Tell him I received a Christmas card he needs to see."

The sergeant took a moment to respond. "This is a difficult time of year for a lot of people," he began. "Let me see if I can get someone you can talk to."

"Look," Ellen said, her face heating up, "I don't need to speak to a goddamned counselor—"

"Hello?" The voice called from behind the door, along with a tidy knock.

Ellen opened the door a little. Two elderly women dressed like Eskimos stood there smiling, one of them holding up a pair of lobster pot holders along with her wallet.

"One sec," Ellen mouthed. She closed the door again and said to the sergeant, "Are you going to take me seriously?"

"We take all calls very seriously, Mrs. Chambers. What we can do is send someone out to see you, we'll assess your situation and take it from there."

"And while you're assessing the situation," Ellen said, "God help you if anything happens to my daughter." She banged open the door, wheeled around the corner, lined up the phone cradle, and slammed the phone down, then turned to the startled women.

"Cash or credit?" she said.

Ten minutes later Detective Gallagher phoned the store. "I have no doubt that Neal nailed the cross to the silo," he said quietly. "His father was a church minister who killed himself in your barn. Neal also killed himself in your barn. He obviously saw great significance in symbolism."

"But I was at that farm in August," Ellen said, trying to hold her anxiety down. "I was there, and that cross was not."

Gallagher sighed tiredly. "Neal Chambers died in November. He apparently erected the cross sometime in the intervening months, September or October."

"Look, this is a riddle, it's a game. To Neal, everything was a game. Let me fax this picture to you."

She heard him sigh again. "I'm at home," he said. "I don't have a fax machine. I understand what you've told me—"

"The ashes you found—your human remains? That was not Neal. It was a man called Gator. He worked for Ray LaFlamme. He came to the farm one night, and Neal murdered him."

"Were you a witness to the murder? Did Neal tell you he did it? Ellen, the only way such a premise is plausible is, one, if your nephew could have somehow kept the corpse from decomposing for three months, without detection; and, two, if Neal himself had survived that barn fire. The first is extremely unlikely. The second is impossible."

"You don't know Neal."

"Neal is gone," he said. "You need to come to grips with that."

"I *want* him gone."

She heard Gallagher clear his throat then take another deep breath. She knew he was having difficulty talking. "Ellen, have you called the person I told you about?"

"I'm sorry I bothered you," she replied, intending to hang up.

"Ellen."

"What?"

"It's not a good time to be alone," he said softly. "Why don't you try to find a friend you can spend time with for a couple of days. Keep yourself busy."

"Thanks."

"I'll be back to work after the holidays," he said. "In the meantime, if you just want someone to chat with, I'll leave instructions with dispatch to page me."

"Thanks," she said again. This time she meant it.

Hard little snowflakes ricocheted off her windshield as she drove home that night, not enough to make her turn on her wipers. In fact, it was too cold to snow in earnest, already minus two and falling. The steam from Ellen's breath seemed to stick to the glass.

When she pulled into the quiet car lot, hundreds of tiny blue Christmas lights blinked at her from the showroom windows. She drove around to the back of the garage and parked her truck.

Stepping out into the cold, she walked briskly to the stairs, her hand cupped under the leather bag so she could feel her .38 in the bottom. The night was so quiet that it fairly crackled as she passed through it. In fact, she could hear the distant hum of traffic on the interstate, ten miles away.

Relieved to see the light on inside the staircase, she hurried up the stairs with her key in her hand, unlocked the door, and flipped on the kitchen light. She locked the door behind her, but before taking off her jacket and cap, she turned up the gas heater on the side of her stove. Then, keeping her hand inside her purse, she walked through the apartment as she did every night checking closets peeking under beds.

Finally satisfied that she was alone, she took off her overclothes but kept her purse slung over her shoulder. To help her sleep, she poured a small glass of tequila, then went into her living room to watch the eleven o'clock news. She set the purse on the floor beside her rocking chair. As she absently watched a report about a Lewiston apartment fire, she sipped the tequila and felt her chest relax by degrees.

Soon she found herself staring at her tapestry loom. The unfinished masterpiece stared back: Scott's father's milk truck, Scott's mother's spinning wheel. Such wholesome endeavors, Ellen thought. Such good people . . . Yet how could they not have seen how desperately Scott tried to win their approval? And why had they constantly withheld it?

Ellen felt the heaviness grow in her chest, and she knew she should stop drinking, but she also knew she needed to silence her chattering mind, so she drank the tequila down then walked out to the kitchen and poured another glass. She returned to the living room with a serrated steak knife.

Standing behind the loom, she carefully pushed the blade through the center of the work and sawed outward to the side, separating warp from weft, sawing up, sawing down, tearing out the colors, freeing the images . . .

A car door closed.

Ellen jumped to the lamp, darkened the room. She dropped to her knees, found her purse, and pulled her revolver out, then turned off the TV and hurried down the hallway into the kitchen, where she switched off the overhead light. In the blackness of her apartment, now she tried to listen for footsteps on the stairs, but she heard only the stove's heater fan blowing. She crept over to it, reaching blindly for the thermostat, knowing she'd burn herself—and she did, twice, before she found the dial and silenced the fan.

Now, rising with her .38 in her hand, she held her breath and listened. But hearing no traitorous creak of stair, she made her way back to the living room. Positioning herself between her two front windows, she inserted a finger in the venetian blinds and spread the slats apart.

Beads of snow drifted like dust motes past the arc sodium lamps. Blue Christmas lights winked off the roofs of the vehicles below like hundreds of eyes, row after row. But nothing else moved. She stared intently at the cars, then returned to her dark hallway, running her hand along the wall until she reached her bathroom. Creeping in and sidling along the bathtub to the small window, she peeled back the shade and peered through the corner of the pane at the seven or eight vehicles parked below her, awaiting repair. She thumbed her breath off the icy window and moved her eyes to the right, over the dumpster to the small pile of wooden pallets.

Behind Ellen, something gulped. She swung the gun around.

The toilet. It gulped again.

Ellen drew a sharp breath, held it, then blew out a shuddering laugh. She lowered the revolver to her knee, then jiggled the flush handle, to stop the toilet from running. Shaking her head at her own nervousness, she walked back to the kitchen and turned the light on, her rational mind returning. Ten below zero, nobody would be out there. Obviously.

She poured herself another glass of tequila, then brought the drink, along with the revolver, into her bedroom. She set them both on her night stand, then sat on the edge of the bed and pulled off her boots, tossing them at the closet, one at a time. She liked the sound of their heels hitting the hollow core door.

With the cold night seeping through the walls, she decided to sleep with her clothes on. Or maybe she was just too tired to take them off. She pushed in under the blankets, took the last sip of tequila, then slid the revolver under her pillow.

She thought of Maddy. She thought of Mo. She was grateful for the alcohol. Under its warm influence, a cross atop a silo no longer seemed threatening. A gulping toilet in the night became nothing more than a plumbing problem. In fact, lying there in her quiet apartment, protected from the icy night outside, it was very easy for Ellen to believe what Gallagher had been trying to tell her all along: that the dangers she had imagined were just the spinnings of her guilt-ridden mind. By degrees, her chest relaxed, her breathing slowed. She reached for the lamp and clicked on the night.

While outside in the frozen dark, her daughter stood at the bottom of the stairway until the cold had worked its way too deeply through her layers of clothes and she could stand there no longer. Then she turned and walked back to her car, the old blue Taurus, and drove quietly home.

Every good thing about me, you know. The bad things arouse you.
This is the conversation Ellen has.
I love your hands, she tells him. I loved your *capabilities.*
My capabilities? He laughs a little. Do you love my mind?
Her eyes go distant. I love the relationship between your neck and your shoulder, she tells him, and he smiles.
I love your depth, he replies, teasing her.
She smiles back at him. "I love the relationship between your brow and your jaw." With her finger, she traces these parts of him as she speaks.
But do you love my mind?
"Your mind scares me," she confesses. "What I love is the relationship between your chest and your stomach." His flesh flows like oil under her palm.
"I love the relationship between your foot and your colors," he says as he kneels at her feet, looking up at her.
She beams curiously. "My colors?"
"Your colors," he says again. His voice is soft as a cello breathing, and his hand running down her leg is even softer.
He cups her heel in his hand, and she realizes they are both naked. She feels a stirring deep in her abdomen. He dips his hand in a bowl

of water, to wash her foot, and she flinches when she feels how cold the water is. He smiles. The muscles of his shoulders flex rhythmically as he works, and the chill rises to her thigh. Her nipples harden.

"I've always loved your hands," she tells him.

"My hands?" He teases her, knowing that she is really looking at his erection, which rises stiffly beside her ankle. His eyes darken as he runs his cold hand up her thigh. She opens her legs for him. He lowers his face, and his beard, soft as a felt cloth, brushes her inner leg. She closes her eyes as she feels his icy fingertips dance down her sides. Her hips ache pleasantly as her thighs open wider.

"I love the relationship," he breathes, "of your length and your depth," his cool words popping off her delicate bud, electrifying her.

"My depth?" she says, with a breathless, luxurious smile.

His mouth descends to her vulva. His hands engulf her breasts, his sudden touch whipping a spasm through her. She arches her back and opens herself wider, and his cool tongue enters. Her nerve endings sparkle. She oils his tongue, and his tongue swells in response. His soft lips press down harder. She moans and tries to warm him more. But his tongue remains cold and moves deeper inside her, incredibly deeper.

"How are you doing that?" she asks in shuddering disbelief, his coldness radiating out through her hips.

His black eyes stare over her pubis. Then, with torturous slowness, his tongue slides deeper, steadily thickening, steadily filling her. Her body writhes, behaving without consent. She forgets to breathe. Her stomach is already filled with him, yet he plunges even deeper, far deeper than she's ever dreamed possible, approaching this secret, ecstatic ache at her very core. Her blood rushes, and she starts to shiver. She can feel her orgasm coming, like the first rumble of an earthquake miles beneath the surface, the rumble of a distant flood.

"Wait," she whispers. All her life she's been vaguely aware of this unreachable place. Now she realizes that he may touch it. And it frightens her, yet she pushes into him. She cannot help herself. She gasps: *"God, how can you possibly do that?"*

His black eyes gleam. His tongue flickers. And all at once a monstrous wave of energy floods around her chest, surging up through the top of her head and down through the deepest part of her.

My heart! she realizes. *He is actually touching my heart.* She clutches his head, pushes into him, as her orgasm pours on, wave after wave of ecstacy.

The rushing waterfall fills her ears, and she realizes they are lying outside in her cucumber patch, immersed in a cool bed of greenery.

"Neal, is this really you?"

Because she knows this cannot be possible. Her orgasm is endless, his hair entwined in her fingers, his cold black eyes staring up through her tangled mound of pubic hair, like the mesmerized eyes of a frog staring out of fat foliage. She feels the fine scratching of cucumber leaves on the backs of her arms. But wait. Not a frog. She feels his tongue flicker again, deep inside her chest. She jumps—

—grabbing for her lamp while he grabs for her ankle, her foot caught in the blankets. The light comes on, piercing her eyes like fangs. She cries out, tears her foot free, throws off her blankets, looking for the snake, but she finds her gun, swinging left and right around the room, heart pounding, mind racing, stopping her aim at the black, open doorway . . .

Did she hear a car door? Toilet gulp? Footsteps in the hall? Did she hear anything but her own heart knocking at her chest?

Awake now, she shivered with the cold and saw her breath clouding the air in front of her face.

The gas heater . . . she had turned it off last night, but forgot to turn it back on. She took a deep breath, a long, steaming sigh, and lay back down, tense with the cold. She rested the revolver on her chest, watched it bump up and down, up and down.

Do you love my mind? he had asked her.

I hate your mind, she wished she had said.

She listened to the incredible stillness outside, the night deeply frozen. She looked at her clock: 2:58.

Chilled as she was, the muscles in her abdomen glowed with an ache that told her she'd had an orgasm in her sleep. She felt the cold wetness between her legs.

Do you love my mind?

Off in the distance, she heard the gong of the church bell two miles away. She thought of the silo and the cross. The bell rang again.

I detest your mind.

Barn with a steeple. Church with a silo.

Ellen sat up in bed.

The bell rang a third time.

Her stockinged foot slid on the floor and she almost went down, but she caught the doorknob and swerved out into the hallway. Her shoulder hit the opposite wall, and she ran into the kitchen and slapped on the kitchen light, grabbed at the phone.

"State Police," the woman said. "What's your emergency?"

"This is Ellen Chambers, I need you to page Detective Gallagher for me. Tell him I know how Neal Chambers survived that fire."

"Is this an emergency, or can it wait till morning?"

Ellen's heart pounded in her temples. "Just tell him!" she yelled, then she hung up.

The farmhouse was dark when she pulled in. But under a bright, misshapen moon the night was bright enough to illuminate the pump house standing alone in the field, the black, rubble-filled foundation off to its right, the white tire tracks winding down through the blackened field, itself ribbed with a dusting of snow along dark harrow grooves.

Ellen picked up her flashlight from the seat beside her—a $2.99 special that occasionally needed a whack to work—and stepped out of her truck. She wore a flannel shirt and sweatshirt, a wool sweater and her jean jacket, with a wool felt hat pulled down to her eyes and thick wool mittens on her hands. She didn't need a thermometer to know it was below zero.

Everything lay so silent under the stars, it was as if the night could hear her every move. As she walked to the foundation, the burned and frozen grass crunched beneath the film of snow like tiny bones breaking. She heard her knee pop when she crouched to lower herself down the aluminum ladder someone had left inside the foundation. Stepping off the lowest rung, her boot squeaked in the frozen coals.

She swung her flashlight toward the front of the foundation, sliding the light over the blackened rocks. But seeing no stone large enough to hide a passageway, she turned her beam to the right, where the eastern wall was interrupted twice: once by a warped steel door hanging by its top hinge—the root cellar—and, farther down, the opening to the bulkhead. Ellen climbed over the frozen ash heaps to the root cellar and shone the light through the angular opening.

She was surprised to see that the destruction inside was not total. In fact the timbers and plank ceiling, although profoundly charred, still managed to support the weight of the frozen ground above. Even the two copper pipes that ran along the ceiling, although destroyed in the main foundation, looked fairly sound inside this protected room. On the back wall, where three wooden bins stood side by side on the floor, the frozen mounds of blackness still held the shape of potatoes—huge, burned casseroles.

Ellen pulled the door open a few inches, until it stopped, then squeezed inside the room. She approached the potato bins gingerly, nervous that a loud noise might bring the earth-covered ceiling down on top of her.

The bins were two feet wide and waist-high, their backs standing flush against the stone wall, their bottoms extending out from the wall at a forty-five-degree angle. The inch-thick plywood was black and blistered like alligator skin, but still solid. Four inches above the middle bin, the two copper pipes emerged through the rock wall and were elbowed up to the ceiling.

Ellen reached her mittened hand to the potato mound in the left-hand bin, found it had solidified into one charred mass. She pushed and pulled on the mound, but it held fast to the wood. When she tried the same thing with the middle bin, she felt a slight rocking—not in the potato mass but in the bin itself. She dropped to her knees and aimed her flashlight underneath, looking for an opening in the wall, but the bottom edge of the bin met the concrete floor square. She got to her feet, pulled off her mitten and reached over the top of the bin. Unable to fit her fingers down behind the wood, even into the seams between the rocks, she climbed up into the potatoes and pressed her cheek and flashlight against the rocks, trying to see down. She couldn't. She ran her hand over the cold rocks above the bins, from left to right, searching for a catch or latch of some kind . . . Then she found it. A small hollow in the underside of a rock. Poking one finger up inside the notch, she felt a metal ring. A small rush of adrenaline spurred her. She folded her finger through the ring and pulled.

The center bin gave way, dropping her to the hard concrete. As she rolled onto the floor, stunned, the bin swung up again, evidently counterweighted, and closed neatly into place between the other two bins.

Ignoring the pain in her knee, Ellen retrieved her flashlight and climbed into the potatoes again. This time when she pulled on the ring, she was ready for the ride. As the bin released, she kept one boot on the floor to ease the lid down, all the while shining her light on the exposed opening in the wall.

Judging from its black mouth, the tunnel was only as wide as the bin—two feet—and not much higher. She saw that its floor was made of plywood, as were the walls. From her vantage point, Ellen could not see the ceiling, but assumed it was also plywood: a wooden, two-by-two chute. She thought of the tunnel between the church and the parsonage, and knew Neal had built a secret passage just like it here, only much more confining.

Forgetting her frozen ears and nose, even ignoring the cold in her fingers, Ellen reached into the fallen bin with both hands and pulled the loosened potato mass halfway out so its weight overhung the top, to keep the bin from closing again.

Then she climbed up and over, holding the rock wall to balance herself as she slid her long legs down the back of the bin and into the mouth of the tunnel. Under her weight, the bin tried to close on her, but she pushed back with her shoulders until she was sitting at its base, with her legs squeezed inside the tunnel. Then she slithered in until only her head leaned against the back of the opened bin.

By the slight tug of gravity, Ellen could tell the tunnel had been built on a decline. She also knew that it led straight to the pump house—the copper pipes running down the center of the ceiling told her that. Additionally, she remembered the night Neal had dug the ditch; he had told her he was replacing water pipes. In truth, he had been preparing his vendetta.

She pressed her knees against the walls of the tunnel and aimed the flashlight between her legs, down the length of the tunnel, raising her head slowly to see its end. Hearing the sudden creak behind her, she threw her head back, but too late. The potato bin swung shut, closing off the night with a solid thud.

She reached over her head and pushed, but succeeded only in sliding down the tunnel floor. Pushing herself up again, she craned her neck and shone her flashlight along the seams between the tunnel and bin, searching for any glimmer of metal that might be a latch. She pressed her heels against the tunnel floor and pushed the bin with her hands again, but it held fast, and once again she slid away.

"I'm down in the root cellar!" she shouted, hoping that if she yelled loud enough, her voice might carry through the water pipes into the house. She stopped and listened for a response, or any sound at all. What she heard, from the foot of the tunnel . . . yes, a quiet humming, almost like the whirring of an electric motor. The water pump, she realized. Someone in the house was awake and running water—probably Scott using the toilet. She rapped her flashlight on the pipes.

"Scott, I'm down here!"

She listened again. Only the whirring replied.

Flicking off her flashlight to conserve batteries, Ellen started pulling herself forward to the pump house inchworm-style, using her boot heels, butt, and elbows, trying to ignore the terrified voice that said Neal had lured her down here and trapped her in the dark. At least the tunnel was warmer than the air outside, she reasoned. But a strange pungency pervaded the air—the sweet smell of pine pitch, fouled by the stench of death.

Noting the thick glassiness of the plywood floor, she had assumed it was another example of Neal's meticulousness—shellacking the tunnel that he intended to use only once. Then she realized another truth: He had also used the shellac to preserve the body.

Yes, he had murdered Gator—she knew that for certain now—and stored his body down here in this passageway. She remembered reading once that ancient Egyptians had preserved their mummies with pine pitch. In Neal's case, the pitch served a second purpose: fuel to destroy the evidence.

Despite the twinge of satisfaction she felt, knowing that she'd been right about Neal, she felt a far more powerful fear knowing for certain that he was still alive. Her boots clunked and squeaked along the shiny floor, her breathing came faster and louder. Then her boot heel splashed.

Ellen stopped moving, confused at first, until the ice water hit her fingers. She jerked on her flashlight, and her heart jumped. She scrambled back a few feet . . . then stared through her legs with a sickening dread.

Less than twenty feet away, the end of the tunnel lay sealed off with cinder blocks that were half-submerged in water . . . which meant the pump house was flooding. Worse, the water was getting deeper, creeping up the tunnel floor.

Her logic ravaged by panic, Ellen banged her flashlight on the water pipes until the light went out. She twisted the lens cap. The light flickered weakly.

"Somebody!" she screamed.

She fought for clarity: whether to continue ahead into the water and try to kick the cinder blocks out, or to retreat back to the root cellar and try again to break through the potato bin. Those were her only options, she told herself. If she pushed ahead to the pump house, she knew she would have to go into the water—and there was no guarantee she could break through the cinder blocks. But if she went back to the root cellar and failed to free herself, she would have lost the chance at the pump house.

As she tried to decide, the water bit at her fingers again. She aimed her light at the opening and now saw only six inches of dry cinder block exposed. She knew that the water pump could exert enough pressure to fill the entire tunnel to the top in a matter of minutes. She had to move. She turned off her flashlight and flung it back up the tunnel, to keep it dry. From here on, she would be less like an inchworm, more like some sightless subterranean fish.

She charged forward, amazed that cold could hurt so much when the icy water poured into her boots. Raising herself onto her hands until her knees rubbed the ceiling and her forehead touched the pipes, she crab-walked ahead. When the water hit her wrists, she yelled to alleviate the pain, simultaneously allowing the assault on her buttocks, but she kept moving ahead, finally submerging her back, the icy water tearing at her kidneys.

Screaming, she splashed deeper, until the water wrapped around her ribs and threatened to paralyze her lungs. Then her boot felt resistance, and she knew she had reached the end. She pushed with her toes, she kicked with her heels. The cinder blocks withstood her kick solidly.

Taking as big a breath as she could, she let her arms collapse, and she plunged completely under water, astonished at the severity of her pain. The aching in her forehead alone was enough to steal her consciousness. She pressed her hands on the ceiling and doubled up her knees. She grabbed hold of the water pipes. Flattening her boots against the cinder blocks, she pounded with her heels until she felt the jolt in her spine, but the cinder blocks refused to budge.

Giving up, Ellen pushed herself back out of the water with a terrified gasp, her frozen heart pounding weakly against her chest, retreating back up the tunnel until her elbow hit the flashlight at the head of the rising water.

"Somebody help me!" she screamed.

She turned on the light, looking around wildly, while the ice water inched steadily toward her heels. Confused as she was, she knew there had to be a latch, some way that Neal had let himself into the pump house. She also knew she would have to go back into the water, this time headfirst.

Pulling her heels to her buttocks, she wrapped her arms around her legs and tried to roll forward onto her knees, jamming her head against the water pipes and pushing off the tunnel's side with her shoulder. She twisted her neck and heard the copper squeak against her cheek. Then it released her, and she fell forward into about two inches of ice water.

She turned off her flashlight and stuffed it in her pocket, then pulled herself out of her wet jacket and wedged a sleeve up over the water pipes, to keep the flashlight dry.

In total darkness, she bellied forward into the water until it reached her chin. Then she took three panting breaths to fill her lungs . . . and dived ahead with her arms outstretched. Streaking through pure weightless cold, she felt the tunnel floor slide under her chest. Her brow throbbing with pain, she frog-legged off the floor and walls until her wrists jammed against the cinder blocks, and, with fingers too numb to feel anything but hard resistance, she vainly searched the sealed opening for a latch, ring, wire, or peg. Then a light came on.

Ellen doubted her eyes at first, thinking that this thin glimmer along the upper edge of blackness was just a hallucination. But the light didn't waver. Someone was in the pump house. Desperate for air, she pushed off the concrete, fighting her way backward through the water, lungs flaring, pressing her shoulders up to the pipes until finally the back of her head broke water. She turned her face to the ceiling, gasping the meager air.

She tried to shout, but her voice wouldn't come. Backing farther out of the water, she waved one arm wildly over her head until her hand hit her jacket. She stripped her revolver from its pocket and fired two shots at the water, the explosions crushing her eardrums, the powder flashes blinding her.

"Help me!" she screamed.

It didn't matter that she was five feet underground, somewhere between the pump house and barn, or that whoever had been in the pump house was looking down into three or four feet of rising water and would already be returning to the house to kill the circuit to the pump.

The water splashed over Ellen's hand again, and she crawled farther backward, until her boot hit the potato bin. Angling the revolver under her arm, she pulled the trigger, and the gun exploded against the wood. With all the fullness of her chest, she screamed.

"SCOTT!"

Her elbow splashed in the water. She fired the gun into the bin again, and screamed louder and longer than she ever had.

"I'M IN THE ROOT CELLAR!"

The water rose up her wrist and knee. She pushed herself upright, pressing her back against the pipes. She heard a voice—or thought she did. She fired the gun again.

"BEHIND THE POTATOES!"

She heard the voice again, muffled, but clear enough to tell it was Scott.

"Reach behind the bin! On the right!"

He yelled again, interrupting her.

"Shut up!" she screamed, rapping the wood with the butt of the revolver. "Find the rock, a hollowed-out rock!"

Suddenly the wall fell forward, Ellen fell with it. She felt the icy bite of the night on her neck and tried to vault over the potatoes, but her legs were too stiff to move. His flashlight beam hit her face.

"Ellie, what the hell are you doing? You almost killed me. And you left the fucking pump house door wide open, so the pipes burst."

Although Ellen's jaw was too frozen to work, she managed a distinct pair of syllables for him.

"I never went near the pump house," she told them. "It's obvious who opened that door—and who shut me in."

Detective Gallagher nodded his head with a blank stare. As bedraggled as he looked—his eyes sunken, his cheekbones prominent—he reminded Ellen of pictures she'd seen of prisoners of war. A state trooper, dressed in a thick, fur-lined parka, stood behind him, just inside the kitchen door.

Ellen reached her hand out of the blankets, retrieved her coffee mug from the floor, and filled her mouth. It was incredible, how good the coffee tasted. She was sitting in a chair in the middle of the room, while a wood fire roared behind her in the cookstove and the electric dryer tumbled her clothes. Underneath the blanket she wore thermal underpants and a shirt.

Gallagher turned to Scott. "Do you remember the last time you went out there, to check on the pump house?"

"I don't know," Scott answered. "Three, four weeks, maybe more. When Ellen got rid of her sheep and moved out, I went down to make sure she shut off the water to the barn."

"Your daughter?"

"What about her?"

"Is there a chance Moreen left the door open?"

Scott shrugged. "There's been no reason for either of us to go out there."

"So the door could've been open for weeks, and you wouldn't have noticed—?"

"I suppose so. This is the first time we've had a deep freeze."

Ellen threw her hands out of her blankets. "I don't believe this," she said. "Scott, did you ever leave that door open? Have you ever forgotten to close the hatch?"

"Hey, the way things are goin, I might've forgotten a lot of things, okay? Half the time I can't remember my own name. It wouldn't surprise me, that's all I'm saying."

Ellen looked directly at Gallagher. "Neal Chambers trapped me inside that tunnel. He knew I was coming. He opened those doors so the pipes would freeze. If Scott hadn't come out, I would've drowned in there."

"And if I'd been a foot to the left, you woulda friggin shot me through the heart. Ellie, what the hell are you doing here?"

"I'm trying to protect Mo!"

"No, you're using Mo," Moreen said sweetly from the living room doorway. "You're still trying to convince yourself that I need you."

Her dark eyes glistened angrily at Ellen, and they lingered—and for some reason, Ellen felt a connection.

"When are you going to understand, Mom?" Moreen went on. "I gave up on you a long time ago."

"Moreen, hon, don't talk to your mother like that," Scott intervened wearily.

As Ellen searched her eyes, Moreen turned and walked back into the living room.

Ellen turned to Gallagher again. "Neal Chambers hid in that tunnel while the barn burned down," she persisted.

"What tunnel?" Scott said, getting louder. "It's a conduit for the water pipes so we could get at them if we ever had a problem. I told Neal to build it that way."

"Or did he tell you?"

"As far as his hiding in there during the fire," Gallagher added with an infuriating calm, "anyone in that narrow space would have suffocated in a matter of seconds. A fire of that magnitude would have sucked out all the oxygen."

"What if he had an oxygen mask, a scuba tank?"

Gallagher cocked his head, not that he was considering her suggestion. He was just too tired to argue.

"Conduit, tunnel, call it what you want," Ellen said, "Neal kept a human corpse down there, then substituted it for himself during the fire. Do the research."

Without looking at her, Gallagher said, "Ellen, I followed up on this Gator character after our last conversation." He shook his head.

"I talked to him. He attacked me."

"Detective Gallagher isn't saying he doesn't exist," the trooper said. "If you say you saw him—"

"I hit him in the face with a fire extinguisher!"

From upstairs a bang shook the house: Moreen slamming her bedroom door.

Gallagher stood up from his chair and zipped his parka. He looked unsteady on his feet. "Ellen, after the holidays, why don't you come down to the barracks and look at some pictures, maybe we can put a better name to this person."

"Neal preserved his body with shellac or pine pitch," Ellen continued, practically yelling. "It's all over the wood in the tunnel."

"That's plywood we scrapped from the tire store," Scott told her, reclining tiredly in the wooden chair. "It was from their paint room. We junked it up and Neal brought it back here."

"All right, who shut the bin?"

"What?"

"When I was inside the tunnel!"

"It could have blown shut. I don't know."

Gallagher's partner, waiting at the door, shrugged his shoulders. "Ma'am, there are no footprints out there, except yours and your husband's."

Ellen rocked her body forward and stood, dropping the blankets to the floor. "You've got answers for everything." Stiff and sore as she was, she brushed past Gallagher and pulled open the clothes dryer. "So you do nothing," she said, jerking out her clothes, hot and humid, far from dry. She bundled them at her chest, then hobbled to the table and snatched her keys in her fist. "Do nothing," she said again, pushing past the cops.

"Come on, El, where are you going like that?" Scott said. "It's below freezing out there."

"What do you care?" she muttered, yanking the door open. Then she snapped her head around. "When you went out to check the pump house, Scott, didn't you see my truck?"

"What?" he said, confused.

She gave him a long look. "Maybe it's you that wants me dead."

"Jesus Christ, Ellie."

She balked in the doorway, knowing she was being scrutinized, knowing also that she'd just blown whatever scrap of credibility she might have had. She thought to say something—an apology, another fuck you, a simple goodbye—but she walked out into the frozen dawn.

Back at the car lot, blue lights blinking, the eastern sky was brightening. Ellen walked up her stairs, realizing that she was no longer thinking of Neal Chambers, no longer wondering where he might be lurking or when he'd make his move. She was too tired and too cold to be frightened of him. Indeed, right now she was more frightened of her own hysteria. Besides, it was much easier to believe what everyone seemed to know, that Neal was dead, which was to say, no longer of this world, no longer walking, thinking, breathing. Obviously. Dead.

Letting herself into her apartment, she dropped her heavy purse on the kitchen table and walked down the hall in semidarkness and turned into her bedroom. She stripped off her damp clothes and frozen socks and threw on her flannel nightgown, then got under the covers. The sheets were cold, her feet were icy. She lay there stiffly and closed her eyes, waiting for sleep to come. She rolled on her side and hugged herself, trying to warm up. She tried to pretend that Mo was five years old again, snuggling in bed with her. She wanted to feel the warmth of her little body, to hear the soft sound of her voice, to recall the particular smell of Mo's hair. But her imagination was barren, and the bed chilled her. She opened her eyes and stared at the pear-toned window shade and let the tears run down her nose. Off in the kitchen, the heater fan blew. Other than that, nothing stirred.

"Forgive *myself?*" she had once yelled at her mother-in-law. "The truth about what?"

Now, she suspected, she was starting to learn.

Ingrid closed the store at noon on the day before Christmas, and for once Ellen looked forward to the solitude of her empty apartment so she could finish making Moreen's gift—a black sweater and matching cap she'd started over a month ago. But when she got home, she found the car dealers having a party in the showroom.

As soon as she got upstairs, she opened the bottle of Pinot Noir that Ingrid had given her, from a winery in the same Oregon town where Ingrid's friend owned the sheep farm. Ellen brought the bottle and a glass into the living room, where she settled on her couch under a quilted comforter and started knitting, listening to the Christmas music that drifted upstairs through the walls, the occasional bursts of laughter.

After her first glass of wine, she set her knitting in her lap, closed her eyes, and fell asleep. When she awoke, it was dark and she was hungry, so she went into the kitchen and cooked up some spaghetti and sauce. She drank a glass of wine while she cooked and another glass while she ate. When she was through, she poured herself a fourth glass and returned to the living room, intending to knit Scott a hat, a way of apologizing for what she'd said to him.

Downstairs a few people were singing "I'll Be Home for Christmas."

Ellen could tell the party was winding down, and it made her wish they'd go on all night. What she really wished was that she could be with Scott and Mo in the morning, opening gifts. She imagined sitting on the couch in her bathrobe, with a mug of hot coffee in her hand. She even wanted to hear the Perry Como album that Scott played every year and *The Beach Boys' Christmas Album.* She wanted to smell turkey roasting, bread baking. She wanted to sit by the tree, reading, while Scott slept in his recliner in front of a football game.

When the singing stopped, Ellen waited for another song. Instead, she heard the sound of doors closing in the parking lot, then car engines starting. This was the hour she dreaded.

She turned on her little television. *It's a Wonderful Life.* Naturally. Jimmy Stewart balancing along the bridge, ready to jump. Great thing to show lonely people on Christmas Eve, she thought, especially people who don't believe in angels. She clicked through a few more channels, then shut the TV off.

She knelt on the couch and opened the venetian blinds, looked out on the car lot. Snow was falling, fat, blue-flashing flakes spinning down, not enough to satisfy the skiers, but enough to cover the cars below . . . except for one. The dark station wagon sat at the back corner of the lot, its dull hood and roof melting the snow that landed, its clear windshield fogged on the passenger side. Gallagher.

Ellen put on her jean jacket and walked down the stairs, turning the corner around the garage, and she saw the detective's head move, saw him pull himself up in his seat. As she approached his door, he opened his window.

"You seemed so sure of yourself," she said. "I almost believed you."

"I am sure of myself," he replied. "I only came here so you could get a good night's sleep."

"You're alone?"

His eyes moved uncomfortably.

"Here, I mean, keeping watch."

"The lieutenant isn't about to authorize personnel to protect you from a dead man," he told her. His thermos mug steamed the windshield.

"Christmas Eve," Ellen said. "Kind of a lousy night to spend alone in a parking lot."

"That's what I get paid for," he replied, but in the blinking lights, the rigidity of his eyes betrayed a darker countenance.

"If you're going to watch my apartment, you might as well do it upstairs," she said. "I have a couch you could sleep on."

He sipped his coffee, watching straight out his windshield.

"We could probably both use someone to talk to," she said.

"I don't think we'd have much of a conversation," he replied, still looking out at the snow. "Not unless you want to talk to me about how Randy Cross got his arm caught in your dam."

Ellen stood at his door for another second or two, waiting for him to make eye contact. He didn't. "Have a good night, Detective," she said, as his window went up.

Back upstairs, she stared at her half-filled wine glass. She'd drunk plenty, to be sure, but probably not enough to make it through this night without curling up in a tiny, self-pitying knot. She picked up the glass and drank it down, then tossed her knitting aside and went to the kitchen to finish the bottle. She picked up the telephone instead.

"I need to apologize," she said when Scott answered. "I didn't mean what I said last night."

He made a low sound in the phone. It made her think he might be feeling as bad about Christmas as she was. How else could he possibly feel about the anniversary of his parents' death?

"How's Mo doing?" she asked.

"Asleep," he told her. "We both went to bed an hour ago."

Ellen looked at the clock, was surprised to see it was past eleven-thirty.

"I'm sorry," she said. "I just wanted to see when I should bring gifts over for you and Mo."

"I didn't get anything for you," Scott told her. "I don't really know how this is done."

"Neither do I," Ellen said. "I'm not finished with yours anyway. Maybe I'll bring them over tomorrow afternoon. Do you guys have plans?"

"I asked her if she wanted to go out for dinner. She didn't really answer me."

"I could stop by in the morning," Ellen said, a little too casually.

He gave an equivocating grunt. Not that she expected anything more.

"Scott, I don't know," she practically blurted . . . then she stopped and started again. "I don't *understand*," she clarified, "what makes people do the things they do."

"It's a rough time of year," Scott said.

"I mean me. I always thought . . . at least I thought I knew myself." She stopped talking again, wishing she had phoned him three glasses of wine earlier. "But I never would've believed I was capable of some of the things I've done."

"El, can we do this another time?"

"Wait—I want to ask you something."

He listened.

"Not that I expect you to answer me," she said, "but just, hypothetically . . . Do you think you could ever forgive me? I'm not asking you to. I'm just wondering if you think it's possible."

While she listened to the silence on the line, she remembered what it was like getting in bed together after setting Christmas gifts under the tree. She imagined crawling under the covers with him tonight.

"I don't think so," he said.

Ellen's mind stopped. She took a slow breath in, then let it out.

"I think you're right," she told him.

"I know I am."

She waited for him to continue, but he hung up.

She returned to the living room and drank the rest of her wine, then considered starting on the tequila. But she didn't. She kept knitting his hat.

Of course, he was right.

How could someone in love even imagine forgiving such a betrayal? Of course, one may agree to remain with an unfaithful partner—passing on the stairs, eating meals together, going to movies—believing that in time the wound will heal over.

But how could she believe she had ever forgiven him—truly for-given him—given the way her stomach wrenched every time she heard April's name? The way her mind blanked whenever she climbed the stairs and found her bedroom door closed. The way she could never feel him enter her without imagining the wandering path of his mind.

So maybe Neal had been right, that the only reason she'd ever fallen in love with him was to get back at Scott.

Time heals all wounds? No. Scars last. They smile and they kiss and they profess loss of memory. But after thirteen years, how ripe she'd been for revenge. Even now she could not deny the small pang of pleasure she felt, picturing Scott lying in his cold bed, regretting one single day—one hour—that happened so long ago it could have been someone else's life.

Ellen awoke to a sharp knocking on her door. Disoriented by the bright sun shining on her blinds, she got out of bed and went into the kitchen.

"Merry Christmas," Ingrid said when she opened the door. "Do you know there's a well-dressed Neanderthal parked outside the building?"

Ellen didn't even try to smile. "No, but if you start it, I'll sing along," she answered sullenly, turning to her coffeemaker.

"Go get dressed," Ingrid told her. "We're having Christmas dinner at my house."

Before Ellen could decline, Ingrid stepped inside and closed the door. "You weren't answering your phone, so I called Scott, to see if you were there."

Ellen brought the coffee pot to the sink.

"No time for coffee," Ingrid said. "I've got people coming and a twenty-pound turkey in the oven."

Ellen gave a half smile, even as she felt the ache in her throat. "Really, I can't."

"They're all women. Most of them make you look like a poster girl for well-adjustment."

Filling the coffeemaker with water, Ellen took a shaky breath. She wished Ingrid would leave.

"You can't refuse," Ingrid told her. "You're at the head of the table this year. It's a spot reserved for anyone who shoots at her husband."

Ellen turned. The older woman's eyes glinted kindly.

"I shot three times," Ellen said. She blurted out a laugh, and tears broke from her eyes.

Ingrid doubled her fist. "That's my girl."

★   ★   ★

The women drank spiced wines and cider, homemade Christmas ale and a Swedish holiday concoction called glögg. A couple of them smoked Cuban cigars out on Ingrid's deck; two or three shared a bowl of Jamaican ganja in the bathroom. Some watched football with the sound muted and remarked on the players' thighs and their potential as sperm donors. One of the women, a licensed massage therapist, gave massages in Ingrid's bedroom. Another read tarot cards in the spinning room. Ellen declined the massage, the cigar, the pot, and the tarot reading, and she limited herself to a single glass of wine.

At the table, the women loosened their belts, unbuttoned their skirts, and ate for nearly two hours. As Ingrid had promised, she seated Ellen at the head of the table. Ellen was relieved that no one asked why.

After dessert, with flames crackling in the fireplace, they drank gourmet coffee and drew names for a gift exchange—Ingrid had thoughtfully brought along one of Ellen's tapestries from the store so that she'd have something to give. Then they sat on pillows and cushions around the coffee table, or huddled together on the couch and shared stories. Ellen learned that some of the women were couples, that one woman had an ovarian cyst, that another had lost her father on Thanksgiving. When five of the women, members of a 200-voice women's chorus in Portsmouth, squeezed together on the couch and sang a gospel song called, "I Feel Like Going On," Ellen struggled to hold back her tears. That's when she slipped into Ingrid's bedroom and picked up the telephone. Moreen answered after the fourth ring.

"Hi, hon," Ellen said. She waited a few seconds for a response. "Sorry I didn't get your gifts over to you today."

"Are you all right?" Moreen asked.

"Better," Ellen said. "Thanks for asking. How are you doing?"

Mo paused. "My expectations are never that high."

Ellen laughed a little. "That's one way to do it," she said. "Listen, I'll bring your gifts over someday this week."

"Don't worry about it."

Ellen smiled. "I miss you, Mo."

She heard Moreen take a deep breath. "I've gotta go," Moreen said. "Merry Christmas, hon."

After Ellen replaced the phone in its cradle, the door opened and Ingrid stepped inside.

"Leaving?"

"My eyes are starting to cross, I'm so tired," Ellen answered, finding her jean jacket under the coats on Ingrid's bed. She pulled her cap out of the sleeve and fit it over her head.

"Feel better?"

Ellen nodded. "Thanks."

Ingrid waved off the gratitude, then shut the door behind her. "I have something for you. I'm afraid it's not too classy, but I'm hoping you'll know what to do with it."

She handed Ellen a simple red card that said GREETINGS. When Ellen opened it, ten one-hundred-dollar bills slid into her palm.

"I didn't want the others to see it," Ingrid said. "A couple of them used to work for me, and I wasn't as generous."

Ellen's shoulders dropped. She felt a compunction to refuse the money, but the glow she felt prevented her from doing anything but folding the bills in half and slipping them into her pocket.

"It's a lot of money for a part-timer," she said.

"You're worth much more. In case no one's told you lately, you're a kind, intelligent, strong, beautiful, and imaginative woman." Ingrid raised a brow. "Sometimes too imaginative."

Ellen smiled. "Thanks," she said again. "But you forgot 'rigid.'"

"Rigid. Really." Ingrid gave her a skeptical look. "Tell me something. How many times have you forgiven your daughter?"

Before Ellen could recover from the small jolt of revelation, Ingrid opened her door. "Busy day tomorrow. Get a good night's sleep."

twenty-four

On the day after Christmas, the store was crowded with people returning gifts or spending their gift money. Ellen put in her hours,
processing exchanges or working at the demonstration loom, weaving
small lighthouse and lobster wall hangings in preparation for the summer
tourist season.

Back in her apartment that night, Ellen found the phone number
Ingrid had given her, of their friend who owned the farm in Oregon.
Although it was eleven o'clock, it was only eight on the West Coast.
She made the call.

In the morning she gave her notice, and Ingrid grinned. "When
are you leaving?"

Ellen shrugged. "End of the month?"

"Go next week, if you want," Ingrid told her. "Once the after-
Christmas rush is over, it's hardly worth opening the doors again till
April."

Ellen took a deep breath.

"Excited?"

"I've never even seen the Pacific Ocean."

Ingrid put her hands on Ellen's arms and turned her toward the
door. "Go talk to your daughter."

Moreen was still sleeping at eleven o'clock, when Ellen knocked
on her bedroom door.

She groaned tiredly when Ellen walked in and sat on the corner of her bed. "Merry late Christmas," she said, setting her sweater and knit hat beside her pillow.

Mo closed her eyes again. In the corner of the room, small arms and legs intertwined in a pile, all her sculptures thrown together, some broken apart.

"Hon, I wanted to talk to you," Ellen began, already knowing how the conversation would go. "I think I'm moving."

Moreen rolled over, facing away from her.

"Do you remember a woman named Priscilla Clancy? She was in the Weavers' Guild with me. She lives in Oregon now, on a farm. She has a guest house that's empty."

Ellen put her hand on Mo's shoulder. Mo drew her arm back.

"There's a state college in the next town, with a good art department. If they saw your work, I know they'd offer you a scholarship."

Moreen pulled her blankets over her head. "Go, if you want. I need to sleep."

Ellen sat for another few moments, then got up. Resisted the temptation to pick Mo's jeans and sweatshirt off the floor. "Honey, I'd like you to come with me. I hope you'll think about it."

Moreen didn't answer.

Ellen left the house, drove to the gun shop.

Scott smirked when she'd told him what she was planning.

"What about Mo?" he said.

"I told her I'd like her to come with me."

"Fat chance of that." He turned and lifted a long cardboard box— a rifle, Ellen guessed—from a wooden shipping crate. "Truck gonna make it?"

"I'll probably sell it and rent a van."

"Yup."

"Anyway, I wanted to look through the attic and see if there's anything I can take—the old toaster, plates and pans and silverware and things. Is that okay?"

Scott scowled over the counter at her, as though it was just dawning on him that she might be serious. "Moreen's not going to go with you, you know that. Are you actually planning to leave her here and go three thousand miles away?"

"Yes, I am," Ellen replied, a bit surprised at her own conviction.

★   ★   ★

As the cold week passed, and Ingrid trimmed Ellen's hours back further, Ellen kept herself busy making arrangements for the move, pricing rental vans and gathering kitchenware from the farmhouse attic. She disassembled her looms and spinning wheel and bagged all her raw wool and yarn, boxed everything and stored it in her spinning room at the house. She did everything but set a date.

On the last day of the year, Ingrid took her to dinner at the York Harbor Inn. They split a bottle of good champagne and talked of ordinary things, not Oregon. Ellen knew Ingrid was trying not to pressure her. In fact, Ellen still hadn't reserved the van. The subject came up only at the end of dinner, when Ingrid promised to visit someday. Her tone of voice said she was wondering if Ellen was still planning to leave. It made Ellen wonder, herself.

Because they'd arrived in separate vehicles, their goodbye in the parking lot was brief.

"Gonna be okay tonight?" Ingrid asked. "Dick Clark can be murder when you're waiting for the phone to ring."

"New Year's Eve never did much for me anyway," Ellen assured her.

"What about tomorrow?"

Ellen rubbed the chill out of her arms. "Anything but football."

"Good day for a long drive," Ingrid said.

"Maybe."

The blues took Ellen by surprise. Almost as though some internal clock were programmed for holiday depression, she spent the night in front of her television with the remote control in her hand, keenly aware of her solitude, keenly disturbed because of it. Finally dozing off during the eleven o'clock news, she practically flew off the couch when the telephone rang.

"What are you doing?" Scott said. He sounded almost as miserable as she felt.

"It's midnight," she said, looking at the clock on the kitchen stove.

"I know."

Neither of them spoke for another moment or two.

"Well, happy New Year," Ellen said.

"Mo's been in bed since ten," Scott replied. "I wish she'd do something, get a job or go back to school."

"I guess we have to give her time to find her way."

"I guess. Trouble is, with you leaving, I just don't know what that's gonna do to her."

Ellen waited him out, wondering about his change in attitude.

"Have you thought any more about it?"

"Leaving? I think about it a lot," Ellen told him, not wanting to admit that she hadn't been able to follow through yet.

"I've been thinking too," he said. If he was drunk, she couldn't detect it in his voice. "Remember what you said the other day, about forgiveness?"

"Yeah—?" She couldn't remember the last time they'd actually had a conversation.

"I guess I could try."

Stunned, Ellen leaned heavily on the kitchen counter.

"El, I know you did the best you could, you know, after me and April." Scott stopped for a moment; cleared his throat. "I guess what I'm saying is, I'd like to believe this marriage isn't over."

Hearing his voice in her ear, she nodded. It was about all she could do.

"Then again, I know you well enough to know that once you set your mind on a course, there's not much that can hold you back." He stopped talking again.

Ellen swallowed hard, to keep her emotions down. "I think I'm going to go to Oregon, Scott."

She heard him sigh. "I understand," he told her. "But maybe before you do, you might think about this as something we can get over someday. I mean, maybe it's not possible. But along the lines of what-ever—curiosity?—I was wondering if I could take you to dinner next Saturday."

She closed her eyes. The tears burned. It was ridiculous, how much her heart ached.

"I was thinking of leaving before then," she said, trying to keep her voice from breaking.

"Okay. If you go, you go. I'm just saying, if you're still around and you want to give dinner a try—that's all I'm saying—just let me know."

Ellen breathed a long, heavy sigh. "I guess another week won't kill me," she told him.

"El, I've really been missing you."

"I miss you too," she said, though she had meant to choose her words more carefully.

★　★　★

For Ellen, the week dragged by. Even though she worked only four hours a day at the store, the lack of customers made those hours seem endless. To make matters worse, early Friday morning a northeaster blew into town, canceling school and keeping most everyone home-bound. The store remained deserted all through the morning, which was fine with Ellen, since Ingrid had called to say she had to tend to her car, which had been vandalized during the night.

As Ellen worked at the loom, the sound system played a tape that Ingrid had made for the shop, a mix of international folk songs by women—not Ellen's favorite music, but after six weeks of Christmas carols played on hammered dulcimers and banjos, she considered any change a relief. Not that she was paying close attention, anyway.

She was far too occupied with thoughts of Scott and Moreen, won-dering if it could be possible for the family ever to live together again, with all they'd been through. Even if it were possible, she wondered if they could continue living in Destin.

As she wove her lighthouse scene—looking out at the snow blan-keting the parking lot—images of Oregon passed through her mind: green vistas of grape vineyards, mountainsides trimmed with tall ever-greens, the wide blue Pacific.

Maybe it was time for all of them to move, she thought. She could teach school anywhere. And Scott, with his business experience, would have no trouble finding work. It was uprooting Moreen that worried her. On the other hand, that far removed from Destin, maybe Mo would find it easier to try on a new personality. Maybe college would inspire her.

The doorbell interrupted her reverie.

"Don't get up," the man said, carrying three cardboard boxes in his arms. He was not a customer but Douglas, the driver from Spruce Bush Farms. Ingrid stocked some offbeat gourmet foods, such as dilly beans and canned fiddleheads, herbed oils and mustards. Douglas visited the shop twice a month to restock the shelves.

"How's the driving?" Ellen asked.

"Terrible," he said, and he stuck an opened jar under her nose.

She wrinkled her nose at the vinegar kick. "What is it?"

"It's a new line we're trying: 'Widow Jimmy's Famous Frickles.' "

"Frickles?"

"Pickled french fries. Try one." He was a roundish balding man with handlebar mustache, rimless glasses and a bump of a chin. His eyes sparkled when he grinned.

"I don't think so," Ellen said.

He brought the opened jar to the cash register and set it on the counter beside a small, free-standing promotional display that held six jars. "We're giving away free samples all over New England, big promotional campaign." He set a box of toothpicks beside the jar.

"Pickled french fries?"

"They're not as bad as they sound. The story's great. Apparently, this woman's husband came up with the recipe, but then he disappeared and all he left her was a barn full of these things. It looked like she was going to lose the farm, but one morning she opened the door and there was a Dunkin Donuts bag on her porch with a hundred grand inside, no name, no explanation. Just the cash—a hundred thousand dollars. She put a bundle into marketing, and now she's making money hand over fist." He shook his head while he popped a Frickle in his mouth and started to chew. "Who said this was a crazy world?"

He picked up the carton and headed down the food aisle.

"Speaking of which," he said over his shoulder, "are you trying to drive yourself nuts in here?"

"What do you mean?"

He stuck his head out of the aisle with a distasteful squint. "For two solid months I've put up with that Christmas shit. Enough already." He waved a hand at the loudspeaker mounted in the corner of the ceiling, as the song sailed through the store: *". . . three French hens, two turtle doves, and a partridge in a pear tree."*

Ellen laughed. "I don't even hear it any more."

"I can tell. But really, once is bad enough."

Ellen looked curiously at him.

" 'The Twelve Days of Christmas,' " he explained. "The song just ended—then started up again. Come on, the holidays are over. Let the dead rest."

Ellen scowled. She got up from the loom and walked around the counter, opened the door to the small back room. On a shelf beside the desk, the tape player was running, as usual. Then she noticed a trail of small puddles leading in from the back door. She stepped over the puddles, turned the knob, and pulled the heavy door open. The blizzard was blowing diagonally out of the colorless sky, the dumpster and woods obscured by whiteness. She checked the knob on the outside of the door—still locked.

"Is everything okay?" the driver said from the doorway, startling her.

Ellen closed the door, then looked at him for a moment. "Yeah," she replied. She went to the tape player and pushed STOP. The shop became perfectly quiet, except for the snow ticking at the door. The driver eyed her curiously.

"What's the date today?" she asked him.

"The sixth," he said. "Why?"

"January sixth," she confirmed.

He nodded his head. "Also called Twelfth Night—if you're a fan of Shakespeare."

Ellen's heart weakened.

"The twelfth day after Christmas," he explained. "I assumed that's why you were playing that god-awful song."

"Twelve days," she breathed, pushing past him into the front of the store, where she turned to the cuckoo clock behind the cash register.

11:45.

"Twelve hours," she whispered.

The man picked up his empty carton, seeming to study her. "Gotta go. I'm running almost two hours late."

Twelve years, twelve months, twelve weeks . . .

She tried to clear the terror from her face, even as her mind raced: *Neal is here.* No, he'd *been* here. Now he was on his way to find Scott and Moreen.

"See you in a couple of weeks?" the driver said, still watching her.

"Yeah," Ellen replied vacantly.

He headed down the main aisle, pushed the door open, then turned to give her one more look. "Have a good one," he said, then he walked out. Ellen watched him fade into the storm.

She grabbed the telephone, wondering what she could possibly say to convince anyone. Then it didn't matter—the phone was dead. She dropped it and ran into the back room, to the desk, reached into her pocketbook, felt around. Her revolver was gone.

Ripping her jacket from the hook, she threw the back door open and charged out into the storm. Her truck was parked about fifty feet away, on the other side of the dumpster. She got in, started the engine and turned on the windshield wipers, but the snow was too heavy to clear, so she jumped out and swiped the snow with her arm until the wipers started moving.

She ducked back in the cab and shifted into gear, turned her defrosters high, punched her emergency flashers, then tore off across the parking lot. At the turn, her truck skated a half circle and slammed backward into the snowbank the plows had made.

"*Shit!*" Ellen yelled, restarting the engine and popping the clutch. The pickup fishtailed wildly, then slid headlong through the lot and into the road, narrowly avoiding a furniture truck that swerved to miss her. She hit a patch of road sand and shot ahead, straight through the stoplight.

The clock on her dash said 11:50. Even on a good day, the drive to her house took ten minutes. Fortunately, the plows had been out all morning, and the road wasn't bad. She passed one car, then another, then swung back into her lane just as a sand truck turned toward her, blasting its horn.

She concentrated on her breathing. Drop the diaphragm. Fill the belly, fill the chest. Full breath in, full breath out.

Clear the mind. *Think.* Cassette tapes are usually forty-five minutes to a side. Which meant Neal couldn't be more than forty-five minutes ahead of her. More likely a half-hour or less. But how long did it take to kill someone?

Twelve years, twelve months, twelve weeks, twelve days, twelve hours: all the twelves in line, at last. It's what Neal had been planning since his twelfth birthday—

—and now he had her gun.

11:51

And she had nine minutes to stop him.

Moreen would still be in bed—she rarely got up before noon. Scott would have come home for lunch a half-hour ago. Ellen's only hope was that Neal would wait for her, wanting them all together.

She pressed the accelerator down. At the intersection with the Reservoir Road, she swerved left through the stop sign and forced a jet-black Altima into the ditch. She never slowed.

11:55

She reached into the glove compartment, felt around for something she could use as a weapon, found a Phillips-head screwdriver about four inches long. She would not hesitate to kill him with it. She pictured herself driving it into his chest, his throat. Whatever it took. She jammed it in her jacket pocket as she made the turn onto River Road.

She knew Scott would have a gun in the house—unless he had gotten rid of it when Moreen moved back home. It didn't matter—he'd never get the chance to use it. Neal would find a way to take them by surprise.

Her keys—

Of course, Neal had copied her keys—the same way he'd let himself into Maddy's house and into the store. Yes, he would let himself in the front door while Scott was in the kitchen with the portable television on, having his lunch.

Then Ellen would steal into the house the same way. She hit her brakes, skidded to a stop at the top of the hill. Her white farmhouse below was completely obscured by the blizzard, and for a moment she felt that gave her an advantage.

11:58

Except that Neal knew she was coming. He had begun constructing this particular road another lifetime ago, and today Ellen had no choice but to follow it. With a sinking fear, she also realized that nothing she might think of to stop him would have escaped his consideration.

She slammed into low gear and her white truck jumped over the crest of the white hill and surged straight down. She pumped the brakes as she approached her driveway. The back end of the truck fishtailed on the ice, she downshifted into second, then hit the gas and plowed into the snowbank beside her driveway. The impact pitched her into the horn—so much for surprises.

11:59

She kicked her door open and fell out into the snowbank, dropping her screwdriver. She picked it up and ran into the dooryard, the snow freezing her wrist. The blizzard was blowing down harder, making it difficult to see more than a few feet ahead, but she could make out Scott's Mercedes parked there, the snow still melting on the dark hood. A fresh set of footprints led from the car to the porch. No other tracks were visible.

Clutching the screwdriver close to her chest, Ellen followed the tracks onto the porch and tried the door, found it unlocked. She pushed it open, looked inside. The kitchen was quiet. She looked up at the clock on the wall, the second hand sweeping up to twelve.

"Scott?" she called, and a fierce chill went through her. *"Moreen!"*

She heard the muffled hum of the noontime fire horn from off in the village. She jerked her head toward the clock as the second hand passed over 12—perfectly synchronized—and silently continued rounding the numbers. Ellen backed against the counter, braced for the attack.

"Scott?"

The sound of her voice slapping off the bare walls sent goosebumps down her sides. Reaching behind her, she quietly pulled out the drawer, where she found a steak knife. She set her screwdriver on the counter.

She thought of the pantry, of Neal lurking that close to her, and she slid along the counter until most of the small room came into view, empty.

A gust of snowflakes tapped at the windows. She looked back at the clock, the second hand sweeping up to 12:01.

Twelve minutes . . . Of course. He would draw this out till the last second. *All the twelves in line.*

She walked into the living room, the steak knife tight in her hand. The stairway rose silently, white stormlight coming in the windows, projecting the shadows of the banister up the wall.

"Scott?"

She listened for a response above her but heard only the wind rattling at the windows . . . and she remembered another time, years ago, when she stood here calling his name.

"Moreen, answer me!" she yelled. Beside her, the VCR blinked from 12:01 to 12:02. On the other side of her—

She stopped.

A Bible lay open on the coffee table, a black circle scrawled around a passage. She bent closer to see: *"And ye shall know the truth, and the truth shall make you free."*

She batted the book on the floor, then crossed to the stairs, transferring the knife to her left hand as she took hold of the railing, climbing steadily, knowing her bedroom door would be closed and terrified of opening it, wondering what she would find this time.

She remembered perfectly the image of Scott and April getting dressed beside the bed, the look in their eyes when she opened the door . . . now she pictured Scott and Moreen lying on the same bed, corpses silently staring.

A tread squawked under her foot and she stopped, nearly paralyzed. But why wait? He knew she was coming. He knew she couldn't refuse. She climbed the last two stairs and stepped around the corner into the hallway. All three doors were shut, as if each held back a secret.

Her hand reached out to the bedroom door.

Neal, we only want to help you.

Yeah. Saying that with a steak knife in her hand wouldn't set any-one free.

She turned the doorknob. Her head hummed, her heart pounded. The door swung open. The room stared back at her. The bed was disheveled. Underpants tossed in the corner with his socks; pocket change scattered on the night table and floor; closet door opened on his permanent-press shirts, his thirty-dollar neckties. A strange feeling washed over Ellen, something akin to relief. *I don't miss this,* she thought.

Was that the truth Neal wanted her to admit?

Scott, living without you the past three months has been the loneliest time of my life. I never imagined anyone could feel such emptiness. But the truth is, I don't miss you.

Maybe it was true, Ellen thought, but not entirely.

Yes, I do miss you. But I don't believe we ever loved each other, not the way love ought to be. Even when we had sex, I felt as if you were having sex with my breasts. I was never part of it.

She opened her own closet, still hung with the skirts and blouses she had no more need of—clothing of a polite woman who would never dream of having sex with her nephew, murdering her son-in-law . . .

When I said I forgave you, Scott, I think what I really meant was that I was afraid to leave you. Or maybe I was afraid you'd kill yourself, like your brother did.

On Scott's night stand, the clock radio whirred.

12:06

Six minutes to save their lives. Ellen went to his bureau and opened the drawers, searched under T-shirts and sweatpants for a weapon she knew wasn't there. She wheeled and hurried out into the hallway, holding the knife out ahead of her as she crossed to Moreen's room and threw the door open. Her heart leaped. Then it fell. Clay body parts littered the room.

Ellen knew it was Moreen's doing, not Neal's, destroying all that was beautiful about herself.

Moreen, every time you came home with a new tattoo or another piece of hardware through your flesh, I felt that it was meant for me.

The disembodied faces—Moreen's faces—glared up at her, scream-ing in a silent rage. Ellen stepped over the discarded clothes, the smashed, twisting limbs, and crossed to the closet, wondering if she'd find Mo's body hanging inside. But there was only the collision of tattered jerseys and T-shirts.

Maybe in my heart I was relieved when your husband died. How's this for truth?

Ellen felt a gnawing deep in her gut.

*And maybe I knew right from the start that Neal was planning to murder
Randy. Maybe I even let it happen—I don't know. But if that's the truth, I
only did it because I love you, and because I knew that Randy was hurting you.*

"Moreen, please answer me!" Ellen shouted.

Her Betty Boop clock turned to 12:10.

Ellen left the room, turned in the hall, and pushed open the door
to her spinning room. Filled with boxes and bags, useless fragments, it
made Ellen wonder if the house was as empty as it seemed, indeed, if
this was all her imagination again.

No. It was Neal who had left the Bible for her. He was here.

A scream spun Ellen into the hall, heart leaping. But it was only
Moreen's alarm clock sounding. Then she heard Scott's radio come on.
"If everybody had an ocean, across the U.S.A . . ." Steak knife in hand,
Ellen hurried down the stairs (the VCR blinking 12:12, 12:12, 12:12,
the stove alarm jangling), burst into the kitchen, turned off the stove
timer. She looked up at the clock on the wall, its second hand
twitching . . . seven . . . eight . . . nine . . . all the twelves. Finally.
All lining up.

Ellen backed against the front door, the knife flashing in front of
her. A deep, distant roll of thunder shook the floor, rattling the dishes
in the cupboard. Then silence.

Ellen opened the door and looked out into the falling snow. Just
the wind in the woods, a deep, steady blowing. Squinting into whiteness, she stepped to the edge of the porch, where the falling snow was
able to reach her. The only footprints she could see were Scott's and her
own, coming into the house. How could they not be inside? Unless—

She turned left and walked to the end of the porch, moving faster
as the answer became apparent. And there they were, tracking down
beside the house and across the dooryard, three sets of prints. They had
gone out the front door.

Ellen made a frightened sound, her voice swallowed by the rush of
wind that seemed to be intensifying . . . except the snow continued
falling straight down. There was no wind.

That's when Ellen realized what was making the sound, and her
heart leaped.

She started to run.

A Gray Ghost sat in the vice, the same unfinished fly that had been
staring at Wes Westerback for a week now, with his magnifying light
hovering over it. Wes himself reclined in his desk chair, watching the

snow tumble down past the glass doors, not listening to the telephone ringing, or the scanner chattering, or the vacuum cleaner that rolled back and forth on the floor over his head, not wondering about the explosion he'd heard, not even thinking about his dead son Sugar. What occupied his mind was watching the blue jays and squirrels battle for a handful of sunflower seeds in the snow—and feeling heartbroken about it. Not the most healthy way for any man to spend his days, let alone the police chief. Wes knew this. But nothing else seemed to hold his attention. Not even the trout fly.

On the seventh ring, Wes picked up his phone and said, "Yup."

"Wes, it's Dave Mercurio, up at the Water District."

"Yeah, Dave."

"I don't know what the hell's going on, but I think some god-damned kids just blew up the dam."

Wes didn't say anything for a second. Outside the glass door, a squirrel dived off a spruce branch and caught the bird feeder in midair, kicking seeds out of the tray as it swung.

"You think?" Wes said.

"We're losing half the goddamned reservoir, Wes. The valley's gonna flood. I don't know what we can do to stop it. I got divers coming, but it's not just the floodgate. Half the friggin dam's blown to smithereens."

Wes inhaled deeply, then let out a long sigh. He watched the squirrel jump off the feeder into the snow and scurry about grabbing his booty. He thought he was going to cry.

"Gotta be kids," Mercurio said. "They're all home from school today."

Wes exhaled another sigh. "Dave, do me a favor and call the state police. They'll handle it. Anyone lives along the river, you'd best get 'em evacuated to the high school. Call Hawkins, the superintendent, and have him open up the school, turn on the heat, and get the cooks in. He'll know what to do."

"I'll make the call, Wes, but who's gonna listen to a Water District engineer?"

"Tell them you're a sergeant with the Destin Police," Wes told him. "I just deputized you."

Ellen ran as fast as she could through the snow, but she kept sinking in the previous tracks and falling to her knees. When she reached the pump house she stopped. Through the falling snow she recognized

Neal's silhouette, sitting ghostly on the middle of the dam. She could tell by the turn of his shoulders that he was watching her. She stepped out beside the cinder-block building and marched down the hill toward him. He had made it impossible for her to do anything but.

"Where is my family?" she screamed at him, slipping as she climbed up the bank to the dam. His hair had grown even longer and his beard was black and full. His eyes gleamed meaningfully through the snow.

When she stepped to the edge of the abutment, she saw her family fifteen feet below her, shackled to the dam: Moreen on the left, Scott on the right, six feet apart, their left arms raised above their heads, handcuffed to the U-rings that Neal had embedded seven feet high in the concrete. Dangling there on the frozen, rocky floor of the pond, they looked like frozen marionettes. Between them, a single handcuff dangled down from the U-ring. Ellen knew it was hers.

Turning to Neal, she shouted, "How do you blame Moreen for what your father did to himself?" She saw the revolver in his hand, resting on his knee. It was her gun, but he was not aiming it at her, nor at anything in particular. He just kept staring.

Moreen had her pea-coat on, along with a wool cap. She wore heavy wool mittens on both hands, even the one that was handcuffed. Scott, however, was dressed in a pin-striped shirt and blue polyester V-neck sweater. His right arm hugged his chest, and he shivered painfully. Then Ellen noticed red drops in the snow by his left shoe.

She reached out and caught the highest rung in the dam, then started climbing down with the knife clutched in her hand, shivering more from fear than the cold. When her boots hit the icy rocks at the bottom, she leaned on the dam for balance as she made her way to Moreen.

"Hon, are you okay?" she asked, reaching up and sawing at the handcuff chain. The blade barely scratched the steel.

Moreen didn't answer but stared off at the distant rushing of sound, the gathering flood.

Ellen looked up to the top of the dam. "Is this what you've lived for?" she yelled at Neal. "This is it?"

Neal looked impassively over the safety cable. "Not the best time to be patronizing, Aunt Ellen. Who knows? Maybe today I'll do things your way. Maybe I'll forgive everybody." He showed her something small and silvery in his fingers. A key?

While snowflakes lit harmlessly on her eyelashes, Ellen could feel the rumbling in her feet. She looked off at the narrow gorge out ahead of them. All she could see above the steep granite walls was the white sky and the tips of three or four scrawny red pines.

"Neal, just let them go. No one wants to hurt you."

He leaned forward and aimed the revolver down at the top of Moreen's head. "That's your last lie, Ellen."

"No!" She dropped the steak knife down into the rocks.

Still he kept his pistol aimed at Moreen. "Ellen, I need you to fasten the center handcuff to your left wrist."

Ellen stared up, knowing it was pointless to try and dissuade him. "Don't hurt Moreen," she said. "Just don't." Reaching up, she took the open cuff in her right hand and snapped it around her left wrist. The icy steel bit into her flesh. "Okay," she called. "Now, please, let Moreen go."

He smiled down imperiously. "James five, sixteen," he said. " 'Confess your faults to one another, that ye may be healed.' "

"Confess what?"

"The truth," he replied. "The truth shall set you free."

"What do you want us to say, Neal?"

Lowering the pistol, he said, "Why not start at the beginning?"

"I don't understand!"

"Ellen, we don't have time to waste. Think back. There was a hurricane."

As the rushing sound intensified out beyond the gorge, she heard a distant crack in the woods, maybe a half mile away, and she imagined the flood waters crashing through the trees, tearing up everything in its path.

"I was teaching," she began. "I came home from school early, to make sure the sheep were safe."

"That's the only reason you came home?"

"That's the reason. I went upstairs and found your mother in our bedroom."

She looked over at Scott, who gazed grimly at the icy walls of the gorge that surrounded them.

"And what was my mother doing in your bedroom, Ellen?"

"She was with Scott, getting dressed."

"Sounds innocent enough," Neal said. He raised his face into the falling snow.

"They'd had sex, all right?"

"Okay," Neal said. "What did you do then?"

"I left them there."

"And?"

"I drove to your house."

"Yes, you did. Why?"

"I didn't know what else to do."

"So you went to my house and what?"

"I told your father."

"Told him what?"

"That they slept together."

"Something wrong with sleeping?"

Ellen closed her eyes. "That they'd had sex!"

He waited.

"That's it," she said. "Then you came home from school. You know the rest."

As the rumble under her feet grew stronger, Ellen looked over at Scott, who was gazing up at the head of the gorge, as if inviting the deluge.

"So that's everything?" Neal asked.

"That's what happened," Ellen told him. "That's the truth."

"*Your* truth," Neal replied. "Now do you want to know what actually happened that day? I came home from school expecting a birthday party, but when I walked in the door, you were there. My mother was hysterical and my father was leaving the house. And you left with him. The next thing I knew, my father was dead, and *nobody*—"

Neal aimed the revolver down at Scott; Ellen caught her breath.

"—nobody ever had the common courtesy to tell me *why*."

"You were twelve years old," Scott said weakly, not realizing he was in Neal's sights. "How the hell could you understand what was going on?"

"Scott," Ellen said, trying to quiet him.

"Uncle Scotty?" Neal asked calmly.

Scott looked up, saw the revolver aiming down. He pulled hard on the chain, trying to protect his face. "Jesus Christ, do you think I didn't regret it?" he shouted at Neal. "Every day! Do you think your mother never regretted it?"

Neal gazed down over the cable at him, the white, snow-filled sky outlining his head and shoulders.

"He's telling you the truth," Ellen called, her voice shaking badly. "How could you expect your mother to tell you something like that?"

Neal reached the key over the dam as if he was about to drop it down to Ellen. "Come on, Ellen, the truth shall set you free."

Ellen whipped her own face skyward. "Quit the pretense, Neal! You came here to indulge yourself with a few more deaths. Just get it over with."

"Would you rather let your daughter die than tell her what she has a right to know?"

"Moreen is not part of this!"

"Moreen is the reason I'm giving you a chance!"

Ellen turned to her daughter—the beautiful eyes, the tattooed teardrops, the fixed hard scowl on her face.

"You want the truth, Neal?" Ellen shouted up at him. "When I thought I was falling in love with you, I was having my revenge against Scott. It meant nothing else."

"Good," he yelled. "So you had sex with your nephew as an expression of resentment."

"That's right!"

"See, that's the way it's done, folks. Come on, Ellen, you're almost there. Tell Mo about Randy."

"I've told her! I hated what he was doing to her."

"That's right," Neal mocked. "Hate the sin, not the sinner."

"Grow up!" Ellen yelled. She turned to Moreen. "When I saw Randy hurt you, I told Neal I felt like killing him. I didn't mean it— not literally. But I said it."

Moreen stared placidly ahead, the tremors around them sounding like a battery of earth-moving machines tearing through the woods.

"The truth," Neal said, exasperated. "Okay? *This isn't that hard, folks.*"

Ellen turned back to Moreen, who refused to meet her eyes. "Maybe I did mean what I said," she continued. "Maybe I knew Neal would do it, I really don't know. And it doesn't matter. I could've stopped him, but I didn't."

Moreen showed no expression beyond her shivering. Rocks around her boots shook off their cover of snow.

"Ellen, up here."

Ellen raised her eyes, and Neal dropped the key. She flashed out her hand as the glitter fell through the snowflakes. She felt the key sting her palm, and she slapped it against her chest. Carefully she cupped her hand around it.

"Don't drop it," Neal said. "It's the only one."

Ellen squeezed the key between her thumb and fingers, then stretched up toward Moreen's handcuff.

"It's yours, not Moreen's," Neal told her. "Mo's going to have to set herself free."

The sound of destruction intensified in the air. Ellen visualized ice chunks tumbling down the hillside, deadwood snapping into splinters. She imagined it all pouring into the gorge on top of them.

"Neal, please! Let her go!"

"Moreen, do you see your mother's dilemma?" Neal called down. "See, she's so torn apart with guilt, she'd rather die than free herself."

Angrily, Ellen reached up and stuck the key in the cuff that held her. She gave it a twist, and the steel snapped open. Her arm fell and her foot slid off the rock. She stumbled against the dam.

"What's worse," Neal continued, "she doesn't know if she's just an overprotective mom or an accessory to murder. Because she doesn't know if it was Randy who hurt you, or her ram."

Moreen's dark eyes lost focus. For the first time since she was a little girl, Ellen thought she looked frightened.

Neal held out another key in his fingers. "Come on, Moreen, was it Randy or the ram?"

"It's okay," Ellen said to her, touching her daughter's cold cheek.

Mo's eyes narrowed. Her jaw clenched. She turned her face to Ellen and said, "I did it."

"Speak up," Neal called down.

Moreen ignored him, focusing her eyes on Ellen, tight with anger. "I used your barbell. I dropped it on myself. Then I let Bucky out."

Ellen stared at her daughter, desperately wanting Moreen to take back what she'd said—to tell her anything else—but Mo's steady gaze told her all she needed to know. Regret gone to resentment, shame to pride, Mo's eyes said it all. She'd been a junkie carrying a junkie in her womb, and in one fleeting act she had spared her baby and punished herself and everyone around her.

Ellen put her hand behind Moreen's head and gripped her as gently as she knew how. She kissed her cheek. "It's okay, Hon." She felt too cold to cry, but hot tears burned her eyes. "It's okay," she whispered.

"Ellen, hold out your hand," Neal called.

Ellen looked up. The key was already falling. Desperately, she reached out, and it bounced off her arm and clinked off the rocks. Ellen dropped to her knees and pinched it out of a crevice. Then she stood and reached for Moreen's wrist. Despite her shaking, she maneuvered the tiny key into the lock, and the handcuff snapped apart. She caught

Moreen's arm and turned her toward the rungs, shouting to Neal: *"Don't you hurt her!"*

"She's free to go," Neal yelled back against the roar above them, while Moreen pulled herself stiffly away from her mother and started climbing the rungs up the face of the dam. "Of course, she might want to stick around and help her dad, who we all know has a little trouble owning up to things."

"All right!" Scott blurted, shivering furiously. "I was involved, too. In the Randy thing."

Moreen pulled herself to the top of the dam, but stopped there, looking down at her father.

"Mo, get out of here!" Ellen yelled at her.

"I think she's waiting for Dad to come clean," Neal said.

Scott looked up at Moreen. "He told me that Randy kicked you, honey. He told me about the hysterectomy. I was only trying to protect you."

He lifted his face expectantly, but Neal only pulled the blanket off his shoulders and threw it over to Moreen, who climbed onto the abutment to retrieve it.

"What the hell do you want from me?" Scott shouted wildly. "Okay, I pushed his arm into the pipe. Jesus." He looked up angrily.

"That's a start," Neal called.

"Neal, Scott made a mistake!" Ellen shouted over the tumult bearing down. "Your mother made a mistake. It was thirteen years ago. Maybe she wasn't as strong as you. Maybe your father beat her down with that religion the same way he beat you."

"And maybe I helped kill my father, as my mother was so fond of saying."

"Maybe you did."

Neal smiled. Then he calmly aimed the revolver down and fired. Stone dust and snow exploded from a rock inches in front of Scott. "I did *not* kill my father," Neal said. "It was my *mother* and your *husband* who killed my father." He fired the .38 twice more to punctuate his words.

"You know that's not true!" Ellen shouted. "They don't deserve to die for having sex!"

"For committing adultery," Neal countered, " *'they shall both of them die.'* Deuteronomy twenty-two."

Neal fired the .38 again, and Scott jerked his arm, rattling the chain. The way he blinked told Ellen he hadn't been hit.

"Moreen, take my truck and get out of here!" Ellen yelled, but Mo stood over them, wrapped in the blanket, watching.

"Come on, Scott. My aunt seems to be convinced that I'm the one who killed Madeleine Sterling."

"Oh, no," Scott cried. "No way, man."

"Daddy, just say whatever he wants," Moreen cried, staring out of the blanket.

"Don't say anything that's not true, Scott," Neal said. "Come on, now. Who shot Maddy?"

"I don't know anything about that!"

Neal leaned over the safety cable and, with both hands, aimed the revolver down at Scott's head.

"Last chance, Uncle."

Scott's head lolled back as if he'd intended to look up at Neal, but he just hung there by his wrist while he hugged himself with his free hand. Then he closed his eyes.

"I went over to talk to her," he said. "That's all." He turned his head and gazed imploringly at Ellen, the words from his mouth sounding increasingly distant. "She was crazy. You know how she got. She was feeling guilty, I don't know. She had the gun to her head, I tried to talk her out of it."

Ellen stared at her husband. Her mind had stopped working. She no longer heard the roar in the sky or the clicking of rocks all around her, nor even the sudden hiss of headwaters. But when Scott's eyes suddenly flared, Ellen looked up to see the monstrous flood head explode over the gorge like an avalanche, as tons of muddy water surged down the falls in a boiling, snowy froth, thundering down the high granite walls. When the full force of the waters hit, Ellen was slammed into Scott, who howled in pain as he swung from his shackle, the water astonishingly icy and immediately thigh-high, rollicking with ice chunks. Ellen held onto Scott, trying to lift him, to keep the handcuff from cutting into his wrist. But, pummeled herself, she reached up and caught the open handcuff beside him.

"Scott, look up here!" Neal shouted down.

Grimacing, Scott raised his face hopefully, as Neal whipped his hand over his shoulder. Clutching the hanging handcuff beside her husband, Ellen watched the silvery glitter as the tiny key arced through the blizzard and disappeared in the waterfall.

"He told you the truth!" Ellen screamed, slapping the dam, though deep inside she knew the truth was far from told.

"Do you believe that Maddy shot herself in the head?" Neal shouted down at her.

As the flood roared into the gorge, he stared down at her for a second or two, and she stared back, while the deluge pressed her against the concrete.

Neal set the revolver on top of the dam, then stood and pulled his sweatshirt over his head. Underneath, he wore a diver's dry suit and a weight harness strapped like suspenders over his shoulders. Picking up the revolver, he walked off the dam toward Moreen.

"Mo, run!" Ellen screamed.

But Moreen remained on the edge of the diving rock, staring out of the hooded blanket, as Neal bent at the abutment and started climbing down the rungs to the water. Five feet above the surface, he dropped feet-first beside Ellen. The roiling water engulfed him at first, and she thought to go for his gun, but he immediately gained his footing and thrust the revolver straight at her. Hanging on the handcuff, she stiffened, waiting to be shot.

"Take it," Neal said, slapping the revolver in her free hand.

She regarded him skeptically, even as she fit her frozen fingers around the grip and aimed the gun at him.

"You be the judge," he told her. "You can shoot me if you want. Or shoot his handcuff chain. Your choice. You've got one bullet left."

She slid her finger into the trigger guard, as a chunk of ice slammed against her hip; she hardly felt the sting.

"If you kill me," Neal told her, "you'll be rid of both of us. It's up to you, Ellen. Forgiveness or revenge."

"Ellen, hurry," Scott groaned, jangling his wrist.

"He's right," Neal said. "If this water gets much deeper, you won't last five minutes before hypothermia kills you both."

Tightening her hand around the open handcuff, she kicked herself closer to Scott, reached out and pressed the muzzle against the middle link of his handcuff chain.

"But I don't think we've heard the reason Maddy was murdered. Have we, Uncle Scott?"

Ignoring the comment, Ellen thumbed the hammer back. She angled the barrel slightly up, hoping to prevent a ricochet or spray of shrapnel, but the water rocked her so badly she was afraid she might miss entirely.

"Turn your head," she said to Scott.

"It wasn't because Maddy was going to tell the cops about Randy. Let's face it, the police knew Randy's death was no accident."

Ellen touched her finger to the trigger. Although she could still feel the water climbing up her waist, she was already growing numb to its cold.

"Just shoot it," Scott whispered, his jaw barely able to move.

"Maybe Maddy had some other information that Scott wanted to be kept secret. Didn't I hear that Mo was seeing your friend on a professional basis?"

A wave of intense shivering attacked Ellen's arm, and the muzzle of her .38 scraped off Scott's handcuff chain.

"El?"

"Like maybe something Moreen saw when she was young—too young to know what to do about it."

As the frigid waters pounded her side, Ellen looked back at Moreen standing high on the diving rock, staring out of her blanket.

"El, shoot it," Scott sputtered. "He's insane."

"I guess it's up to you, Mo," Neal called. "Can you tell us what you saw that day? The day my father died."

Up on the high rock, Moreen seemed to be entranced, the way she raised her beautiful, ornamented face into the falling snow, the way her head shook almost imperceptibly, back and forth.

"See, she's telling you!" Scott cried. "She never saw a thing!"

"Oh, yes," Moreen said, and now she looked directly at her father. "I did see. Daddy—"

To Ellen, it seemed like the entire world had spun off its axis. For that moment, she did not feel the iciness that rocked her body. For that moment, nothing existed except Scott and his desperate denial.

"I heard you out in the barn fighting with Uncle Jon," Mo continued. "Yes, you were. He was yelling and you were yelling. I was scared, so I went in the house and hid in the pantry. Then you came into the kitchen and got a chair, and you went back out again."

Shaking and gray-faced, Scott tried to smile, as he shook his head and repeated, as though he were drunk, "Nope. Nope. Nope."

"I ran out the door, and you ran after me. You caught me in the pasture and said if I ever told anyone you'd been there, the police would take you away and we'd never see you again."

Scott turned to Ellen, the icy flood assailing his chest. "He was trying to kill me!"

Ellen remembered her mother-in-law's words. *Face the truth. If you want to save Moreen . . .*

"You stretched out his necktie when you strangled him," Neal asserted. "So you tied it to the chainfall. Then you hoisted him up and dropped the chair under him."

Ellen fixed her frozen gaze on her husband, but he refused to meet her eyes.

"He was the town preacher!" Scott cried, throwing his face out of the water. "I was a high school dropout with a brand-new Mercedes. Who the hell was gonna believe me, that I killed him in self-defense?"

"So you see, Aunt Ellen," Neal explained behind her, "that's the day that Moreen and her dad became lifelong allies—the same day that made allies out of you and me."

Ellen tried to ignore him, but she knew it was true. Now she stared at this man, her husband, as if she were seeing him for the first time— his downcast eyes, the incredible sadness in his gaze.

"Scott, you could have told me the truth," she said to him. "Didn't you know I would have understood?"

"Lie!" The invective echoed off the woods, as a wave of ice water splashed down Ellen's jacket. She peered up through the snow, immobilized, her vision filled with the image of Moreen standing high on the rock, the little girl who had once stood speechless in her doorway, trying to tell her something—while Ellen stripped the bed that had always been their meeting place.

"You never understood a thing!" Moreen cried.

Ellen stared up at her daughter, a grown woman now, a perfect stranger. The world went white.

"Mom, save him!"

Ellen felt as if she'd lost consciousness. She looked at Scott hanging heavily from the handcuff, while a floating plate of ice played against his armpit. He had stopped shivering. His eyes stared down at the water, nearly shut.

Ellen heard a splash behind her and turned to see Neal holding the handcuff Mo had hung from. He was only an arm's length away. Afraid he'd try to take the revolver from her, she raised it beside her ear.

"We're running out of time, Aunt Ellen," he said quietly. "Forgiveness or revenge?"

Matching his electric stare with her own, she shook her head at him. Then she turned back to Scott, reached the .38 to the handcuff, pressing the muzzle firmly against the chain. As she was about to fire, however, his handcuff chain snapped out of the line of fire.

"Scott, hold still," she gasped, trying to follow the chain with the weapon.

But he shook his wrist again, a reckless flash of confidence shining in his eye. In other circumstances, Ellen would have thought him playfully drunk—in this circumstance he was telling her something: Use the last bullet on Neal.

The ice water splashed against her chin as she shook her head.

He scowled at her, telling her to get on with it.

She scowled back at him.

Then he gave her a strange, forced smile. And before she could question him, he dropped his face into the water. She saw his back lurch powerfully, as a great cough of bubbles exploded around his ears.

"Scott!"

She started in after him, but Neal's arm locked around her throat, and his other hand grabbed for the revolver. She drove her left elbow into his ribs and Neal hauled her under water into a skull-crushing freeze, wrenching her arm back until it felt as if her shoulder would rip from its socket.

She threw her skull at him, got her chin up over his shoulder and bit down on his ear. He jerked his head into her nose, throwing her off. She swung the gun around. He caught it in his hand. She squeezed the trigger, and her ears shattered with the blast. She dropped the revolver and sprang for the sky, blindly catching the open handcuff and pulling herself up, but Neal caught her ankle and kept her underwater. She held tight to the cuff, even as he tried to drag her back down. But he wasn't anchored, and she was, and she reached her other hand up and caught the U-bolt, pulling for the light with every last fiber of her strength, while he climbed her body as if he were climbing a rope, crawling up her legs and hips, her stomach and chest. With the bright sky dancing only inches above her mouth, every morsel of Ellen's being screamed for a taste of air. But then Neal captured her hand that held the U-bolt, and he wrapped his legs around her waist. Now, while she beat at his face with the handcuff, he concentrated on tearing her hand free with his teeth. Suddenly she felt a fierce sharpness in the knuckle of her index finger, an incredible pressure at its base. She looked through the murk and saw her finger in his mouth, then she heard the snap of her bone breaking. Pain flared behind her eyes and she lost hold of the U-bolt.

But not the handcuff.

She slammed it over his wrist. The chain snapped taut as he tried to yank free. With all her strength, Ellen jammed his wrist against the dam until she felt the handcuff catch, then she broke free.

Splashing into the air, she ripped an agonizing breath into her lungs as she pulled for the ladder. But, hearing a groan behind her, she turned.

"Mo!" she screamed.

Her daughter's dark eyes stared out of the water, the dark hair spread across the surface. Ellen could tell that she was holding onto Scott, shivering helplessly.

"Mo," Ellen gasped, reaching back for her. "He's gone, Mo. Hurry."

Grabbing her daughter under the arms, Ellen pulled, and Mo's hand came out of the water, losing hold of her father. She moaned defiantly and tried to fight. Then her eyes flared in fear.

Ellen turned, saw Neal's head rise above the surface right beside her, eyes open, dark and glinting. She pulled Moreen back, grabbing onto the U-bolt just under the surface, the one Scott was shackled to. The ladder rungs were less than ten feet away, but they couldn't reach them without going through Neal. Neither could they go around him, lacking the strength to swim against the current, even though the flood seemed, oddly, to have subsided somewhat.

"Honey, stay awake," Ellen said, giving Mo a shake, although she struggled to stay conscious herself. Moreen could do little more than hang shivering in her arm.

As the water rocked quietly around his nose, Neal reached his face out of the water, pursed his lips and made a long, steady hissing sound, sucking a volume of icy air into his lungs. His bloody hand came out like a serpent, and he brushed the hair from his eyes, pink water streaming down his face. Then he turned the hand toward Ellen, showing her the crimson, gulping hole in his palm.

"Now do you understand?" he declaimed. "Now do you understand my life?"

Easily within reach of the hand that she'd shot, Ellen held tight to Moreen, while she curled her wrist around the U-bolt, fixing herself to the dam. Then, with a fearsome shudder, she nodded her head compliantly. "Yes, I understand," she gasped.

Raising his mouth out of the water again, Neal refilled his lungs with a windy whistle, his eyes sparkling with validation.

"I understand perfectly, Neal," she said, and she matched the gleam in his eye with one of her own. "You didn't get your birthday party."

In that one frozen moment, as Neal's gaze lost its light, Ellen's boot shot out of the water. Numb as she was, she nevertheless felt a solid impact, the cartilage of his nose snapping under her heel.

She leaped ahead, grabbing the U-bolt that held his handcuff and pulling Moreen over the top of him. Catching hold of the last U-bolt, she shoved Moreen toward the ladder. "Mo, swim!" she gasped.

As Mo's hand came weakly out of the water, reaching for the rungs, Ellen heard the splash behind her, saw the bloody hand arc past her face. Moreen's head was yanked back.

Ellen lunged, caught his wrist in her hand. She felt Moreen's hands there too, fighting to free her hair from his fingers. Clutching the U-bolt, Ellen wrapped her arm around Neal's elbow and tried to pull him to the surface, but he was too strong. When he started pulling Mo's head deeper, Ellen felt the U-bolt slipping through her frozen fingers. Then she lost it, and she grabbed desperately for the hanging handcuff, felt its chain scrape the web of her hand until her thumb hooked its base. With every bit of her remaining strength, she focused on her right elbow, refusing to lose her daughter. She pulled to the right. He pulled left. She heard her own groans straining in her ears as she tried to bring her arms together. Incredibly, she felt Mo's head bump against her chin, and there was Neal's bloody hand hard against her breast.

Seeing her chance, Ellen jabbed the handcuff at his wrist. He deflected her attack effortlessly, snapping his hand around, gathering more of Mo's hair. Then he started dragging her away. Ellen screamed and attacked his wrist with the handcuff again, but struck the heel of his hand, the base of his thumb, the side of his fingers. Then he stopped pulling. Holding his position with his wrist just out of her reach, he shone his black eyes at her from behind the veil of Mo's floating hair, his grim, self-satisfied grin.

Meeting his eyes with her own, she shook her head intently at him, then snapped her own hand around, sinking the hook of the open handcuff through his bullet hole. Reflexively, his fingers sprang open, trying to shake the manacle out of his hand, but Ellen slammed the cuff into the dam, engaging the lock. He shook his hand violently, and Mo's head shook too. Desperate for air, Ellen fought to free her, when suddenly she was knocked roughly aside. Fighting back through an explosion of bubbles, she grasped for Moreen, but grasped at only water. Then, in amazement, she watched her daughter ascend into the light.

Ellen burst up into the snowstorm with a furious gasp. She heard Moreen coughing, saw her rising up the rungs, caught in the arm of Rooftop Paradise.

The giant looked down at Ellen. "Can you get out?"

Ellen wrapped her arm around a ladder rung. Breathlessly, she tried to nod her head, but it took all her strength just to hang on.

"I'll be right back," Rooftop told her, climbing.

Amazed to be alive, Ellen clutched the iron and watched her other arm come stiffly out of the water and reach for a higher rung. She felt firmness under her boot and strained to straighten her leg, trembling weakly as she tried to push herself up. Then she stopped, to gather strength. Every movement ached deeply, even though the surface of her body felt numb. She stared at the gray concrete in front of her eyes, trying to grasp the reality of Scott's death. But Moreen was safe, she told herself, and that was more than she had hoped for.

Shivering desperately, she began to notice the silence around her. In fact, it seemed the entire world had become quiet, offering up no sound but the bright trickle of waters melting down the sides of the gorge. Then she heard the burst of bubbles behind her. Her heart jumped and she clutched at the rungs, steeling herself against another attack. But she realized it was Neal exhaling his last breath. And then she wanted nothing more than to forget the sound forever. She closed her eyes. She listened to the silence. She began to drift.

When the arm wrapped around her chest, she cried out.

"I've got you," Rooftop said softly, and she felt herself pulled upward, watching the dam falling swiftly past her face, her boots bouncing off the rungs as she rose. At the top of the dam he carried her to the snow-covered embankment, where Moreen sat on the blanket, wrapped in Rooftop's fur-lined parka. Mo's face was white, her lips as blue as her teardrop tattoos. Shivering intently, she looked out over the gorge.

"There's an ice jam up at the Rez, so the water's stopped for now," Rooftop explained, setting Ellen down on the blanket beside her. "I'm going to run Moreen up to the house and call for an ambulance. Then I'll come back for you." He lifted Moreen effortlessly into his arms, taking care that the parka stayed on her.

"Get Mo warmed up. I can make it back myself," Ellen said, although she was surprised that her frozen jaw even moved.

"I've got to come back anyway," he said. "Cover up."

He lifted a corner of the blanket over her shoulder, and Ellen caught it in her frozen hand, huddling inside, closing her eyes, still trying to fathom everything that had happened. Then she heard the bubbles again. She turned, her body tingling.

"You got bolt cutters up at the house?" Rooftop asked her. "I shoved a little emergency tank in his mouth, but it's only good for five minutes or so. I'm going to have to cut him out of there."

Ellen stared up at him.

"Maybe I've got something in my truck," he said. "Hang on, I'll be right back."

As he walked briskly away with Moreen in his arms, Ellen rolled to her shoulder and pressed the heel of her hand in the snow. She bent her leg, painfully, leaned her elbow on her knee and pushed herself upward until, incredibly, she felt her frozen body rising. Holding the blanket around her like a shawl, she straightened her back and, more painfully, her knees, then took her first unsteady step toward the dam, her stiff legs aching inside her heavy, hardening jeans.

She heard the bubbles below her.

She took two more steps until she stood at the point where the abutment narrowed to the top of the curved dam. Gathering all her strength, she stepped up. To her left, a bed of snow-covered granite lay at the bottom of a twenty-foot drop; to her right, the surface of the pond lay six feet below, floating with ice chunks and driftwood, silent and still, except for a small pocket of turbulence over the spot where Neal was shackled.

Ellen took another step onto the dam, feeling the slight resistance of the safety cable against the right side of her shin. Carefully, she brought her other foot even with it, steadying herself. Out near the opposite bank, she could see the pale image of Scott's hand dangling under the water. Closer to her, she could see Neal looking skyward, a white tank the size of a liter bottle jutting sideways from his mouth.

Lashed with his back to the dam, his upturned eyes seemed to track her movements as she shuffled farther out onto the dam, until she was directly above him. In the distance she heard a siren start, and she knew he would be rescued soon.

As though reading her mind, Neal blinked once, calmly. Then a small flurry of bubbles jostled up, laughing as they broke the surface. When the water cleared, she saw his eyes again, glinting triumphantly up at her.

She stared back, horrified, almost mesmerized, wishing she had the strength to jump in the water and tear the tank from his mouth. Then she saw Neal's eyes dart to the side.

"Is that him?" came a man's voice.

Ellen turned slowly, as Wes Westerback stepped onto the dam from the woods on the other side of the pond, carrying a long, black rifle strapped to his shoulder. Wearing a red hunting jacket and snow-frosted crusher, his cheeks were bright, his eyes dull.

"Can you make it back to the house?" he asked her.

She looked down again, saw Neal's eyes move from Westerback to her. She nodded her head.

Suddenly Neal's elbows began flapping, and his body jerked, resembling a fat bass fighting a line. When Ellen heard the quick, hard catch of a shell being chambered, Neal's struggling ceased. His eyes targeted Wes, widening in a scowl of protest. A scowl of warning. Then his eyes sprang back to Ellen.

"Ellie, go look after your daughter," said Wes.

Gazing at Neal for another second, she took a breath, then turned her eyes away. She heard Neal's bubbles again, breaking furiously on the water, but she ignored him, keeping her eyes hard on the dam as she turned her body and began shuffling stiffly along, listening to the siren wailing from the top of the hill. Stepping off the dam onto the abutment, she followed Rooftop's big boot prints down over the bank to the farm road. As she started uphill, she heard the first rifle shot, a hard, flat slap that died in the surrounding snow. She did not flinch, nor did she stop walking. But before she'd taken two more steps, she heard the second shot.

She saw Rooftop run out beside the pump house and peer down through the whiteness. Then he started running again, his long black legs looking like sticks as he lifted one after the other out of the snow. Reaching Ellen, he bent to lift her.

"Police are on their way," he said, wheezing thickly. "Let's get you up to the house."

She shook her head in protest, even as she felt herself falling. He caught her.

"Okay?" he asked, bending tentatively for her legs. She leaned back on his arm and closed her eyes, letting him lift her.

The ache of thawing was the worst pain Ellen had ever felt. She stepped in her bathtub fully clothed and turned on the shower. Even though the water was barely lukewarm, it gnawed ravenously at the deepest part of her body. She moaned, withstanding the ache, but stopped when she heard a knock.

"Mrs. Chambers, the EMTs are here." It was Rooftop, outside the door.

"I'll be right out," she answered.

She stripped off her frozen jean jacket and dropped it in the tub. Gradually, as she was able to make the water warmer, she removed the rest of her clothes and let the water work on her. When she was through, she shut off the shower and slid the plastic curtain back.

A thick, green bath towel sat folded on the corner of the sink, along with her bra, jersey, a flannel shirt and sweater, a pair of cotton underpants and loose-fitting jeans, and heavy wool socks. She wondered if Mo had put them there for her, hoped she had. Stepping out of the tub, she noted with some relief the fiery redness of her skin, hoping it meant she hadn't gotten frostbite. The touch of the towel on her arm sent a fierce, burning pain through her.

When she opened the bathroom door, two men and a woman in blue, fleece-lined jackets were sitting at the kitchen table. The ambulance crew, Ellen guessed. A state trooper stood by the door, watching out the window. Moreen sat close to the cookstove with her hair wrapped in a towel and her dark eyes downcast. Rooftop sat on the floor in front of the chair, rubbing her stockinged feet tenderly in his hands.

Ellen went over to her. "You okay, hon?" She touched Mo's head. "I love you, Mo."

"We'd like to run you and your daughter to the hospital, Mrs. Chambers," one of the EMTs said, "if you're ready."

Ellen turned to respond and saw Wes Westerback through the window. He was sitting on the porch steps with his rifle laid across his knees. Detective Gallagher was coming up the farm road from the pond with a broad-shouldered young trooper beside him.

"Give me a minute," Ellen said, and she went to the door.

"Put something on," one of the EMTs told her. She ignored him and opened the door. Wes turned around, his jaw clenched tight.

Gallagher slowed his pace about fifteen feet from the porch. He was wearing his dark brown trench coat and matching fedora, but he was not wearing them well. Regarding Ellen tentatively, he put his hand to his brim, as though holding his hat against the wind. Ellen imagined he was thinking of a way to deflect the blame for his mistakes, or maybe improvise an apology. She was wrong.

"Condolences on your loss," he said stiffly, speaking louder than usual. "Is that Neal down there with your husband?"

"It's Neal," she said. "Is he dead?"

Gallagher nodded. "As far as we can see, he has a gunshot wound in the head, maybe two." The detective took three steps closer. "Do you mind if I come inside and talk with you and your daughter?"

Ellen took a deep, shivering breath. "Neal shot Scott in the foot, then handcuffed him to the dam. He tried to handcuff Moreen and me, but we fought him." The words steamed from her mouth.

"Who's 'we?' "

"I fought him," Ellen said. "Me alone."

Gallagher gave her a nod, pulling a pad and pen from his pocket, as a gust of snow blew across his shoulders.

"When we fought for the gun, I shot him in the hand. Then I handcuffed him to the dam."

"Shot him with—?"

"The gun's at the bottom of the pond. Are you going to write this down?"

Gallagher looked down at Wes, then back to Ellen. "Mrs. Chambers, I only have a few questions. You shouldn't be out here."

"Moreen and I are going to the hospital now, Detective," Ellen said. "Am I under arrest?"

"Not at all. Chief Westerback already told me that he fired the shots that killed your nephew. I just need a more thorough statement from you and your daughter, but nothing that can't wait a day or two."

Ellen shook her head. "I don't want you talking to Mo. Not today, tomorrow, not ever. She's been through enough."

The detective's eyes left hers, hung suspended for a moment or two in the snow. Then he put his hands, along with his notepad, in his pockets. The young trooper standing at his side seemed to be studying him.

"Detective Gallagher," Wes interrupted. He labored to stand up, taking his rifle off his lap. "Would you mind picking me up at my house?"

"What for?"

Wes came off the porch and handed Gallagher his rifle. "I'd like to drop off my vehicle, save my wife from having to come over here to get it."

Holding the old man's weapon, Gallagher's eyes wandered down Wes's wool trousers to his rubber-bottomed boots, then back up again. Then he turned his head toward the trooper and said, "Go ahead and warm up your car, we're not going to be long."

The trooper nodded and left them. When he was out of earshot,

Gallagher turned back to Wes. "Chief, why would I be picking you up?"

Wes stood, stone-faced.

Gallagher looked back toward the trooper's patrol car. "Unless someone tells me differently," he said, avoiding eye contact with the older man, "my report's going to say that when you fired your rifle into the water, you were aiming for the handcuff, trying to break Neal Chambers free."

Ellen watched the detective carefully, curiously, as he returned the rifle to the older man.

"Bullets do unpredictable things when they hit the water," Gallagher said, "even high-velocity shells. That's what I'll be writing in my report." He shoved his hands in his pockets and looked off toward the pond.

"Under the circumstances," he said, turning toward Ellen with a halting glance, "I also wanted you to know that I'll be closing the book on the diving accident that claimed your daughter's husband."

The detective touched his brim again. She didn't know if he was protecting his hat from the wind or if he expected thanks. She didn't feel especially thankful, so she said nothing.

Gallagher pulled up his collar. He gave her one more look, then he put his hands in his pockets and walked to his car.

epilogue

Ellen popped awake in the dark, heart pounding. The green light lay flat on her eyelids, then went black again. Her pillow was wet with perspiration. But she was safe, she told herself. Moreen was safe. She tried to relax her breathing. She tried to convince herself.

She had hoped the nightmares would stop once she got out of Maine. But even at the edge of this desert, two thousand miles away, she'd been jolted by some snap of silence. Not that it surprised her. She hadn't had a full night's sleep since the flood, alerted to every tick from the water pipes, each creak of roof rafters objecting to the cold. Sometimes she'd wake with a shout, and then she'd lie in the dark trying to rid her mind of images—Neal's black eyes blinking up out of the water; the handcuff through his hand; the supreme confidence of Scott's last smile. More often, it was her body's memories she'd need to exorcize—Neal's fingers from her flesh, or hers from his; his taste from her tongue, his weight from her thighs.

The green light came on. The green light went off again, the Green Oasis Motor Inn flashing its seven-second greeting over the highway. In a strange way, the light was a comfort. Every time it lit, the room looked the same: the Royal Crown Cola bottle standing atop the TV; the opened suitcase beside it; Moreen sleeping in the other bed; Roof-top spread out on the floor in front of the radiator, his long, noisy breathing drifting just out of sync with the cadence of the motel light. Ellen turned away from the window and closed her eyes, burying her ear in the pillow, covering her other ear with her arm. She tried to focus on her breathing.

For two nights and a day the Boston Whaler had followed the black panel truck across the country, Rooftop driving, Moreen sitting beside him, staring out at the snow fields, while Ellen sat squeezed in the back seat between cardboard boxes and grocery bags. Finally in the desert somewhere in western South Dakota, they pulled off the highway. Moreen had barely said a word for the duration of the trip. Aside from a few obligatory replies, neither had she spoken to Ellen at all since the flood, not even during Scott's funeral.

At least Mo had agreed to the move. Ellen took encouragement from that and hoped she could get Mo into counseling once they landed in Oregon. She was also heartened by Mo's relationship with Rooftop; it wasn't difficult to see that they found great comfort in each other's company.

Ellen's eyes opened again. The green motel light came on, lighting the closed bathroom door, the hanging jackets, the boots. The room darkened again. On for seven seconds, off for seven seconds. She closed her eyes and tried to close her mind to everything but her own breathing, as she'd learned in yoga.

Full breath in.

Full breath out.

Pause. Peace. Repeat:

Fullness in.

Fullness out.

Pause. Peace. Soon she began slowing her breaths, pacing her respiration to the cycles of the motel light. By degrees, she felt her body relax.

Full breath in when the light comes on.

Full breath out when the light goes out.

Pause. Peace. Repeat:

Full breath in when the light comes on.

Full breath out when the light goes out.

Pause. Peace . . .

But the light stayed off.

Ellen's eyes opened, saw the dark figure standing over her.

"No!"

She thrashed out of her blankets. Her wrists were caught. A bright light flashed on. Ellen stared up into the glare, stark and shaking. At first, Moreen appeared to be laughing, the way her shoulders shook.

"Hon?" said Ellen.

All at once, Mo let out a pitiful sob. Her arms collapsed, and she fell heavily onto Ellen, shaking so hard that even the bedsprings seemed to cry.

"Honey, it's okay," Ellen whispered, combing her fingers gently through her daughter's hair. Behind her, Rooftop stood tensed, his body covering the door. Ellen could see his chest expanding, could hear him wheezing. Her own heart was pounding. And it was breaking, the way Moreen nestled in the warmth of her body as she had when she was five years old, the way she pushed her grown-up hand under her mother's arm.

Ellen pulled the blankets over her, steadily stroking her hair as Moreen's tears fell down her neck.

Then Rooftop turned off the room light.

"It's okay," Ellen whispered again, even as her own tears ran from her eyes.

Moreen cried and cried until only weariness quieted her. When she finally fell asleep, Ellen held onto her, fit her warm head in the hollow of her neck, her warm breast under her arm. A welling of happiness rose inside her, a great warmth of joy, and she knew she wouldn't be able to sleep, but she didn't care. She looked over toward the window and saw Rooftop sitting tall in the dark, his back against the door. The way his glasses reflected the green light in slow, silent intervals—Ellen was reminded of a lighthouse on the coast.

He would sit there like that until morning, keeping watch. Ellen would lie there, gazing at the ceiling until it paled with the desert light. And Moreen would sleep peacefully. In the morning they would emerge from the room and continue their journey together.